A Brief History & Selected Readings of English and American Literature

英美文学简史及名篇选读

主　编　田祥斌　朱甫道
编　者　冯军霞　高　倩
　　　　赵格亚　刘　蕾

外语教学与研究出版社
FOREIGN LANGUAGE TEACHING AND RESEARCH PRESS
北京 BEIJING

图书在版编目（CIP）数据

英美文学简史及名篇选读 ：英文 / 田祥斌，朱甫道主编 ；冯军霞等编. -- 北京 ：外语教学与研究出版社，2017.4（2021.8 重印）
ISBN 978-7-5135-8859-1

Ⅰ. ①英… Ⅱ. ①田… ②朱… ③冯… Ⅲ. ①英国文学－文学研究－高等学校－教材－英文②文学研究－美国－高等学校－教材－英文③英国文学－文学欣赏－高等学校－教材－英文④文学欣赏－美国－高等学校－教材－英文 Ⅳ. ①I561.06②I712.06

中国版本图书馆 CIP 数据核字 (2017) 第 110152 号

出 版 人　徐建忠
责任编辑　程　序
封面设计　锋尚设计
版式设计　黄　浩
出版发行　外语教学与研究出版社
社　　址　北京市西三环北路 19 号（100089）
网　　址　http://www.fltrp.com
印　　刷　廊坊十环印刷有限公司
开　　本　787×1092　1/16
印　　张　25.75
版　　次　2017 年 8 月第 1 版　2021 年 8 月第 21 次印刷
书　　号　ISBN 978-7-5135-8859-1
定　　价　79.90 元

购书咨询：（010）88819926　电子邮箱：club@fltrp.com
外研书店：https://waiyants.tmall.com
凡印刷、装订质量问题，请联系我社印制部
联系电话：（010）61207896　电子邮箱：zhijian@fltrp.com
凡侵权、盗版书籍线索，请联系我社法律事务部
举报电话：（010）88817519　电子邮箱：banquan@fltrp.com
物料号：288590001

记载人类文明
沟通世界文化
www.fltrp.com

前 言

英美文学是我国高等学校本科英语专业的一门必修课程。学生既可以从文学发展中了解英美的社会文化，还可以通过阅读经典英语文学作品增强语言运用能力和思辨能力。英美文学以英语语言文字为工具，形象化地反映出不同时代的客观现实和意识形态；文学是表现和诠释人之心灵的艺术，是文化的一种美学表现形式，包括小说、诗歌、戏剧和散文。

本教材融英美文学史及经典阅读为一体，旨在让英语专业的学生对英美文学的起源和发展有较全面的了解，能汲取英美文化中的精髓。还能在欣赏文学精品的阅读过程中，学习地道的英语，感受语言文字的魅力。《英美文学简史及名篇选读》严格按照教育部《高等学校英语专业教学大纲》的要求编写。教材以文学史为主线，简明扼要地介绍文学发展史和重点作家作品，精选经典作品或片段选读，以便学生从文学中获取宽广的知识面，在作品阅读中提升英语语言理解能力；用英美文学精品培育学生，提高大学生的道德、文化、心理等素质。

教材包括背景介绍、重点作家作品概览、名篇选读、注释、文本思考题、章节练习等。背景介绍中包括主要文学思潮、文学运动、代表作家、文学术语等，时间跨度从英国的中古文学和美国的独立时期到21世纪。名篇选读包括经典的小说节选、诗歌、戏剧节选、短篇小说、散文，以提高学生分析不同体裁文学的能力和提升写作能力。

本教材适合高等学校英语专业学生使用。编写过程中，文学发展主线梳理和文学理论的阐释参考了网络及前人的专著或教材，也汲取了国内外英美文学研究的近期成果，在此向这些编著者表示衷心的谢意。第一、二、三、六、八、九章由田祥斌编写；第五、七章由冯军霞编写；第四、十一章由高倩编写；第十章由赵格亚编写；第十二章由刘蕾编写。田祥斌统稿，朱甫道审稿，冯军霞负责校对。编者力求重点突出、语言通俗易懂、篇幅短而精。若有不足，恳请指正。

编者
2017 年 7 月

CONTENTS

PART I

ENGLISH LITERATURE

CHAPTER I

English Literature in the Old and Middle Ages

(449-1485)

General Introduction

Old English literature, or Anglo-Saxon literature, began in the period after the settlement of the Teutonic tribes of Angles, Saxons and Jutes about 449 AD and ended after the Norman Conquest in 1066. The Angles settled in the central part of the island, calling their new home Angle-land, then shortened into England. The greatest Old English poem is *Beowulf*.

Beowulf

Beowulf is the greatest and first English epic. It belongs to the seventh century which tells us a story of a brave young man, Beowulf, who is from southern Sweden to help Hrothgar, King of the Danes. The poem consists of 3182 lines and the author is unknown. *Beowulf* is a valuable narrative poem, which records the valuable custom of that time and gives us an interesting picture of life in those old days. The epic tells us of fierce fights and brave deeds of the leader and the sufferings of his men. It is mainly about Beowulf's three major adventures and praises the bravery, keeping promise, and loyalty.

Hrothgar is in trouble because his great hall, called Heorot, is visited at night by the terrible monster Grendel, which lives in a lake and comes to kill and devours many of Hrothgar's warriors while they sleep. Beowulf leaves his homeland with his king's permission to help Hrothgar. One night, Beowulf waits secretly for the monster in the hall and attacks it. Beowulf pulls Grendel's arm off with his bare hands. Grendel runs to his home and slowly dies.

The Grendel's mother comes to the hall in revenge for Grendel's defeat. Beowulf attacks her and follows her to the bottom of the lake. There he kills Grendel's mother. He returns to Heorot, where Hrothgar gives Beowulf many gifts.

Later in his life, Beowulf is the king of his people. In order to defend his country against a fire-breathing creature, Beowulf and his warriors come to fight the creature. Although he kills the animal, Beowulf is badly wounded and dies. The poem ends with a sorrowful description of Beowulf's funeral fire.

The original poem written in old language is not easy to read, but *Beowulf* has its own value. The poem is of no rhyme. Instead, each half-line is joined to the other by alliteration. Alliteration is the repetitions of the same consonant sounds in a line, especially at the beginning of words. Here are two lines of it.

Of men he was the mildest and most beloved,
To his kin the kindest, keenest to praise.

Another feature is the use of a lot of metaphors and understatements in the poem in which things are described indirectly and in combinations of words. A ship is not only a ship. It is a sea-goer, a sea-boat, a sea-wood, or a wave-floater.

Epic is a long narrative poem that records the adventures of a hero, whose exploits are important to the history of a nation.

Middle English literature, or Medieval English Literature, refers to the literature written from about 1066 to about 1500. The Norman conquest of England began with the battle of Hastings in 1066 when the Normans headed by Duke William II of Normandy defeated the Anglo-Saxons. The Norman Conquest marked the end of the Anglo-Saxon period.

After the Norman Conquest, three languages co-existed in England. French became the official language used by the king and Norman lords; Latin became the principal tongue of church affairs and in universities. And Old English was spoken only by the common English people.

The greatest poet of the time was Geoffrey Chaucer who is often called the father of English poetry. As we know, the language had changed a great deal in the seven hundred years since the time of *Beowulf* and it is much easier to read Chaucer than to read anything written in Old English.

In the medieval period, the prevailing literary form was the romance. **Romance** was a long composition, sometimes in verse, sometimes in prose, describing the life and adventures of a noble hero. The central character of romances was the knight, a man of noble birth skilled in the use of weapons. The knight was commonly described as riding forth to seek adventures, or fighting for his lord in battle. He was devoted to the church and the king.

The subjects of English romances mainly deal with three types of historical material: the matter of Rome and Greece, the matter of France, and the matter of Britain which refers to Arthurian stories. The famous romance is adventures of *King Arthur and His Knights of the Round Table.* One of the main subjects is the search for The Holy Grail. Another subject is Arthur's battles against his enemies, including *Sir Gawain and the Green Knight* which is one of the very popular stories.

Sir Gawain and the Green Knight

The poem's author is anonymous. Sir Gawain is the King Arthur's nephew, one of the Knights of the Round Table. *Sir Gawain and the Green Knight* is the most accomplished example of medieval romance and a poem of rich psychological and moral interest. It tells of the adventures of one of King Arthur's Knights in a struggle against an enemy with magic powers as well as great strength and cunning. Sir Gawain finishes the adventure with all honors.

In the first canto, Green Knight challenges the bravest knight and Gawain accepts the challenge. He takes the battle ax to cut off the Green Knight's head. In the second canto, Gawain keeps his promise to look for the Green Chapel and lives in the castle near the chapel. The third canto shows the life of Gawain spent in the castle to get three kisses and the girdle within three days. In the fourth canto, Gawain is brought to the Green Chapel. The Green Knight wounds him because he conceals the green girdle.

Geoffrey Chaucer
(1343-1400)

INTRODUCTION

Geoffrey Chaucer, known as the father of English literature, is widely considered the greatest poet of the Middle Ages. He is regarded as the first realist in English literature because he gives us the ordinary daily life of the 14th century. It is Chaucer alone who, for the first time in English literature, presented to us a comprehensive realistic picture of the English society of his time and created a whole gallery of vivid characters from all walks of life in his masterpiece, *The Canterbury Tales*.

Chaucer is often called the father of English poetry. His contribution to English poetry lies chiefly in the fact that he introduced from France the rhymed stanzas of various types to English poetry instead of the old alliterative verse, especially **heroic couplet**, a verse form with iambic pentameter, which rhymes in pairs or couplets.

As a first realistic writer, Chaucer is considered as the founder of English realism because he shows us the realistic pictures of 14th-century English society in his *The Canterbury Tales*.

As a forerunner of humanism, Chaucer praises man's energy, intellect, quick wit and love of life. His tales expose and satirize the evils of the time.

His language is vivid and exact. Chaucer is the first great poet who wrote in the current English language. He did much in making the dialect of London the foundation for modern English speech. Chaucer is recorded in the *Oxford English Dictionary* as the first author to use many common English words in his writings. So we can say he is the master of the English language.

Chaucer was born about 1340 in London. He was the son of a well-to-do wine merchant who had connections with the Court. The poet is said to have studied at Cambridge and Oxford. His learning was wide in scope. He obtained a good knowledge of Latin, French and Italian. In 1359, in the early stages of the Hundred Years' War, Chaucer went to France and he was captured in 1360. Edward III paid £16 for his ransom and Chaucer was released. After his return, he married Philippa, a lady-in-waiting to Edward III's queen. Several times he was sent to the Continent on diplomatic missions, two of which took him to Italy. Then he was appointed Controller of customs at London. He died in 1400 and was buried in Westminster Abbey in

London. Chaucer is the first writer who was interred in the area now known as "Poets' Corner".

Chaucer went Italy twice and was influenced by Italian Renaissance, especially by Dante and Boccaccio. His major works include *The Book of the Duchess* (1370), *The Parliament of Fowls* (1380), *The House of Fame* (1374-1384), *Troilus and Criseyde* (1385), *The Legend of Good Women* (1385), and his masterpiece *The Canterbury Tales*.

SELECTED READING

The Canterbury Tales

Overview

The *Canterbury Tales* is a framed story which is called one of the monumental works in English literature. The plan of this narrative poem shows the evident influence of Boccaccio's *Decameron*. According to Chaucer's plan, he will tell us over 120 tales, more than the number of *Decameron*, but he has only finished *General Prologue* and 24 tales, of which four are incomplete. However, *The Canterbury Tales* shows us the real society of the fourteenth-century England. The gallery of portraits in the *General Prologue* covers almost the whole range of fourteenth-century occupations and professions. And the tales deal with important social and domestic issues. The poem as a whole gives a vivid and comprehensive picture of the social conditions of the 14th century England.

Chaucer meets a party of twenty-nine other pilgrims at the Tabard Inn on their way to Canterbury. He joins the company to visit the shrine of Saint Thomas à Becket. At the suggestion of the host of the inn, the pilgrims agree to tell stories to pass the time on their journey on horseback from London to Canterbury. Each of them will tell two tales on the way to Canterbury and two on the way back. The best story-teller shall be treated with a fine supper at general expense at the end. The host is to be the judge of the contest.

In the famous *General Prologue* to the *Canterbury Tales*, Chaucer describes the pilgrims for us in great detail, from which we get to know the pilgrims themselves. Most of them, such as the merchant, the lawyer, the cook, the sailor, the plowman, and the miller, are ordinary people, but each of them can be recognized as a real person with his or her own character. One of the most enjoyable characters is the Wife of Bath. She tells her story to manage her five husbands strictly.

The selection is from the *General Prologue* which provides a framework for the tales. The poet begins his poem with a flowery description of the English countryside in the spring time. All the birds are prodded into participation in the processes of nature and sing all the night through. Then people have been stirred by the beautiful nature to go off on pilgrimages. The description of the rain, the west wind, the sun, the birds and human beings gives us beautiful and harmonious scenery in April.

General Prologue

(Excerpt)

As soon as April pierces to the root
The drought of March, and bathes each bud and shoot
Through every vein of sap with gentle showers
From whose engendering liquor spring the flowers;
When Zephyrus[1] have breathed softly all about
Inspiring every wood and field to sprout,
And in the zodiac[2] the youthful sun
His journey halfway through the Ram[3] has run;
When little birds are busy with their song
Who sleep with open eyes the whole night long
Life stirs their hearts and tingles in them so,
Then off as pilgrims people long to go,
And palmers[4] to set out for distant strands
And foreign shrines renowned in many lands.
And specially in England people ride
To Canterbury from every countryside

1 Zephyrus: the west wind

2 Zodiac: an area of the sky through which the sun, moon and most of the planets appear to move, or the representation of this area in the form of a usually circular drawing. The area of sky is divided into twelve equal parts, each of which has a name, is connected with a time of year, and is represented by a symbol.

3 Ram: Ram is one of the signs of the Zodiac. The sun is supposed to run through the sign of the Ram annually from March 21st to April 21st, so the sun is young.

4 palmers: pilgrims to foreign countries

To visit there the blessed martyred saint[1]
Who gave them strength when they were sick and faint.

In Southwark at the Tabard one spring day
It happened, as I stopped there on my way,
Myself a pilgrim with a heart devout
Ready for Canterbury to set out,
At night came all of twenty-nine assorted
Travellers, and to that same inn resorted,
Who by a turn of fortune chanced to fall
In fellowship together, and they were all
Pilgrims who had it in their minds to ride
Toward Canterbury. The stables doors were wide,
The rooms were large, and we enjoyed the best,
And shortly, when the sun had gone to rest,
I had so talked with each that presently
I was a member of their company
And promised to rise early the next day
To start, as I shall show, upon our way.

But none the less, while I have time and space,
Before this tale has gone a further pace,
I should in reason tell you the condition
Of each of them, his rank and his position,
And also what array they all were in;
And so then, with a knight I will begin.

1 saint: Here Saint refers to St. Thomas à Becket, murdered in Canterbury cathedral in 1170. In February 1173, he was formally canonized by Pope Alexander III.

QUESTIONS

1 What does *liquor* refer to here?
2 What makes wood and field to sprout?
3 In the seventh line, why does the author use "youthful" to describe the sun?
4 Why do the little birds sleep with open eyes during the whole night?
5 Why do the pilgrims long to set out?
6 What is the significance of the setting of the pilgrimage?

English Ballads

INTRODUCTION

During the fifteenth century, the continuous wars affected the development of English literature. Yet popular ballads and songs were widely spread in England and Scotland. **Ballad** is a narrative poem written in four-line stanzas, characterized by swift action and narrated in a direct style. Usually only the second and fourth lines rhyme. Ballads are anonymous narrative songs that have been preserved by oral transmission. The most famous English ballads at that time centered on the stories about a legendary outlaw called Robin Hood, who was described as a popular folk figure in the late-medieval period, and continues to be widely represented in literature, films and television. English ballads include historical, legendary, and humorous ballads. The following selection, *Get Up and Bar the Door*, is a good example of humorous ballad.

SELECTED READING

Get Up and Bar the Door

Overview

This is a medieval Scots ballad about a common life between a husband and wife. The ballad shows us a battle of wills between a husband, who tries to maintain his power, and wife, who refuses to be treated like a doormat. Both of them are too stubborn to bar the door. The song begins with the wife busy in her cooking. As the wind picks up, the husband asks his wife to close and bar the door. They make a pact that the person who speaks first must bar the door, and the door remains open. At midnight two thieves enter the house and eat the puddings that the wife has just made. The husband and wife watch them, but still neither speaks. Amazed, one of the thieves proposes to kiss the wife. Finally, the husband shouts "Will ye kiss my wife before my eye/And scald me with pudding-broth?" The wife, having won the pact, tells the husband, "Goodman, you've spoken the foremost word; Get up and bar the door."

It fell about the Martinmas time[1],
And a gay time it was then,
When our goodwife[2] got puddings to make,
And she's boiled them in the pan.

The wind so cold blew south and north,
And blew into the floor;
Quoth our goodman[3] to our goodwife,
"Go out and bar the door."

"My hand is in my hussyfscap[4],
Goodman, as ye may see;
If it should not be barr'd this hundred year,
It's not be barr'd by me."

They made a paction[5] 'tween them two,
They made it firm and sure,
That the first word whoe'er should speak,
Should rise and bar the door.

1 Martinmas time: the feast of St. Martin, Nov. 11th of each year

2 goodwife: wife

3 goodman: husband

4 hussyfscap: a small case for needles, thread, etc.

5 paction: pact, i.e., agreement

Then by there came two gentlemen,
At twelve o'clock at night,
And they could neither see house nor hall,
Not coal, nor candlelight.

"Now whether is this a rich man's house,
Or whether is it a poor?"
But ne'er a word would one of them speak,
For barring of the door.

And first they ate white puddings,
And then they ate the black;
Though much thought the goodwife to herself,
Yet ne'er a word she spake.

Then said the one unto the other,
"Here, man, take ye ma[1] knife;
Do you take off[2] the old man's beard,
And I'll kiss the goodwife."

"But there's no water in the house,
And what shall we do then?"
"What ails ye at the pudding-broth[3],
That boils into the pan?"

O, up then started our goodman,
An angry man was he;
"Will ye kiss my wife before my eye,
And scald me with pudding-broth?"

1 ma: my

2 take off: to shave off.

3 What ails ye at the pudding-broth: What's the matter with the pudding broth? Why not use the pudding-broth?

O, up then started our goodwife,
Made three skips on the floor;
"Goodman, you've spoken the foremost word;[1]
Get up and bar the door."

QUESTIONS

1 What is the agreement made between the husband and wife?
2 Why could the two gentlemen neither see the house, nor hall, nor candlelight?
3 What did they do after they ate the puddings?
4 Why was the goodman so angry at last?
5 What is the rhyme scheme of the poem?
6 What kind of life does this ballad reflect?
7 What is the tone of the ballad?

EXERCISES OF CHAPTER I

I Fill in the following blanks.

1 Different tribes of Teutons include ____________, ______________, and ____________.

2 ____________ is the oldest poem in the English language which is called English national epic.

3 After the Norman Conquest, three languages co-existed in England. ____________ became the official language used by the king and the Norman lords; ____________ was spoken in church affairs and in universities, and ____________ was spoken only by the common English people.

II Find the relevant match from Column B for each item in Column A.

Column A	Column B
1 ( ) Geoffrey Chaucer	A. *Angle-land*
2 ( ) popular ballad	B. *Sir Gawain and the Green Knight*
3 ( ) the best of Arthurian romances	C. *Get Up and Bar the Door*
4 ( ) the oldest English epic	D. *The Canterbury Tales*

1 You've spoken the foremost word: You have been the first to speak.

5 ( ) England E. *Beowulf*

III Choose the best answer for each statement.

1 *The Canterbury Tales* is written for the greater part in ______ couplets.
A. epic B. heroic C. narrative D. lyric

2 Chaucer died on the 25th of October 1400, and was buried in ______.
A. Italy B. France C. Oxford D. Westminster Abbey

3 Geoffrey Chaucer is the founder of the English ______.
A. romantic poetry B. realistic literature
C. classical novels D. heroic epic

4 "When little birds are busy with their song/Who sleep with open eyes the whole night long/Life stirs their hearts and tingles in them so," (From *The Canterbury Tales*). This means the birds cannot sleep because they ______.
A. keep singing the whole night
B. are excited by the beauty of nature
C. have a heart full of love
D. are busy with picking seeds

IV Answer the following questions.

1 What are the main contributions of Chaucer to British literature?
2 What are the features of *Beowulf*?

CHAPTER II

English Literature in the Renaissance Period

(1485-1620)

General Introduction

The century and a half following the death of Chaucer (1400-1550) was full of significant changes. The Hundred Years' War with France took place from 1336 to 1453. After the Hundred Years' War, a series of wars for control of the throne of England called The War of the Roses were fought between supporters of two rival branches in Lancaster and York during 1455 and 1483. The discovery of America and the new sea routes promoted the development of commerce, sea navigation and industry. King Henry VIII (reigned 1509-1547) set up absolute monarchy in England at the beginning of the 16th century and started the Reformation. He declared the break with Rome and became head of the English church.

During the reign of Queen Elizabeth I from 1558 to 1603, the absolute monarchy in England reached its summit. England's defeat of the Spanish Armada in 1588, associated Elizabeth with one of the greatest military victories in English history, made Great Britain become more powerful on the high seas and in world trade. The contradiction between the wealth of the ruling classes and the poverty of the people aggravated to result in many uprisings of the peasantry which were ruthlessly suppressed. The social and economic conditions mentioned above brought about great changes in the development of science and art, including the prosperity of national culture known as the English Renaissance.

The English Renaissance was a cultural and artistic movement in England dating from the late 15th to the early 17th century, usually seen as the end of Middle Ages and the beginning of the modern world. The Renaissance is also known as the rebirth of letters and sprang first in Italy in the 14th century and gradually spread all over Europe, which reached England slowly in the latter half of the 15th century. The beginning of the English Renaissance is often taken to be 1485, and the Elizabethan era in the second half of the 16th century is usually regarded as the height of the

English Renaissance. Two features are striking of this movement. The one is a thirsting curiosity for classical literature. Old manuscripts were dug out. There arose a current of the study of Greek and Latin authors. Another feature of the Renaissance is the keen interest in human activities. People ceased to look upon themselves as living only for God and a future world. Thinkers, artists and poets arose to the new feeling of admiration for human beauty and human achievement. Hence the thought of Humanism arose which was the keynote of the Renaissance.

Humanism is a belief system based on the principle that people's spiritual and emotional needs can be fulfilled without following a religion. It reflected the new outlook of the rising bourgeois class. The greatest of the English humanists was Thomas More, the author of *Utopia*.

This period is perhaps England's Golden Age in literature. Among the giants are William Shakespeare, Christopher Marlowe, Edmund Spenser, Sir Thomas More, Francis Bacon, and Ben Jonson.

Thomas More (1478-1535) was an English lawyer, social philosopher, author, statesman and noted Renaissance humanist. More's masterpiece is *Utopia*, which was written in Latin in 1516 and in the form of a conversation between More and Hythloday, a returned voyager. It's divided into two books. The first book contains a long discussion on the social conditions of England and shows us a realistic picture of early 16th century England. In the second book, an ideal country of utopia is described in detail, which is the first sketch of an ideal commonwealth, where property is held in common and there is no poverty. The name "Utopia" comes from two Greek words meaning "no place" or "nowhere".

Thomas Wyatt (1503-1542) was a 16th-century English ambassador and lyrical poet. Thomas Wyatt followed his father to court after his education at St John's College, Cambridge. It was Wyatt who first brought the sonnet to England. However, none of Wyatt's poems were published during his lifetime.

Edmund Spenser (1552-1599) was the "poet's poet" of the period because of his love of beauty and exquisite melody. He was born in a minor noble family, his father being a merchant in London. Spenser once received a good education at Pembroke College, Cambridge, and received his MA degree in 1576. His masterpiece is *The Faerie Queene* (*The Fairy Queen*) which is a long poem planned in 12 books, but he finished only six. Spenser invented a special meter, Spenserian stanza, for *The Faerie Queene*. It was written in a 9-line stanza form, consisting of eight lines of iambic pentameter and a concluding line of iambic hexameter, rhyming ABABBCBCC. Spenserian stanza, named after Edmund Spenser, influenced Shelley, Byron, Keats, and Tennyson.

Ben Jonson (1573-1637) was an English playwright, poet, actor and literary critic of the 17th century. He is best known for the satirical plays *Every Man in His Humour* (1598) and *Volpone, or the Foxe* (1605) which is his most savage comedy. He is generally regarded as the second most important English dramatist, after William Shakespeare, during the period of the English Renaissance. Jonson is the father of English literary criticism. In his *Timber or Discoveries* (1640), collection of notes and ideas on various subjects, Jonson began to make clear the true work of a critic, his aims and limitations. Ben Jonson said that a critic ought to judge a work as a whole, and that the critic himself must have some poetic abilities.

Christopher Marlowe (1564-1595) was an English playwright, poet, and translator. He was the most gifted of the "University Wits". Marlowe was the greatest of the pioneers of English drama and greatly influenced William Shakespeare. It is Marlowe what first made blank verse the principal instrument of English drama. He attended Corpus Christi College, Cambridge to study and received his BA and MA there. His dramatic achievement lies chiefly in his epical, and at times lyrical, verse. His works paved the way for the plays of the greatest English dramatist, Shakespeare. Marlowe's best-known plays are *Tamburlaine the Great* (1587), *The Jaw of Malta* (1592), and *The Tragical History of Doctor Faustus* (1588).

University Wits refers to a group of English poets and playwrights who established themselves in London in the 1580s and 1590s after attending university at either Oxford or Cambridge. The most important member of the group was Christopher Marlowe whose powerful blank-verse plays prepared the way for Shakespeare. Other prominent members of this group included Robert Greene, Thomas Nashe from Cambridge, and John Lyly, Thomas Lodge, George Peele from Oxford. They are identified as among the earliest professional writers in English. They were all of humble birth and struggled for a livelihood by writing.

William Shakespeare (1564-1616)

INTRODUCTION

William Shakespeare was an English poet, playwright, and actor. He was one of the founders of realism in world literature. Shakespeare is widely regarded as the greatest writer in the English language and the world's pre-eminent dramatist. His close friend, Ben Jonson, spoke highly of Shakespeare, "He is the greatest playwright all over the world, not of an age, but for all the time". He is also a great poet or often called England's national poet. Apart from his sonnets and long poems, his dramas were written in blank verse. They are rich in images, conceit, metaphors and symbols. Shakespeare is a humanist. He reflects the spirit of his age. Shakespeare is known as a great master of the English language. It is estimated that he had used about 15,000 words. Many of his quotations and phrases have been absorbed into the English language. His complete works include 37 plays, 2 long narrative poems and 154 sonnets.

Shakespeare was born in Stratford-Upon-Avon, in central England. His father, John Shakespeare, was a merchant. His mother was the daughter of a well-to-do farmer. At the age of 7, he attended the local grammar school and there he studied for six years and learned Latin and a little Greek. When he was 14, his father fell into debt, the boy probably left schools, and went to work. At 18 he married Anne Hathaway, who was eight years senior and they had three children.

About 1586 he left his family for London. Shortly after his arrival in the great city, he went to work at odd jobs in a theatre. Then he became an actor and later started to write for the stage. About 1611, he retired from London to his native town, though he continued to write. He died in 1616, at the age of 52.

Shakespeare's writing life can be divided into three periods: The first period is from 1590 to 1600. In this period, he completed most of his comedies, historical plays, 2 long narrative poems and most of the sonnets. Among the outstanding comedies *The Merchant of Venice* (1598) is the best, which contains a portrayal of the vengeful Jewish moneylender Shylock and reflects Elizabethan views. Portia is one of Shakespeare's ideal women in the play. Other famous comedies include *A Midsummer Night's Dream* (1595), *Twelfth Night* (1601), *As You Like It* (1599), *Romeo and Juliet* (1595), *Henry IV* and *Henry V*. *A Midsummer Night's Dream* shows Shakespeare's growing power in comedy, a witty mixture of romance, fairy magic, and comic lowlife scenes; *Twelfth Night* has been called the perfection of English comedy, the lively merrymaking story which centres on the twins Viola and Sebastian who cause confusion when the girl dresses like her brother. The whole play is alive with humour and action. *As You Like It* is a beautiful love story about heroine Rosalind, another ideal woman who dresses herself as a man to be admired for her intelligence, quick wit, and beauty. *Romeo and Juliet* is very popular, but it is called as tragicomedy by some critics because the deaths of Romeo and Juliet make two hostile families conciliatory. The two remarkable historical plays are *Henry IV* and *Henry V* which deal with the troubled events of 15th century. In the plays, the playwright depicts successfully a never-to-be forgotten character, John Falstaff, who is only a social parasite, moving about with a big belly, eating, drinking and doing nothing.

The second period is from 1601 to 1608, which is his Period of Tragedies, years of greater achievement. It contains a series of tragedies headed by the famous *Hamlet* (1601). Others include *Othello* (1604), *King Lear* (1605), and *Macbeth* (1606). These plays reflect the social contradiction of the age.

Othello is a tragic story of love and marriage between a brave Moorish general, Othello, and his beautiful wife, Desdemona. Lago hates Othello and devises a plan to destroy him. Othello so easily believes lago's evil words that his wife, Desdemona and his loyal lieutenant, Cassio are lovers, that he kills Desdemona. When he realizes his mistake, he wounds lago and kills himself. It reflects the themes of racism, love, jealousy, betrayal revenge and repentance.

King Lear reaches into the deepest places of the human spirit. King Lear's weakness is his openness to flattery. He is thrown out of his home by two wicked daughters because he gives his kingdom only to the two evil daughters who flatter him and nothing to the youngest girl, Cordelia, who tells the truth but loves him best.

Macbeth is about a brave Scottish general named Macbeth who receives a prophecy from three witches that one day he will become King of Scotland. Consumed by ambition and spurred to action by his wife, Macbeth murders King Duncan and takes the Scottish throne for himself. But Duncan's son, Malcolm brings an army against Macbeth and takes Macbeth and Lady Macbeth into the realms of madness and death.

Shakespeare's writing life ended with his third period during 1609 and 1612, in which there are three comedies and a minor historical play. Plays of this period show a general tone of conciliation and a falling off from his previous height, because he had then gradually abandoned the active dramatic work in London for the quiet life of a country gentleman. This period has sometimes been called the Period of Romance. *The Tempest* (1612) is the best in this period. Other two are *Cymbeline* (1969) and *The Winter's Tale* (1611). In these last plays we see his optimistic faith in the future of humanity, at the same time we also see the dramatist's Utopianism.

SELECTED READING

Hamlet

Overview

This is the story of murder and revenge. The prince, Hamlet, is told by his father's ghost, the former King of Denmark, that the latter has been murdered by hamlet's uncle Claudius who is now ruling as king and has married Hamlet's mother. Hamlet must try to find the proof of the murder. He pretends to be mad while planning for revenge and at the same time trying to make sure about his uncle's guilt. He asks a group of actors to stage a play to be sure of his uncle's crime and decides to kill him. But he kills an important courtier Polonius. For this slaughter Hamlet is sent to England by his uncle, to be beheaded there upon arrival. But Hamlet escapes and comes home, and he meets Polonius's son Laertes and the brother of Ophelia in a fancying match as arranged by his uncle. At last, Hamlet kills all his enemies and avenges his father. Hamlet and other principal characters die in the final scene. Hamlet is a great humanist and a hero of the Renaissance. His learning, wisdom, noble nature, as well as his limitation and tragedy are all representative of the humanists at the turn of the century.

The excerpt given below is the best known of Hamlet's soliloquy. "To be, or not to be" reveals the inner contradiction of the hero as well as the poet's penetrating comments on the social reality of his time. **Soliloquy** is a dramatic convention in which a character, alone on stage, speaks aloud and thus shares his or her thoughts with the audience. The whole soliloquy is written in **blank verse**, a line of poetry or prose in unrhymed iambic pentameter.

Act III Scene 1

(Excerpt)

Hamlet: To be, or not to be[1]—that is the question:
Whether 'tis nobler in the mind to suffer
The slings and arrows[2] of outrageous fortune,

1 To be, or not to be: to live on in this world or to die. To be: to exist, to live on.

2 slings and arrows: injuries (sling refers to a simple weapn used mainly in past for throwing stones)

Or to take arms against a sea of[1] troubles,
And by opposing end them? To die, to sleep—
No more—and by a sleep to say we end
The heartache and the thousand natural shocks
That flesh is heir to[2]. 'Tis a consummation[3]
Devoutly to be wish'd. To die, to sleep,
To sleep, perchance[4] to dream: ay, there's the rub,
For in that sleep of death what dreams may come
When we have shuffled off this mortal coil[5],
Must give us pause. There's the respect
That makes calamity of so long life,
For who would bear the whips and scorns of time,
The oppressor's wrong, the proud man's contumely,
The pangs of despis'd love, the law's delay,
The insolence of office and the spurns
That patient merit of the unworthy takes,
When he himself might his quietus make
With a bare bodkin[6]? Who would these fardels[7] bear,
To grunt and sweat under a weary life,
But that the dread of something after death,
The undiscover'd country, from whose bourn[8]
No traveller returns, puzzles the will,
And makes us rather bear those ills we have
Than fly to others[9] that we know not of?
Thus conscience does make cowards of us all;

---

1 a sea of: large quantities of

2 That flesh is heir to: The human body must suffer from."Flesh" here refers to human body.

3 consummation: conclusion, final settlement of everything.

4 perchance: possibly, maybe

5 mortal coil: it refers to human life.

6 bare bodkin: bare dagger (small bare knife)

7 fardels: burdens

8 bourn: boundary

9 fly to others: to go to others

And thus the native hue of resolution
Is sicklied o'er[1] with the pale cast[2] of thought,
And enterprises of great pith and moment[3]
With this regard[4] their currents turn awry
And lose the name of action[5].—Soft you now,[6]
The fair Ophelia—Nymph[7], in thy orisons[8]
Be all my sins remember'd.

QUESTIONS

1 What does "To be or not to be—that is the question..." here mean?
2 What comfort can sleep bring about according to the soliloquy?
3 What puzzles people's will to sleep?
4 What is Hamlet's dilemma?
5 Do you think Hamlet simply thinks about a personal revenge? What broader problem is he pondering about?
6 What kind of character does the soliloquy reveal of Hamlet?
7 What does the line "That patient merit of the unworthy takes" mean?
8 What are the figures of speech the poet used in the soliloquy? What do they refer to?

Sonnet

Overview

A sonnet is a fourteen-line poem in iambic pentameter with a fixed rhyme scheme. This verse form was introduced into English literature mainly by Thomas Wyatt in the 16th century. The two basic types of sonnets are the Italian or Petrarchan sonnet and the English or Shakespearean sonnet. The *Shakespearean* or *English sonnet* is arranged as three quatrains and couplet,

---

1 sicklied o'er: covered with a sickly color
2 cast: shade of color
3 enterprises of great pith and moment: actions of great importance
4 with this regard: in consideration of this
5 lose the name of action: fail to be put into action
6 Soft you now: Wait for a moment.
7 Nymph: a nymphlike maiden
8 orisons: prayers

rhyming *abab cdcd efef gg*.

Shakespeare wrote 154 sonnets which can be divided into two distinct groups. The first 126 are addressed to a "fair youth" (W. H., a handsome friend), and the others refer to a new association with the "Dark Lady". Shakespeare's sonnets are very important in history of literature.

In sonnet 18, the poet writes beautifully on the traditional theme that his poetry will bring eternity to the one he loves and highly praises.

In sonnet 29, the poet complains of his own miseries and dissatisfaction in life and then becomes happy upon the thought of the one he loves. Here Shakespeare is supposed to reveal his own thoughts and feelings.

Sonnet 18

Shall I compare thee to a summer's day[1]?
Thou art more lovely and more temperate[2]:
Rough winds do shake the darling buds of May,
And summer's lease[3] hath all too short a date:
Sometime[4] too hot the eye of heaven[5] shines,
And often is his gold complexion dimm'd:
And every fair from fair sometime declines,
By chance, or nature's changing course[6] untrimm'd[7];
But thy eternal summer shall not fade,
Nor lose possession of that fair thou ow'st[8],
Nor shall death brag[9] thou wander'st in his shade,
When in eternal lines[10] to time thou grow'st;
　So long as men can breathe or eyes can see,
　So long lives this[11], and this gives life to thee.

1 summer's day: a day in summer. In England, summer is the best season of a year.
2 temperate: neither hot nor cold
3 lease: a space of time, allotted time
4 sometime: sometimes
5 the eye of heaven: The eye of heaven here refers to the sun.
6 By chance or nature's changing course: either by fortune or by the normal course of change in the natural world
7 untrimmed: stripped of its beauty
8 thou ow'st: you own; you possess.
9 brag: boast
10 eternal lines: immortal lines of poetry, such as the lines of this sonnet
11 this: this poem

QUESTIONS

1 Why does Shakespeare use the "summer's day" as an image?
2 What are the different meanings of "fair" in "every fair from fair"?
3 What does "thy eternal summer" refer to here?
4 What does "eternal lines" refer to?
5 What kinds of rhetorical devices are used in the sonnet?
6 What is the effect of the final couplet?
7 Whom does he praise?
8 What is the theme of this sonnet?

Sonnet 29

When in disgrace[1] with Fortune and men's eyes
I all alone beweep[2] my outcast state,
And trouble deaf heaven with my bootless[3] cries,
And look upon myself, and curse my fate,
Wishing me like to one more rich in hope,
Featur'd like him, like him with friends possess'd,
Desiring this man's art[4], and that man's scope,
With what I most enjoy contented least;
Yet in these thoughts myself almost despising,
Haply[5] I think on thee,—and then my state,
Like to the lark at break of day arising
From sullen[6] earth, sings hymns at heaven's gate;
  For thy sweet love remember'd such wealth brings
  That then I scorn to change my state[7] with kings.

QUESTIONS

1 How many complains can be listed in the first eight lines?

1 in disgrace: out of favor, despised by others
2 beweep: to weep over; deplore, lament
3 bootless: useless
4 art: skill; ability, literary or other accomplishment
5 haply: fortunately, by chance
6 sullen: gloomy
7 state: condition, state of mind; or chair of state. Pay attention to a pun used here.

2 What does "my outcast state" in the second line mean?
3 Explain the speaker's change of thoughts in the whole poem.
4 Does "thee" here refer to a beautiful lady? Why?
5 What devices are used by the poet?
6 How can you associate this sonnet with humanism?

Francis Bacon
(1561-1626)

INTRODUCTION

Francis Bacon was an English author, philosopher, statesman, and scientist. He is the founder of English materialist philosophy and is known as the founder of modern science in England. Above all, Bacon is the first famous essayist in England.

Bacon was born to the family of Sir Nicholas Bacon. Associated with the court for his family connections, the boy early won the favor of the Queen. He went to Trinity College, Cambridge at 12 and, after graduating at 16, took up law. At twenty-three, he became a member of the House of Commons. At the height of his career, he was accused of taking bribes in office. He admitted accepting presents but defended the justice of his act. He was convicted, deprived of his office, fined and banished from London in 1621. Bacon retired in disgrace and resumed his writing and died in 1626.

Bacon's famous scientific works include *Advancement of Learning* (1605), *Novum Organum (New Instrument,* 1620). Bacon's philosophy emphasized the belief that people are the servants and interpreters of nature, that truth is not derived from authority, and that knowledge is the fruit of experience. *The New Atlantic* (1626) contains social ideas in the form of a story.

Bacon is famous for his *Essays*. These essays cover a wide variety of subjects, such as love, truth, friendship, parents and children, beauty, studies, riches, youth and age, garden, death and many others. His earlier essays are short, sharp and effective; the style of the later essays is rather more flowing. The essays are well-ordered and precisely arranged. Some of the best-known sayings in English come from Bacon's *Essays*, such as:

> Men fear death as children fear to go in the dark.
> That is the best part of beauty which a picture cannot express.

The famous pieces among these essays are *Of Studies*, *Of Truth*, *Of Travel* and *Of Wisdom*.

SELECTED READING

Of Studies

Overview

Of his 58 essays, *Of Studies* is one of the shortest, but the one of the better known and the more widely read. It analyzes what studies chiefly serve for, the different ways adopted by different people to pursue studies, and how studies influence human character. Many of its sentences have become wise old sayings.

Studies serve for delight, for ornament, and for ability. Their chief use for delight is in privateness and retiring[1]; for ornament, is in discourse[2]; and for ability, is in the judgment and disposition[3] of business. For expert men[4] can execute, and perhaps judge of particulars, one by one; but the general counsels, and the plots[5] and marshalling of affairs, come best from those that are learned. To spend too much time in studies is sloth; to use them too much for ornament is affectation; to make judgment wholly by their rules is the humour[6] of a scholar. They perfect nature, and are perfected by experience: for natural abilities are like natural plants, that need pruning by study; and studies themselves do give forth directions too much at large, except they be bounded in by experience. Crafty men[7] contemn studies, simple men[8] admire them, and wise men use them, for they teach not their own use; but that is a wisdom without them, and above them, won by observation. Read not to contradict and confute, nor to believe and take for granted, nor to find talk and discourse, but to weigh and consider. Some books are to be tasted, others to be swallowed, and some few to be chewed and digested; that is,

1 in privateness and retiring: when a person is alone and away from company.

2 discourse: formal conversation or speech

3 disposition: arrangement

4 expert men: men with much experience

5 plots: plans

6 humour: [archaic] the mental peculiarity

7 crafty men: skillful men; men who have some special skill

8 simple men: men having little intelligence

some books are to be read only in parts; others to be read, but not curiously[1]; and some few to be read wholly, and with diligence and attention. Some books also may be read by deputy[2], and extracts made of them by others, but that would be only in the less important arguments[3] and the meaner sort of books; else[4] distilled books[5] are like common distilled waters, flashy things[6]. Reading maketh a full man, conference[7] a ready man[8], and writing an exact man. And therefore, if a man write little, he had need have a great memory; if he confer[9] little, he had need have[10] a present wit, and if he read little, he had need have much cunning, to seem to know that he doth not. Histories make men wise; poems, witty; the mathematics, subtle; natural philosophy, deep; moral[11] grave; logic and rhetoric, able to contend. *Abeunt studia* in mores.[12] Nay, there is no stond[13] or impediment in the wit[14] but may be wrought out by fit studies like as[15] diseases of the body may have appropriate exercises. Bowling is good for the stone and reins[16], shooting for the lungs and breast, gentle walking for the stomach, riding for the head, and the like. So if a man's wit be wandering[17], let him study the mathematics; for in demonstrations, if his wit be called away never so little, he must begin again. If his wit be not apt to distinguish or find differences, let him study the

1 not curiously: not with care

2 be read by deputy: to be read with the assistance of others

3 arguments: contents or subject matter of books

4 else: or else

5 distilled books: books whose better parts have been extracted from other books

6 flashy things: tasteless things

7 conference: conversations, meetings

8 a ready man: a man who can respond readily and freely

9 confer: to converse, speak

10 had need have: ought to have

11 moral: moral philosophy

12 *abeunt studia in mores*:[Latin] "Studies have an influence upon the manners of those that are conversant in them".

13 stond: hindrance, difficulty

14 in the wit: in the mind

15 like as:[archaic] as

16 the stone and reins: the gall bladder and kidneys

17 if a man's wit be wandering: if a man's mind cannot concentrate on anything.

schoolmen[1], for they are *Cymini sectores*[2]. If he be not apt to beat over matters[3] and to call up one thing to prove and illustrate another, let him study the lawyers' cases. So every defect of the mind may have a special receipt[4].

QUESTIONS

1 Why does the author say, "Studies serve for delight, for ornament, and for ability"?
2 What are "three abuses of studies"?
3 How do you remedy the abuses according to the instruction?
4 How do you read and study?
5 What is the function of reading different books?
6 What does the last sentence mean?

EXERCISES OF CHAPTER II

I Fill the following blanks.

1 Thomas More wrote his famous prose work "____________".

2 In Elizabethan Period, ____________wrote more than fifty excellent essays, which made him one of the best essayists in English literature.

3 Shakespeare's four great tragedies generally refer to "____________", "____________", "____________", and "____________".

4 Two features are striking of this Renaissance movement. The one is a thirsting curiosity for ____________ literature. Another feature of the Renaissance is the keen interest in ____________. Humanism is the ____________of the Renaissance.

II Find the relevant match from Column B for each item in Column A.

Part I

Column A	Column B
1 ( ) William Shakespeare	A. *Tamburlaine the Great*
2 ( ) Thomas More	B. *The Faerie Queene*
3 ( ) Edmund Spenser	C. *Of Truth*

1 schoolmen: medieval philosophers or theologians

2 *Cymini sectores*: [Latin] dividers of cumin-seeds, i.e., hairsplitters

3 beat over matters: discuss a subject thoroughly

4 receipt: cure, prescription

4 ( ) Francis Bacon — D. *Othello*

5 ( ) Christopher Marlowe — E. *Utopia*

Part II

Column A	Column B
6 ( ) *The Merchant of Venice*	F. Desdemona
7 ( ) *As You Like It*	G. Cordelia
8 ( ) *Hamlet*	H. Juliet
9 ( ) *King Lear*	I. Ophelia
10 ( ) *Othello*	J. Falstaff
11 ( ) *Romeo and Juliet*	K. Rosalind
12 ( ) *Henry IV*	L. Portia

III Choose the best answer for each statement.

1 The English Renaissance Period was an age of ________.

A. ballads and songs B. poetry and drama

C. essays and journals D. prose and novel

2 The well-known soliloquy by Hamlet "To be, or not to be...And lose the name of action." shows his ________.

A. hatred for his uncle B. love for life

C. resolution of revenge D. inner contradiction

3 The first poet to introduce the sonnet into English literature is ________.

A. William Shakespeare B. Thomas Wyatt

C. Francis Bacon D. Thomas More

4 It was ________ who made blank verse the principal vehicle of expression in drama.

A. Thomas More B. Christopher Marlowe

C. Francis Bacon D. William Shakespeare

5 Choose the one author who does not belong to the group of "University Wits" from the following playwrights.

A. John Lyly B. Robert Greene

C. William Shakespeare D. Christopher Marlowe

6 Whom does the poet praise in the Sonnet 18 and Sonnet 29?
The person is ________.

A. a young beautiful lady B. a dark lady

C. a handsome young man D. the poet's girl friend

IV Answer the following questions.

1 How can you associate Sonnet 18 with the Renaissance humanism?

2 What is your interpretation on Hamlet's melancholy?

CHAPTER III
English Literature in the Seventeenth Century

General Introduction

English literature in the 17th century is related to the bourgeois revolution and the restoration. The English bourgeois revolution (or civil war) broke out between Charles I and the Parliament in 1642. All the classes in England soon split up into two camps. The royalist troops were defeated by Oliver Cromwell and Charles I himself was captured and imprisoned. In January, 1649, Charles I was tried and beheaded. The civil war ended and England was declared a commonwealth.

In 1653, Oliver Cromwell imposed a military dictatorship on the country. After his death in 1658, monarchy was again restored. In 1660, the son of the beheaded king was welcomed back as King Charles II until 1688, which has been known as the period of the Restoration.

In 1688, the country invited Prince William of Orange, Mary's husband, to be the King of England. It is called "Glorious Revolution" because it was bloodless. After that, the state structure of England was settled, within which capitalism could develop freely.

The literature in the Revolution Period is different from the literature of Elizabethan Period in the following three aspects: one is that the king became the open enemy of the people, and the country was divided by the struggle for political and religious liberty. So literature was divided in spirit into two groups. Another is that the literature in the Puritan Age expressed rage and sadness. Even its brightest hours were followed by gloom and pessimism. However, the Revolution period produced one of the most important poets in English literature, John Milton, and in his works, the indomitable revolutionary spirit found its noblest expression. Therefore, this period is also called Age of Milton. It is generally agreed that the English poet second after Shakespeare is John Milton. John Milton towers over his age as William Shakespeare towers over the Elizabethan Age and as Chaucer towers over the medieval period. Moreover, the main literary form of the period was poetry. Besides Milton, there were two other groups of poets, the *Metaphysical Poets* and the *Cavalier Poets*.

Metaphysical Poets appeared in England at about the beginning of the 17th century. The works of these poets, **Metaphysical poetry**, are characterized by mysticism in content and fantasticalith in form. John Donne is the founder of **the Metaphysical School.** The Metaphysical poets wrote verses which were generally less beautiful and less musical, and which contained tricks of style and unusual images to attract attention. These poets mixed strong feelings with reason and the mixture is strange. They emphasized the intellectual and psychological aspects of emotion and religion.

Most of the **Cavalier Poets** were courtiers and soldiers. Their poetry expresses the spirit of pessimism.

The period also produced a great prose writer, John Bunyan. The famous playwright is John Dryden.

John Dryden (1631-1700) was an English poet, literary critic, translator, and playwright. He is the greatest literary figure of the Restoration, the greatest poet between Milton and Pope. He was the first poet in England to attain the posts of Poet Laureate conferred by letters patent in 1670. The post became a regular institution. But it is his *An Essay of Dramatic Poesy* that established his position as the leading critic of the day to such a point that the period came to be known in literary circles as the Age of Dryden. His celebrated *An Essay of Dramatic Poesy* discusses the principles of drama and compares the qualities of Ben Jonson and Shakespeare, which made him become the foremost critic of his age.

Dryden once studied in the famous Westminster school and then in Cambridge. In the political affairs, he was quite changeable in attitude. He once supported Cromwell and wrote a poem upon Cromwell's death. When the Restoration period began, he turned to the Royalists. In order to make a living he wrote nearly 30 plays and did a series of distinguished translations of Virgil and other classical authors.

John Donne
(1572?- 1631)

INTRODUCTION

John Donne was an English poet and a cleric in the Church of England. He is considered the pre-eminent representative of the metaphysical poets, the founder of the Metaphysical school.

Donne was the son of a merchant in London. He went first to Oxford (1584) and then to Cambridge (1587), but left without taking a degree, because of his Roman Catholic background. And then he studied law in London at Lincoln's Inn (1592). He spent much of his time studying law, languages, literature, and theology. Many of his poems were written before 1600, including most of his *Songs and Sonnets*. In 1621, Donne was appointed the Dean of St. Paul's Cathedral and kept that post until his death. He also served as the Member of Parliament in 1601 and in 1614. In the 18th and 19th centuries his poetry was neglected, but in the 20th century he was much praised and even imitated by a number of poets in England and America, including T. S. Eliot, John Ransom, and Allen Tate.

His poetry involves a certain kind of argument. He seems to be speaking to an imagined hearer, raising the topic and trying to persuade, or convince him. With the brief, simple language, the argument is continuous throughout the poem. The diction is simple, and the imagery is drawn from the actual life. His *Songs and Sonnets*, a collection of his 55 love lyrics, are probably his finest work. Donne was also a lawyer and a priest. His greatest prose works are his sermons, which are both rich and imaginative. He can say effective things in a few words. John Donne is among the best preachers in England.

> No man is an island, entire of itself; every man is a piece of the continent, a part of the main;...any man's death diminishes me, because I am involved in mankind; and therefore never send to know for whom the bell tolls; it tolls for thee.

The most remarkable feature of metaphysical poetry is its use of **the conceit** which is a clever comparison made in a piece of writing. It is an elaborate extended simile or figurative comparison within a poem, used especially by the metaphysical poets. The metaphysical conceits bring together things that are primarily unlike, such as *fleas* and *marriage temples* in the following poem. John Donne is undoubtedly the master of conceits and achieves surprisingly good effects in his poetry. He has got his fame as "the great writer of conceited verse." His poem may be composed of a group of conceits based on a central one.

SELECTED READING

The Flea

Overview

In the poem, *The Flea*, John Donne gives us a vivid image. The flea's sucking both the man's and the lady's blood is compared to be a worldly marriage; the flea then unifies them; when the lady angrily kills the flea, she commits suicide as well as a murder. The central conceit—the flea as the combination of the two—is reinforced through different levels. Through some images and metaphors, the poet expresses his thoughts, and through the thoughts to express his emotion.

Mark[1] but this flea, and mark in this,
How little that which thou deniest me is;
Me it sucked first, and now sucks thee,
And in this flea our two bloods mingled be;
Thou know'st that this cannot be said
A sin, nor shame, nor loss of maidenhead;
Yet this enjoys before it woo,
And pampered swells with one blood made of two[2],
And this, alas, is more than we would do[3].

Oh stay[4], three lives in one flea spare[5],
Where we almost, yea, more than married are.
This flea is you and I, and this
Our marriage bed and marriage temple is;

1 mark: [archaic] pay attention to; notice

2 And pampered swells with one blood made of two: The condition of *pampered swells* suggests pregnancy.

3 this, alas, is more than we would do: we, alas, don't dare to hope for this consummation of our love, which the flea freely accepts.

4 stay: stop

5 three lives in one flea spare: spare three lives in one flea

Though parents grudge, and you, we are met,
And cloistered in these living walls of jet[1].
Though use[2] make you apt to kill me,
Let not to that, self-murder added be[3],
And sacrilege[4], three sins in killing three.

Cruel and sudden, hast thou since
Purpled thy nail in blood of innocence?
Wherein could this flea guilty be,
Except in that drop which it sucked from thee?
Yet thou triumph'st, and say'st that thou
Find'st not thy self nor me the weaker now.[5]
'Tis true; then learn how false fears be;
Just so much honour, when thou yield'st to me,
Will waste, as this flea's death took life from thee.

QUESTIONS

1 Who is the speaker in this poem?
2 What is the typical comparison in the poem?
3 What does "three lives in one flea spare" mean?
4 Why does the speaker say that to kill the flea would be "three sins in killing three"?
5 What is the real purpose of the male speaker's argument?
6 What is the tone of the poem?

Death, Be Not Proud

Overview

This is a sonnet written in the strict Petrarchan pattern, with 14 lines of iambic

---

1 these living walls of jet: "These living walls of jet" refer to the body of the flea.

2 use: custom, habit

3 Let not to that, self-murder added be: Don't do that (killing the flea) to add new crime of self-murder.

4 sacrilege: disrespectful treatment of what should be sacred

5 Find'st not thy self nor me the weaker now: You do not find both of us weaker now.

pentameter rhyming abba abba cddcee. The poem reveals the poet's belief in life after death. Donne compares death to rest or sleep. He believes that death is only momentary, while happiness after death is eternal. John Donne expresses his religious idea peculiarly in the supposed dialogue with "death". In the poem, various reasons are listed to argue against the common belief in death as "mighty and dreadful". This sonnet is regarded as a typical work of the school of metaphysical poetry.

Death, be not proud, though some have called thee
Mighty and dreadful, for thou art not so;
For those whom thou think'st thou dost overthrow
Die not, poor Death, nor yet canst thou kill me.
From rest and sleep, which but thy pictures[1] be,
Much pleasure; then from thee much more[2] must flow,
And soonest[3] our best men with thee do go,
Rest of their bones, and soul's delivery[4].
Thou art slave to fate, chance, kings, and desperate men,
And dost with poison, war, and sickness dwell,
And poppy[5] or charms can make us sleep as well
And better[6] than thy stroke; why swell'st thou then?
One short sleep past, we wake eternally
And death shall be no more; Death, thou shalt die.

QUESTIONS

1 What do some people call Death?
2 Why is the speaker not afraid of death?
3 What does "Rest of their bones, and soul's delivery" mean here?
4 Why does the speaker say that "death" is the "slave to fate, chance, kings, and desperate men"?
5 What does "One short sleep past, we wake eternally" imply?
6 List the personification that the poet uses in the sonnet.

---

1 pictures: images, likeness
2 much more: much more pleasure
3 soonest: most willingly
4 delivery: freedom
5 poppy: opium
6 better: easier

John Milton
(1608-1674)

INTRODUCTION

John Milton (1608-1674) was an English poet, polemicist, man of letters, and a civil servant for the Commonwealth of England under Oliver Cromwell. He is best known for his epic poem *Paradise Lost* (1667), written in blank verse. Writing in English, Latin, Greek, Hebrew, and Italian, he achieved international renown within his lifetime. It is generally agreed that John Milton is the English poet second after Shakespeare.

He is called the greatest writer of the 17th century, and one of the giants of English literature. He towers over his age as Shakespeare towers over the Elizabethan age, and as Chaucer towers over the medieval period. He made a strong influence on the later English poetry.

Milton is a great revolutionary poet of the 17th century, an outstanding political pamphleteer. During the civil war and the commonwealth, there were two leaders in England, Cromwell, the man of action, and John Milton, the man of thought.

Milton is a great stylist. His poetry has a grand style. That is because he made a study of classical and Biblical literature. His poetry is famous for sublimity of thought and majesty of expression.

He is a great master of blank verse and the glorious pioneer to introduce blank verse into non-dramatic poetry. Milton also contributed 24 sonnets.

Milton was born in London, whose father was a merchant, a lover of music and literature, and a radical Puritan in politics and religion. His mother was a woman of refinement and social grace, with a deep interest in religion and in local charities. Young Milton was educated at the famous St. Paul's School in London, where he showed talent for mastering the ancient languages and literatures. He went on to distinguish himself at Christ's College, Cambridge University, where he got BA in 1629 and MA in 1632. He was famous for his personal beauty and the strictness of his life and was nicknamed "the Lady of the Christ's" by the students of the college. After his graduation he lived and studied in his father's country house at Horton in Buckinghamshire. There he devoted himself to study and to the writing of poetry. In 1638 he left England to complete his education with two years of travel in Europe.

When he returned home in 1639, England was on the verge of a civil war between Charles I and Parliament (Cromwell) from 1642 to 1651. During these years, he worked hard at his pamphlets, supported Cromwell. He was the spokesman of the Revolution and wrote a number of pamphlets defending the English revolution, such as *A Defense of the English People* (1651) and *Second Defense of the English People* (1654). He published his best prose work *Areopagitica* in 1644, in which the style is fairly simple. Milton's sincere belief in the importance of freedom of writing and speech fills the book with honest feeling. After the Revolution succeeded and the commonwealth was established, Milton became Latin Secretary to the council of Foreign Affairs. His eyesight began to fail, and by 1651 he was totally blinded. When Charles II was made king in 1660, he became unpopular. He was once arrested and fined but finally released, and left in peace to produce his poetic works. From then on he wrote his three greatest works: *Paradise Lost* (1667), *Paradise Regained* (1671), and the poetical drama, *Samson Agonistes* (1671). The stories of three works were taken from the Old Testament.

Milton was married to Mary Powell, a member of a Royalist family, in June, 1642. Six weeks after the marriage she left to return to her parents. In 1645, she returned and bore her husband three daughters and a son who died infancy. She died herself in 1652 in giving birth to the third daughter. For several years Milton issued pamphlets in which he argued that all Englishmen should have the right to get a divorce. Milton got married three times. His blindness forced him to depend on his daughters for assistance with his reading and writing. In his last years he suffered more and more from gout, and he died of it in 1674.

Samson Agonistes is the most perfect example of the verse drama after the Greek style in English. This tragedy describes the last days of Samson, when he is blind and a pioneer of the Philistines at Gaza. He is forced to go away to provide amusement for the Philistine lords; but later Samson pulls down the whole theatre on their heads and his own. When Milton wrote this play, he had been blind for about twenty years. Samson's sorrows no doubt reminded him of his own. The poetical play suggests Milton's longing that he too could bring destruction down upon the enemy at the cost of his own life. In this sense, Samson is Milton.

Milton's poetry is not easy reading and does not sound natural. His Biblical and classical allusions and his epic similes are often obscure and their beauty is difficult to be caught even with the help of explanatory notes.

SELECTED READING

Paradise Lost

Overview

Milton's reputation rests largely on *Paradise Lost,* his masterpiece and an epic poem in blank verse, which was written between 1658 and 1663, in 12 books. The story of the epic was taken from the Bible (Old Testament). It is about Satan's revolt against god and man's loss of paradise.

Satan was once Lucifer, the highest angel in Heaven. In an attempt to make himself equal to God, he had rebelled and persuaded one-third of the angels to rebel with him. But they were defeated by god and put into Hell. They have lain in torment on a burning lake for 9 days. Satan and his followers, though defeated by God and thrown into Hell, are not discouraged.

The epic begins with a detailed description of Satan and his followers' meeting in Hell and planning to take their revenge on God. Satan chooses for his battlefield the most perfect of spots ever created by God—the Garden of Eden, where live the first man and woman, Adam and Eve. Satan's plan is to tear the first man and woman away from the influence of God. It is Satan who deceives Eve and Adam to eat the fruit on the tree of knowledge. In doing so, they disobey God and therefore are driven out of Paradise. They lose their innocence, happiness, and immortality, and are doomed to an earthly life full of sufferings.

The selection below is taken from Book I, and includes Satan's powerful speech as they denounce the tyranny of God and plot for revenge. Satan is not a bit discouraged and he still plans to take revenge on God.

Book I

(Excerpt)

...

What though the field be lost[1]?
All is not lost: the unconquerable will,
And study[2] of revenge, immortal hate,
And courage never to submit or yield:
And what is else not to be overcome? [3]
That glory never shall his wrath or might
Extort from me. To bow and sue for grace[4]

1 What though the field be lost?: What does it matter though we have lost the battle with God? field: battlefield

2 study: pursuit

3 And what is else not to be overcome: What are other things that cannot be conquered?

4 sue for grace: beg for mercy

With suppliant knee, and deify[1] his power
Who from the terror of this arm so late
Doubted his empire[2]—that were low[3] indeed,
That were an ignominy[4] and shame beneath
This downfall[5]; since by fate the strength of gods
And this empyreal substance cannot fail;[6]
Since through experience of this great event[7]
In arms not worse, in foresight much advanced,
We may with more successful hope resolve
To wage by force or guile eternal war
Irreconcilable to our grand Foe[8],
Who now triumphs, and in th' excess of joy
Sole reigning holds the tyranny of Heaven.

QUESTIONS

1 What does "That glory never shall his wrath or might/Extort from me." mean here?
2 What does Satan consider the "ignominy" and "shame" as?
3 Why does God doubt his "empire" after the battle?
4 What would Satan like to do for the eternal way?
5 What is the image of Satan in the poem?
6 What does "God" symbolize in *Paradise Lost*?

---

1 deify: worship

2 doubted his empire: doubted whether he could maintain his empire. doubted: feared for, lost confidence in; empire: authority and power

3 low: mean, degraded

4 ignominy: shame, disgrace

5 shame beneath/This downfall: a more shameful thing than this defeat

6 by fate the strength of gods/And this empyreal substance cannot fail: The essence of Satan's fault is his claim to the position of a god, subject to fate but to nothing else. His substance is "empyreal" and cannot be destroyed.

7 this great event: It refers to the battle between God and Satan.

8 our grand foe: It refers to God.

John Bunyan
(1628-1688)

INTRODUCTION

John Bunyan (1628-1688) was an English writer and Baptist preacher best remembered as the author of the Christian allegory *The Pilgrim's Progress*. In the field of prose writing of the Puritan Age, John Bunyan occupies the most important place.

His father was a poor village tinker, and Bunyan received only the simplest education before taking up his father's trade. He eventually married and fought with the parliamentary army during the Civil War.

After the Restoration, he was imprisoned in 1660 for preaching without a licence. Bunyan spent most of the next years writing nine books in Bedford Jail. After his release in 1672, he was imprisoned again for a short period in 1677. During his second imprisonment he wrote his most important work, *The Pilgrim's Progress*.

John Bunyan's prose set an example of clear, simple expression, especially in *The Pilgrim's Progress* and *The Holy War* (1682). His style was influenced by his regular reading of the Authorised Version of the Bible and it reflects the beauty and earnest simplicity of that translation.

SELECTED READING

The Pilgrim's Progress

Overview

The Pilgrim's Progress (1678) is John Bunyan's great allegory of Christian journey to heaven through the evils of the world. This prose set an example of clear, simple expression. *The Pilgrim's Progress* was written as a book of religious instruction for simple folk, in the form of allegory and dream. The traveller's name is Christian, and he represents every Christian in human world. The figures and places Christian encounters on his journey stand for the various experiences every Christian must go through in the quest for salvation.

The whole book falls into two parts. At the beginning of the first part the author tells us that he has a dream. In the dream, he sees a man called

Christian setting out with a book in hand and a great load on his back from the city of Destruction. Christian has two objects: one is to get rid of his burden, which holds the sins and fears of his life, and the other is to make his way to the Holy City. As Christian goes forward, his neighbours, friends, wife and children call to him to come back; but he puts his fingers in his ears, crying out, "Life, life, eternal life" and rushes across the plain, starting his journey. On the way he overcomes many obstacles and encounters various personages, such as, Mr. Worldly Wiseman, Faithful, Hopeful, Giant Despair, Apollyon and some others. He passes the Palace Beautiful, the Valley of Humiliation, the Valley of Shadow, and Vanity Fair. Finally he accomplishes his journey and arrives at the Celestial City. The second part describes the subsequent conversion of his wife and their children, and their similar journey with a group of friends.

The excerpt is taken from *Vanity Fair*, one part of *The Pilgrim's Progress.* In the Vanity Fair, all sorts of vanity are sold. All of the relationship may be business. This is the symbol of London at the time of Restoration. William Thackeray used this subheading to write a long novel, *Vanity Fair.*

Vanity Fair

(Excerpt)

Then I saw in my dream, that when they were got out of the wilderness, they presently saw a town before them, and the name of that town is Vanity[1]; and at the town there is a fair kept, called Vanity Fair; it is kept all the year long. It beareth the name of Vanity Fair, because the town where it is kept is lighter than vanity; and also because all that is there sold, or that cometh thither is vanity. As is the saying of the wise, "All that cometh is vanity."

This fair is no new-erected business; but a thing of ancient standing; I will show you the original of it.

Almost five thousand years agone[2], there were pilgrims walking to the Celestial City, as these two honest persons[3] are; and Beelzebub, Apollyon, and Legion[4], with their companions, perceiving by the path that the pilgrims

1 "I" here refers to the author who saw the pilgrim's journey in his dream; "they" refer to Christian and his friend Faithful who are on their way to the Celestial City.

2 agone (archaic): ago

3 these two honest persons: Christian and Faithful

4 Beelzebub, Apollyon and Legion: Here they are used by author to refer to all the devils and evil spirits.

made, that their way to the city lay through this town of Vanity, they contrived here to set up a fair; a fair wherein should be sold of all sorts of vanity, and that it should last all the year long. Therefore at this fair are all such merchandise sold: as houses, lands, trades, places, honours, preferments, titles, countries, kingdoms; lusts, pleasures, and delights of all sorts, as whores, bawds, wives, husbands, children, masters, servants, lives, blood, bodies, souls, silver, gold, pearls, precious stones, and what not[1].

And, moreover, at this fair there is at all times to be seen jugglings, cheats, games, plays, fools, apes, knaves, and rogues and that of every kind.

Here are to be seen, too, and that for nothing, thefts, murders, adulteries, false-swearers, and that of a blood-red colour.

And as in other fairs of less moment[2], there are the several rows[3] and streets, under their proper names, where such and such wares are vended; so here likewise you have the proper places, rows, streets (viz.[4], countries and kingdoms), where the wares of this fair are soonest[5] to be found. Here is the Britain Row; the French Row; the Italian Row; the Spanish Row; the German Row—where several sorts of vanities are to be sold. But as in other fairs, some one commodity is as the chief of all the fair, so the ware of Rome and her merchandise is greatly promoted in this fair: only our English nation, with some others[6], have taken a dislike thereat.

Now, as I said, the way to the Celestial City lies just through this town, where this lusty fair is kept; and he that will go to the City, and yet not go through this town, must needs "go out of the world". The Prince of princes[7] himself, when here, went through this town to his own country, and that upon a fair day too; and as I think, it was Beelzebub, the chief lord of this fair, that invited him to buy of his vanities; yea, would have made him lord of

1 and what not: and other things of similar kind

2 less moment: less importance

3 rows: short streets or narrow streets

4 viz.: (Latin) namely

5 soonest: easiest

6 only our English nation, with some others: The sentence refers to the Reformation in England and other European countries.

7 The prince of princes: Jesus Christ

the fair, would he but have done him reverence as he went through the town. Yea, because he was such a person of honour, Beelzebub had him from street to street, and showed him all the kingdoms of the world in a little time, that he might, if possible, allure the Blessed One[1], to cheapen and buy some of his vanities; but he had no mind to the merchandise; and therefore left the town without laying out[2] so much as one farthing upon these vanities. This fair, therefore, is an ancient thing, of long standing, and a very great fair.

Now, these pilgrims, as I said, must needs go through this fair. Well, so they did: but, behold, even as they entered into the fair, all the people in the fair were moved[3], and the town itself as it were in a hubbub about them, and that for several reasons: for—

...

QUESTIONS

1 Who built this Vanity Fair?
2 Why is the market known as Vanity Fair?
3 What can be seen in Vanity Fair?
4 What would be sold in this market?
5 Why does the author list the names of streets?
6 Do you think that Bunyan has satirized England in the story? Why?

EXERCISES OF CHAPTER III

I Fill in the following blanks.

1 The English bourgeois revolution broke out between ____________ and the ____________ in 1642.

2 1649, Charles I was tried and ____________. The civil war ended and England was declared a ____________.

3 In 1660, the son of the beheaded king was welcomed back as ____________ until 1688, which has been known as the period of

1 the Blessed One: Jesus Christ
2 laying out: expending
3 moved: excited

the ____________.

4 In this period, John Milton towers over his age as ____________ towers over the Elizabethan Age and as ____________ towers over the Medieval period.

II Find the relevant match from Column B for each item in Column A.

Part I

Column A	Column B
1 ( ) John Milton	A. *An Essay of Dramatic Poesy*
2 ( ) John Bunyan	B. *Songs and Sonnets*
3 ( ) John Donne	C. *Samson Agonistes*
4 ( ) John Dryden	D. *The Pilgrim's Progress*

Part II

5 ( ) Metaphysical poetry	E. *Paradise Lost*
6 ( ) Satan	F. *Vanity Fair*
7 ( ) Allegory	G. John Milton
8 ( ) blank verse	H. John Donne

III Choose the best answer for each statement.

1 *Paradise Lost is* ______ except one. Which one?
A. Milton's masterpiece　B. a great epic in 12 books
C. written in blank verse　D. Metaphysical poetry

2. Milton has the following titles, except one. Which one?
A. a great revolutionary poet of the 17th century
B. an outstanding political pamphleteer
C. foremost critic of his age
D. a great master of blank verse

3. The most remarkable feature in *The Flea* is its use of ______.
A. metaphor　B. simile　C. personification　D. conceit

4. The stories of *Paradise Lost* were taken from ______.
A. Greek mythology　B. the Old Testament
C. the New Testament　D. Chinese ancient tales

5. John Bunyan wrote *The Pilgrim's Progress* in the form of ______.
A. religious instruction　B. clear, and simple expression
C. allegory and dream　D. conceit and satire

IV Answer the following questions.

1 What does Satan in *Paradise Lost* symbolize?

2 What is conceit? How does John Donne use conceit in his poetry?

CHAPTER IV

English Literature in the Eighteenth Century

General Introduction

The eighteenth century is an era of peace, prosperity, optimism, balance and glory for Great Britain. Politically, Glorious Revolution of the 1688 helped the bourgeoisie came to power without a bloody revolution. A well-balanced state-system of two parties, Whigs and Tories, allowed peaceful shift of power. In order to keep balance of votes, London was flooded with pamphlets. Most of talented writers of this age became the willing servants of the Whigs or Tories. The famous pamphleteers included Richard Steele (1672-1729), Joseph Addison (1672-1719), Daniel Defoe (1660-1731), and Jonathan Swift (1667-1745).

Economically, Industrial Revolution and fast-expanding colonization boosted the development of capitalism and made Great Britain become the empire on which "the sun never sets" with great wealth, which filled the middle class with the spirit of optimism.

Great changes of social life happened with the emergency of social clubs and coffee-houses. In London, about three thousand public coffee-houses and a large number of private clubs appeared in the first half of the 18th century, where nearly all the writers went to the coffee-houses talking and arguing about social problems and the matters discussed there became the materials of literature.

Intellectually, the 18th century witnessed the spread of Enlightenment Movement which was an intellectual movement dominating the world of ideas in Europe in the 18th century. The Enlightenment included a range of ideas centered on reason as the primary source of authority and legitimacy, and advocated liberty, progress, tolerance, fraternity, constitutional government, and separation of church and state. The English Enlighteners, different from those of France, appealed more to reformation instead of revolution, replacing the feudal ideas with the bourgeois ideology. They fought against class inequality, stagnation, prejudices and other survivals of feudalism. The enlighteners proved that man was born kind and honest. The corrupted social environment would make a man depraved. The English Enlightenment literature is intended much for the interest of the middle class.

There were many literature trends in the 18th century England, Neo-classism, Realistic novel, and Sentimentalism. Richard Steele, Joseph Addison and Alexander Pope were among the important figures of English Enlightenment, who drew some fixed rules, laws, disciplines from Greek and Latin works, using rimed couplet instead of blank verse, preferring to regularity in construction. Alexander Pope is the greatest enlightener and poets, famous for heroic couplets he used in his poems. Samuel Johnson (1709-1784) was a poet, essayist, and lexicographer, whose *A Dictionary of the English Language* is a landmark in the study of English language.

Robinson Crusoe (1719) by Daniel Defoe (1660-1731) is the first English realistic novel. Jonathan Swift (1667-1745), Henry Fielding (1707-1754) and Toblas George Smollet (1721-1771) gave a panorama of the English society from many perspectives, exposing and attacking the political system and the avaricious aristocracy and middle-class. Swift was the most influential and outstanding one, for his fierce and ruthless exposure of attack on the social problems especially in his masterpiece, *Gulliver's Travels* (1726).

Samuel Richardson (1689-1761) was a writer and printer, who showed interest in psychoanalysis in his novel *Pamela* (1740), which is the first English psycho-analytical novel and the first epistolary novel. *Pamela* is a novel written in the form of letters. When the letters began to appear, the ladies of the time were excited. They could read about the feelings of an English girl, Pamela Andrews. The story is simple about a good girl who receives the rewards of virtue. Because the story came out in letters, the ladies could try to persuade Richardson to let Pamela do what they wanted. Some critics think that *Pamela* is the first English novel in the modern sense. Another famous epistolary novel by Richardson is *Clarissa: Or the History of a Young Lady* (1748).

Sentimentalism is the practice of being sentimental, or the tendency to base actions and reactions from emotions and feelings as opposed to reason. And Sentimentalists express their discontent with both of the survival of feudalism and the progress of bourgeois. They resorted to sentiment instead of reason for happiness and social justice, for the latter one was not sufficient. Lawrence Sterne (1713-1768), Oliver Goldsmith (1730-1774) and Thomas Gray (1716-1771) were the representatives of Sentimentalism. Lawrence Sterne is the most outstanding figure of English sentimentalism. To him sentiment is more important than reason. His masterpieces are *Tristram Shandy* (1760-1767) and *A Sentimental Journey* (1768). Sentimentalism is named after *A Sentimental Journey*. Sterne gave detailed descriptions of the characters' inner thoughts and feelings. His characters are ordinary persons who are like real persons with faults and merits.

The 18th century showed a decline of drama, and the only brief flowering could be found in the comedies of Richard Brinsley Sheridan (1751-1816) and Oliver Goldsmith (1728-1774). Sheridan is the most important playwright of English literature in the 18th century, who is also a satirist and poet. His masterpiece is *The School for Scandal* (1777). Oliver Goldsmith is an Irish novelist, playwright, essayist and poet. He is best known for his novel *The Vicar of Wakefield* (1766).

William Blake (1757-1827) and Robert Burns (1759-1796) are known as pre-romantic poets in the 18th century.

Daniel Defoe
(1660-1731)

INTRODUCTION

Daniel Defoe (1660-1731) is the first writer to create an image of enterprising capitalist English society, who is one of the forerunners of English realistic novel. Defoe was born in London in 1660, a son of a butcher. He was a jack-of-all-trades, taking up various occupations, a merchant, politician, journalist, pamphleteer, publicist, and novelist. He had been through upheavals of prosperity, poverty, power, influence, and imprisonment.

In his journalistic works and pamphlets, he exposed and lashed the vices and follies of the ruling class, and touched upon many subjects, which provided materials for his novels to make them vivid and true to life. He wrote in simple, easy, colloquial, precise and plain language, a language of common people.

Robinson Crusoe (1719) is his masterpiece, which makes him immortal as a great writer. His other major works are *Captain Singleton* (1720), *Moll Flanders* (1722), *A Journal of the Plague Year* (1722).

SELECTED READING

Robinson Crusoe

Overview

Robinson Crusoe (1719) is Defoe's representative work. It's based on a real story of a Scottish sailor's adventure in the Atlantic. Robinson Crusoe, a young man from an old English gentleman's family, refuses to take a decent job in law as his father wishes and leaves home to be a sailor. On his voyage to Africa, their ship is wrecked off the coast of an uninhabited island, and he is the only one who has survived. He has nothing but some bread, rice, corn, lead and gunpowder, an axe and two saws to live on alone on the island.

With strenuous and consistent effort and indomitable persistence, he manages to live and live better by planting grains, building a boat, hunting and domesticating wild animals, exploring the island, in spite of failures, disappointment and hostile conditions. One day, Crusoe saves a black young man, a victim of a group of cannibals who came to the island to celebrate their victory. Crusoe names him Friday, who turns out a loyal and helpful companion. After 28 years of living on the island, Crusoe is saved by an English ship and comes back to the civilized world of England.

In the novel, Crusoe is celebrated as a hero for his capability, persistence and optimism in adversity. He feeds himself with food and hope through his hard labour. The optimistic enterprising spirit is a mirror of the bourgeoisie in its early stage of development.

Part 1

(Excerpt)

When I came down from my apartment in the tree I looked about me again, and the first thing I found was the boat, which lay as the wind and the sea had tossed her upon the land, about two miles on my right hand. I walked as far as I could upon the shore to have got to her, but found a neck or inlet of water between me and the boat, which was about half a mile broad; so I came back for the present, being more intent upon getting at the ship, where I hoped to find something for my present subsistence.

A little after noon I found the sea very calm, and the tide ebbed so far out, that I could come within a quarter of a mile of the ship; and here I found a fresh renewing of my grief, for I saw evidently, that if we had kept on board, we had been all safe, that is to say, we had all got safe on shore, and I had not been so miserable as to be left entirely destitute of all comfort and company, as I now was; this forced tears from my eyes again, but as there was little relief in that, I resolved, if possible, to get to the ship, so I pull'd off my clothes, for the weather was hot to extremity, and took the water, but when I came to the ship, my difficulty was still greater to know how to get on board, for as she lay a ground, and high out of the water, there was nothing within my reach to lay hold of; I swam round her twice, and the second time I spied a small piece of a rope, which I wondered I did not see at first, hang down by the fore-chains so low, as that with great difficulty I got hold of it, and by the help of that rope, got up into the forecastle of the ship; here I found that the ship was bulged, and had a great deal of water in her hold, but that she lay so on the side of a bank of hard sand, or rather earth, that her stern lay lifted up upon the bank, and her head low almost to the water; by this means all her quarter was free[1], and all that was in that part was dry; for you may be sure my first work was to search and to see what was spoiled and what was free[2]; and first I found that all the ship's provisions were dry and untouched by the water, and being very well disposed to eat, I went to the bread-room and filled my pockets with biscuit, and eat it as I went about other things[3], for I had no time to lose; I also found some Rum[4] in the great cabin, of which I took a large dram, and which I had indeed need enough of to spirit me for what was before me. Now I wanted nothing but a boat to furnish myself with many things which I foresaw would be very necessary to me.

QUESTIONS

1 What was Crusoe's "present subsistence"?
2 What was he grieving over the most?
3 How did Crusoe get to the ship?
4 What did Crusoe find in the ship?
5 What kind of character can you find of Crusoe from "as there was little relief in that, I resolved, if possible, to get to the ship"?
6 How does the writer make the story real and credible?

1 all her quarter was free: There was no water in all the after part of the ship. quarter: the upper portion of the after side of a ship

2 what was spoiled and what was free: Here "what" refers to the food.

3 and eat it as I went about other things: At that time "eat" could be used as the past tense.

4 rum: an alcoholic liquor distilled from fermented molasses or sugar cane

Jonathan Swift
(1667-1745)

INTRODUCTION

Jonathan Swift is an unsurpassable master of pamphlets in his time and one of the most important writers in English literature. His novels of *Gulliver's Travels* (1726), *A Tale of a Tub* (1704) and pamphlet of *A Modest Proposal* (1729) are the greatest satires in English literature with ruthless and bitter sarcasm, irony of the arrogance, cruelty, and follies of aristocracy, the ruling class, and the two parties.

Swift was born in Dublin, Ireland, in 1667. He had to live with his relatives with his father dead and mother poor. After a repressive and unpleasant time of schooling in Dublin University, he came under patronage of another relative, Sir William Temple, a statesman and a diplomat to be his private secretary. During the time he worked for Temple, Swift finished his first notable work, *Battle of the Books* (1704), which is a satire on the two-party state-system. After 10 years of hard work and humiliation of being treated as a servant, Swift left to serve in the Church of England. And then he settled in a little church in Ireland where he finished *A Tale of a Tub*, published with *Battle of the Books*, both works bringing him great success and fame as the most influential and powerful satirist. After several years living as a prominent figure participating in political strife in London, Swift went back to Ireland with the Tories getting out of power, and he died there in illness and anguish.

Gulliver's Travels is his masterpiece, one of the best-read and known works in English literature. It is a bitter irony of the corruption, hypocrisy, and vices of politics, ruling class, government, church, and human nature. The novel is in four books. The young readers usually read the first two books: Gulliver's voyages to Lilliput where the people are six inches high and Brobdingnag where the people are immense. Gulliver is then found by a farmer who was about 72 feet tall and the grass of that country is as tall as a tree. The Lilliputians fight wars as the English do, which seem foolish. The king of Brobdingnag thinks that the people in Gulliver's country must be the most hateful race of creature on earth after hearing about Gulliver's motherland. The novel is known as most famous satire.

SELECTED READING

A Modest Proposal[1]

Overview

Swift's pamphlets on Ireland is very important part of his works, *A Modest Proposal* (1729), which was the most powerful and striking one. It exposes and attacks the English Government for exploiting and draining Ireland of wealth and resources. The Irish people have to live in such extreme poverty that the writer proposes them to sell their babies to the rich as food to pay the tax to English government, to pay the rent of the landlord's, to lessen the burden of the destitute parents. It's a heart-breaking, horrifying yet fiercely indignant satire and accusation of the oppression and exploitation of English government on Ireland. It features simple language with a mask of gravity and calmness, and bitter irony concealed.

For Preventing the Children of Poor People
in Ireland from Being a Burden to Their
Parents or Country, and for Making
Them Beneficial to the Public

It is a melancholy object to those who walk through this great town[2] or travel in the country, when they see the streets, the roads, and cabin-doors, crowded with beggars of the female sex, followed by three, four, or six children, all in rags and importuning every passenger for an alms. These mothers, instead of being able to work for their honest livelihood, are forced to employ all their time in strolling to beg sustenance for their helpless infants, who, as they grow up, either turn thieves for want of work, or leave their dear native country to fight for the Pretender in Spain[3], or sell themselves to the Barbadoes.

I think it is agreed by all parties that this prodigious number of children

1 *A Modest Proposal* is an example of Swift's favorite satiric devices used with superb effect.

2 this great town: Here it refers to the city of Dublin.

3 the Pretender in Spain: The Pretender was the descendant of King James II of the House of Stuart, expelled from Britain in 1689.

in the arms, or on the backs, or at the heels of their mothers, and frequently of their fathers, is in the present deplorable state of the kingdom a very great additional grievance; and therefore whoever could find out a fair, cheap and easy method of making these children sound, useful members of the commonwealth would deserve so well of the public as to have his statue set up for a preserver of the nation.

But my intention is very far from being confined to provide only for the children of professed beggars; it is of a much greater extent, and shall take in the whole number of infants at a certain age who are born of parents in effect as little able to support them as those who demand our charity in the streets.

As to my own part, having turned my thoughts for many years upon this important subject, and maturely weighed the several schemes of other projectors[1], I have always found them grossly mistaken in their computation. It is true, a child just dropped from its dam may be supported by her milk for a solar year, with little other nourishment; at most not above the value of two shillings, which the mother may certainly get, or the value in scraps, by her lawful occupation of begging; and it is exactly at one year old that I propose to provide for them in such a manner as instead of being a charge upon their parents or the parish, or wanting food and raiment for the rest of their lives, they shall on the contrary contribute to the feeding, and partly to the clothing, of many thousands.

There is likewise another great advantage in my scheme, that it will prevent those voluntary abortions, and that horrid practice of women murdering their bastard children, alas, too frequent among us, sacrificing the poor innocent babes, I doubt, more to avoid the expense than the shame, which would move tears and pity in the most savage and inhuman breast.

The number of souls in this kingdom[2] being usually reckoned one million and a half, of these I calculate there may be about two hundred thousand couples whose wives are breeders; from which number I

1 projectors: devisers of schemes

2 kingdom: Here it refers to Ireland.

subtract thirty thousand couples who are able to maintain their own children, although I apprehend there cannot be so many under the present distresses of the kingdom; but this being granted, there will remain an hundred and seventy thousand breeders. I again subtract fifty thousand for those women who miscarry, or whose children die by accident or disease within the year. There only remain an hundred and twenty thousand children of poor parents annually born. The question therefore is, how this number shall be reared and provided for, which, as I have already said, under the present situation of affairs, is utterly impossible by all the methods hitherto proposed. For we can neither employ them in handicraft or agriculture; we neither build houses (I mean in the country) nor cultivate land. They can very seldom pick up a livelihood by stealing till they arrive at six years old, except where they are of towardly[1] parts; although I confess they learn the rudiments much earlier, during which time they can however be properly looked upon only as probationers, as I have been informed by a principal gentleman in the county of Cavan, who protested to me that he never knew above one or two instances under the age of six, even in a part of the kingdom so renowned for the quickest proficiency in that art.

I am assured by our merchants that a boy or a girl before twelve years old is no saleable commodity; and even when they come to this age they will not yield above three pounds, or three pounds and half a crown at most on the Exchange; which cannot turn to account either to the parents or kingdom[2], the charge of nutriments and rags having been at least four times that value.

I shall now therefore humbly propose my own thoughts, which I hope will not be liable to the least objection.

I have been assured by a very knowing American of my acquaintance in London, that a young healthy child well nursed is at a year old a most delicious, nourishing, and wholesome food, whether stewed, roasted, baked,

1 towardly: dutiful, tractable

2 which cannot turn to account either to the parents or the kingdom: which cannot be useful or profitable to their parents or Ireland.

or boiled; and I make no doubt that it will equally serve in a fricassee or a ragout[1].

I do therefore humbly offer it to public consideration that of the hundred and twenty thousand children, already computed, twenty thousand may be reserved for breed, whereof only one fourth part to be males, which is more than we allow to sheep, black cattle, or swine; and my reason is that these children are seldom the fruits of marriage, a circumstance not much regarded by our savages, therefore one male will be sufficient to serve four females. That the remaining hundred thousand may at a year old be offered in sale to the persons of quality and fortune through the kingdom, always advising the mother to let them suck plentifully in the last month, so as to render them plump and fat for a good table. A child will make two dishes at an entertainment for friends; and when the family dines alone, the fore or hind quarter will make a seasonable dish, and seasoned with a little pepper or salt will be very good boiled on the fourth day, especially in winter.

I have reckoned upon a medium that a child just born will weigh twelve pounds, and in a solar year if tolerably nursed increases to twenty-eight pounds.

I grant this food will be somewhat dear, and therefore very proper for landlords, who, as they have already devoured most of the parents, seem to have the best title to the children.

Infant's flesh will be in season throughout the year, but more plentiful in March, and a little before and after. For we are told by a grave author, an eminent French physician[2], that fish being a prolific diet, there are more children born in Roman Catholic countries about nine months after Lent[3] than at any other season; therefore, reckoning a year after Lent, the markets will be more glutted than usual, because the number of popish infants in at least three to one in this kingdom; and therefore

1 ragout: a highly seasoned meat stew

2 French physician: Here it refers to Francois Rabelais (494-1553), a humorist and a satirist.

3 Lent: the 40 weekdays from Ash Wednesday until Easter observed by Christians as a season of fasting and penitence in preparation for Easter

it will have one other collateral advantage, by lessening the number of Papists among us.

I have already computed the charge of nursing a beggar's child (in which list I reckon all cottagers, labourers, and four fifths of the farmers) to be about two shillings per annum, rags included; and I believe no gentleman would repine to give ten shillings for the carcass of a good fat child, which, as I have said, will make four dishes of excellent nutritive meat, when he hath only some particular friend or his own family to dine with him. Thus the squire will learn to be a good landlord, and grow popular among the tenants; the mother will have eight shillings net profit, and be fit for work till she produces another child.

Those who are more thrifty (as I must confess the times require) may flay the carcass; the skin of which artificially[1] dressed will make admirable gloves for ladies, and summer boots for fine gentlemen.

As to our city of Dublin, shambles[2] may be appointed for this purpose in the most convenient parts of it, and butchers we may be assured will not be wanting; although I rather recommend buying the children alive, and dressing them hot from the knife as we do roasting pigs.

A very worthy person, a true lover of his country, and whose virtues I highly esteem, was lately pleased in discoursing on this matter to offer a refinement upon my scheme. He said, that many gentlemen of this kingdom, having of late destroyed their deer, he conceived that the want of venison might be well supplied by the bodies of young lads and maidens, not exceeding fourteen years of age nor under twelve, so great a number of both sexes in every country being now ready to starve for want of work and service; and these to be disposed of by their parents, if alive, or otherwise by their nearest relations. But with due deference to so excellent a friend and so deserving a patriot, I cannot be altogether in his sentiments; for as to the males, my American acquaintance assured

1 artificially: skillfully

2 shambles: slaughterhouses

me from frequent experience that their flesh was generally tough and lean, like that of our school-boys, by continual exercise, and their taste disagreeable; and to fatten them would not answer the charge. Then as to the females, it would, I think with humble submission, be a loss to the public, because they soon would become breeders themselves: and besides, it is not improbable that some scrupulous people might be apt to censure such a practice (although indeed very unjustly) as a little bordering upon cruelty; which, I confess, hath always been with me the strongest objection against any project, how well soever intended.

But in order to justify my friend, he confessed that this expedient was put into his head by the famous Psalmanazar[1], a native of the island Formosa, who came from thence to London above twenty years ago, and in conversation told my friend that in his country when any young person happened to be put to death, the executioner sold the carcass to persons of quality as a prime dainty; and that in his time the body of a plump girl of fifteen, who was crucified for an attempt to poison the emperor, was sold to his Imperial Majesty's prime minister of state, and other great mandarins of the court, in joints from the gibbet, at four hundred crowns. Neither indeed can I deny that if the same use were made of several plump young girls in this town, who without one single groat to their fortunes cannot stir abroad without a chair, and appear at a playhouse and assemblies in foreign fineries which they never will pay for, the kingdom would not be the worse.

Some persons of a desponding spirit are in great concern about that vast number of poor people who are aged, diseased, or maimed, and I have been desired to employ my thoughts what course may be taken to ease the nation of so grievous an encumbrance. But I am not in the least pain upon that matter, because it is very well known that they are every day dying and rotting by cold and famine, and filth and vermin, as fast as can be reasonably expected. And as to the young laborers, they are now in almost as hopeful a condition. They cannot get work, and

1 Psalmanazar: George Psalmanazar, a famous imposter

consequently pine away from want of nourishment to a degree that if at any time they are accidentally hired to common labor, they have not strength to perform it; and thus the country and themselves are happily delivered from the evils to come.

I have too long digressed, and therefore shall return to my subject. I think the advantages by the proposal which I have made are obvious and many, as well as of the highest importance.

For first, as I have already observed, it would greatly lessen the number of Papists, with whom we are yearly overrun, being the principal breeders of the nation as well as our most dangerous enemies; and who stay at home on purpose with a design to deliver the kingdom to the Pretender, hoping to take their advantage by the absence of so many good Protestants, who have chosen rather to leave their country than stay at home and pay tithes[1] against their conscience to an Episcopal curate.

Secondly, the poorer tenants will have something valuable of their own, which by law may be made liable to a distress[2], and help to pay their landlord's rent, their corn and cattle being already seized and money a thing unknown.

Thirdly, whereas the maintenance of an hundred thousand children, from two years old and upwards, cannot be computed at less than ten shillings a piece per annum, the nation's stock will be thereby increased fifty thousand pounds per annum, besides the profit of a new dish introduced to the table of all gentlemen of fortune in the kingdom who have any refinement in taste. And the money will circulate among ourselves, the goods being entirely of our own growth and manufacture.

Fourthly, the constant breeders, besides the gain of eight shillings sterling per annum by the sale of their children, will be rid of the charge of maintaining them after the first year.

Fifthly, this food would likewise bring great custom to taverns, where the vintners will certainly be so prudent as to procure the best receipts for

1 tithes: a tenth part of one's annual income contributed voluntarily or due as a tax, especially for the support of the clergy and church.

2 distress: to hold the property of (a person) against the payment of debts

dressing it to perfection, and consequently have their houses frequented by all the fine gentlemen, who justly value themselves upon their knowledge in good eating; and a skilful cook, who understands how to oblige his guests, will contrive to make it as expensive as they please.

Sixthly, this would be a great inducement to marriage, which all wise nations have either encouraged by rewards or enforced by laws and penalties. It would increase the care and tenderness of mothers towards their children, when they were sure of a settlement for life to the poor babes, provided in some sort by the public, to their annual profit instead of expense. We should see an honest emulation among the married women, which of them could bring the fattest child to the market. Men would become as fond of their wives during the time of their pregnancy as they are now of their mares in foal, their cows in calf, or sows when they are ready to farrow; nor offer to beat or kick them (as is too frequent a practice) for fear of a miscarriage.

Many other advantages might be enumerated. For instance, the addition of some thousand carcasses in our exportation of barrelled beef, the propagation of swine's flesh, and improvement in the art of making good bacon, so much wanted among us by the great destruction of pigs, too frequent at our tables, which are no way comparable in taste or magnificence to a well-grown, fat, yearling child, which roasted whole will make a considerable figure at a lord mayor's feast or any other public entertainment. But this and many others I omit, being studious of brevity.

Supposing that one thousand families in this city would be constant customers for infants' flesh, besides others who might have it at merry meetings, particularly at weddings and christenings, I compute that Dublin would take off annually about twenty thousand carcasses, and the rest of the kingdom (where probably they will be sold somewhat cheaper) the remaining eighty thousand.

I can think of no one objection, that will possibly be raised against this proposal, unless it should be urged, that the number of people will be thereby much lessened in the kingdom. This I freely own, and 'twas indeed one principal design in offering it to the world. I desire the reader will observe, that I calculate my remedy for this one individual Kingdom of Ireland, and for no other that ever was, is, or, I think, ever can be upon Earth. Therefore let no man talk to me of other expedients: Of taxing our absentees at five shillings a pound: Of using neither clothes, nor household furniture, except what is of our own growth and manufacture: Of utterly rejecting the materials and instruments that promote foreign luxury: Of curing the expensiveness of pride, vanity, idleness, and gaming in our women: Of introducing a vein of parsimony, prudence and temperance: Of learning to love our country, wherein we differ even from Laplanders, and the inhabitants of Topinamboo:[1] Of quitting our animosities and factions, nor acting any longer like the Jews, who were murdering one another at the very moment their city was taken: Of being a little cautious not to sell our country and consciences for nothing: Of teaching landlords to have at least one degree of mercy towards their tenants. Lastly, of putting a spirit of honesty, industry, and skill into our shop-keepers, who, if a resolution could now be taken to buy only our native goods, would immediately unite to cheat and exact upon us in the price, the measure, and the goodness, nor could ever yet be brought to make one fair proposal of just dealing, though often and earnestly invited to it.

Therefore I repeat, let no man talk to me of these and the like expedients, 'till he hath at least some glimpse of hope, that there will ever be some hearty and sincere attempt to put them into practice.

But, as to myself, having been wearied out for many years with offering vain, idle, visionary thoughts, and at length utterly despairing of success, I fortunately fell upon this proposal, which, as it is wholly new, so it hath something solid and real, of no expense and little trouble, full in our own power, and whereby we can incur no danger in disobliging

1 We differ even from Laplanders, and the inhabitants of Topinamboo: Even Laplanders and the savage tribes of Brazil love their country and their jungle more than that the Anglo-Irish love Ireland.

England. For this kind of commodity will not bear exportation, and flesh being of too tender a consistence, to admit a long continuance in salt, although perhaps I could name a country, which would be glad to eat up our whole nation[1] without it.

After all, I am not so violently bent upon my own opinion, as to reject any offer, proposed by wise men, which shall be found equally innocent, cheap, easy, and effectual. But before something of that kind shall be advanced in contradiction to my scheme, and offering a better, I desire the author or authors will be pleased maturely to consider two points. First, as things now stand, how they will be able to find food and raiment for a hundred thousand useless mouths and backs. And secondly, There being a round million of creatures in humane figure throughout this kingdom, whose whole subsistence put into a common stock, would leave them in debt two million of pounds sterling, adding those who are beggars by profession, to the bulk of farmers, cottagers and labourers, with their wives and children, who are beggars in effect; I desire those politicians who dislike my overture, and may perhaps be so bold to attempt an answer, that they will first ask the parents of these mortals, whether they would not at this day think it a great happiness to have been sold for food at a year old, in the manner I prescribe, and thereby have avoided such a perpetual scene of misfortunes, as they have since gone through, by the oppression of landlords, the impossibility of paying rent without money or trade, the want of common sustenance, with neither house nor clothes to cover them from the inclemencies of the weather, and the most inevitable prospect of entailing the like, or greater miseries, upon their breed forever.

I profess, in the sincerity of my heart, that I have not the least personal interest in endeavouring to promote this necessary work, having no other motive than the public good of my country, by advancing our trade, providing for infants, relieving the poor, and giving some pleasure to the rich. I have no children by which I can propose to get a single

1 nation: Here it refers to England.

penny; the youngest being nine years old, and my wife past childbearing.

QUESTIONS

1 What are the mothers and children in the first paragraph doing?
2 What is Swift's argument?
3 Why is it that "we can neither employ them in handicraft or agriculture; we neither build houses (I mean in the country) nor cultivate land"?
4 Why does the writer give a very detailed way of raising and cooking children?
5 What are the attitudes of the writer's toward the churches and English government?
6 What are the rhetorical features used in the prose?

Henry Fielding
(1707-1754)

INTRODUCTION

Henry Fielding is called the "Father of the English novel", and one of the founders of the English realism, who sets up the standard and theory of realism in English literature. Fielding portrays the real life of men without disguise, exposes the hypocrisy of the ruling class, and gives a comprehensive picture of the life of 18th century England.

Fielding was born to a poor family of a retired general in 1704, well-educated but not finishing his study in university due to financial problem. He is a man of versatility, working hard and successfully as a dramatist, a political pamphleteer, a magistrate, a novelist; whatever he took as a job, he did it with diligence, passion and intellect. Throughout his life, he had been fighting against adversities of illness, poverty, death of his beloved wife and daughter, persecution from the government, attacks from the enemies, but with optimism and strong will power. In 1754, he died in Lisbon from illness.

Fielding took the earthly life of common people for the material of his novels, depicting human nature faithfully and accurately as he observed. His works feature satire with humor, lashing and ridiculing the follies of human beings, the corruption and evils of the ruling class. His style is easy, vivid and vigorous. He began a novel, *Joseph Andrews,* in 1742, as a kind of satire on *Pamela.* Fielding's greatest novel is *The History of Tom Jones, a Foundling* (1749). Other major works are *Jonathan Wild* (1743) and *Amelia* (1751).

SELECTED READING

The History of Tom Jones, a Foundling

Overview

The History of Tom Jones, a Foundling tells a story of the adventurous life of Tom Jones, who is a foundling. The novel is often known simply as Tom Jones, which is a comic novel. The novel is both a Bildungsroman and a picaresque novel.

Tom is an orphan abandoned in Mr. Allworthy's house, and he is brought up there with kindness. Shortly afterwards Miss Bridget, Mr. Allworthy's sister, gets married to a certain Captain Blifil, and gives birth to a boy. After young Blifil's parents died, the orphan is left in the care of Mr. Allworthy who brings two boys up together. The two boys are quite different in character. Tom is kind, frank, open with a good nature, and respects Mr. Allworthy for his benevolence and love; while Blifil is sly, wicked, full of hatred and jealousy against Tom. Then Tom falls in love with the beautiful Sophia, daughter of a neighboring Squire Western. He does several other things that Allworthy does not like and Tom is driven out of the house. Tom has to leave his lover, Sophia, to go to London. Fearing of being forced to marry Blifil by her father, Sophia flees to London. Tom and Sophia travel independently. In London, Tom experiences a series of adventures and immature love affairs, but in the end he meets Sophia there and all ends happily. Mr. Allworthy learns from a letter by his sister Bridget on her death-bed that Tom is the illegitimate son of Miss Bridget. At the end of the story, Tom becomes the heir of Mr. Allworthy and marries Sophia, while Blifil is banished by Mr. Allworthy.

Book IV: Chapter 13

(Excerpt)

A dreadful accident which befell Sophia; the gallant behaviour of Jones, and the more dreadful consequence of that behaviour to the young lady; with a short digression in favour of the female sex.

Mr. Western grew every day fonder and fonder of Sophia, insomuch that his beloved dogs themselves almost gave place to her in his affections; but as he could not prevail on himself to abandon these, he contrived very cunningly to enjoy their company, together with that of his daughter, by insisting on her riding a hunting with him.

Sophia, to whom her father's word was a law, readily complied with his desires, though she had not the least delight in a sport, which was of too rough and masculine a nature to suit with her disposition. She had however another motive, beside her obedience, to accompany the old gentleman in the chase; for by her presence she hoped in some measure to restrain his impetuosity, and to prevent him from so frequently exposing his neck to the utmost hazard.

The strongest objection was that which would have formerly been an inducement to her, namely, the frequent meeting with young Jones, whom she had determined to avoid; but as the end of the hunting season now approached, she hoped, by a short absence with her aunt, to reason herself entirely out of her unfortunate passion; and had not any doubt of being able to meet him in the field the subsequent season without the least danger.

On the second day of her hunting, as she was returning from the chase, and was arrived within a little distance from Mr. Western's house, her horse, whose mettlesome[1] spirit required a better rider, fell suddenly to prancing and capering[2] in such a manner that she was in the most imminent peril of falling. Tom Jones, who was at a little distance behind, saw this, and immediately galloped up to her assistance. As soon as he came up, he leapt from his own horse, and caught hold of hers by the bridle. The unruly beast presently reared himself an end on his hind legs, and threw his lovely burthen[3] from his back, and Jones caught her in his arms.

She was so affected with the fright, that she was not immediately able to satisfy Jones, who was very solicitous to know whether she had received any hurt. She soon after, however, recovered her spirits, assured him she was safe, and thanked him for the care he had taken of her. Jones answered, "If I have preserved you, madam, I am sufficiently repaid; for I promise you, I would have secured you from the least harm at the expense of a much greater misfortune to myself than I have suffered on this occasion."

"What misfortune?" replied Sophia eagerly; "I hope you have come to no mischief ?"

"Be not concerned, madam," answered Jones. "Heaven be praised you have escaped so well, considering the danger you was in. If I have broken my arm, I consider it as a trifle, in comparison of what I feared upon your account."

Sophia then screamed out, "Broke your arm! Heaven forbid."

"I am afraid I have, madam," says Jones: "but I beg you will suffer me first

1 mettlesome: dashing and spirited

2 prancing and capering: The horse is springing and bounding.

3 burthen: burden

to take care of you. I have a right hand yet at your service, to help you into the next field, whence[1] we have but a very little walk to your father's house."

Sophia seeing his left arm dangling by his side, while he was using the other to lead her, no longer doubted of the truth. She now grew much paler than her fears for herself had made her before. All her limbs were seized with a trembling, insomuch that Jones could scarce support her; and as her thoughts were in no less agitation, she could not refrain from giving Jones a look so full of tenderness, that it almost argued a stronger sensation in her mind, than even gratitude and pity united can raise in the gentlest female bosom, without the assistance of a third more powerful passion.

Mr. Western, who was advanced at some distance when this accident happened, was now returned, as were the rest of the horsemen. Sophia immediately acquainted them with what had befallen Jones, and begged them to take care of him. Upon which Western, who had been much alarmed by meeting his daughter's horse without its rider, and was now overjoyed to find her unhurt, cried out, "I am glad it is no worse. If Tom hath broken his arm, we will get a joiner to mend it again."

The squire alighted from his horse, and proceeded to his house on foot, with his daughter and Jones. An impartial spectator, who had met them on the way, would, on viewing their several countenances, have concluded Sophia alone to have been the object of compassion: for as to Jones, he exulted in having probably saved the life of the young lady, at the price only of a broken bone; and Mr. Western, though he was not unconcerned at the accident which had befallen Jones, was, however, delighted in a much higher degree with the fortunate escape of his daughter.

The generosity of Sophia's temper construed[2] this behaviour of Jones into great bravery; and it made a deep impression on her heart: for certain it is, that there is no one quality which so generally recommends men to women as this; proceeding, if we believe the common opinion, from that natural timidity of the sex, which is, says Mr Osborne[3], "so great, that a woman is the most

1 whence: from where

2 construe: interpret

3 Osborne: Francis Osborne (1593-1659) was an English essayist, and the quotation is from his *Advice to a Son.*

cowardly of all the creatures God ever made;"—a sentiment more remarkable for its bluntness than for its truth. Aristotle, in his Politics, doth them, I believe, more justice, when he says, "The modesty and fortitude of men differ from those virtues in women; for the fortitude which becomes a woman, would be cowardice in a man; and the modesty which becomes a man, would be pertness in a woman." Nor is there, perhaps, more of truth in the opinion of those who derive the partiality which women are inclined to show to the brave, from this excess of their fear. Mr. Bayle[1] (I think, in his article of Helen) imputes this, and with greater probability, to their violent love of glory; for the truth of which, we have the authority of him who of all others saw farthest into human nature, and who introduces the heroine of his Odyssey, the great pattern of matrimonial love and constancy, assigning the glory of her husband as the only source of her affection towards him.

The English reader will not find this in the poem; for the sentiment is entirely left out in the translation.

However this be, certain it is that the accident operated very strongly on Sophia; and, indeed, after much enquiry into the matter, I am inclined to believe, that, at this very time, the charming Sophia made no less impression on the heart of Jones; to say truth, he had for some time become sensible of the irresistible power of her charms.

QUESTIONS

1 What is the "more dreadful consequence" of "the gallant behaviour of Jones" to Sophia?
2 What is the tone of the first paragraph?
3 What is Sophia's character?
4 What are Tom's characters and his attitude towards Sophia shown in the accident?
5 Does the writer agree that "a woman is the most cowardly of all the creatures God ever made"?
6 What is the writer's attitude towards women?

1 Bayle: Pierre Bayle (1647-1706) was a French philosopher and writer best known for his seminal work the *Historical and Critical Dictionary*.

Thomas Gray
(1716-1771)

INTRODUCTION

Thomas Gray was an English poet and scholar, born in London, educated in Eton College and Cambridge. He is one of the leading figures of Sentimentalism of English literature. He was one of the most learned men of his time. In 1768 he was made professor of History and modern languages at Cambridge.

Gray suffered in his childhood from separation from his abusive father and a weak constitution, both of which contributed to his lifelong melancholy, a noticeable feature of his poetry. Gray is known as one of the "Graveyard poets" of the late 18th century, who enjoyed meditating on death, mortality, and the finality and sublimity of death. He spent most of his life as a quiet scholar in Cambridge. His major work is *Elegy Written in a Country Churchyard* (1751), enjoying an internationally great fame as a representative work of Sentimentalism and a masterpiece of elegy.

SELECTED READING

Elegy Written in a Country Churchyard

Overview

Elegy Written in a Country Churchyard is Gray's representative work, a model of sentimentalist poetry of the eighteenth-century English literature. The poem is one of the most beautiful and famous of English poems, which describes his thoughts as he looks at the graves of country people buried near the church at Stoke Poges. He wonders what they might have done in the world if they had had better opportunities. It shows poet's interest and appreciation of the beauty of nature in countryside, and sincere sympathy for common people in a melancholy tone.

The curfew tolls the knell of parting day,
  The lowing herd winds slowly o'er the lea,

The ploughman homeward plods his weary way,
And leaves the world to darkness and to me.

Now fades the glimmering landscape on the sight,
And all the air a solemn stillness holds,
Save where the beetle wheels his droning flight,
And drowsy tinklings lull the distant folds[1];

Save that from yonder ivy-mantled tower[2]
The moping owl does to the moon complain
Of such as, wandering near her secret bower[3],
Molest her ancient solitary reign.

Beneath those rugged elms, that yew-tree's shade,
Where heaves the turf in many a mouldering heap,
Each in his narrow cell for ever laid,
The rude Forefathers of the hamlet sleep.

The breezy call of incense-breathing morn,
The swallow twittering from the straw-built shed,
The cock's shrill clarion, or the echoing horn,
No more shall rouse them from their lowly bed[4].

For them no more the blazing hearth shall burn,
Or busy housewife ply her evening care;
No children run to lisp their sire's return,
Or climb his knees the envied kiss to share.

Oft did the harvest to their sickle yield,

---

1 folds: sheepfolds

2 yonder ivy-mantled tower: Here it refers to the tower of the church at Stoke Poges.

3 bower: a woman's chamber

4 lowly bed: the grave

Their furrow oft the stubborn glebe has broke;
How jocund did they drive their team afield!
How bowed the woods beneath their sturdy stroke!

Let not Ambition mock their useful toil,
Their homely joys, and destiny obscure;
Nor Grandeur hear with a disdainful smile
The short and simple annals of the Poor.

The boast of heraldry[1], the pomp of power,
And all that beauty, all that wealth e'er gave,
Awaits alike the inevitable hour:—
The paths of glory lead but to the grave.

Nor you, ye Proud, impute to these the fault
If Memory o'er their tomb no trophies raise,
Where through the long-drawn aisle and fretted vault
The pealing anthem swells the note of praise.

Can storied urn[2] or animated[3] bust
Back to its mansion call the fleeting breath?
Can Honour's voice provoke the silent dust,
Or Flattery soothe the dull cold ear of Death?

Perhaps in this neglected spot is laid
Some heart once pregnant with celestial fire;
Hands, that the rod of empire might have swayed,
Or waked to ecstasy the living lyre.

1 heraldry: noble birth

2 storied urn: a funeral urn with an epitaph inscribed on it

3 animated: lifelike

But Knowledge to their eyes her ample page,
Rich with the spoils of time, did ne'er unroll;
Chill Penury repressed their noble rage,
And froze the genial current of the soul.

Full many a gem of purest ray serene,
The dark unfathomed caves of ocean bear;
Full many a flower is born to blush unseen,
And waste its sweetness on the desert air.

Some village-Hampden[1], that with dauntless breast
The little tyrant of his fields withstood;
Some mute inglorious Milton here may rest,
Some Cromwell, guiltless of his country's blood.

The applause of listening senates to command,
The threats of pain and ruin to despise,
To scatter plenty o'er a smiling land,
And read their history in a nation's eyes,

Their lot forbade: nor circumscribed alone
Their growing virtues, but their crimes confined;
Forbade to wade through slaughter to a throne,
And shut the gates of mercy on mankind,

The struggling pangs of conscious truth to hide,
To quench the blushes of ingenuous shame,
Or heap the shrine of Luxury and Pride
With incense kindled at the Muse's flame.

1 Hampden: John Hampden (1594-1643), an English politician who was both as a private citizen and as one of the leading parliamentarians involved in challenging the authority of Charles I of England in the run-up to the English Civil War. He zealously defended the rights of the people against Charles I and he mortally wounded in a skirmish near Oxford.

Far from the madding crowd's ignoble strife,
  Their sober wishes never learned to stray;
Along the cool sequestered vale of life
  They kept the noiseless tenor of their way.

Yet even these bones from insult to protect
  Some frail memorial still erected nigh,
With uncouth rhymes and shapeless sculpture decked,
  Implores the passing tribute of a sigh.

Their name, their years, spelt by the unlettered Muse,
  The place of fame and elegy supply:
And many a holy text around she strews,
  That teach the rustic moralist to die.

For who, to dumb forgetfulness a prey,
  This pleasing anxious being e'er resigned,
Left the warm precincts of the cheerful day,
  Nor cast one longing lingering look behind?

On some fond breast the parting soul relies,
  Some pious drops the closing eye requires;
E'en from the tomb the voice of Nature cries,
  E'en in our ashes live their wonted fires.

For thee, who, mindful of the unhonored dead,
  Dost in these lines their artless tale relate;
If chance, by lonely contemplation led,
  Some kindred spirit[1] shall inquire thy fate, —

1 kindred spirit: person like you

Haply[1] some hoary-headed swain may say,
  "Oft have we seen him at the peep of dawn
Brushing with hasty steps the dews away
  To meet the sun upon the upland lawn.

"There at the foot of yonder nodding beech
  That wreathes its old fantastic roots so high.
His listless length at noontide would he stretch,
  And pore upon the brook that babbles by.

"Hard by yon wood, now smiling as in scorn,
  Muttering his wayward fancies he would rove;
Now drooping, woeful wan, like one forlorn,
  Or crazed with care, or crossed in hopeless love.

"One morn I missed him on the customed hill,
  Along the heath, and near his favourite tree;
Another came; nor yet beside the rill,
  Nor up the lawn, nor at the wood was he;

"The next with dirges due in sad array
  Slow through the church-way path we saw him borne[2].
Approach and read (for thou canst read) the lay
  Graved on the stone beneath yon aged thorn."

The Epitaph

Here rests his head upon the lap of Earth
  A youth to Fortune and to Fame unknown.
Fair Science frowned not on his humble birth,

1 haply: perhaps.

2 borne: in his coffin.

And Melancholy marked him for her own.

Large was his bounty, and his soul sincere,
Heaven did a recompense as largely send:
He gave to Misery all he had, a tear,
He gained from Heaven ('twas all he wished) a friend.

No farther seek his merits to disclose,
Or draw his frailties from their dread abode
(There they alike in trembling hope repose),
The bosom of his Father and his God.

QUESTIONS

1 What is the tone in the first stanza?
2 What kind of people do "Hampden", "Milton", and "Cromwell" symbolize?
3 What is the purpose of the writer by putting the "Grandeur" and the "Poor" together?
4 What are the figures of speech used in the poem?
5 What is the basic rhyme scheme of the poem?
6 What is the theme of the poem?

William Blake
(1757-1827)

INTRODUCTION

William Blake is one of the representative poets and painters of English Pre-Romanticism, which goes against the principle of reason of Neo-Classism, by appealing to passion and emotion. His poetry and paintings have been characterized as part of the Romantic Movement and as "Pre-Romantic". Blake did not believe in the reality of matter, or in the power of earthly rulers, or in punishment after death. Blake is famous for his short lyrics. His poetry strikes us with its childish vision and simplicity. His poems often carry the lyric beauty with immense compression of meaning, implying romantic spirit, natural sentiment, and individual originality. Blake writes his poems in plain, simple and direct language.

Blake was the son of a London tradesman. He was a strange and imaginative child. Without going to school, he managed to learn to read and write. The only formal education he received was in a drawing school and the Royal Academy of Arts, where he learned arts. Working as an apprentice to a famous engraver for seven years, Blake read widely in his free time and began to compose poetry himself.

His best known works include two collections of short lyrics, *Songs of Innocence* (1787) and *Songs of Experience* (1794), which are his best but quite different short poems. *Songs of Innocence* are poems for children, bright in color, jolly in mood, presenting a picture of a beautiful nature, innocent children, and a harmonious world. The only darkness can be found in *The little Black Boy* and *The Chimney Sweeper*, which gives a glimpse of children suffering poverty under the same shining sun. *Songs of Experience* is much more mature but also gloomier, darker in theme and tone. It presented the world as full of misery and pains, in the shadow of evil power. Freedom and salvation come only through revolt and revolution against ruling authority. In his *The French Revolution, a Prophecy* (1791), and *America a Prophecy* (1793), he depicted the events and saw them as the triumph of freedom, advocating revolting against the authority. Blake's poetry features natural sentiment and individual originality. His other works include *The Marriage of Heaven and Hell* (1790) and *Milton* (1804).

SELECTED READING

The Chimney Sweeper

Overview

Two different versions of *The Chimney Sweeper* appeared in Blake's two different volumes of early lyrics. This is from *The Songs of Experience*. The short lyric contains chiefly the simple yet somewhat ironical speech of a boy chimney-sweeper. In the poem, Blake describes vividly about the child's miserable condition and attacks the hypocritical religion and capitalist system. The poet uses the sad tone from a chimney sweeper to condemn the parents' cruelty and show his sympathy for the children. The language of the poem is concise, fluent, plain and with deep implication.

A little black thing[1] in the snow,
Crying, "'weep! 'weep![2]" in notes of woe!
"Where are thy father and mother? Say!"—
"They are both gone up to the church to pray.

"Because I was happy upon the heath,
And smiled among the winter's snow,
They clothed me in the clothes of death,
And taught me to sing the notes of woe.

"And because I am happy and dance and sing,
They think they have done me no injury,
And are gone to praise God and his priest and king,
Who make up a heaven of our misery."

QUESTIONS

1 What does "A little black thing" in the first line refer to?
2 Why was the boy crying "weep"?

---

1 a little black thing: a little boy who is a chimney sweeper

2 "weep! " weep!: sweep! sweep! The sound "sweep, sweep" sounds very like "weep, weep".

3 What does it mean that "They clothed me in the clothes of death"?
4 Where did the parents go and what did they do?
5 What is the rhyme scheme of each stanza?
6 What kind of social reality has been reflected in this poem?

Robert Burns
(1759-1796)

INTRODUCTION

Robert Burns is the greatest Scottish poet, a national poet of Scotland, and a poet of peasants and common people. He is another representative of Pre-Romanticism in the Eighteenth-century. Burns drew on traditional Scottish folk songs for material. His poems sang of the simplicity, dignity, love and friendship of the common people.

Burns was a son of a Scottish peasant, plowing hard on the soil to help make a living for the family even when he was a child. He taught himself to read and write in his very little free time. He was greatly influenced by the Scottish folk songs. He practiced writing poems by writing lyrics to the old Scottish tunes in his mind while working in the fields. He did a good deal of reading and knew the old Scottish songs and ballads. In 1786, Burns couldn't support the family any longer with his father's death years ago. He decided to go abroad to make a living. To make money for the journey, he printed and sold *Poems, Chiefly in the Scottish Dialect* and got 20 pounds. He bought his ticket and wrote his *Farewell to Scotland* on the night before the ship sailed. But in the morning he received news that his collection of poems was a great success. All the people spent their hard-earned shillings for this little book. Therefore, he changed his mind and went to Edinburgh, but failed to get due attention or respect. He went back home to soil and lived in a farm with his wife. For the rest of his life, they lived a meager life with the salary of Burns' job as an exciseman. In the last 12 years of his life, Burns devoted all his free time to collect Scottish folk songs.

Burns is famous for his songs written in the Scottish dialect. His works express the feelings and daily life of the working people, singing the optimism and dignity of the common people and mocking the folly and cruelty of the church and ruling classes. A new and fresh spirit of romanticism can be noticed in his poems of love and friendship in a simple and vivid language. His poems are characterized by simplicity, humour, directness, optimism, and satire.

Burn's major works include *Holy Willie's Prayer* (1785), *Poems, Chiefly in the Scottish Dialect* (1786), *The Two Dogs* (1786), *My Heart's in the Highlands* (1789), *Scots Wha Hae* (1793), *The Tree of Liberty* (1794), *A Red, Red Rose* (1794), *A Man's Man for a That* (1795), *John Anderson, My Jo* (1796).

SELECTED READING

A Red, Red Rose

Overview

This poem is composed of four quatrains with alternate lines of four and three feet. The rimes fall on the second and fourth lines of each stanza. *A Red, Red Rose* is one of Burn's popular love lyrics. It is a good example of how Burns made use of old Scottish folk poetry to create immortal lines by revising the old folk material. The simplicity of the language and the charming rhythmic beat of the verse express the poet's own emotions better than anything else.

O, my Luve's[1] like a red, red rose,
  That's newly sprung in June;
O, my Luve's like the melodie[2],
  That's sweetly played in tune[3].

As fair art thou[4], my bonnie lass[5],
  So deep in luve am I;
And I will luve thee still, my dear,
  Till a' the seas gang dry.

Till a' the seas gang dry[6], my dear,
  And the rocks melt wi' the sun;
And I will luve thee still, my dear,
  While the sands o' life shall run[7].

1 Luve: love
2 melodie: melody
3 in tune: in harmony
4 fair art thou: you are fair.
5 bonnie lass: [Scotch] pretty girl, sweetheart
6 Till a' the seas gang dry: till all the seas go dry.
7 While the sands o' life shall run: as long as I live.

And fare-thee-weel[1], my only Luve!
  And fare-thee-weel, a while!
And I will come again, my Luve,
  Tho''t were[2] ten thousand mile!

QUESTIONS

1 What does the poet compare his love to according to the first paragraph?
2 What is the meaning of "As fair art thou" in Line 5?
3 What does "the sands o' life" in Line 12 refer to?
4 What is the rhyme scheme of the third stanza and the fourth stanza?
5 What are the figures of speech in this poem?
6 What are the language features of the poem?

My Heart's in the Highlands

Overview

My Heart's in the Highlands is a 1789 song and poem by Robert Burns. The Highlands refers to a mountainous region of northern Scotland, famous for its rugged beauty and known for the style of dress of the kilt and tartan. The lyric poem sings the praises of the beauty of nature and the life of the people in Highlands.

Farewell to the Highlands, farewell to the North,
The birthplace of Valour[3], the country of Worth;
Wherever I wander, wherever I rove,
The hills of the Highlands forever I love.

My heart's in the Highlands[4], my heart is not here;
My heart's in the Highlands, a-chasing[5] the deer;

1 fare-thee-weel: farewell, good-bye to you.
2 Tho''t were: though it were
3 valour: courage and boldness as in battle
4 the Highlands: the mountainous northern part of Scotland
5 a-chasing: chasing

A-chasing the wild-deer, and following the roe,
My heart's in the Highlands, wherever I go.

Farewell to the mountains, high-covered with snow;
Farewell to the straths[1] and green valleys below;
Farewell to the forests and wild-hanging woods[2];
Farewell to the torrents and loud-pouring floods.

My heart's in the Highlands, my heart is not here;
My heart's in the Highlands, a-chasing the deer;
A-chasing the wild-deer, and following the roe,
My heart's in the Highlands, wherever I go.

QUESTIONS

1 What kind of feeling does this poem express?
2 Why does the writer bid farewell to the Highlands?
3 What figures of speech have been used in this poem?
4 What is the rhyme scheme of the poem?
5 What do the Highlands symbolize?
6 What are the possible themes of the poem?

EXERCISES OF CHAPTER IV

I Fill in the following blanks.

1 Thomas Gray is a representative of ____________ in poetry.
2 The poetry of ____________ is inspired by the old Scottish songs and dialect.
3 ____________ is called the "Father of the Realistic Novels" of English literature.

II Choose the best answer for each statement.

1 The most important and influential Neo-Classist writers are

1 strath: [Scotch] a flat, wide river valley
2 wild-hanging woods: woods covering steep mountain slopes or reaching the edge of cliffs

__________, Addison and Steele.

A. Burns B. Defoe C. Pope D. Swift

2 The first English realistic novel is __________.

A. *Robinson Crusoe* B. *Pamela*

C. *Gulliver's Travels* D. *Tom Jones*

3 The most famous pamphlets written by Jonathan Swift is __________.

A. *Essays on Criticism* B. *A Modest Proposal*

C. *Gulliver's Travels* D. *The Battle of the Books*

4 __________was an intellectual movement in the first half of the 18th century.

A. The English Renaissance B. The Enclosure Movement

C. Romanticism D. The Enlightenment

III Find the relevant match from Column B for each item in Column A.

Column A	Column B
1 ( ) William Blake	A. *Gulliver's Travels*
2 ( ) Sophia	B. *Songs of Innocence*
3 ( ) yahoo	C. *Tom Jones*
4 ( ) Friday	D. *Robert Burns*
5 ( ) Pre-Romanticism	E. *Robinson Crusoe*

IV Answer the following questions.

1 What are the main differences between Neo-Classism and Pre-romanticism?

2 What are the literature trends in 18th century England?

CHAPTER V
English Literature in Romantic Age
(1798-1832)

General Introduction

The Romantic Period was one of major social changes in England. Romanticism appeared in England as a literary movement influenced both by the domestic contradictions, such as the Industrial Revolution and the "Enclosure Movement", and by the international atmosphere of French Revolution and American Revolution.

Romanticism is a literary trend. It prevailed in England during the period of 1798-1832, beginning with the publication of Wordsworth and Coleridge's joint work *Lyrical Ballads* in 1798, ending with Walter Scott's death in 1832. The English Romanticism was greatly influenced by the Industrial Revolution and the French Revolution. Generally speaking, the romanticists expressed the ideology and sentiment of those classes and social strata who were discontented with, and opposed to, the development of capitalism.

During the Romantic Period, the laboring people and the progressive intellectuals of Britain hailed the doctrine of "Liberty, Equality and Fraternity", which were the watchwords of the Revolution and became the national spirit of English people. Many British writers got their inspirations from the revolution and wrote beautiful poems or prose. William Blake and Robert Burns are usually called the poets of Pre-Romanticism. In English literature, the key figures of the Romantic movement include such poets as Wordsworth, Coleridge, Southey, Keats, Byron, and Shelley.

Romanticism, as a violent reaction against the Enlightenment, focuses on passion, individual and inner life. Romantic writers lay emphasis on mystery and the supernatural power, showing their admiration and love for nature.

The Romantic Period was one of poetical revival, an age of verse. It is the second great age in English literary history; for poetry is the highest form of literary expression and poetry seems to have been most in harmony with the noblest powers of the English genius. Wordsworth, Coleridge and Southey are called **Lake Poets**, because this group of romantic poets lived in the Lake District most of their lives and wrote about that area and its people in their poems.

Besides these famous poets, two influential novelists in this age are Walter Scott, who is the first to write historical novel, and Jane Austen, a famous realistic female novelist.

William Wordsworth (1770-1850)

INTRODUCTION

Wordsworth (1770-1850) is a leading English Romantic poet, the most talented member of "Lake Poets". His work *Lyrical Ballads* (1798) marked the beginning of the Romantic Age. He was named as "Laureate Poet" in 1843. Wordsworth was called poet of nature because he was so filled with the love of nature that he said that the language of poetry ought to be the same as the language of a simple farm-worker.

Wordsworth was born in the scenic region in northwestern England known as the Lake District. The young Wordsworth roamed the area freely, engaged in various activities and got to learn the life of the cottagers, shepherds, and other ordinary people. The experiences provided an important background and source for his later creation. In 1787, he went to St. John's College, Cambridge. Before his final semester, he went on a walking tour of Europe. These experiences influenced both his poetry and his political sensibilities. While touring to Europe, he came into contact with the French Revolution. This experience, as well as a subsequent period of living in France, made him full of sympathy for the lives and troubles of the "common men." These issues proved to be reflected in his works.

Equally important in the poetic life of Wordsworth was that he met the poet Samuel Taylor Coleridge in 1795. The two poets became very good friends. They collaborated on a book of poems entitled *Lyrical Ballads,* first published in 1798. In 1798 and 1799, Wordsworth with his sister, Dorothy, and Coleridge made a trip to Germany. In 1799, Wordsworth went back to his native Lake District and settled down in the Dove Cottage, Grasmere. He married Mary Hutchinson, a childhood friend, in 1802. The poet Robert Southey as well as Coleridge lived nearby, and the three men became known as the "Lake Poets". In 1843, he succeeded Southey as "Poet Laureate". Wordsworth died at Rydal Mount in 1850 and was buried in the Grasmere churchyard.

His best-known works include *Lyrical Ballads* (1798), *Lucy Poems* (1799), *Poems, in Two Volumes* (1807), *The Excursion* (1814) and *The Prelude* (1805-1850). Some short poems are very popular, such as *She Dwelt Among the Untrodden Ways* (1799), *The Solitary Reaper* (1803), and *I Wandered Lonely As a Cloud* (1807).

SELECTED READING

She Dwelt Among the Untrodden Ways[1]

Overview

The poem, with three stanzas, is written by William Wordsworth in 1799. It describes the beauty and dignity of Lucy who lives in solitude near the source of the River Dove. It is the best known of "Lucy" series by Wordsworth.

She dwelt among the untrodden ways
  Beside the springs of Dove,
A Maid whom there were none to praise
  And very few to love:

A violet by a mossy stone
  Half hidden from the eye!
Fair as a star, when only one
  Is shining in the sky.

She lived unknown, and few could know
  When Lucy ceased to be;
But she is in her grave, and, oh,
  The difference to me!

QUESTIONS

1 What is the symbolic meaning of "untrodden ways"?
2 What does the poet compare the girl to?

1 This is one of the "Lucy Poems" written by Wordsworth in 1799.

3 Why does the poet use "only one" in the second stanza?
4 What is the importance of the imagery in this poem?
5 What are the possible themes of the poem?
6 What do you think of the living condition of Lucy?

The Solitary Reaper

Overview

The poem is a ballad by William Wordsworth, and one of his best-known works. The poem is inspired by his sister Dorothy's stay at the village in Scotland in September 1803. The words of the reaper's song are incomprehensible, so the poet focuses on the tone, impressive beauty, and the blissful mood. The poem functions to praise the beauty of music and its fluid impressive beauty.

Behold her, single in the field,
Yon[1] solitary Highland Lass!
Reaping and singing by herself;
Stop here, or gently pass!
Alone she cuts and binds the grain,
And sings a melancholy strain;
O listen! for the Vale profound
Is overflowing with the sound.

No Nightingale did ever chaunt
More welcome notes to weary bands
Of travellers in some shady haunt,
Among Arabian sands[2]:
A voice so thrilling ne'er was heard
In spring-time from the Cuckoo-bird,
Breaking the silence of the seas

1 Yon: yonder. It is a synonym for *there*, which tends to mean "only a few feet from the speaker".

2 Arabian sands: the deserts in Arabia

Among the farthest Hebrides[1].

Will no one tell me what she sings?—
Perhaps the plaintive numbers flow
For old, unhappy, far-off things,
And battles long ago:
Or is it some more humble lay,
Familiar matter of today?
Some natural sorrow, loss, or pain,
That has been, and may be again?

Whatever the theme, the Maiden sang
As if her song could have no ending;
I saw her singing at her work,
And o'er the sickle bending;—
I listened, motionless and still;
And, as I mounted up the hill
The music in my heart I bore,
Long after it was heard no more.

QUESTIONS

1 How does the first stanza emphasize the solitary state of the reaper?
2 What is the meaning of "Yon solitary Highland Lass!"?
3 Is it possible to hear the song of the nightingale in the Arabian deserts or the cry of the cuckoo-bird in the Hebrides? If not, why did Wordsworth use these comparisons?
4 What does the poet think of the song of the reaper?
5 What are the possible themes of the poem?
6 What figures of speech are used in the poem?

1 Hebrides: islands off the northwest tip of Scotland

I Wandered Lonely as a Cloud

Overview

The poem is a lyric poem, first published in *Poems, in Two Volumes* in 1807. It is one of Wordsworth's most famous poems and is based on the poet's experience of coming across a great many golden daffodils when he and his sister wander in the countryside. The poem expresses not only the happiness of seeing the natural beauty, but the feeling of the poet's recollection of this experience.

I wandered lonely as a cloud
That floats on high o'er vales and hills,
When all at once I saw a crowd,
A host, of golden daffodils;
Beside the lake, beneath the trees,
Fluttering and dancing in the breeze.

Continuous as the stars that shine
And twinkle on the Milky Way,
They stretched in never-ending line
Along the margin of a bay:
Ten thousand saw I at a glance,
Tossing their heads in sprightly dance.

The waves beside them danced; but they
Out-did the sparkling waves in glee:
A poet could not but be gay,
In such a jocund company:
I gazed—and gazed—but little thought
What wealth the show to me had brought:

For oft, when on my couch I lie
In vacant or in pensive mood,
They flash upon that inward eye

Which is the bliss of solitude;
And then my heart with pleasure fills,
And dances with the daffodils.

QUESTIONS

1 Why does the poet describe the cloud first?
2 What kind of scenery does the poet come across?
3 What is the change of the poet's thought before and after he came across the scenery?
4 How does the beauty of daffodils influence the poet afterwards?
5 What does this poem mainly describe?
6 What is the rhyme scheme in each stanza?

George Gordon Lord Byron
(1788-1824)

INTRODUCTION

George Gordon Lord Byron was an English leading poet in the Romantic Movement. In his works, he described the characters known as "Byronic heroes", who are men with fiery passions and unbending will and express the poet's own ideal of freedom. These heroes rise against tyranny and injustice, but they are merely lone fighters striving for personal freedom and some individualistic ends. Although Byron was widely condemned on moral grounds by his contemporaries, his influence on European poetry, music, novel, opera, and painting has been extremely huge.

Byron was born in a noble family and his mother petted and abused him. He was handsome, but he had been born with a clubfoot and became extremely sensitive about his lameness. In 1805 Byron entered Trinity College, Cambridge. In Cambridge, he led an unbalanced life. He spent much of his money on expensive clothes and on decorations for his college rooms. Byron entertained lavishly and kept a pet bear.

Byron's first published volume of poetry, *Hours of Idleness*, appeared in 1807. In 1809, Byron took his seat in the House of Lords, and then began a grand tour in European countries. The experience in Europe provided material for his creation and his creative work soon reached a new stage. In 1812, he published the first two cantos of *Childe Harold's Pilgrimage* (1809-1817), which, written in the Spenserian stanza, tells the story of a man who goes off to travel far and wide because he is disgusted with life's foolish pleasures.

In 1815, Byron got married to Anna Isabella and a year later, his wife left him after the birth of their daughter Ada. Byron found himself surrounded by scandal and left England in 1816 and never returned. Byron first went to Switzerland, where he made acquaintance with Shelley. He next established his residence in Venice, where he produced a series of dramas, including *Manfred* (1817) and *Cain* (1821). At the same time, he began to create *Don Juan* (1818-1824). In 1823, at the news of the Greek revolt against the Turks, Byron headed for the Greece and supported Greek. Because of several months' hard work under bad weather, Byron fell ill and died in 1824.

Byron was regarded as the perverted man, the satanic poet, in England; while on the Continent, he was described as the champion of liberty, poet of the people. Because of the English prejudice, Byron was refused to be buried in the "Poets' Corner" when he died. Only in 1969 was this prejudice against Byron finally overcome by the British critical circle. A white marble-floor memorial to Lord Byron was set up in Westminster Abbey.

Among his best-known works are the lengthy narrative poems *Don Juan* and *Childe Harold's Pilgrimage,* and the short lyrics *She Walks in Beauty*. Other influential works include *Oriental Tales* (1813-1816), *The Prisoner of Chillon* (1816), *Manfred, Cain, The Vision of Judgment* (1822) , *The Age of Bronze* (1823), etc.

She Walks in Beauty

Overview

The poem is considered one of Byron's most powerful works. It is said to have been inspired by an event in Byron's life. At the evening party on June 11, 1814, Byron for the first time met his young cousin, Lady Wilmot Horton, who was newly widowed and wore a black mourning gown brightened with spangles. Her exquisite good looks dazzled Byron and he was so struck by her beauty that, on returning home, he wrote this poem in a single night.

She walks in beauty, like the night
　Of cloudless climes[1] and starry skies;
And all that's best of dark and bright
　Meet in her aspect and her eyes:
Thus mellowed to that tender light
　Which heaven to gaudy day denies.

One shade the more, one ray the less,
　Had half impaired the nameless grace
Which waves in every raven tress[2],
　Or softly lightens o'er her face;
Where thoughts serenely sweet express
　How pure, how dear their dwelling place.

And on that cheek, and o'er that brow,
　So soft, so calm, yet eloquent,
The smiles that win, the tints that glow,

1 clime: climate

2 raven tress: black and shiny hair

But tell of days in goodness spent,
A mind at peace with all below,
A heart whose love is innocent!

QUESTIONS

1 What is the color of the lady's dress? How do you know?
2 What is the meaning of "their dwelling place" in the last line of second stanza?
3 What are the personalities of the lady according to the poet?
4 What are the comparisons used by the poet in this poem?
5 Can you describe the beauty of the lady in your own words?
6 What is the relationship between the physical beauty and the inner beauty according to the poem?

Don Juan

(The Isles of Greece)

Overview

The poem *The Isles of Greece* with 16 six-line stanzas is taken from *Don Juan* which is a satire to attack some of Byron's enemies and a long poem of astonishing adventures in Spain, Turkey, Russia, and England. *The Isles of Greece* is famous for its extensive use of allusions, references and citations. In the early 19th century, Greece was under the rule of Turks. In the poem, Byron praises Greece's ancient brilliant culture, splendid civilization, great military achievements and heroic militant tradition. Meanwhile he satirizes the Greek's indifference towards their country's being enslaved by Turks, with the hope to encourage and impel the Greek people to fight for their national liberty and independence, which shows the poet's enthusiastic support for people against all forms of oppression.

(From Canto III)

1

The Isles of Greece, the Isles of Greece!
Where burning Sappho[1] loved and sung,
Where grew the arts of War and Peace,

1 Sappho: Greek lyric poetess

Where Delos[1] rose, and Phoebus[2] sprung!
Eternal summer gilds them yet,
But all, except their Sun, is set.

2

The Scian and Teian muse,
The Hero's harp, the Lover's lute,
Have found the fame your shores refuse;
Their place of birth alone is mute
To sounds which echo further west
Than your Sires' "Islands of the Blest".

3

The mountains look on Marathon[3]—
And Marathon looks on the sea;
And musing there an hour alone,
I dreamed that Greece might still be free;
For standing on the Persians' grave,
I could not deem myself a slave.

4

A King[4] sate on the rocky brow
Which looks o'er sea-born Salamis;
And ships, by thousands, lay below,
And men in nations;—all were his!
He counted them at break of day—
And, when the Sun set, where were they?

1 Delos: name of a small island, which is said to be the birthplace of Apollo in Greek mythology

2 Phoebus: Greek sun god, god of music or poetry

3 Marathon: a plain in Greeks, where the Persian invaders were completely annihilated by the Greek in 490 BC

4 King: Xerxes, king of Persia, who invaded Greece by sea and land in 480 BC

5

And where are they? And where art thou,
   My country? On thy voiceless shore
The heroic lay is tuneless now—
   The heroic bosom beats no more!
And must thy Lyre, so long divine,
Degenerate into hands like mine?

6

'T is something, in the dearth[1] of Fame,
   Though linked among a fettered race,
To feel at least a patriot's shame,
   Even as I sing, suffuse my face;
For what is left the poet here[2]?
For Greeks a blush—for Greece a tear.

7

Must we but weep o'er days more blest?
   Must we but blush?—Our fathers bled.
Earth ! render back from out thy breast
   A remnant of our Spartan dead!
Of the three hundred grant but three,
To make a new Thermopylae[3]!

8

What, silent still? and silent all?
   Ah ! no;—the voices of the dead
Sound like a distant torrent's fall,
   And answer, "Let one living head,
But one arise,—we come, we come!"

---

1 dearth: lack of

2 "For what is left the poet here?": What is left for a poet to do here?

3 Thermopylae: It was a narrow mountain pass in Greece.

'T is but the living who are dumb.

9

In vain—in vain: strike other chords;
   Fill high the cup with Samian wine!
Leave battles to the Turkish hordes,
   And shed the blood of Scio's vine!
Hark ! rising to the ignoble call[1]—
How answers each bold Bacchanal!

10

You have the Pyrrhic dance[2] as yet,
   Where is the Pyrrhic phalanx gone?
Of two such lessons, why forget
   The nobler and the manlier one?
You have the letters Cadmus gave—
Think ye he meant them for a slave?

11

Fill high the bowl with Samian wine!
   We will not think of themes like these!
It made Anacreon's song divine:
   He served—but served Polycrates—
A Tyrant; but our masters then
Were still, at least, our countrymen.

12

The Tyrant of the Chersonese
   Was Freedom's best and bravest friend;
That tyrant was Miltiades!

1 ignoble call: call for drinking wine

2 Pyrrhic dance: a kind of dance during wartime

Oh ! that the present hour would lend
Another despot of the kind!
Such chains as his were sure to bind.

13

Fill high the bowl with Samian wine!
On Suli's rock, and Parga's shore,
Exists the remnant of a line
Such as the Doric mothers bore;
And there, perhaps, some seed is sown,
The Heracleidan[1] blood might own.

14

Trust not for freedom to the Franks[2]—
They have a king who buys and sells;
In native swords, and native ranks,
The only hope of courage dwells;
But Turkish force, and Latin[3] fraud,
Would break your shield, however broad.

15

Fill high the bowl with Samian wine!
Our virgins dance beneath the shade—
I see their glorious black eyes shine;
But gazing on each glowing maid,
My own the burning tear-drop laves[4],
To think such breasts must suckle slaves.

---

1 Heracleidan: of Hercules

2 Franks: the Europeans

3 Latin: Here it refers to Europeans.

4 lave: wash

16

Place me on Sunium's[1] marbled steep,
　Where nothing, save[2] the waves and I,
May hear our mutual murmurs sweep;
　There, swan-like[3], let me sing and die:
A land of slaves shall ne'er be mine—
Dash down yon cup of Samian wine!

QUESTIONS

1 What is the rhyme scheme of the poem?
2 What is the meaning of "But all, except their Sun, is set." in Stanza 1?
3 Allusions are frequently used in this poem. Try to interpret the function of allusions in the stanza.
4 What is the symbolic meaning of "Pyrrhic phalanx" in Stanza 10?
5 What does the poet hope for in Stanza 12?
6 What are the possible themes of the poem?

1 Sunium: the high rocky promontory near Athens, on which was situated an ancient temple
2 save: except
3 swan-like: It is said that the swan sings beautifully just before its death, which is called last song.

Percy Bysshe Shelley
(1792-1822)

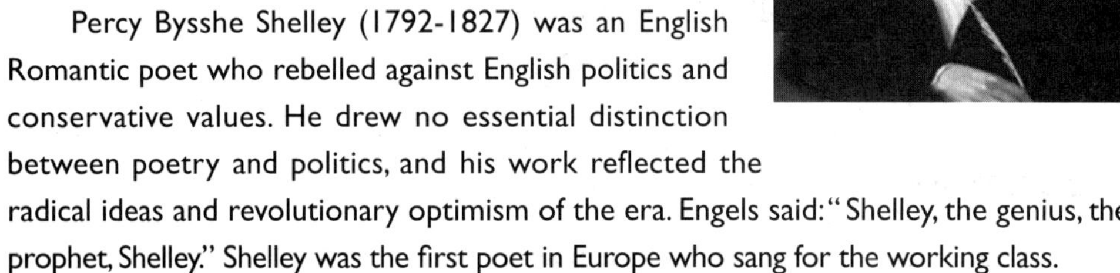

INTRODUCTION

Percy Bysshe Shelley (1792-1827) was an English Romantic poet who rebelled against English politics and conservative values. He drew no essential distinction between poetry and politics, and his work reflected the radical ideas and revolutionary optimism of the era. Engels said: " Shelley, the genius, the prophet, Shelley." Shelley was the first poet in Europe who sang for the working class.

Shelley was born in an aristocratic family. His father was a Sussex squire and a Member of Parliament. Shelley had written two romances and published a collection of poems before he was 18, showing his talent in writing. At Eton, because of his sensitive nature and crazy rebellion against injustice, he was called "Mad Shelley". In 1810 he entered Oxford University and the next year, he was expelled from the University for publishing *The Necessity of Atheism* which is a pamphlet against religion. Shelley disowned by his father because he quarreled fiercely with his father. Homeless, Shelley went to London where he met Harriet Westbrook and married this 16-year-old school girl in 1811. In 1813, Shelley published his first important poem, the atheistic *Queen Mab*. Shelley's marriage with Harriet had proved short-lived and the couple agreed to separate in 1814. Harriet was drowned in the river in 1816, for which Shelley was attacked by his political enemies. In 1818, he was forced to leave England with the novelist William Godwin's gifted daughter Mary. He moved to Italy and met Byron there. In 1822 Shelley was drowned at the coast of Italy because of a storm.

Shelley's four-act lyrical drama, *Prometheus Unbound* (1819), is widely considered to be his masterpiece. His other important poems include *Queen Mab* (1813),*The Cenci* (1819), *Song to the Men of England* (1819), *England in 1819* (1819). However, Shelley is perhaps best known for his odes, such as *Ode to the West Wind* (1819) and *Ode to a Skylark* (1820). Shelley is also famous for his *A Defence of Poetry* (1821), a great theory of poetry.

SELECTED READING

Ode to the West Wind

Overview

The poem *Ode to the West Wind* (1819) is one of Shelley's famous political lyrics. It describes the power of the west wind and the cycle of the seasons. One day, the poet was in a wood with a cold wind, which was the inspiration for the poem. The poet describes vividly the activities of the West Wind on the earth, in the sky and on the sea and then expresses his envy for the boundless freedom of the west wind and his wish to be free like the wind and to scatter his words among mankind. The poem consists of five stanzas of iambic pentameter, written in terza rima. Each section contains four tercets (ABA, BCB, CDC, DED) and a rhyming couplet (EE). The poem can be divided into two parts: the first three cantos are about the qualities of the powerful wind and each ends with the invocation "Oh hear!" The last two cantos give a relation between the wind and the speaker. The celebrated final line of the poem, "If Winter comes, can Spring be far behind?" can best express Shelley's optimistic belief in the future of mankind.

I

O wild West Wind, thou breath of Autumn's being,
Thou, from whose unseen presence the leaves dead
Are driven, like ghosts from an enchanter fleeing,

Yellow, and black, and pale, and hectic red,
Pestilence-stricken multitudes[1]: O thou,
Who chariotest to their dark wintry bed

The winged seeds, where they lie cold and low,
Each like a corpse within its grave, until
Thine azure sister of the Spring shall blow

Her clarion o'er the dreaming earth, and fill

1 Pestilence-stricken multitudes: It refers to the dead leaves mentioned above.

(Driving sweet buds like flocks to feed in air)
With living hues and odours plain and hill:

Wild Spirit, which art moving everywhere;
Destroyer and preserver; hear, O hear!

II

Thou on whose stream, 'mid the steep sky's commotion,
Loose clouds like earth's decaying leaves are shed,
Shook from the tangled boughs of Heaven and Ocean,

Angels of rain and lightning: there are spread
On the blue surface of thine aery surge,
Like the bright hair uplifted from the head

Of some fierce Maenad[1], even from the dim verge
Of the horizon to the zenith's height,
The locks of the approaching storm. Thou dirge

Of the dying year, to which this closing night
Will be the dome of a vast sepulchre,
Vaulted with all thy congregated might

Of vapours, from whose solid atmosphere
Black rain, and fire, and hail will burst: O hear!

III

Thou who didst waken from his summer dreams
The blue Mediterranean, where he lay,
Lulled by the coil of his crystalline streams,

1 Maenad: a very frenzied woman in Greek mythology, a priestess of the God of wine, Bacchus

Beside a pumice isle in Baiae's bay[1],
And saw in sleep old palaces and towers
Quivering within the wave's intenser day,

All overgrown with azure moss and flowers
So sweet, the sense faints picturing them! Thou
For whose path the Atlantic's level powers

Cleave themselves into chasms, while far below
The sea-blooms and the oozy woods which wear
The sapless foliage of the ocean, know

Thy voice, and suddenly grow gray with fear,
And tremble and despoil themselves: O hear!

IV

If I were a dead leaf thou mightest bear;
If I were a swift cloud to fly with thee;
A wave to pant beneath thy power, and share

The impulse of thy strength, only less free
Than thou, O uncontrollable! If even
I were as in my boyhood, and could be

The comrade of thy wanderings over Heaven,
As then, when to outstrip thy skiey speed
Scarce seemed a vision; I would ne'er have striven

As thus with thee in prayer in my sore need.
Oh, lift me as a wave, a leaf, a cloud!

1 Baiae's bay: a favourite resort of the ancient Romans on the coast of Campania, at the western end of the Bay of Naples

I fall upon the thorns of life! I bleed!

A heavy weight of hours has chained and bowed
One too like thee: tameless, and swift, and proud.

V

Make me thy lyre, even as the forest is:
What if my leaves are falling like its own!
The tumult of thy mighty harmonies

Will take from both a deep, autumnal tone,
Sweet though in sadness. Be thou, Spirit fierce,
My spirit! Be thou me, impetuous one!

Drive my dead thoughts over the universe
Like withered leaves to quicken a new birth!
And, by the incantation of this verse,

Scatter, as from an unextinguished hearth
Ashes and sparks, my words among mankind!
Be through my lips to unawakened Earth

The trumpet of a prophecy! O Wind,
If Winter comes, can Spring be far behind?

QUESTIONS

1 According to the first three cantos, what are the qualities of the Wind?
2 What is the relationship between the West Wind and the poet?
3 As "the trumpet of a prophecy", what does the West Wind predict in physical reality?
4 What does the writer refer to when he said "If winter comes, can spring be far behind" in the last sentence?
5 What does the West Wind generally symbolize in the poem?
6 What are the themes of the whole poem?

John Keats
(1795-1821)

INTRODUCTION

John Keats was an English Romantic poet. The poetry of Keats is characterized by sensual imagery. He was good at using the device of description to create poetry, combining perfectly a variety of emotions and nature and getting the inspiration of creation from life. Keats is a writer of "pure poetry", a sort of "art for art's sake". His leading principle is: "Beauty is truth, truth beauty."

He was born to a poor family. And he lost his parents early in life, and was apprenticed at 15 to a doctor. During his studying as an apprentice, he showed a strong interest in the literature. After passing the medical examinations, he gave up his profession though skillful enough as a surgeon and decided to pour his energy into the poetry. In 1817, Keats published his first important poem *On First Looking into Chapman's Homer*. In the second year, he published his second book of poetry, *Endymion*. As a result of this, he met with hostile criticism from conservative magazines. But Keats did not feel frustrated by the attack and continued to write poems.

His greatest works were created from 1818 to 1821, including *The Eve of St. Agnes, Ode to Psyche, Ode to a Nightingale* and *To Autumn*. Unfortunately, he was ill with tuberculosis. In the summer of 1818 he left London and started on a walking tour through England and Scotland. In the fall of 1820, Keats went to Rome to seek a warm climate for the winter. But his health was already in such a hopeless state that the warmer climate in southern Europe could not save him. He died in Rome shortly after his arrival there in 1821.

Keats' contribution to English literature mainly lies in his long poems and odes. His major works include *Ode to a Nightingale* (1819), *Ode on a Grecian Urn* (1819), *To Autumn* (1819), *Ode on Melancholy* (1819), *Ode to Psyche* (1819), *Isabella* (1820), *Lamia* (1820), *The Eve of St. Agnes* (1820), and *Hyperion* (1820).

SELECTED READING

Ode to a Nightingale

Overview

One of Keats' beautiful odes is *Ode to a Nightingale*. One day, the poet saw a nightingale was building her nest near a house of his friend. Inspired by the bird's joyful and peaceful song, Keats composed the poem. This ode consists of 8 stanzas of iambic pentameter. In the poem, this ode expresses the contrast between the happy world of natural loveliness and human world of agony. The ode is free in its movement, sensuous in imagery and is full of passion without any embedded philosophy.

1

My heart aches, and a drowsy numbness pains
  My sense, as though of hemlock I had drunk,
Or emptied some dull opiate to the drains
  One minute past, and Lethe-wards had sunk:
'Tis not through envy of thy happy lot,
  But being too happy in thine happiness,—
    That thou, light-winged Dryad[1] of the trees,
      In some melodious plot
  Of beechen green, and shadows numberless,
    Singest of summer in full-throated ease.

2

O, for a draught of vintage! that hath been
  Cool'd a long age in the deep-delved earth,
Tasting of Flora[2] and the country green,
  Dance, and Provencal song, and sunburnt mirth!
O for a beaker full of the warm South,
  Full of the true, the blushful Hippocrene[3],
    With beaded bubbles winking at the brim,
      And purple-stained mouth;
  That I might drink, and leave the world unseen,

1 Dryad: a nymph inhabiting a tree, sometimes personifying features of nature such as trees, waters, and mountains, and here referring to the nightingale.

2 Flora: the goddess of flowers in Roman mythology. Here it refers to flower.

3 Hippocrene: a fountain on Mount Helicon, Greece, sacred to the Muses and regarded as a source of poetic inspiration. Here it refers to the wine mentioned above.

And with thee fade away into the forest dim:

3

Fade far away, dissolve, and quite forget
What thou among the leaves hast never known,
The weariness, the fever, and the fret
Here, where men sit and hear each other groan;
Where palsy shakes a few, sad last gray hairs,
Where youth grows pale, and spectre-thin, and dies;
Where but to think is to be full of sorrow
And leaden-eyed despairs,
Where Beauty cannot keep her lustrous eyes,
Or new Love pine at them beyond to-morrow.

4

Away! away! for I will fly to thee,
Not charioted by Bacchus and his pards[1],
But on the viewless wings of Poesy,
Though the dull brain perplexes and retards:
Already with thee! tender is the night,
And haply the Queen-Moon is on her throne,
Cluster'd around by all her starry Fays[2];
But here there is no light,
Save what from heaven is with the breezes blown
Through verdurous glooms and winding mossy ways.

5

I cannot see what flowers are at my feet,
Nor what soft incense hangs upon the boughs,
But, in embalmed darkness, guess each sweet

1 Bacchus and his pards: Bacchus is the god of wine in Roman mythology and his chariot is drawn by leopards.

2 Fays: [archaic] Fairies

Wherewith the seasonable month endows
The grass, the thicket, and the fruit-tree wild;
White hawthorn, and the pastoral eglantine;
Fast fading violets cover'd up in leaves;
And mid-May's eldest child,
The coming musk-rose, full of dewy wine,
The murmurous haunt of flies on summer eves.

6

Darkling I listen; and, for many a time
I have been half in love with easeful Death,
Call'd him soft names in many a mused rhyme,
To take into the air my quiet breath;
Now more than ever seems it rich to die,
To cease upon the midnight with no pain,
While thou art pouring forth thy soul abroad[1]
In such an ecstasy!
Still wouldst thou sing, and I have ears in vain—
To thy high requiem become a sod.

7

Thou wast not born for death, immortal Bird!
No hungry generations tread thee down;
The voice I hear this passing night was heard
In ancient days by emperor and clown:
Perhaps the self-same song that found a path
Through the sad heart of Ruth[2], when, sick for home,
She stood in tears amid the alien corn;
The same that oft-times hath
Charm'd magic casements, opening on the foam

1 abroad: in the open air

2 Ruth: In the Old Testament, a widow who left home voluntarily with her mother-in-law and went to a foreign country. Here the poet assumes that she was sad at heart while she gleaned the ears of corn in a strange land.

Of perilous seas, in faery lands forlorn.

8

Forlorn! the very word is like a bell
To toll me back from thee to my sole self!
Adieu! the fancy cannot cheat so well
As she is fam'd to do, deceiving elf.
Adieu! adieu[1]! thy plaintive anthem[2] fades
Past the near meadow, over the still stream,
Up the hill-side; and now 'tis buried deep
In the next valley-glades:
Was it a vision, or a waking dream?
Fled is that music:—Do I wake or sleep?

QUESTIONS

1 What does the Nightingale generally symbolize in the poem?
2 According to the poem, what are the poet's unhappy experiences?
3 What is the relationship between nightingale and poetry?
4 What images are used in the poem?
5 What is the meaning of "Do I wake or sleep?" in the last line?
6 What is the theme of the whole poem?

1 adieu: goodbye, mainly used in poetry

2 anthem: song, hymn

Walter Scott
(1771-1832)

INTRODUCTION

Walter Scott is a Scottish historical novelist, playwright and poet and is regarded as the founder and great master of the historical novel. And Scott's death in 1832 is considered to mark the end of the English Romantic period. His novels marked the transition from Romanticism to realism.

Walter Scott was born in Edinburgh. His father was a respected solicitor and his mother was an educated woman who influenced the son greatly. Scott was educated at the University of Edinburgh where he studied law. As a child, Scott was delicate and lame in the right leg. He spent his childhood at his paternal grandparents' farm in the rural Scottish Borders, where he became versed in his family's history, and in Borders culture in general, laying a foundation for his later historical novel writing. In 1803, he gave up his profession as a lawyer and devoted himself entirely to literature. At first, Walter Scott wrote poems. However, he soon discovered that he could not write poetry as good as Byron's, so he turned to the historical novel, because he has no rival as a historical novelist. In 1814, he published his first novel *Waverley*, which gained a great success. Since the success of *Waverley*, novels came from his pen rapidly: *Guy Mannering* (1815), *The Black Dwarf* (1816), *Old Mortality* (1816), *Rob Roy* (1817), and *Ivanhoe* (1819). But in 1826 he suffered a huge financial crisis. Scott lost all his money through the business failure of his publisher and printer. His indebtedness was over 100,000 pounds. He began to write novels to pay the huge debt after he refused the money that his friends offered to help him. Then Scott turned himself into a writing machine. His books brought him enough money to pay the last pound after his death.

Scott wrote 25 novels. His major works include: *The Minstrelsy of the Scottish Border* (1802), *The lady of the Last Minstrel* (1805), *Marmion* (1808), *The lady of the Lake*(1810), *Waverley*, *The Black Dwarf*, *Rob Roy* and *Ivanhoe*. Scott's novels combine historical fact with romantic imagination, which give a picturesque representation of many historical personages and events but his novels are difficult to read because of the dialect. Scott's books are long for the modern readers.

SELECTED READING

Ivanhoe

Overview

The novel about English history is regarded as Scott's masterpiece. It is set in the late 12th century, portraying the enmity of Saxons and Normans during the reign of Richard I.

The novel *Ivanhoe* concerns the rivalry between King Richard I and his wicked brother John who has taken over his authority during his absence, and between Saxons and the ruling Norman aristocrats. Ivanhoe, the protagonist of the novel, falls in love with Rowena. However, his father, a Saxon nobleman, plans to restore the rule of Saxon over the Normans, by trying to marry Rowena to Saxon Lord. Therefore, Ivanhoe is forced to leave home and joins King Richard. The novel begins with Ivanhoe's return to England. Then Ivanhoe is severely wounded in the competition organized by Prince John and is taken into the care of Rebecca. Later, Ivanhoe and his friends are taken captive by the Norman nobles. King Richard and his fellowman Robin Hood (named as Locksley) saved them. The book ends with the union of Ivanhoe and Rowena and the compromise between the Saxon and the ruling Normans under King Richard I. Rebecca, stifling her love for Ivanhoe, accompanies her father to Spain, where they hope to find a more tolerant society. The real protagonist of the novel is Richard, who is depicted as a Knight, a brave and just man, representing the Norman Lords.

Chapter 13

(Excerpt)

...

"My grandsire[1]," said Hubert[2], "drew a good bow at the battle of Hastings, and never shot at such a mark in his life; and neither will I. If this yeoman can cleave that rod, I give him the bucklers; or rather, I yield to the devil that is in his jerkin, and not to any human skill; a man can but do his best, and I will not shoot where I am sure to miss. I might as well shoot at the edge of our parson's whittle, or at a wheat straw, or at a sunbeam, as at a

1 grandsire: ancestry

2 Hubert: winner of the first round of the archery contest

twinkling white streak which I can hardly see."

"Cowardly dog!" said Prince John. "Sirrah Locksley[1], do thou shoot; but, if thou hittest such a mark, I will say thou art the first man ever did so. However it be, thou shalt not crow over us with a mere show of superior skill."

"I will do my best, as Hubert says," answered Locksley; "no man can do more."

So saying, he again bent his bow, but on the present occasion looked with attention to his weapon, and changed the string, which he thought was no longer truly round, having been a little frayed by the two former shots. He then took his aim with some deliberation, and the multitude awaited the event in breathless silence. The archer vindicated their opinion of his skill: his arrow split the willow rod against which it was aimed. A jubilee of acclamations followed; and even Prince John, in admiration of Locksley's skill, lost for an instant his dislike to his person. "These twenty nobles[2]," he said, "which, with the bugle, thou hast fairly won, are thine own; we will make them fifty, if thou wilt take livery and service with us as a yeoman of our body guard, and be near to our person. For never did so strong a hand bend a bow, or so true an eye direct a shaft."

"Pardon me, noble Prince," said Locksley; "but I have vowed, that if ever I take service, it should be with your royal brother King Richard. These twenty nobles I leave to Hubert, who has this day drawn as brave a bow as his grandsire did at Hastings. Had his modesty not refused the trial, he would have hit the wand as well I."

Hubert shook his head as he received with reluctance the bounty of the stranger, and Locksley, anxious to escape further observation, mixed with the crowd, and was seen no more.

The victorious archer would not perhaps have escaped John's attention so easily, had not that Prince[3] had other subjects of anxious and more

1 Locksley: Robin Hood, an English yeoman

2 nobles: (late medieval) British gold coin (about six old British shillings eight pence or half Mark)

3 Prince: Prince John, brother of King Richard

important meditation pressing upon his mind at that instant. He called upon his chamberlain as he gave the signal for retiring from the lists, and commanded him instantly to gallop to Ashby, and seek out Isaac the Jew. "Tell the dog," he said, "to send me, before sun-down, two thousand crowns[1]. He knows the security; but thou mayst show him this ring for a token. The rest of the money must be paid at York within six days. If he neglects, I will have the unbelieving villain's head. Look that thou pass him not on the way; for the circumcised slave was displaying his stolen finery amongst us."

So saying, the Prince resumed his horse, and returned to Ashby, the whole crowd breaking up and dispersing upon his retreat.

QUESTIONS

1 Who did take part in the archery competition?
2 What is the result of the archery competition?
3 What will be awarded to the winners in the archery competition?
4 How does Locksley deal with the award?
5 Can you describe the character of Hubert according to the words of Prince John?
6 Try to analyze the position of Jew in England according to John's order about the Jew Isaac.

1 crowns: English name of the monetary unit of Norway, Denmark and other countries

Jane Austen
(1775-1817)

INTRODUCTION

Jane Austen was an English novelist known primarily for her six major novels which interpret critique and comment upon the life of the British middle class at the end of the 18th century. She was the founder of the novel which deals with unimportant middle-class people and of which there are many fine examples in latter English fiction. Austen's plots often explore the dependence of women on marriage in the pursuit of favourable social standing and economic security. She is famous for her accurate observation and vivid representation of different types of people and their lives. Her most highly praised novel during her lifetime was *Pride and Prejudice*. As one of the greatest English novelists, Austen is a gifted, bright, and attractive little woman. Although she belonged to the age of Walter Scott, Austen's realism would place her in the group of the realistic novelists.

Jane Austen was born in Steventon, Hampshire in England. She was the daughter of a country-clergyman, the seventh of eight children and one of two girls. Austen passed all her life in doing small domestic duties in the countryside. In her childhood, she and her sister were sent to Oxford to be educated, but due to the illness, she and her sister had to come back and continued their education at home. Austen spent her life very quietly, cheerfully and uneventfully at home.

Despite this, she received a broader education than many women of her time. Her brother Henry, a banker whose friends are bankers, merchants, publishers, painters, and actors, provided Jane Austen with a social world not visible from a small parish in rural Hampshire. Extensive reading and contact with people from various lines provided materials for her creation.

But probably due to the prevailing prejudice at the time about the female writer, she published her novels anonymously. Different from her contemporary romanticists, she focused on England's local middle-class countryside, never touching upon the class conflicts and wars of her time, which are calm pictures of society life, though Austen wrote her books in troubled years which included the French Revolution. It is Austen who brought the novel of family life to its highest point of perfection.

Austen was never married, but her social life was active and she had suitors and romantic dreams. In 1816, Austen got serious illness and died in Winchester on 18th,

July 1817, at the age of 41. Austen's brother Henry made her authorship public after her death.

Her major works include *Sense and Sensibility* (1811), *Pride and Prejudice* (1813), *Northanger Abbey* (1818), *Mansfield Park* (1814), *Emma* (1815), and *Persuasion* (1818).

SELECTED READING

Pride and Prejudice

Overview

Austen completed the original manuscript of *Pride and Prejudice*, titled *First Impressions*, between 1796 and 1797. A publisher rejected the manuscript, and it was not until 1809 that Austen began the revisions that would bring it to its final form. The novel deals with the everyday life of small and big landlords and their families in the English countryside, particularly with the love and marriage of the younger members of those families. The story centers round the heroine Elizabeth Bennet who stands for "prejudice" and the hero Fitzwilliam Darcy who stands for "pride" and a minor couple, her sister Jane and his friend Charles Bingley. One of the themes is prudent conduct in getting married: prudent choice in finding a mate.

The story follows the main character, Elizabeth Bennet, as she deals with issues of manners, upbringing, morality, education, and marriage in the society. At first, Mr. Darcy slights and offends Elizabeth with his pride. Later, he is fascinated by Elizabeth. However, due to the slander from Mr. Wickham, Elizabeth is full of prejudice against Mr. Darcy. After a succession of twists and turns, things are cleared up. Elizabeth finally changes her feeling toward Darcy from original prejudice to now admiration and marries herself to Darcy. Bingley and Jane get married too with the help of Darcy. The novel ends with the marriage of the happy couples.

By describing several kinds of marriage, Jane Austen expresses her own views on the love and marriage. Although the theme in her story is narrow, Jane Austen succeeds in producing very vivid portraits of her major characters and in painting realistic and colorful pictures of the life and manners of the upper middle class in rural England of her time.

Chapter 1 of *Pride and Prejudice* has been universally acknowledged to be very well written as an opening chapter. The style is lucid and graceful, with touches of humor and mild satire.

Chapter 1

It is a truth universally acknowledged, that a single man in possession of a good fortune must be in want of a wife.

However little known the feelings or views of such a man may be on his first entering a neighbourhood, this truth is so well fixed in the minds of the surrounding families, that he is considered as the rightful property of some one or other of their daughters.

"My dear Mr. Bennet," said his lady to him one day, "have you heard that Netherfield Park[1] is let at last?"

Mr. Bennet replied that he had not.

"But it is," returned she; "for Mrs. Long[2] has just been here, and she told me all about it."

Mr. Bennet made no answer.

"Do not you want to know who has taken it?" cried his wife impatiently.

"You want to tell me, and I have no objection to hearing it."

This was invitation enough.

"Why, my dear, you must know, Mrs. Long says that Netherfield is taken by a young man of large fortune from the north of England; that he came down on Monday in a chaise and four[3] to see the place, and was so much delighted with it that he agreed with Mr. Morris[4] immediately; that he is to take possession before Michaelmas[5], and some of his servants are to be in the house by the end of next week."

"What is his name?"

"Bingley."

"Is he married or single?"

"Oh! single, my dear, to be sure! A single man of large fortune; four or five thousand a year. What a fine thing for our girls!"

"How so? how can it affect them?"

1 Netherfield Park: the name of an estate near the home of the Bennets

2 Mrs. Long: a neighbour of the Bennets

3 a chaise and four: a lightweight carriage driven with four horses

4 Mr. Morris: the owner of the Netherfield Park

5 Michaelmas: September 29th, a religious festival

"My dear Mr. Bennet," replied his wife, "how can you be so tiresome! You must know that I am thinking of his marrying one of them."

"Is that his design in settling here?"

"Design! nonsense, how can you talk so! But it is very likely that he may fall in love with one of them, and therefore you must visit him as soon as he comes."

"I see no occasion for that. You and the girls may go, or you may send them by themselves, which perhaps will be still better; for, as you are as handsome as any of them, Mr. Bingley might like you the best of the party."

"My dear, you flatter me. I certainly have had my share of beauty, but I do not pretend to be anything extraordinary now. When a woman has five grown up daughters, she ought to give over thinking of her own beauty."

"In such cases, a woman has not often much beauty to think of."

"But, my dear, you must indeed go and see Mr. Bingley when he comes into the neighbourhood."

"It is more than I engage for, I assure you."

"But consider your daughters. Only think what an establishment it would be for one of them. Sir William and Lady Lucas[1] are determined to go, merely on that account, for in general, you know they visit no new comers. Indeed you must go, for it will be impossible for us to visit him, if you do not."

"You are over-scrupulous, surely. I dare say Mr. Bingley will be very glad to see you; and I will send a few lines by you to assure him of my hearty consent to his marrying whichever he chooses of the girls; though I must throw in a good word for my little Lizzy[2]."

"I desire you will do no such thing. Lizzy is not a bit better than the others; and I am sure she is not half so handsome as Jane[3], nor half so good humoured as Lydia[4]. But you are always giving her the preference."

"They have none of them much to recommend them," replied he; "they are all silly and ignorant like other girls; but Lizzy has something more of quickness than her sisters."

1 Sir William and Lady Lucas: Sir William Lucas and his wife, neighbours of the Bennets

2 Lizzy: Mr. and Mrs Bennet's second daughter

3 Jane: Mr. and Mrs Bennet's eldest daughter

4 Lydia: Mr. and Mrs Bennet's youngest daughter

"Mr. Bennet, how can you abuse your own children in such way? You take delight in vexing me. You have no compassion on my poor nerves."

"You mistake me, my dear. I have a high respect for your nerves. They are my old friends. I have heard you mention them with consideration these twenty years at least."

"Ah, you do not know what I suffer."

"But I hope you will get over it, and live to see many young men of four thousand a year come into the neighbourhood."

"It will be no use to us if twenty such should come, since you will not visit them."

"Depend upon it, my dear, that when there are twenty I will visit them all."

Mr. Bennet was so odd a mixture of quick parts, sarcastic humour, reserve, and caprice, that the experience of three and twenty years had been insufficient to make his wife understand his character. Her mind was less difficult to develop. She was a woman of mean understanding, little information, and uncertain temper. When she was discontented, she fancied herself nervous. The business of her life was to get her daughters married; its solace was visiting and news.

QUESTIONS

1 What is the meaning of the first sentence of the first paragraph?
2 What do you know about Mr. Bingley according to the dialogue between Mrs. Bennet and her husband?
3 Can you describe the character of Mr. Bennet according to the dialogue of the couple?
4 Can you give a character analysis about Mrs. Bennet?
5 What do Mr. and Mrs. Bennets think of an ideal husband for their daughter?
6 What is the language feature of the chapter? And give us some examples.

EXERCISES OF CHAPTER V

I Fill in the following blanks.

1 The Romantic period began with____________and ended with____________in 1832.

2 The Lake Poets consist of ____________, ____________ and ___________.

3 ____________ is considered the father of historical novelist in the English Romantic Age.

II Find the relevant match from Column B for each item in Column A.

Column A	Column B
1 ( ) William Wordsworth	A. *A Red, Red Rose*
2 ( ) George Byron	B. *Lyrical Ballads*
3 ( ) John Keats	C. *She Walks in Beauty*
4 ( ) Walter Scott	D. *Ode to the West Wind*
5 ( ) Jane Austen	E. *Ode to a Nightingale*
6 ( ) Robert Burns	F. *Ivanhoe*
7 ( ) Percy Bysshe Shelley	G. *Sense and Sensibility*

III Choose the best answer for each statement.

1 "If Winter comes, can Spring be far behind?" This line of poem is from ______.

A. Wordsworth's *I Wandered Lonely as a Cloud*

B. Keats' *Ode to a Nightingale*

C. Byron's *The Isles of Greece*

D. Shelley's *Ode to the West Wind*

2 Who is a realistic writer during the Romantic Period? ______.

A. Walter Scott B. William Wordsworth

C. Jane Austen D. Percy B. Shelley

3 In *Pride and Prejudice*, "pride" stands for ______.

A. Mr. Bingley B. Elizabeth Bennet

C. Fitzwilliam Darcy D. Mr. Bennet

4 Whose principle is "Beauty is truth, truth beauty" among the romantic poets?

A. William Wordsworth B. George Byron

C. Percy Shelley D. John Keats

5 What does Wordsworth mainly describe in his poem *I Wandered Lonely as a Cloud*? ______.

A. A floating cloud B. A great number of golden daffodils

C. The shining stars in the sky D. The danced waves

IV Answer the following questions.

1 Discuss Jane Austen's greatest contributions to English literature.

2 What is John Keats' style of poetry and the subject matter in odes?

CHAPTER VI

English Literature in the Victorian Age

(1832-1902)

General Introduction

Queen Victoria ruled over England from 1837 to 1901. In the history of England, the period has generally been regarded as one of the most remarkable in the development of the country, marked by a great expansion of the British Empire. It was a long period of peace, prosperity, refined sensibilities and national self-confidence for Britain, which is known as the Victorian era or Victorian Age. Some scholars date the beginning of the period in terms of sensibilities and political concerns to the passage of the Reform Act 1832. During this age, Britain had reached its highest point of development. And the literature, science and arts in the United Kingdom were also in prosperity.

Literature is closely related to the development of society and it is inevitable to reflect the social reality. The social problems such as the political power passed into the hands of the middle-class industrial capitalists, the House of Commons headed by the two parties: the Liberal and the Conservative, the problem of women influenced by the Industrial Revolution, the contradiction between the rich and the poor, the conflicts between capital and labour, the widespread unemployment, severe depression, the system of workhouses, and the flourish of new philosophical ideas, etc. found their expression in the novels of the critical realists like Dickens, Mrs. Gaskell, Charlotte Brontë, Thomas Hardy and other realistic writers. Thus, critical realism, a new literary trend, appeared in mid and late 19th century.

English critical realism of the 19th century flourished in the forties and in the early fifties. The critical realists described with much vividness and artistic skill the chief traits of the English society and criticized the capitalist system from a democratic viewpoint. It found its expressions in the form of novel. The greatest English realist of the time was Charles Dickens. With striking force and truthfulness, he created pictures of bourgeois civilization, showing the misery and sufferings of the common people. Another critical realist was William Makepeace Thackeray. His novels are mainly a satirical portrayal of the upper strata of society. Others are Brontë sisters, Mrs.

Elizabeth Gaskell, George Eliot, and Thomas Hardy. The novelists exposed and criticized the corrupted society mercilessly. They are generally known as critical realists.

Although in this period, some outstanding women appeared, old convention and prejudice remained dominant. Cheap labour and very hard jobs made women unbearable and thousands of women were driven into prostitution. So in the late period of Victorian Age, a feminist movement started, fighting for women's equality and freedom, and for their educational and employment opportunities. The spirit of the movement was reflected in the writings of women writers, such as Brontë sisters, Mrs Gaskell, George Eliot, etc.

Elizabeth Cleghorn Gaskell (1810-1865), often referred to as **Mrs. Gaskell**, was an English novelist and short story writer. Her novels offer a detailed portrait of the lives of many strata of society, including the very poor. Her first novel, *Mary Barton* (1848), contains a vivid picture of the class conflicts. In the novel, Gaskell shows great sympathy for the workers and highly praises the workers' struggle against the capitalists. Her other novels include *Cranford* (1853) which gives readers a picture of life in a village. *Ruth* (1853) is a sad story of a girl whose parents are dead. *North and South* (1854-1855) is a novel to study the different lives of English people. *Sylvia's Lovers* (1863) and *Wives and Daughters* (1864-1866) are Gaskell's two finest novels, both of which trace the growth and development of their contrasted heroines. *Wives and Daughters*, by contrast, examines family relationships and social class. Mrs. Gaskell was the close friend of Charlotte Brontë. Her *The Life of Charlotte Brontë*, published in 1857, was the first biography about Charlotte Brontë.

George Eliot (1819-1880) was the pseudonym of Mary Ann Evens. She was one of the leading writers of the Victorian era. George Eliot was the most probably intelligent of the great mid-Victorian novelists. Her seriousness was readily praised and acclaimed by the reviewers. She was the author of seven novels, of which four novels are best-known. *Adam Bede* (1859) is a rural tragedy; *The Mill on the Floss* (1860) tells a story of the daughter and son of a country miller. The novel reinforces family values. In this novel, Eliot examines a very different pattern of loyalties and relationships. *Silas Marner* (1861) explores a series of dense ethical, social, and spiritual dilemmas. And *Middlemarch* (1872) discusses some significant themes, including the status of women, the nature of marriage, idealism, self-interest, religion, hypocrisy, political reform, and education. *Middlemarch* has been described by Martin Amis and Julian Barnes as the greatest novel in the English language.

In the late of 19th century, other popular novelists published some readable and colourful novels.

Lewis Carroll (1832-1898) was the penname of Charles Lutwidge Dodgson, a university teacher of mathematics at Oxford. He is remembered more for his two books for children than for his excellent mathematics. Carroll's two Alice novels, *Alice's*

Adventure in Wonderland (1865) and *Through the Looking-Glass* (1871), were written for a young girl, Alice, but they are read now by grown-ups, too, because the nonsense in it is not only delightful but strangely reasonable.

Anthony Trollope (1815-1882) was one of the most successful, prolific and respected English novelists of the Victorian era. He once worked in the General Post Office, but by 1879 he had earned 70,000 pounds by his books. Among his 47 novels, *The Warden* (1855) is the first of those that are known as the Barsetshire novels. Barsetshire is the name given to the (imaginary) county. Trollope wrote like a machine, for three hours a day in the early morning, forcing himself to write 1,000 words an hour. It is surely very unusual for him to have one or two complete novels waiting for his publisher. He also published dozens of short stories and a few books on travel. Critics generally acknowledge *The Way We Live Now* (1875) as his masterpiece.

William Wilkie Collins (1824-1889) is regarded as the first English novelist to write detective stories, who occasionally worked with Dickens. Collins possessed an extraordinary narrative gift to suit to his pioneering interest in the evolution of the detective story. His *The Woman in White* (1860) treats of insanity, selfishness, and guilty secrets. Collins's *The Moonstone* (1868) is a multiple narrative which subtly explores the nature of detection. This is a tale of mystery which tells us that a precious stone from India disappears, and the search for it brings out the character of Sergeant Cuff, one of the first detectives in English literature.

Robert Louis Stevenson (1850-1894) was a Scottish novelist and poet. He is known as the representative of New Romanticism, another literary trend prevailing at the end of the 19th century. Stevenson studied engineering and the law before he wrote books. His weak lungs drove him to travel in search of health. His most famous works are *Treasure Island* (1883), *The New Arabian Nights* (1882), *Kidnapped* (1886) and *Strange case of Dr Jekyll and Mr Hyde* (1886). *Treasure Island*, the boys' popular story, is an adventure story. *The New Arabian Nights* is a book of stories which almost make us believe the impossible. *Kidnapped* is a story of adventure in Scotland. His best story is perhaps *Strange Case of Dr Jekyll and Mr Hyde*. In this exciting novel the reader follows the struggle between two forms of the same man: the good Dr Jekyll and the evil Mr. Hyde.

Arthur Conan Doyle (1859-1930) was as an Irish-Scots writer, most noted for creating the fictional detective Sherlock Holmes in *A Study in Scarlet* (1887), which is generally considered a milestone in the field of crime fiction.

Samuel Butler (1835-1902) was a representative writer of the late 19th century realism. He was educated at Cambridge University. Then he went to New Zealand where he became a successful sheep breeder. Five years later, he returned to England and began his literary career. He is famous for his two books. One is his utopian fantasy *Erewhon* (Nowhere) which shows his most prominent feature, use of antiphrasis; the other is *The Way of All Flesh*, a novel published after his death, which is Butler's autobiographical study of parents and children. His *Erewhon* (1872) is a satire on English customs. Erewhon is a strange country. The beautiful people have different ideas from those of Europe. If a man is poor in Erewhon, he is a criminal. If he is sick, he is a criminal. If he is ugly, he is a criminal. But if he does something that we consider to be a crime, he is sent to hospital, not to prison. There he is cured of his crimes by doctors. Their special sort of money is, in fact, useless. Machines are not allowed; they have all been destroyed because the rulers think them dangerous. They might rule the country themselves if they were allowed to develop. This unusual book was followed by another, *Erewhon Revisited* (1901).

During the Victorian Age, the most famous work of scientific literature should be *On the Origin of Species* (1859) written by **Charles Robert Darwin** (1809-1882), which has introduced his theory of evolution with compelling evidence.

The Victorian Age was largely an age of prose, especially of novels. Although poetry was no longer a major form of literature, English poetry did not stop development. The most famous poet of the age was Alfred Tennyson. His influence in his own time was immense. Tennyson reflected the changing ideas of his age in his various poems. Other two famous poets were Robert Browning and Mrs. Browning.

The famous playwrights in the late 19th century were Oscar Wilde and George Bernard Shaw. Wilde was an Irish playwright and novelist. He was a spokesman for aestheticism. The masterpiece of his plays is *The Importance of Being Earnest* (1895). George Bernard Shaw published his first play in 1880s but most of his plays were published in 20th century.

Charles Dickens (1812-1870)

INTRODUCTION

Charles Dickens was an English writer and social critic. He is regarded as the greatest novelist of the Victorian era and remains one of the best-known and most-read of English authors. Dickens is the greatest representative of English critical realism. By the twentieth century, critics and scholars had recognized him as a literary genius. His novels and short stories enjoy lasting popularity and he is one of the few whose works did not become unpopular after his death.

Dickens was born in 1812 at Portsmouth, where his father was a clerk in the Navy Pay Office. When he was 9 years old, his family moved to London. There his father fell into debt, and was thrown into the poor-debtors' prison. At 11 years of age the boy was taken out of school and sent to earn his living in a blacking factory. Work there began at eight in the morning and ended at eight at night. He can get 6 shillings a week. This was the unhappiest time of all his life. He was lonely and hungry. Afterwards a small legacy brought the father out of prison, and Charles was sent to school once more. At 15 he left school and went to work as clerk in a lawyer's office. In his spare time he studied shorthand and visited the British Museum library, where he did much reading. At the age of 19 he became a Parliamentary reporter. In 1836, when he was only 24, his *Pickwick Papers* came into being. It tells of the adventures of Mr. Pickwick and his club. *Pickwick Papers* swept across England and Dickens became the most popular living novelist of his day.

In his novels, Dickens gives us a realistic and vivid picture of the English society of his age and depicts the everyday life of the ordinary people. In his different novels Dickens describes and attacks many kinds of unpleasant people and places, such as bad schools and school masters, government departments, bad prisons, and dirty houses. His characters cover thieves, murderers, hungry children, men in debt, stupid and unwashed men and women, etc. Dickens used fiction as his vehicle against what he saw as injustice. His name continues to be popularly associated with good causes and with remedies for social abuses because he was quite the wittiest, the most persuasive, and the most influential voice.

Dickens provides readers with a fantasy, a fairy-tale, and a nightmare world. It is a world seen through the eyes of a child: the shadows are blacker, the fog is denser, the houses are higher, and the midnight streets are emptier and more terrifying than in reality. The characters, too, are seen as children see people.

Oliver Twist (1837-1838) is the story of a poor boy's cruel treatment and miserable adventures, including descriptions of hunger, stealing, murder and hanging.

The Old Curiosity Shop (1841) is a story of the suffering and hardships of an old man named Trent, and his granddaughter, Nell, who keep and live in an old curiosity shop in London. Driven by poverty and misery, they escape from the capital. Little Nell's mortality has so profoundly moved the first readers of the novel.

David Copperfield (1849-1850) is based on Dickens's own life, which has a sad beginning. It is one of the most popular of his novels. Dickens wrote: "Of all my books, I like this the best."

Bleak House (1852-1853) attacks the law's delay. The novel exposes the abuses of the English courts, and the plot is built around the law-suit of Jarndyce and Jarndyce over the inheritance of a family fortune, which has dragged on for many generations.

Hard Times (1854) is set in industrial surroundings, where Gradgrind's children are brought up among hard facts and without any help for the spirit. The son robs a bank, and the girl makes an unhappy marriage; but luckily the father suddenly understands his own foolishness. Dickens attacks the Industrial Revolution in this novel.

Little Dorrit (1855-1857) attacks the prisons and imprisonment for debt. It has a broader European frame of reference.

A Tale of Two Cities (1859) is set in the French Revolution. The "two cities" are Paris and London in the time of that revolution. The theme is revolution. Underlying the novel there is the idea "Where there is oppression, there is revolution."

Great Expectations (1860-1861) is the story about the development of Pip. In the novel, Pip is manipulated and gentrified and left empty. He learns from his bad fortune and gets rid of his snobbishness. Many critics have called it the best of his novels. To many readers, it remains the most completely satisfying and haunting of Dickens' works.

The Mystery of Edwin Drood (1870) is Dickens' unfinished murder story.

SELECTED READING

Oliver Twist

Overview

Oliver Twist tells the story of an orphan boy, who starts his life in a workhouse. He is brought up under miserable conditions and is then sold to an undertaker. After serving an unhappy apprenticeship to the undertaker, he runs away and travels to London, where he falls into the hands of a gang of pickpockets led by the elderly criminal Fagin. His stepbrother Monks wants to keep him in the gang in order to get his whole property. In breaking into Mrs. Maylie's house, Twist receives a gun-shot wound and is abandoned. Luckily, he is kindly cared for by Mrs. Maylie and Rose who is his aunt. Oliver then is adopted by Mr. Brownlow, a good gentleman. In this novel, Dickens exposes the terrible conditions in the English workhouse of the time and the cruel treatment of a poor orphan. In the famous scene in Chapter 2, Oliver is beaten up and punished only because he ventures to ask for an extra portion of gruel, which is only one of the many details to show the extreme brutality and corruption of the oppressors and their agents.

Chapter 2

(Excerpt)

Oliver had not been within the walls of the workhouse a quarter of an hour, and had scarcely completed the demolition of a second slice of bread, when Mr. Bumble[1], who had handed him over to the care of an old woman, returned; and, telling him it was a board night, informed him that the board had said he was to appear before it forthwith.

Not having a very clearly defined notion of what a live board[2] was, Oliver was rather astounded by this intelligence, and was not quite certain whether he ought to laugh or cry. He had no time to think about the matter, however; for Mr. Bumble gave him a tap on the head, with his cane, to wake him up: and another on the back to make him lively: and bidding him to follow, conducted him into a large white-washed room, where eight or ten fat gentlemen were sitting round a table. At the top of the table, seated in an arm-chair rather higher than the rest, was a particularly fat gentleman with a very round, red face.

"Bow to the board," said Bumble. Oliver brushed away two or three tears that were lingering in his eyes; and seeing no board but the table[3],

1 Mr. Bumble: a parish beadle who put Oliver into the workhouse

2 live board: The pun is used here. Pay attention to the different understanding of "board".

3 no board but the table: Note the pun again on the words "board" and "table".

fortunately bowed to that.

"What's your name, boy?" said the gentleman in the high chair.

Oliver was frightened at the sight of so many gentlemen, which made him tremble: and the beadle gave him another tap behind, which made him cry. These two causes made him answer in a very low and hesitating voice; whereupon a gentleman in a white waistcoat said he was a fool, which was a capital way of raising his spirits, and putting him quite at his ease.

"Boy," said the gentleman in the high chair, "listen to me. You know you're an orphan, I suppose?"

"What's that, sir?" inquired poor Oliver.

"The boy IS a fool—I thought he was," said the gentleman in the white waistcoat, in a very decided tone. If one member of a class be blessed with an intuitive perception of others of the same race, the gentleman in the white waistcoat was unquestionably well qualified to pronounce an opinion on the matter.

"Hush!" said the gentleman who had spoken first. "You know you've got no father or mother, and that you were brought up by the parish, don't you?"

"Yes, sir," replied Oliver, weeping bitterly.

"What are you crying for?" inquired the gentleman in the white waistcoat. And to be sure it was very extraordinary. What COULD the boy be crying for?

"I hope you say your prayers every night," said another gentleman in a gruff voice; "and pray for the people who feed you, and take care of you—like a Christian."

"Yes, sir," stammered the boy. The gentleman who spoke last was unconsciously right. It would have been very like a Christian, and a marvellously good Christian too, if Oliver had prayed for the people who fed and took care of HIM. But he hadn't, because nobody had taught him.

"Well! You have come here to be educated, and taught a useful trade," said the red-faced gentleman in the high chair.

"So you'll begin to pick oakum to-morrow morning at six o'clock," added the surly one in the white waistcoat.

For the combination of both these blessings in the one simple process of picking oakum, Oliver bowed low by the direction of the beadle, and was then hurried away to a large ward; where, on a rough, hard bed, he sobbed himself to sleep. What a novel illustration of the tender laws[1] of England! They let the paupers go to sleep!

Poor Oliver! He little thought, as he lay sleeping in happy unconsciousness of all around him, that the board had that very day arrived at a decision which would exercise the most material influence over all his future fortunes. But they had. And this was it:

The members of this board were very sage, deep, philosophical men; and when they came to turn their attention to the workhouse, they found out at once, what ordinary folks would never have discovered—the poor people liked it! It was a regular place of public entertainment for the poorer classes; a tavern where there was nothing to pay; a public breakfast, dinner, tea, and supper all the year round; a brick and mortar elysium, where it was all play and no work. "Oho!" said the board, looking very knowing; "we are the fellows to set this to rights; we'll stop it all, in no time." So, they established the rule, that all poor people should have the alternative (for they would compel nobody, not they), of being starved by a gradual process in the house, or by a quick one out of it. With this view, they contracted with the water-works to lay on an unlimited supply of water; and with a corn-factor to supply periodically small quantities of oatmeal; and issued three meals of thin gruel a day, with an onion twice a week, and half a roll of Sundays. They made a great many other wise and humane regulations, having reference to the ladies, which it is not necessary to repeat; kindly undertook to divorce poor married people, in consequence of the great expense of a suit in Doctors' Commons[2]; and, instead of compelling a man to support his family, as they had theretofore done, took his family away from him, and made him a bachelor! There is no saying how many applicants for relief, under these last two heads, might have started up in all classes of society, if it had not

1 the tender laws: It is an allusion to the New Poor Laws passed by Parliament in 1834, which would like to modify the existing system of poor relief and encourage the large-scale development of workhouses.

2 Doctor's Commons: a civil law court in London

been coupled with the workhouse; but the board were long-headed men, and had provided for this difficulty. The relief was inseparable from the workhouse and the gruel; and that frightened people.

For the first six months after Oliver Twist was removed, the system was in full operation. It was rather expensive at first, in consequence of the increase in the undertaker's bill, and the necessity of taking in the clothes of all the paupers, which fluttered loosely on their wasted, shrunken forms, after a week or two's gruel. But the number of workhouse inmates got thin as well as the paupers; and the board were in ecstasies.

The room in which the boys were fed was a large stone hall, with a copper at one end, out of which the master, dressed in an apron for the purpose, and assisted by one or two women, ladled the gruel at mealtimes. Of this festive composition each boy had one porringer, and no more—except on occasions of great public rejoicing, when he had two ounces and a quarter of bread besides.

The bowls never wanted washing. The boys polished them with their spoons till they shone again; and when they had performed this operation (which never took very long, the spoons being nearly as large as the bowls), they would sit staring at the copper, with such eager eyes, as if they could have devoured the very bricks of which it was composed; employing themselves, meanwhile, in sucking their fingers most assiduously, with the view of catching up any stray splashes of gruel that might have been cast thereon. Boys have generally excellent appetites.

Oliver Twist and his companions suffered the tortures of slow starvation for three months: at last they got so voracious and wild with hunger, that one boy, who was tall for his age, and hadn't been used to that sort of thing (for his father had kept a small cook-shop), hinted darkly to his companions, that unless he had another basin of gruel per diem[1], he was afraid he might some night happen to eat the boy who slept next him, who happened to be a weakly youth of tender age. He had a wild, hungry eye; and they implicitly believed him. A council was held; lots were cast who should walk up to

1 per diem [Latin]: per day

the master after supper that evening, and ask for more; and it fell to Oliver Twist.

The evening arrived; the boys took their places. The master, in his cook's uniform, stationed himself at the copper; his pauper assistants ranged themselves behind him; the gruel was served out; and a long grace was said over the short commons[1]. The gruel disappeared; the boys whispered each other, and winked at Oliver; while his next neighbours nudged him. Child as he was, he was desperate with hunger, and reckless with misery. He rose from the table; and advancing to the master, basin and spoon in hand, said: somewhat alarmed at his own temerity:

"Please, sir, I want some more."

The master was a fat, healthy man; but he turned very pale. He gazed in stupefied astonishment on the small rebel for some seconds, and then clung for support to the copper. The assistants were paralyzed with wonder; the boys with fear.

"What!" said the master at length, in a faint voice.

"Please, sir," replied Oliver, "I want some more."

The master aimed a blow at Oliver's head with the ladle; pinioned him in his arm; and shrieked aloud for the beadle.

The board were sitting in solemn conclave, when Mr. Bumble rushed into the room in great excitement, and addressing the gentleman in the high chair, said—

"Mr. Limbkins, I beg your pardon, sir! Oliver Twist has asked for more!"

There was a general start. Horror was depicted on every countenance.

"For MORE!" said Mr. Limbkins. "Compose yourself, Bumble, and answer me distinctly. Do I understand that he asked for more, after he had eaten the supper allotted by the dietary?"

"He did, sir," replied Bumble. "That boy will be hung," said the gentleman in the white waistcoat. "I know that boy will be hung."

Nobody controverted the prophetic gentleman's opinion. An animated discussion took place. Oliver was ordered into instant confinement; and a

1 short commons: insufficient daily food

bill was next morning pasted on the outside of the gate, offering a reward of five pounds to anybody who would take Oliver Twist off the hands of the parish. In other words, five pounds and Oliver Twist were offered to any man or woman who wanted an apprentice to any trade, business, or calling.

"I never was more convinced of anything in my life," said the gentleman in the white waistcoat, as he knocked at the gate and read the bill next morning: "I never was more convinced of anything in my life, than I am that that boy will come to be hung."

As I purpose to show in the sequel whether the white waist coated gentleman was right or not, I should perhaps mar the interest of this narrative (supposing it to possess any at all), if I ventured to hint just yet, whether the life of Oliver Twist had this violent termination or no.

QUESTIONS

1 Who is Bumble? What does he do to Oliver Twist?
2 What does Oliver Twist understand "board"?
3 What are the images of the eight or ten gentlemen?
4 What is the alternative for all the poor people described in this selection?
5 Why does the novelist describe the clothes of all the paupers?
6 How does the author describe the paupers' meal?
7 What has Oliver Twist done to make all of the gentlemen and assistants shocked?
8 What is the consequence of Oliver Twist's behaviour?

William Makepeace Thackeray (1811-1863)

INTRODUCTION

Thackeray was an English novelist of the 19th century. He is famous for his satirical works, particularly *Vanity Fair*, a panoramic portrait of English society. He is another representative of critical realism in 19th century England.

He was born to the family of an English official. Thackeray studied at Trinity College of Cambridge University, but left it without taking a degree. Then he travelled in Germany, France and Italy. On his return to England, he went into politics and wrote articles for various magazines. In the forties of 19th century he had already become a good realistic writer. In 1847 he published his masterpiece *Vanity Fair*, which marks the peak of his literary career. Later he wrote some other novels but it is *Vanity Fair* that established his position in the literature. His novels are mainly a satirical portrayal of the upper strata of society. In his opinion, the existing society was corrupted as well as corrupting. He took it as his duty to expose the vices of his age, esp. those in the upper-middle class. Instead of the poor, he described the nobility.

SELECTED READING

Vanity Fair: A Novel without a Hero

Overview

Thackeray's best-known work, *Vanity Fair*, describes the adventures of two girls of different sorts: Rebecca (Becky) Sharp, a clever, brave and poor girl without a conscience; and Amelia Sedley, the gentle daughter of a rich Londoner. The title of the novel comes from Bunyan's *Pilgrim's Progress*.

Vanity Fair's subtitle is "A Novel without a Hero". It suggests the fact that the writer's intention was not to portray individuals, but the bourgeois and aristocratic society as a whole. The plot is around the lives of Amelia Sedley and Becky Sharp. William Dobbin, finally wins Amelia, the woman he has always loved. The selection given below is taken from Chapter 36 of the novel. Here it is on Becky Sharp's adventures in Paris.

Chapter 36

(Excerpt)

How to Live Well on Nothing a Year

I suppose there is no man in this Vanity Fair of ours so little observant as not to think sometimes about the worldly affairs of his acquaintances, or so extremely charitable as not to wonder how his neighbour Jones, or his neighbour Smith, can make both ends meet at the end of the year.

...

The truth is, when we say of a gentleman that he lives elegantly on nothing a year, we use the word "nothing" to signify something unknown; meaning, simply, that we don't know how the gentleman in question defrays the expenses of his establishment. Now, our friend the Colonel had a great aptitude for all games of chance: and exercising himself, as he continually did, with the cards, the dice-box, or the cue, it is natural to suppose that he attained a much greater skill in the use of these articles than men can possess who only occasionally handle them.

...

In fact, our friends may be said to have been among the first of that brood of hardy English adventurers who have subsequently invaded the Continent and swindled in all the capitals of Europe. The respect in those happy days of 1817-18 was very great for the wealth and honor of Britons. They had not then learned, as I am told, to haggle for bargains with the pertinacity which now distinguishes them. The great cities of Europe had not been as yet open to the enterprise of our rascals. And whereas there is now hardly a town of France or Italy in which you shall not see some noble countryman of our own, with that happy swagger and insolence of demeanor which we carry everywhere, swindling inn-landlords, passing fictitious cheques upon credulous bankers, robbing coach-makers of their carriages, goldsmiths of their trinkets, easy travelers of their money at cards, even public libraries of their books—thirty years ago you needed but to be a Milor Anglais[1], traveling in a private carriage, and credit was at your hand wherever

1 Milor Anglais [French]: English lord

you chose to seek it, and gentlemen, instead of cheating, were cheated. It was not for some weeks after the Crawleys' departure that the landlord of the hotel which they occupied during their residence at Paris found out the losses which he had sustained: not until Madame Marabou, the milliner, made repeated visits with her little bill for articles supplied to Madame Crawley; not until Monsieur Didelot from Boule d'Or in the Palais Royal had asked half a dozen times whether cette charmante Miladi[1] who had bought watches and bracelets of him was de retour[2]. It is a fact that even the poor gardener's wife, who had nursed madame's child, was never paid after the first six months for that supply of the milk of human kindness with which she had furnished the lusty and healthy little Rawdon. No, not even the nurse was paid —the Crawleys were in too great a hurry to remember their trifling debt to her. As for the landlord of the hotel, his curses against the English nation were violent for the rest of his natural life. He asked all travelers whether they knew a certain Colonel Lor Crawley—avec sa femme une petite dame, tres spirituelle[3]. "Ah, Monsieur!" he would add—"ils m'ont affreusement vole.[4]" It was melancholy to hear his accents as he spoke of that catastrophe.

Rebecca's object in her journey to London was to effect a kind of compromise with her husband's numerous creditors, and by offering them a dividend of nine-pence or a shilling in the pound, to secure a return for him into his own country. It does not become us to trace the steps which she took in the conduct of this most difficult negotiation; but, having shown them to their satisfaction that the sum which she was empowered to offer was all her husband's available capital, and having convinced them that Colonel Crawley would prefer a perpetual retirement on the Continent to a residence in this country with his debts unsettled; having proved to them that there was no possibility of money accruing to him from other quarters, and no earthly chance of their getting a larger dividend than that which she

1 cette charmante Miladi [French]: this charming madame

2 de retour [French]: to return

3 avec sa femme, une petite dame, tres spirituelle [French]: with his wife, a little lady with high spirit

4 "Ah, Monsieur!" ..."ils m'ont affreusement vole [French]: Ah, Sir, they have robbed me terribly.

was empowered to offer, she brought the Colonel's creditors unanimously to accept her proposals, and purchased with fifteen hundred pounds of ready money more than ten times that amount of debts.

Mrs. Crawley employed no lawyer in the transaction. The matter was so simple, to have or to leave, as she justly observed, that she made the lawyers of the creditors themselves do the business. And Mr. Lewis representing Mr. Davids, of Red Lion Square, and Mr. Moss acting for Mr. Manasseh of Cursitor Street (chief creditors of the Colonel's), complimented his lady upon the brilliant way in which she did business, and declared that there was no professional man who could beat her.

Rebecca received their congratulations with perfect modesty; ordered a bottle of sherry and a bread cake to the little dingy lodgings where she dwelt, while conducting the business, to treat the enemy's lawyers: shook hands with them at parting, in excellent good humour, and returned straightway to the Continent, to rejoin her husband and son and acquaint the former with the glad news of his entire liberation. As for the latter, he had been considerably neglected during his mother's absence by Mademoiselle Genevieve, her French maid; for that young woman, contracting an attachment for a soldier in the garrison of Calais, forgot her charge in the society of this militaire[1], and little Rawdon very narrowly escaped drowning on Calais sands at this period, where the absent Genevieve had left and lost him.

And so, Colonel and Mrs. Crawley came to London: and it is at their house in Curzon Street, May Fair, that they really showed the skill which must be possessed by those who would live on the resources above named.

QUESTIONS

1 Who does "Jones" or "Smith" in the first paragraph refer to?
2 What does "nothing" here mean?
3 What does Colonel do to get money in the second paragraph?
4 What does the gardener's wife do to Sharp? Has Sharp paid what she should pay?
5 How does Rebecca Sharp deal with their debtors?
6 What do you think of the subtitle of the novel?

1 militaire [French]: military man

Brontë Sisters

Charlotte Brontë

Emily Brontë

Anne Brontë

INTRODUCTION

The Brontës were a 19th century literary family who ever lived in the isolated village of Thornton on the edge of the moors in Yorkshire, England. The sisters, Charlotte (1816-1855), Emily (1818-1848), and Anne (1820-1849), are well known as poets and novelists. Their books have been translated into many languages and are always high in reading popularity. Their home, Haworth Parsonage in Yorkshire, has been set up as the Brontë Parsonage Museum, which has become a place of pilgrimage for hundreds of thousands of visitors from many nations.

They received some education in a charity school. The conditions there were very bad. Charlotte exposed the evil conditions of that school in her masterpiece *Jane Eyre*. Their father was a poor clergyman. Their childhood was not so happy, for they lost their mother when they were quite young.

In 1846, the three sisters published their small joint volume of poems, entitled *Poems by Currer, Ellis and Acton Bell*, the pseudonyms of Charlotte, Emily and Anne. Then each sister started novel writing. In 1847, they published their representative novels, *Jane Eyre* by Charlotte Brontë, *Wuthering Heights* by Emily Brontë, and *Agnes Grey* by Anne Brontë. Their stories immediately attracted attention.

Brontë sisters' father, Patrick Brontë, met and married 29-year-old Maria Branwell in 1812. And by 1820, the family moved into the parsonage at Haworth where Patrick took up the post of *Perpetual curate*. Then misfortunes came to the family one after another. The mother, Maria Branwell, died of cancer in 1821. Mrs. Brontë's elder sister, Aunt Branwell, came to look after the children and the house. In 1824, Maria, Elizabeth, Charlotte, and Emily were sent to Cowan Bridge School to get education, but two elder sisters, Maria and Elizabeth, died within a few weeks in 1825. In 1848, Emily, with books planned which she was never able to write, and Branwell, the only boy and the hope of his sisters, died of tuberculosis. The following year, Anne, the youngest and the gentlest, died of same illness. Charlotte lived to win the fame and independence they had all longed for. However, she died in 1855, less than a year after she got married to her father's curate Nicholls.

Anne Brontë wrote two novels, *Agnes Grey*, and *The Tenant of the Wildfell Hall*. Her novels are not so good as those by her two elder sisters. Emily Brontë wrote only one novel entitled *Wuthering Heights*. It is one of the best novels in English literature. Charlotte Brontë produced four novels. *The Professor* was written in 1846 and published in 1857. It describes events in the life of a schoolmaster in Brussels; *Jane Eyre* is her masterpiece; *Shirley* deals with themes of industrial unrest and the role of women in society, published in 1849; and *Villette* reflects the writer's experiences in Brussels, in which the heroine becomes a teacher and wins respect although she is not beautiful and has no money.

Chronology of the Brontës

- 1812 Patrick Brontë and Maria Branwell married.
- 1813 Maria Brontë was born.
- 1815 Elizabeth Brontë was born.
- 1816 Charlotte Brontë was born.
- 1817 Patrick Branwell Brontë was born.
- 1818 Emily Jane Brontë was born.
- 1820 Anne Brontë was born.
- 1820 The Brontë family moved to Haworth
- 1821 Her mother died of cancer (poet and painter), leaving five daughters and a son to be taken care of by her sister, Elizabeth Branwell.
- 1824 Maria, Elizabeth, Charlotte, and Emily Brontë were sent to Cowan Bridge School.
- 1825 Maria and Elizabeth Brontë died.
- 1831-2 Charlotte continued her education at Roe Head School.
- 1835-8 Charlotte returned to Roe Head School as a teacher.
- 1842 Charlotte and Emily went to Brussels; Emily returned late that year, Charlotte returned in January 1844.
- 1846 *Poems* were published.
- 1847 *Jane Eyre*, *Wuthering Heights*, *Agnes Grey* were published.
- 1848 Branwell and Emily died and *Tenant of Wildfell Hall* was published.
- 1849 Anne died and *Shirley* was published.
- 1852 *Villette* was published.
- 1854 Charlotte and Arthur Bell Nicholls married.
- 1855 Charlotte died.
- 1857 Mrs. Gaskell's *Life of Charlotte Brontë* was published.
- 1861 Mr. Patrick Brontë died.
- 1906 Mr. Arthur Bell Nicholls died.

Charlotte Brontë (1816-1855)

Charlotte Brontë was the eldest of the three Brontë sisters who survived into adulthood and whose novels have become classics of English literature. She first published her works under the pen name Currer Bell. As a result of a stay in Brussels, she wrote *The Professor* which was written in 1846, which describes events in the life of a schoolmaster in that city. The novel was rejected by many publishing houses and was published posthumously in 1857. *Villette* (1853) uses the same material and reflects the personal experiences of Charlotte when she was in Brussels. Charlotte Brontë's second published novel after *Jane Eyre* is *Shirley* which is a social novel published in 1849. Her finest and very successful novel is *Jane Eyre* which was published in 1847.

SELECTED READING

Jane Eyre

Overview

Jane Eyre is a novel by the English writer Charlotte Brontë. It was published in 1847. The novel describes the life of a poor and unbeautiful girl who is brought up by a cruel aunt in Gateshead Hall and sent to a miserable Lowood School. After that she goes to teach the daughter of Mr Rochester at Thornfield Hall. Although she is neither beautiful nor rich, Rochester falls in love with her; but when she discovers that his (mad) wife is still alive, she runs away and meets St. John Rivers, her cousin, in Moor House. Later the Thornfield Hall is burnt down and the mad wife is killed. In trying to save her, Rochester is blinded and loses all hope of happiness. He moves to Ferndean Manor. On hearing all of this, Jane marries him and so is able to bring comfort into the remaining part of his life. Jane's struggle for self-realization and her longing for love and fulfilment are both realized without violating her integrity or her conscience.

The selection is from Chapter 23. The conversation took place after Mr. Rochester told that he would marry Miss Ingram and pretended he had found a governess position for her in Ireland. Jane began to cry quietly, because she would be so far away from him. When he told her to listen to the nightingale, she was overcome with emotion and sobbed convulsively. Jane confessed her love for Rochester, and to her surprise, he asked her to be his wife and admitted that he brought up marrying Ingram in order to arouse Jane's jealousy. Pay attention to Jane's speech about spirit equality. The dialogue is more realistic and less formal than in many novels of the period.

Chapter 23

(Excerpt)

...

"Jane, do you hear that nightingale singing in the wood? Listen!"

In listening, I sobbed convulsively; for I could repress what I endured no longer; I was obliged to yield, and I was shaken from head to foot with acute distress. When I did speak, it was only to express an impetuous wish that I had never been born, or never come to Thornfield.

"Because you are sorry to leave it?"

The vehemence of emotion, stirred by grief and love within me, was claiming mastery, and struggling for full sway, and asserting a right to predominate, to overcome, to live, rise, and reign at last: yes,—and to speak.

"I grieve to leave Thornfield: I love Thornfield:—I love it, because I have lived in it a full and delightful life,—momentarily at least. I have not been trampled on[1]. I have not been petrified. I have not been buried with inferior minds, and excluded from every glimpse of communion with what is bright and energetic and high. I have talked, face to face, with what I reverence, with what I delight in,—with an original, a vigorous, an expanded mind. I have known you, Mr. Rochester; and it strikes me with terror and anguish to feel I absolutely must be torn from you for ever. I see the necessity of departure; and it is like looking on the necessity of death."

"Where do you see the necessity?" he asked suddenly.

"Where? You, sir, have placed it before me."

"In what shape?"

1 be trampled on: be treated cruelly

"In the shape of Miss Ingram; a noble and beautiful woman,—your bride."

"My bride! What bride? I have no bride!"

"But you will have."

"Yes;—I will!—I will!" He set his teeth.

"Then I must go:—you have said it yourself."

"No: you must stay! I swear it—and the oath shall be kept."

"I tell you I must go!" I retorted, roused to something like passion. "Do you think I can stay to become nothing to you? Do you think I am an automaton?—a machine without feelings? and can bear to have my morsel of bread snatched from my lips, and my drop of living water dashed from my cup? Do you think, because I am poor, obscure, plain, and little, I am soulless and heartless? You think wrong!—I have as much soul as you,—and full as much heart! And if God had gifted me with some beauty and much wealth, I should have made it as hard for you to leave me, as it is now for me to leave you. I am not talking to you now through the medium of custom, conventionalities, nor even of mortal flesh;—it is my spirit that addresses your spirit; just as if both had passed through the grave, and we stood at God's feet, equal,—as we are!"

"As we are!" repeated Mr. Rochester—"so," he added, enclosing me in his arms, gathering me to his breast, pressing his lips on my lips: "so, Jane!"

"Yes, so, sir," I rejoined: "and yet not so; for you are a married man—or as good as a married man, and wed to one inferior to you—to one with whom you have no sympathy—whom I do not believe you truly love; for I have seen and heard you sneer at her. I would scorn such a union: therefore I am better than you—let me go!"

"Where, Jane? To Ireland?"

"Yes—to Ireland. I have spoken my mind, and can go anywhere now."

"Jane, be still; don't struggle so, like a wild frantic bird that is rending its own plumage in its desperation."

"I am no bird; and no net ensnares me; I am a free human being with an independent will, which I now exert to leave you."

Another effort set me at liberty, and I stood erect before him.

"And your will shall decide your destiny," he said: "I offer you my hand, my heart, and a share of all my possessions."

"You play a farce, which I merely laugh at."

"I ask you to pass through life at my side—to be my second self, and best earthly companion."

"For that fate you have already made your choice, and must abide by it."

"Jane, be still a few moments: you are over-excited: I will be still too."

A waft of wind came sweeping down the laurel-walk and trembled through the boughs of the chestnut: it wandered away—away—to an indefinite distance—it died. The nightingale's song was then the only voice of the hour: in listening to it, I again wept. Mr. Rochester sat quiet, looking at me gently and seriously. Some time passed before he spoke; he at last said—

"Come to my side, Jane, and let us explain and understand one another."

"I will never again come to your side: I am torn away now, and cannot return."

"But, Jane, I summon you as my wife: it is you only I intend to marry."

I was silent: I thought he mocked me.

"Come, Jane—come hither."

"Your bride stands between us."

He rose, and with a stride reached me.

"My bride is here," he said, again drawing me to him, "because my equal is here, and my likeness. Jane, will you marry me?"

Still I did not answer, and still I writhed myself from his grasp: for I was still incredulous.

"Do you doubt me, Jane?"

"Entirely."

"You have no faith in me?"

"Not a whit."

"Am I a liar in your eyes?" he asked passionately. "Little sceptic, you shall be convinced. What love have I for Miss Ingram? None: and that you know. What love has she for me? None: as I have taken pains to prove: I caused a rumour to reach her that my fortune was not a third of what was supposed, and after that I presented myself to see the result; it was coldness both from her and her mother. I would not—I could not—marry Miss Ingram. You—you strange, you almost unearthly thing!—I love as my own flesh. You—poor and obscure, and small and plain as you are—I entreat to accept me as a husband."

"What, me!" I ejaculated, beginning in his earnestness—and especially in his incivility—to credit his sincerity: "me who have not a friend in the world but you—if you are my friend: not a shilling but what you have given me?"

"You, Jane, I must have you for my own—entirely my own. Will you be mine? Say yes, quickly."

"Mr. Rochester, let me look at your face: turn to the moonlight."

"Why?"

"Because I want to read your countenance—turn!"

"There! you will find it scarcely more legible than a crumpled, scratched page. Read on: only make haste, for I suffer."

His face was very much agitated and very much flushed, and there were strong workings in the features, and strange gleams in the eyes.

"Oh, Jane, you torture me!" he exclaimed. "With that searching and yet faithful and generous look, you torture me!"

"How can I do that? If you are true, and your offer real, my only feelings to you must be gratitude and devotion—they cannot torture."

"Gratitude!" he ejaculated; and added wildly—"Jane, accept me quickly. Say, Edward—give me my name—Edward—I will marry you."

"Are you in earnest? Do you truly love me? Do you sincerely wish me to be your wife?"

"I do; and if an oath is necessary to satisfy you, I swear it."

"Then, sir, I will marry you."

"Edward—my little wife!"

"Dear Edward!"

"Come to me—come to me entirely now," said he; and added, in his deepest tone, speaking in my ear as his cheek was laid on mine, "Make my happiness—I will make yours."

"God pardon me!" he subjoined ere long; "and man meddle not with me: I have her, and will hold her."

"There is no one to meddle, sir. I have no kindred to interfere."

"No—that is the best of it," he said. And if I had loved him less I should have thought his accent and look of exultation savage; but, sitting by him, roused from the nightmare of parting—called to the paradise of union—I thought only of the bliss given me to drink in so abundant a flow. Again and again he said, "Are you happy, Jane?"And again and again I answered, "Yes," after which he murmured, "It will atone—it will atone. Have I not found her friendless, and cold, and comfortless? Will I not guard, and cherish, and solace her? Is there not love in my heart, and constancy in my resolves? It will expiate at God's tribunal. I know my Maker sanctions[1] what I do. For the world's judgment—I wash my hands thereof. For man's opinion—I defy it."

But what had befallen the night? The moon was not yet set, and we were all in shadow: I could scarcely see my master's face, near as I was. And what ailed the chestnut tree? it writhed and groaned; while wind roared in the laurel walk, and came sweeping over us.

"We must go in," said Mr. Rochester: "the weather changes. I could have sat with thee till morning, Jane."

"And so," thought I, "could I with you." I should have said so, perhaps, but a livid, vivid spark leapt out of a cloud at which I was looking, and there was a crack, a crash, and a close rattling peal; and I thought only of hiding my dazzled eyes against Mr. Rochester's shoulder.

The rain rushed down. He hurried me up the walk, through the grounds, and into the house; but we were quite wet before we could pass the threshold. He was taking off my shawl in the hall, and shaking the water out of my loosened hair, when Mrs. Fairfax emerged from her room. I did not observe her at first, nor did Mr. Rochester. The lamp was lit. The clock was on the stroke of twelve.

"Hasten to take off your wet things," said he; "and before you go, good-

1 sanction: officially accept or allow something

night—good-night, my darling!"

He kissed me repeatedly. When I looked up, on leaving his arms, there stood the widow, pale, grave, and amazed. I only smiled at her, and ran upstairs. "Explanation will do for another time," thought I. Still, when I reached my chamber, I felt a pang at the idea she should even temporarily misconstrue what she had seen. But joy soon effaced every other feeling; and loud as the wind blew, near and deep as the thunder crashed, fierce and frequent as the lightning gleamed, cataract-like as the rain fell during a storm of two hours, duration, I experienced no fear and little awe. Mr. Rochester came thrice to my door in the course of it, to ask if I was safe and tranquil: and that was comfort, that was strength for anything.

Before I left my bed in the morning, little Adèle came running in to tell me that the great horse-chestnut at the bottom of the orchard had been struck by lightning in the night, and half of it split away.

QUESTIONS

1 How does Rochester make Jane confess her love for him?
2 Find out some sentences to show Jane's view of equality.
3 Why does Jane say "You play a farce, which I merely laugh at"?
4 Why are they forced to run into the house after the proposal?
5 What does Adèle tell in the morning?
6 What do the storm and the great horse-chestnut symbolize?

Emily Brontë
(1818-1848)

INTRODUCTION

Emily was a poet and novelist. According to Charlotte Brontë's description, Emily was clever, benevolent, but very stubborn: "Stronger than a man, simpler than a child, her nature stood alone." Now Emily has been described as an outstanding woman poet in English literature.

When her only novel, *Wuthering Heights*, appeared in 1847, it didn't attract the attention of her time. It was once considered controversial because its depiction of mental and physical cruelty was unusually stark, and it challenged strict Victorian ideals of the day, including religious hypocrisy, morality, social classes and gender inequality. But now the novel is widely regarded as a great work and a classic of English literature.

SELECTED READING

Wuthering Heights

Overview

The novel deals mainly with the story of Heathcliff, who was picked up by Mr. Earnshaw in the street and brought up with his children in Wuthering Heights. Heathcliff and Catherine love each other even as children, but Heathcliff hears her say that she could never marry such a low sort of creature, and so he leaves the house. Three years later, when he returns as a wealthy man, he finds that Catherine has married Edgar Linton, whom she does not love. Heathcliff then begins his cruel revenge. Heathcliff still loves Catherine. After giving birth to a daughter, Cathy Linton, Catherine dies heart-broken. Heathcliff marries Linton's sister Isabella but treats her badly only as a part of his revenge. Heathcliff with his wealth prevails completely over Hindley and his son Hareton. He treats Hareton cruelly in revenge of Hindley's former treatment of himself. Eventually Heathcliff forces Cathy Linton to marry his own sickly son. But the son dies, and Cathy falls in love with Hareton. Only then does Heathcliff, now an old man and still tortured by the memory of

Catherine, see the futility of revenge. Then he dies. And Hareton and Cathy are united.

Some critics think that *Wuthering Heights* is a morbid story of love, but a powerful attack on the bourgeois marriage system. The innocent love between Heathcliff and Catherine is poisoned by class prejudice founded on wealth.

The quality that readers have most admired is its unconventional narration. Different from the first person singular or the third person omniscient, the story is told chiefly by two characters in the story: Mr. Lockwood, one of the tenants of Heathcliff, and Nelly Dean, a housekeeper in the service of Catherine, in addition to some supplementary aids. The unusual way of narration adds much to the truthfulness of the story and the complexity of its plot. Precision is regarded as another successful characteristic.

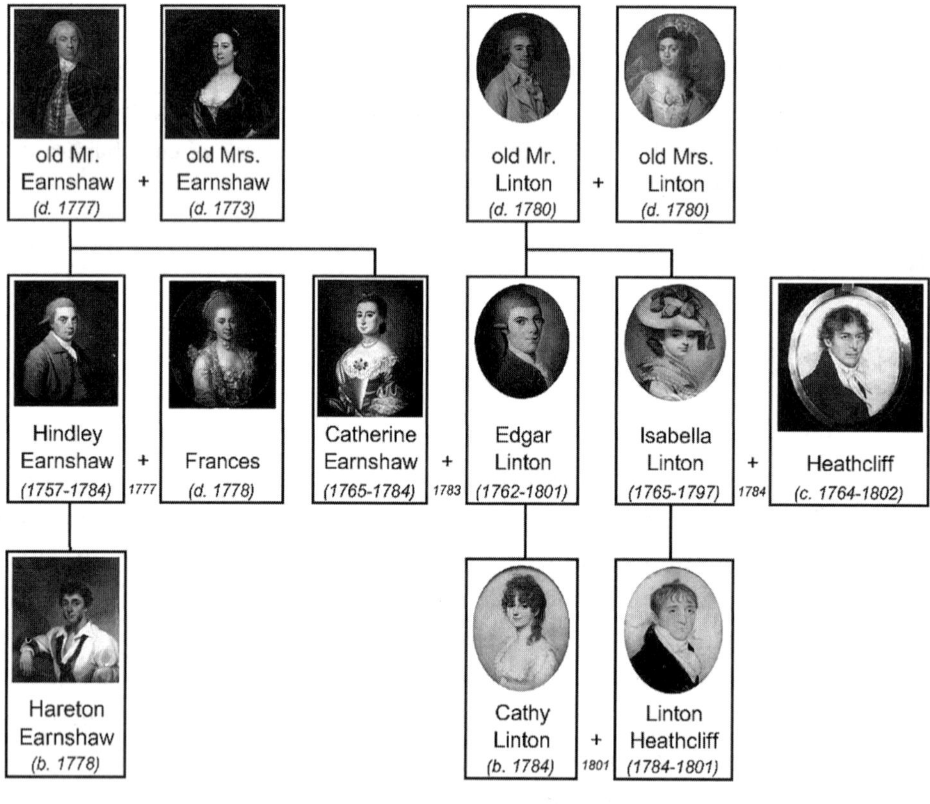

(From internet)

The following selection is from Chapter 15. It is the last meeting of Heathcliff and Catherine, which is the climax of development of the story.

Chapter 15

[Excerpt]

...

"What now?" said Catherine, leaning back, and returning his look with a suddenly clouded brow[1]: her humour was a mere vane[2] for constantly varying caprices. "You and Edgar[3] have broken my heart, Heathcliff! And you both came to bewail the deed to me, as if you were the people to be pitied! I shall not pity you, not I. You have killed me—and thriven on it, I think. How strong you are! How many years do you mean to live after I am gone?"

Heathcliff had knelt on one knee to embrace her; he attempted to rise, but she seized his hair, and kept him down.

"I wish I could hold you," she continued bitterly, "till we were both dead! I shouldn't care what you suffered. I care nothing for your sufferings. Why shouldn't you suffer? I do! Will you forget me? Will you be happy when I am in the earth[4]? Will you say twenty years hence, 'That's the grave of Catherine Earnshaw. I loved her long ago, and was wretched to lose her; but it is past. I've loved many others since: my children are dearer to me than she was; and at death, I shall not rejoice that I am going to her: I shall be sorry that I must leave them!' Will you say so, Heathcliff?"

"Don't torture me till I am as mad as yourself," cried he, wrenching his head free, and grinding his teeth.

The two, to a cool spectator, made a strange and fearful picture. Well might Catherine deem that heaven would be a land of exile to her, unless with her mortal body she cast away her moral character also. Her present countenance had a wild vindictiveness[5] in its white cheek, and a bloodless lip and scintillating[6] eye; and she retained in her closed fingers a portion of

1 clouded brow: gloomy and sorrowful expression

2 vane: arrow or pointer on the top of a building, turned by the wind so as to show its direction

3 Edgar: Edgar Linton, Catherine's husband and the master of Thrushcross Grange

4 in the earth: in the grave

5 vindictiveness: having or showing a desire for revenge

6 scintillate: to sparkle, to be brilliant

the locks she had been grasping. As to her companion, while raising himself with one hand, he had taken her arm with the other; and so inadequate was his stock of gentleness to the requirements of her condition, that on his letting go I saw four distinct impressions left blue in the colourless skin.

"Are you possessed with a devil," he pursued savagely, "to talk in that manner to me when you are dying? Do you reflect that all those words will be branded[1] on my memory, and eating deeper eternally after you have left me? You know you lie to say I have killed you: and, Catherine, you know that I could as soon forget you as my existence![2] Is it not sufficient for your infernal selfishness, that while you are at peace[3] I shall writhe in the torments of hell?"

"I shall not be at peace," moaned Catherine, recalled to a sense of physical weakness by the violent, unequal throbbing of her heart, which beat visibly and audibly under this excess of agitation. She said nothing further till the paroxysm[4] was over; then she continued, more kindly—

"I'm not wishing you greater torment than I have, Heathcliff. I only wish us never to be parted: and should a word of mine distress you hereafter, think I feel the same distress underground, and for my own sake, forgive me! Come here and kneel down again! You never harmed me in your life. Nay, if you nurse anger[5], that will be worse to remember than my harsh words! Won't you come here again? Do!"

Heathcliff went to the back of her chair, and leant over, but not so far as to let her see his face, which was livid[6] with emotion. She bent round to look at him; he would not permit it: turning abruptly, he walked to the fireplace, where he stood, silent, with his back towards us. Mrs Linton's glance followed him suspiciously: every movement woke a new sentiment in her. After a pause and a prolonged gaze, she resumed; addressing me in accents

1 branded: marked with

2 I could as soon forget you as my existence!: I could not forget you just like that I could not forget my own existence.

3 while you are at peace: while you pass away

4 paroxysm: sudden attack or outburst (of pain, anger, laughter, etc.)

5 nurse anger: be angry all the time

6 livid: of the colour of lead, blue grey

of indignant disappointment—

"Oh, you see, Nelly, he would not relent a moment to keep me out of the grave. That is how I'm loved! Well, never mind. That is not my Heathcliff. I shall love mine yet; and take him with me: he's in my soul. And", added she, musingly, "the thing that irks[1] me most in this shattered prison[2], after all. I'm tired, tired of being enclosed here. I'm wearying to escape into that glorious world[3], and to be always there: not seeing it dimly through tears, and yearning for it through the walls of an aching heart; but really with it, and in it. Nelly, you think you are better and more fortunate than I; in full health and strength: you are sorry for me—very soon that will be altered. I shall be sorry for you. I shall be incomparably beyond and above you all. I wonder he won't be near me!" She went on to herself. "I thought he wished it. Heathcliff, dear! you should not be sullen now. Do come to me, Heathcliff."

In her eagerness she rose and supported herself on the arm of the chair. At that earnest appeal he turned to her, looking absolutely desperate. His eyes, wide and wet, at last flashed fiercely on her; his breast heaved convulsively. An instant they held asunder[4], and then how they met I hardly saw, but Catherine made a spring, and he caught her, and they were locked in an embrace from which I thought my mistress would never be released alive: in fact, to my eyes, she seemed directly insensible. He flung himself into the nearest seat, and on my approaching hurriedly to ascertain if she had fainted, he gnashed at me, and foamed like a mad dog, and gathered her to him[5] with greedy jealousy. I did not feel as if I were in the company of a creature of my own species: it appeared that he would not understand, though I spoke to him; so I stood off, and held my tongue, in great perplexity.

A movement of Catherine's relieved me a little presently: she put up her hand to clasp his neck, and bring her cheek to his as he held her; while

1 irk: to trouble, to annoy

2 this shattered prison: It refers to the mortal world.

3 that glorious world: It refers to the next world.

4 held asunder: kept away from each other; stood wide apart from each other

5 gathered her to him: embraced her

he, in return, covering her with frantic caresses, said wildly—

"You teach me now how cruel you've been—cruel and false. Why did you despise me? Why did you betray your own heart, Cathy? I have not one word of comfort. You deserve this. You have killed yourself[1]. Yes, you may kiss me, and cry; and ring out my kisses and tears: they'll blight[2] you—they'll damn you. You loved me—then what right had you to leave me? What right—answer me—for the poor fancy you felt for Linton? Because misery and degradation, and death, and nothing that God or Satan could inflict would have parted us, you, of your own will, did it. I have not broken your heart—you have broken it; and in breaking it, you have broken mine. So much the worse for me, that I am strong. Do I want to live? What kind of living will it be when you—oh, God! Would *you* like to live with your soul[3] in the grave?"

"Let me alone. Let me alone," sobbed Catherine. "If I have done wrong, I'm dying for it. It is enough! You left me too: but I won't upbraid[4] you! I forgive you. Forgive me!"

"It is hard to forgive, and to look at those eyes, and feel those wasted hands," he answered. "Kiss me again; and don't let me see your eyes! I forgive what you have done to me. I love *my* murderer—but *yours*! How can I?"

They were silent—their faces hid against each other, and washed by each other's tears. At least, I suppose the weeping was on both sides; as it seemed Heathcliff *could* weep on a great occasion like this.

I grew very uncomfortable, meanwhile; for the afternoon wore fast away[5], the man whom I had sent off returned from his errand, and I could distinguish, by the shine of the westering[6] sun up the valley, a concourse[7] thickening outside Gimmerton chapel porch.

1 You have killed yourself: It refers to Catherine's marriage to Linton, which destroyed her life.

2 blight: to destroy, to bring evil influence on

3 soul: Here it refers to Catherine.

4 upbraid: to blame, to scold, to reproach

5 wear away: to consume or impair sth. by constant use, etc.

6 westering: going west

7 concourse: a crowd of people

"Service is over," I announced. "My master[1] will be here in half an hour."

Heathcliff groaned a curse, and strained Catherine closer: she never moved.

Ere long I perceived a group of the servants passing up the road towards the kitchen wing. Mr Linton was not far behind; he opened the gate himself and sauntered slowly up, probably enjoying the lovely afternoon that breathed as soft as summer.

"Now he is here," I exclaimed. "For Heaven's sake, hurry down! You'll not meet anyone on the front stairs. Do be quick; and stay among the trees till he is fairly in."

"I must go, Cathy," said Heathcliff, seeking to extricate[2] himself from his companion's arms. "But if I live, I'll see you again before you are asleep. I won't stay five yards from your window."

"You must not go!" she answered, holding him as firmly as her strength allowed. "You shall not, I tell you."

"For one hour," he pleaded earnestly.

"Not for one minute," she replied.

"I must—Linton will be up immediately," persisted the alarmed intruder.

He would have risen, and unfixed her fingers by the act—she clung fast, gasping: there was mad resolution in her face.

"No!" she shrieked. "Oh, don't, don't go. It is the last time! Edgar will not hurt us. Heathcliff, I shall die! I shall die!"

"Damn the fool! There he is," cried Heathcliff, sinking back into his seat. "Hush, my darling! Hush, hush, Catherine! I'll stay. If he shot me so, I'd expire[3] with a blessing on my lips."

And there they were fast again[4]. I heard my master mounting the stairs—the cold sweat ran from my forehead: I was horrified.

1 my master: Here it refers to Mr. Linton.

2 extricate…from…: to be free from , to disentangle

3 expire: die

4 they were fast again: they held firmly again

"Are you going to listen to her ravings[1]?" I said passionately. "She does not know what she says. Will you ruin her, because she has not wit to help herself? Get up! You could be free instantly. That is the most diabolical[2] deed that ever you did. We are all done for—master, mistress, and servant.

I wrung my hands, and cried out; Mr Linton hastened his step at the noise. In the midst of my agitation, I was sincerely glad to observe that Catherine's arms had fallen relaxed, and her head hung down.

QUESTIONS

1 Who is the narrator to tell the story in this chapter? How is Nelly behaving in this chapter?
2 How can you understand their accusations against each other?
3 What does "I love *my* murderer—but *yours*" imply?
4 How do they express their romantic love?
5 What do you think of the love between Heathcliff and Catherine?
6 What causes the love tragedy of Heathcliff and Catherine?

1 ravings: delirious, irrational speeches

2 diabolical: of or like a devil, very cruel or wicked

Thomas Hardy
(1840-1928)

INTRODUCTION

Thomas Hardy was one of English famous novelists and poets, one of the representatives of English critical realism at the turn of the 19th century. Many of his novels concern tragic characters struggling against their passions and social circumstances, and they are often set in the semi-fictional region of Wessex. Hardy is one of the relatively few well-known English writers who did not have a university education, but he got honorary degrees from Cambridge and Oxford.

Hardy was born in Dorset, a southern county of England, which he called Wessex in his books, in 1840. His father taught Hardy the violin and his mother greatly encouraged his early interest in books. At the age of 16, he left school and was apprenticed to an architect. Although his formal studies stopped, he continued to educate himself. Before leaving for work, he would arise early in the morning and study for an hour or two every day. When he was 22, he left Dorset for London, where he worked for the architect Arthur Bloomfield and also found time for extensive reading. He returned home in 1867 and continued architectural work in Dorcet and began to write novels and stories. In 1868, he completed his first novel: *The Poor Man and the Lady*, which was rejected and not published. In 1871 his first published novel *Desperate Remedies* proved successful. So he gave up architecture and made literature his profession. Then he wrote some good works and became an outstanding realist in English literature.

The dominant theme of his novels is the futility of man's effort to struggle against cruel and unintelligible fate, chance, and circumstances, which are all predestined by the Immanent Will. Hardy believed that the past has built up a mass of conditions, which remain to influence people's lives; and he also thought that blind chance has a very important effect. The best way of life is therefore to accept calmly the blows of fate. His novels, spread over the years 1870-1896, are mostly pictures of human beings struggling against fate or chance.

Hardy's novels and short stories, according to his own classification, fall into three groups: Romances and Fantasies, Novels of Ingenuity, and Novels of Character and Environment. Of the three, the last group is the most outstanding and most of his better-known novels to it, including: *Under the Greenwood Tree* (1872), *Far from the Madding Crowd* (1874), *The Return of the Native* (1878), *The Mayor of Casterbridge* (1886),

Tess of the D'Urbervilles (1891), and *Jude the Obscure* (1896).

Under the Greenwood Tree is the first of the novels to have a rural setting.

Far from the Madding Crowd is the earliest of the novels which are generally read today and receive very favourable reviews.

The Return of the Native is a sad story of love affairs and jealousy, among his best and most popular novels.

The Mayor of Casterbridge is a tragic story about Michael Henchard who sells his wife and children for a few pounds while he is drunk. Although he works hard to be made a Mayor, he is still ruined and dies miserably.

Tess of the d'Urbervilles reflects the author's concern with several of the most pressing problems of his time.

Jude the Obscure is Hardy's last and extremely miserable novel. It may be true that such terrible novel of his imagination made him turn to poetry in order to escape from public criticism. The novel explores several social problems in Victorian England, especially those relating to the issues of class, education, religion and marriage.

The last two novels have been regarded as the summit of his realism. But both books were given a hostile reception by the bourgeois public and they caused Hardy to undergo some very severe criticism. This criticism, which sometimes amounted to personal abuse, combined with his continuing love for poetry, caused him to give up the writing of fiction and began to assemble his first volume of verse, *Wessex Poems* (1898). From then on, Hardy published only poetry. He wrote over 900 poems, published in eight volumes.

SELECTED READING

Tess of the d'Urbervilles

Overview

Tess of the d'Urbervilles is the tragic story of a poor girl, a pure woman, ruined by the bourgeois society. The novel is Hardy's fictional masterpiece, but it received mixed reviews when it first appeared, in part because it challenged the sexual morals of late Victorian England.

In the story, Tess' poor father's life is upset when he learns that he is descended from an ancient family, the D'Urbervilles. Sent by her mother to the D'Urberville family, Tess is seduced by the young master of the house, Alec, and has to return home in disgrace. After giving birth to a child who dies in infancy, she goes to work at a dairy farm. There Tess meets Angel Clare, son of a clergyman, and he falls in love with her and marries her. On their wedding night Tess and Clare tell each other about their past. And Clare, after hearing Tess' confession, leaves her abruptly for Brazil. Misfortune follows Tess one after another. Poverty forces Tess to seek for work and she works on a capitalist farm. Then her father dies and her family has to leave their old cottage. The poverty drives her to seek for assistance from Alec. When repentant Angel Clare returns and is ready to be reconciled to Tess, he finds that her living with Alec hinders her from returning to Clare. She kills Alec and then is arrested, tried and hanged.

Tess is portrayed as a brave, hard-working, sweet-natured and innocent girl, and yet she is not free from the influence of social conventions and moral standards of the day. Though much of the story has to do with love and marriage, the real theme of the novel has a much wider significance. It is the social tragedy of a person from the labouring mass against the moral and religious prejudices as well as the legal and educational systems of a class society. Although Hardy tries to explain the misfortune of Tess from the viewpoint of fatalism, in fact, the misfortune is determined by the social causes. **Fatalism** is a philosophical doctrine that man is powerless to do anything other than what we actually do. Man has no power to influence the future. As a rural young lady, it is very difficult for Tess to struggle against the hypocrisy of the traditional rules in the whole society.

The selection is taken from Chapter 35, when Tess told Clare of her affair with Alec in the hope of his forgiveness. But to her surprise, Clare is stunned and then he tells Tess that she is not the woman he loves and marries. After the sleepless night, Clare leaves Tess for Brazil. The incident highlights the selfishness and hypocrisy of Clare in striking contrast with the frankness and honesty of Tess. Her tragedy lies in her purity.

Phase the Fifth: The Woman Pays

Chapter 35

(Excerpt)

Her narrative ended; even its re-assertions and secondary explanations were done. Tess's voice throughout had hardly risen higher than its opening tone; there had been no exculpatory phrase of any kind, and she had not wept.

…

Clare performed the irrelevant act of stirring the fire; the intelligence had not even yet got to the bottom of him. After stirring the embers he rose to his feet; all the force of her disclosure had imparted itself now. His face had withered. In the strenuousness[1] of his concentration he treadled fitfully on the floor. He could not, by any contrivance[2], think closely enough; that was the meaning of his vague movement. When he spoke it was in the most inadequate, commonplace voice of the many varied tones she had heard from him.

"Tess!"

"Yes, dearest."

"Am I to believe this? From your manner I am to take it as true. O you cannot be out of your mind! You ought to be! Yet you are not… . My wife, my Tess—nothing in you warrants such a supposition as that?"

"I am not out of my mind," she said.

"And yet—" He looked vacantly at her, to resume with dazed senses: "Why didn't you tell me before? Ah, yes, you would have told me, in a way—but I hindered you, I remember!"

These and other of his words were nothing but the perfunctory babble of the surface while the depths remained paralyzed. He turned away, and bent over a chair. Tess followed him to the middle of the room where he was, and stood there staring at him with eyes that did not weep. Presently she slid down upon her knees beside his foot, and from this position she crouched in a heap.

"In the name of our love, forgive me!" she whispered with a dry mouth. "I have forgiven you for the same!"

And, as he did not answer, she said again—

"Forgive me as you are forgiven! I forgive *you*, Angel."

"You—yes, you do."

"But you do not forgive me?"

1 strenuousness: using or needing great effort, full of energy

2 contrivance: sth. contrived, stratagem

"O Tess, forgiveness does not apply to the case! You were one person; now you are another. My God—how can forgiveness meet such a grotesque—prestidigitation[1] as that!"

He paused, contemplating this definition; then suddenly broke into horrible laughter—as unnatural and ghastly as a laugh in hell.

"Don't—don't! It kills me quite, that!" she shrieked. "O have mercy upon me—have mercy!"

He did not answer; and, sickly white, she jumped up.

"Angel, Angel! what do you mean by that laugh?" she cried out.

"Do you know what this is to me?"

He shook his head.

"I have been hoping, longing, praying, to make you happy! I have thought what joy it will be to do it, what an unworthy wife I shall be if I do not! That's what I have felt, Angel!"

"I know that."

"I thought, Angel, that you loved me—me, my very self! If it is I you do love, O how can it be that you look and speak so? It frightens me! Having begun to love you, I love you forever—in all changes, in all disgraces, because you are yourself. I ask no more. Then how can you, O my own husband, stop loving me?"

"I repeat, the woman I have been loving is not you."

"But who?"

"Another woman in your shape."

She perceived in his words the realization of her own apprehensive foreboding in former times. He looked upon her as a species of impostor; a guilty woman in the guise of an innocent one. Terror was upon her white face as she saw it; her cheek was flaccid[2], and her mouth had almost the aspect of a round little hole. The horrible sense of his view of her so deadened her that she staggered; and he stepped forward, thinking she was going to fall.

---

1 prestidigitation: juggle, conjuring

2 flaccid: soft and weak instead of firm, flabby.

"Sit down, sit down," he said gently. "You are ill; and it is natural that you should be."

She did sit down, without knowing where she was, that strained look still upon her face, and her eyes such as to make his flesh creep.

"I don't belong to you any more, then; do I, Angel?" she asked helplessly. "It is not me, but another woman like me that he loved, he says."

The image raised caused her to take pity upon herself as one who was ill-used. Her eyes filled as she regarded her position further; she turned round and burst into a flood of self-sympathetic tears.

Clare was relieved at this change, for the effect on her of what had happened was beginning to be a trouble to him only less than the woe of the disclosure itself. He waited patiently, apathetically, till the violence of her grief had worn itself out, and her rush of weeping had lessened to a catching gasp at intervals.

"Angel," she said suddenly, in her natural tones, the insane, dry voice of terror having left her now. "Angel, am I too wicked for you and me to live together?"

"I have not been able to think what we can do."

"I shan't ask you to let me live with you, Angel, because I have no right to! I shall not write to mother and sisters to say we be married[1], as I said I would do; and I shan't finish the good-hussif[2] I cut out and meant to make while we were in lodgings."

"Shan't you?"

"No, I shan't do anything, unless you order me to; and if you go away from me I shall not follow you; and if you never speak to me any more I shall not ask why, unless you tell me I may."

"And if I do order you to do anything?"

"I will obey you like your wretched slave, even if it is to lie down and die."

"You are very good. But it strikes me that there is a want of harmony

1 we be married: The word "be" is a dialect, meaning "are".

2 good-hussif: (dialect) literally "the good housewife", referring to a bag holding needles and thread

between your present mood of self-sacrifice and your past mood of self-preservation."

These were the first words of antagonism. To fling elaborate sarcasms at Tess, however, was much like flinging them at a dog or cat. The charms of their subtlety passed by her unappreciated, and she only received them as inimical sounds which meant that anger ruled. She remained mute, not knowing that he was smothering his affection for her. She hardly observed that a tear descended slowly upon his cheek, a tear so large that it magnified the pores of the skin over which it rolled, like the object lens of a microscope. Meanwhile reillumination as to the terrible and total change that her confession had wrought in his life, in his universe, returned to him, and he tried desperately to advance among the new conditions in which he stood. Some consequent action was necessary; yet what?

"Tess," he said, as gently as he could speak, "I cannot stay—in this room—just now. I will walk out a little way."

He quietly left the room, and the two glasses of wine that he had poured out for their supper—one for her, one for him—remained on the table untasted. This was what their Agape[1] had come to. At tea, two or three hours earlier, they had, in the freakishness of affection, drunk from one cup.

The closing of the door behind him, gently as it had been pulled to, roused Tess from her stupor[2]. He was gone; she could not stay. Hastily flinging her cloak around her she opened the door and followed, putting out the candles as if she were never coming back. The rain was over and the night was now clear.

She was soon close at his heels, for Clare walked slowly and without purpose. His form beside her light gray figure looked black, sinister, and forbidding, and she felt as sarcasm the touch of the jewels of which she had been momentarily so proud. Clare turned at hearing her footsteps, but his recognition of her presence seemed to make no difference in him, and he went on over the five yawning arches of the great bridge in front of the

1 Agape: the love feast accompanied by Eucharistic celebration in the early Christian Church.

2 stupor: almost unconscious condition

house.

The cow and horse tracks in the road were full of water, the rain having been enough to charge them, but not enough to wash them away. Across these minute pools the reflected stars flitted[1] in a quick transit as she passed; she would not have known they were shining overhead if she had not seen them there—the vastest things of the universe imaged in objects so mean.

The place to which they had travelled today was in the same valley as Talbothays[2], but some miles lower down the river; and the surroundings being open she kept easily in sight of him. Away from the house the road wound through the meads, and along these she followed Clare without any attempt to come up with him or to attract him, but with dumb and vacant fidelity.

At last, however, her listless walk brought her up alongside him, and still he said nothing. The cruelty of fooled honesty is often great after enlightenment, and it was mighty in Clare now. The outdoor air had apparently taken away from him all tendency to act on impulse; she knew that he saw her without irradiation—in all her bareness; that Time was chanting his satiric psalm at her then—

> Behold, when thy face is made bare, he that loved thee shall hate;
> Thy face shall be no more fair at the fall of thy fate.
> For thy life shall fall as a leaf and be shed as the rain;
> And the veil of thine head shall be grief, and the crown shall be pain.[3]

He was still intently thinking, and her companionship had now insufficient power to break or divert the strain of thought. What a weak thing her presence must have become to him! She could not help addressing Clare.

"What have I done—what *have* I done! I have not told of anything

---

1 flit: to fly or move lightly and quickly

2 Talbothays: the Talbothays Dairy in the Froom Valley, where Tess worked as a dairymaid and met Angel

3 This is a poem about fate from Swinburne's long poem, *Atalanta in Calydon*, and the poem is full of tragic colour.

that interferes with or belies my love for you. You don't think I planned it, do you? It is in your own mind what you are angry at, Angel; it is not in me. O, it is not in me, and I am not that deceitful woman you think me!"

"H'm—well. Not deceitful, my wife; but not the same. No, not the same. But do not make me reproach you. I have sworn that I will not; and I will do everything to avoid it."

But she went on pleading in her distraction; and perhaps said things that would have been better left to silence.

"Angel!—Angel! I was a child—a child when it happened! I knew nothing of men."

"You were more sinned against than sinning[1], that I admit."

"Then will you not forgive me?"

"I do forgive you, but forgiveness is not all."

"And love me?"

To this question he did not answer.

"O Angel—my mother says that it sometimes happens so!—she knows several cases where they were worse than I, and the husband has not minded it much—has got over it at least. And yet the woman has not loved him as I do you!"

"Don't, Tess; don't argue. Different societies, different manners. You almost make me say you are an unapprehending peasant woman, who have never been initiated into the proportions of social things. You don't know what you say."

"I am only a peasant by position, not by nature!"

She spoke with an impulse to anger, but it went as it came.

"So much the worse for you. I think that parson who unearthed your pedigree would have done better if he had held his tongue. I cannot help associating your decline as a family with this other fact—of your want of firmness. Decrepit families imply decrepit wills, decrepit conduct. Heaven, why did you give me a handle for despising you more by informing me of

1 more sinned against than sinning: It is from Shakespeare's *King Lear*, Act III, Scene II: "a man more sinned against than sinning."

your descent! Here was I thinking you a new-sprung child of nature; there were you, the belated seedling[1] of an effete[2] aristocracy!"

"Lots of families are as bad as mine in that! Retty[3]'s family were once large landowners, and so were Dairyman Billett's. And the Debby houses, who now are carters, were once the De Bayeux family. You find such as I everywhere; "tis a feature of our county, and I can't help it."

"So much the worse for the county."

She took these reproaches in their bulk simply, not in their particulars; he did not love her as he had loved her hitherto, and to all else she was indifferent.

QUESTIONS

1 Please infer what Tess has told Angel according to the first sentence "Her narrative ended" and the next description in the selection.
2 Does Angel behave as his name indicates? Give some examples to support your idea.
3 Why does Clare "perform the irrelevant act of stirring the fire"?
4 What do Angel's words "You were one person; now you are another" imply?
5 What has Tess said to show her love to Angel?
6 What has Clare said and behaved to show his hypocrisy?

---

1 seedling: young plant newly grown from a seed. Here it means offspring.

2 effete: exhausted, weak and worn

3 Retty: Retty Priddle, one of the milkmaids at Talbothays, also in love with Angel

Oscar Wilde (1854-1900)

INTRODUCTION

Oscar Wilde is an Irish playwright, novelist, essayist, and poet, who is regarded as the representative among the writers of aestheticism and decadence. He is remembered for his epigrams, his novel *The Picture of Dorian Gray* (1891), his plays, as well as his imprisonment and early death. His writing in different forms throughout the 1880s made him become one of London's most popular playwrights in the early 1890s.

Wilde was born in Dublin, distinguished by both his class and his education. His father was a surgeon and his mother was a literary hostess. Wilde was educated at Trinity College, Dublin. Then he won a scholarship to continue his study at Oxford where he was under the influence of aesthetic theories of Professor John Ruskin and posed as a leader of the aestheticism. In 1895, he was sentenced to two years' imprisonment for homosexual offences. Then he went to France after his release. In his essays and lectures he expounds the theory of "art for art's sake", and his fiction is devoted to the propaganda of this principle. His novel *The Picture of Dorian Gray* and his play *The Importance of Being Ernest* (1895) are regarded as his masterpieces. *The Picture of Dorian Gray* is a typical decadent novel describing the author's aesthetic view and immorality.

Aestheticism was a literary movement in the nineteenth century supporting the emphasis of aesthetic values more than social-political themes for literature and other arts. This particular movement focused more on being beautiful rather than having a deeper meaning. The aesthetes used slogan "art for art's sake". Key figures of the aesthetic movement were Walter Pater and Oscar Wilde. Aestheticism was related to another movement, **decadence** which means simply "decline" in an abstract sense. Now it is most often used to refer to a perceived decay in standards, morals, dignity, and religious faith. Oscar Wilde is also one of the leading figures associated with the decadent movement in Britain.

Wilde's best-known comedies are: *A Woman of No Importance* (1892), *Lady Windermere's Fan* (1892), *The Importance of Being Earnest* (1895), and *An Ideal Husband* (1895).

SELECTED READING

The Picture of Dorian Gray

Overview

The Picture of Dorian Gray is a philosophical novel by Oscar Wilde. It is the representative work of aestheticism and decadence. As literature of the 19th century, *The Picture of Dorian Gray* is an example of Gothic fiction and features an aphoristic preface—a defense of the artist's rights and of art for art's sake.

The Preface

The artist is the creator of beautiful things. To reveal art and conceal the artist is art's aim.

The critic is he who can translate into another manner or a new material his impression of beautiful things. The highest as the lowest form of criticism is a mode of autobiography.

Those who find ugly meanings in beautiful things are corrupt without being charming. This is a fault. Those who find beautiful meanings in beautiful things are the cultivated. For these there is hope. They are the elect to whom beautiful things mean only beauty.

There is no such thing as a moral or an immoral book. Books are well written, or badly written. That is all.

The nineteenth century dislike of realism is the rage of Caliban seeing his own face in a glass. The nineteenth century dislike of romanticism is the rage of Caliban not seeing his own face in a glass.

The moral life of man forms part of the subject-matter of the artist, but the morality of art consists in the perfect use of an imperfect medium.

No artist desires to prove anything. Even things that are true can be proved. No artist has ethical sympathies. An ethical sympathy in an artist is an unpardonable mannerism of style.

No artist is ever morbid. The artist can express everything.

Thought and language are to the artist instruments of an art.

Vice and virtue are to the artist materials for an art. From the point of view of form, the type of all the arts is the art of the musician. From the point of view of feeling, the actor's craft is the type.

All art is at once surface and symbol.

Those who go beneath the surface do so at their peril.

Those who read the symbol do so at their peril. It is the spectator, and not life, that art really mirrors.

Diversity of opinion about a work of art shows that the work is new, complex, and vital.

When critics disagree, the artist is in accord with himself.

We can forgive a man for making a useful thing as long as he does not admire it. The only excuse for making a useless thing is that one admires it intensely.

All art is quite useless.

QUESTIONS

1 What is the aim of the art according to the author?
2 Who can become the elect in Oscar Wilde's opinion?
3 What are instruments of an art to the artist?
4 What are materials for an art to the artist?
5 What does the sentence "It is the spectator, and not life, that art really mirrors." imply?
6 What do you think of the author's attitude towards an art?

Alfred, Lord Tennyson
(1809-1892)

INTRODUCTION

Tennyson was the famous poet in The Victorian Age. He began writing poetry before he was ten. In 1827 he went to study at Cambridge University. But in 1831 he had to leave Cambridge without a degree because of financial difficulties. In 1850, he was appointed the Poet Laureate of Great Britain and Ireland and was finally able to marry the woman he had loved for many years.

His main poetical works include: *The Princess* (1847), *In Memoriam* (1850), *The Idylls of the King* (1859), *Ulysses* (1833).

The Princess is a long poem over 3000 lines, which deals with a story happened in the Middle Ages. This narrative poem contains fine lyrics and shows Tennyson's interest in women's rights and liberation.

In Memoriam is a collection of 131 short poems, an elegy for the death of his friend Hallam, his closest friend and the fiancé of his sister. Hallam died in 1833 at the age of 22 when he was studying in Cambridge. The sudden death of his friend plunged Tennyson into great sorrow. We can see his sorrow from his short poem "Break, Break, Break". But actually it becomes a discussion of the relations and science.

The Idylls of the King consists of 12 metrical tales telling the stories of King Arthur and his Knights of the Round Tables, which is his most ambitious work which took him over 30 years to complete and is regarded as a masterpiece.

Ulysses is a poem in blank verse. The poem is popularly used to illustrate the dramatic monologue form.

In general, Tennyson's shorter poems are better than the long ones. His best-known short poems are Break, Break, Break; The Eagle; Tears, Idle Tears; Crossing the Bar, etc.

SELECTED READINGS

Break, Break, Break

Overview

This short lyric was written in memory of the poet's very dear friend

Arthur Hallam whose death was felt very keenly by Tennyson throughout his life and was the occasion also of other poems by the same poet, notably the long elegy *In Memoriam*. This poem is typical of Tennyson as lyrical poet, for here, as the writer contrasts his own feelings of sadness first with the innocent joys of a fisherman's boy and of a sailor lad and then with the unfeeling waves of the sea that break upon the shore and with the insensate ships that enter into a harbour. The whole effect is one of real personal grief revealed through simple imagery and very musical language.

This short lyric contains four quatrains. The rimes fall on the second and fourth lines of each stanza. The first lines in the first and last stanzas contain only three words of one syllable each: "Break, break, break," but each of these three words reads with much strong feeling.

Break, break, break,
On thy cold gray stones, O Sea!
And I would[1] that my tongue could utter
The thoughts that arise in me.

O, well for the fisherman's boy,
That he shouts with his sister at play!
O, well for the sailor lad,
That he sings in his boat on the bay!

And the stately ships go on
To their haven[2] under the hill;
But O for the touch of a vanished hand,
And the sound of a voice that is still![3]

Break, break, break,
At the foot of thy crags, O Sea!
But the tender grace of a day[4] that is dead

1 would: wish

2 haven: harbour

3 a vanished hand/And the sound of a voice that is still: the hand and the voice of Arthur Hallam

4 the tender grace of a day: It refers to the happy memory of the past when the poet was enjoying the company.

Will never come back to me.

QUESTIONS

1 What does "Break, break, break" symbolize?
2 What is the contrast in the first stanza?
3 Why does the poet describe the pleasant sights?
4 What do the ships used here symbolize?
5 Which is the dominant image of the poem?
6 What figures of speech are used in the poem?

The Eagle

Overview

This is another lyric poem in memory of his friend Hallam. The poet creates an eagle standing in the top of the towering crag. The eagle stands for his friend.

He clasps the crag with crooked hands;
Close to the sun[1] in lonely[2] lands,
Ringed with the azure world, he stands.

The wrinkled sea beneath him crawls;
He watches from his mountain walls,
And like a thunderbolt he falls.

QUESTIONS

1 What do you understand the eagle's nature?
2 What is the symbol of the sun here?
3 What is the image of the eagle?
4 What do you think of "the wrinkled sea"?
5 What does the word "falls" imply?
6 What are the contrast images in the short poem?

---

1 the sun: truth, seeking self-confidence

2 lonely: isolated from the dirty world

Robert Browning (1812-1889) & Mrs. Browning (1806-1861)

INTRODUCTION

Robert Browning (1812-1889) is thought of today as the most important Victorian poet after Tennyson. Mr. Browning was also an English playwright famous for his mastery of the dramatic monologue. He was realistic, much concerned with presenting facts and analyzing human psychology. Browning was optimistic and believed in the progress of mankind.

Mr. Browning was born to a very comfortable and cultivated family. His father was an official of the Bank of England. Browning attended a boarding school, but he was also tutored at home in ancient and modern languages, in music and in horsemanship. He began writing poetry at a very early age. He wrote his first poem when he was only five years old.

Robert Browning met **Elizabeth Barrett** (1806-1861), one of the most prominent English poets of the Victorian era, in 1845. She was six years older and much better known as a poet than he was. She was in poor health and living a life of unhappy seclusion. In 1846, Browning married Elizabeth Barrett (Elizabeth Barrett Browning or Mrs Browning), which started one of history's most famous literary marriages. The story of the life and courtship of Browning and Elizabeth is well known through the letters they exchanged and through Elizabeth's own love sonnets. During their courtship she wrote a series of 44 sonnets celebrating their love. The poems were published with the title of *Sonnets from the Portuguese*, as if she had translated the poems from that language. She is remembered for such poem as *How Do I Love Thee?*

As Elizabeth's father did not agree to their marriage, they were secretly married and lived in Italy until Elizabeth's death in 1861. By the time of her death in 1861, Mr. Browning had published the crucial collection *Men and Women* (1855), his finest volume of poems. It displays his complete mastery of the poetic form the dramatic monologue. The followed collection *Dramatis Personae* (1864) and the epic poem *The Ring and the Book* (1868-1869) made him a leading British poet. When his wife died, he returned to London.

The Ring and the Book is Browning's masterpiece. It is a very long poem, more specifically, a verse novel, of 21,000 lines, which tells a horrible story of a man's murder of his beautiful young wife. The stories in the poem are told in various ways by different people, who do not always have the same view of the details.

Robert Browning's great contribution to poetry is his **dramatic monologue,** which is a kind of narrative poem in which one character speaks to one or more listeners whose replies are not given in the poem. The occasion is usually a crucial one in the speaker's life, and the dramatic monologue reveals the speaker's personality as well as the incident that is the subject of the poem. One of the best-known dramatic monologues is *My Last Duchess* by Robert Browning.

SELECTED READING

My Last Duchess

(Ferrara)

Overview

The poem takes its sources from the life of Alfonso II, duke of Ferrara of the 16th-century Italy. After three years of marriage, his young wife died suspiciously. Then the duke managed to marry with the niece of another noble man. This narrative poem in dramatic monologue is the duke's speech addressed to the agent who comes to negotiate the marriage. He reveals himself as a self-conceited, cruel and tyrannical man. The poem is written in heroic couplets, but with no regular metrical system. He draws a curtain to reveal a painting of a woman, explaining that it is a portrait of his late wife; he invites his guest to sit and look at the painting. As they look at the portrait, the duke describes her happy, cheerful and flirtatious nature, which had displeased him.

That's my last Duchess painted on the wall,
Looking as if she were alive. I call
That piece a wonder, now: Frà Pandolf's[1] hands
Worked busily a day, and there she stands.
Will 't please you sit and look at her? I said
"Frà Pandolf" by design[2], for never read

1 Frà Pandolf: Frà is an Italian word , meaning "brother". Brother Pandolf is a fictitious painter who painted the portrait of the Duchess.

2 by design: purposely

Strangers like you that pictured countenance[1],
The depth and passion of its earnest glance[2],
But to myself they turned[3] (since none puts by
The curtain I have drawn for you, but I[4])
And seemed as they would ask me, if they durst[5],
How such a glance came there; so, not the first
Are you to turn and ask thus[6]. Sir, 't was not
Her husband's presence only, called[7] that spot
Of joy into the Duchess' cheek: perhaps
Frà Pandolf chanced to say, "Her mantle laps
Over my lady's wrist too much[8]", or "Paint
Must never hope to reproduce the faint
Half-flush that dies along her throat"[9]: such stuff
Was courtesy[10], she thought, and cause enough
For calling up that spot of joy. She had
A heart—how shall I say?—too soon made glad,
Too easily impressed; she liked whate'er
She looked on, and her looks went everywhere[11].
Sir, 't was all one[12]! My favour at her breast[13],
The dropping of the daylight in the West,
The bough of cherries some officious fool

---

1 for never read/Strangers like you that pictured countenance: For strangers like you never looked at that face in the picture.

2 The depth and passion of its earnest glance: the deep feelings showed on her face as she glanced in earnest

3 But to myself they turned: Strangers always turned to me.

4 since none puts by/The curtain I have drawn for you, but I: since only I have the right to draw the curtain behind which the portrait is hung.

5 durst: dare

6 not the first/Are you to turn and ask thus: You are not the first to turn to me and ask thus.

7 called: caused

8 Her mantle laps/Over my lady's wrist too much: Her cloak covers up to much of my lady's wrist.

9 the faint/Half-flush that dies along her throat: the light reddish blush that gradually disappears along her throat

10 such stuff/Was courtesy: Such foolish words were acts of politeness and respect.

11 her looks went everywhere: She loved to see everything.

12 't was all one: It was all the same.

13 my favour at her breast: a gift I gave her which she wore at her breast

Broke in the orchard for her, the white mule
She rode with round the terrace—all and each
Would draw from her alike the approving speech,
Or blush, at least. She thanked men,—good! but thanked
Somehow—I know not how—as if she ranked
My gift of a nine-hundred-years-old name
With anybody's gift[1]. Who'd stoop to blame
This sort of trifling[2]? Even had you skill
In speech—(which I have not)—to make your will
Quite clear to such an one[3], and say, "Just this
Or that in you disgusts me; here you miss,
Or there exceed the mark"[4]—and if she let
Herself be lessoned[5] so, nor plainly set
Her wits to yours[6], forsooth[7], and made excuse,
—E'en then would be some stooping[8]; and I choose
Never to stoop. Oh, sir, she smiled, no doubt,
Whene'er I passed her; but who passed without
Much the same smile? This grew; I gave commands[9];
Then all smiles stopped together[10]. There she stands[11]
As if alive. Will 't please you rise? We'll meet
The company below[12] then. I repeat,

---

1 she ranked/my gift of a nine-hundred-years-old name /With anybody's gift: She regarded my gift, the title of the Duchess of Ferrara with a history of nine hundred years to be of the same value as the gifts given to her by some insignificant persons.

2 Who'd stoop to blame/This sort of trifling : Who would lower himself to find fault with this kind of trivial things? (Pay attention to the haughty and hypocritical tone of the Duke.)

3 such an one: Here it refers to the Duchess.

4 here you miss/Or there exceed the mark: You have not done this quite enough, while you are doing too much.

5 be lessoned: be given a lesson

6 nor plainly set/Her wits to yours: She did not argue with you.

7 forsooth: indeed

8 stooping: lowering

9 This grew; I gave commands: This kind of things grew worse and worse; I gave orders.

10 Then all smiles stopped together: Then she passed away.

11 There she stands: It refers to the portrait on the wall.

12 We'll meet/The company below: We shall meet the others downstairs.

The Count your master's known munificence
Is ample warrant that no just pretense[1]
Of mine for dowry will be disallowed[2];
Though his fair daughter's self, as I avowed
At starting[3], is my object. Nay, we'll go
Together down, sir. Notice Neptune[4], though,
Taming a sea-horse, thought a rarity,
Which Claus of Innsbruck[5] cast in bronze for me!

QUESTIONS

1 Who is speaking in the poem?
2 Whom do you think he is speaking to?
3 Why is the speaker not satisfied with his wife?
4 How did the last Duchess die? How do you know that?
5 How many characters are there in this poem?
6 What is the Duke's opinion about the Duchess' personality?

SELECTED READING

How Do I Love Thee

(Sonnet 43)

Overview

Some of Mrs. Browning's poems are too long, but in a sonnet she could not write too much because the form is limited to fourteen lines. Thus much of her best work is contained in *Sonnets from the Portuguese* (1850), a collection of 44 love sonnets. She pretended at first that these sonnets were translated

1 pretense: demand, claim

2 disallowed: rejected

3 At starting: at the beginning of our conversation

4 Neptune: Here it refers to the statue of Neptune, the god of the sea in Roman myth. The Duke is showing to the envoy as they are going downstairs to meet the others.

5 Claus of Innsbruck: Claus is an imaginary name of a sculptor: Innsbruck is a place in Austria, famous for its sculpture, which Browning visited in 1838.

from the Portuguese; they were really an entirely original expression of her love for Robert Browning. The collection was acclaimed and popular in the poet's lifetime and it remains so today.

How do I love thee? Let me count the ways.
I love thee to the depth and breadth and height
My soul can reach, when feeling out of sight
For the ends of Being and ideal Grace.
I love thee to the level of everyday's
Most quiet need, by sun and candle-light.
I love thee freely, as men strive for Right;
I love thee purely, as they turn from Praise.
I love thee with a passion put to use
In my old griefs, and with my childhood's faith.
I love thee with a love I seemed to lose
With my lost saints, — I love thee with the breath,
Smiles, tears, of all my life! — and, if God choose,
I shall but love thee better after death.

QUESTIONS

1 What is the key word in the poem?
2 How many ways does the speaker love her husband according to the sonnet?
3 What kind of sonnet does this poem belong to?
4 What is the rhyme scheme of the sonnet?
5 What is the main figure of speech used in the poem?
6 What is the function of the main figure of speech in the sonnet?

EXERCISES OF CHAPTER VI

I Fill in the following blanks.

1 Queen Victoria ruled over England from ____________ to ____________. In the history of England, the period has generally been regarded as one of the most ____________ in the development of the country, marked by a

great ______ of the ______.

2 The social problems appeared during Victorian Age, including ______, ______, ______; ______.

3 The first biography about Brontë, published in 1857, is ______ written by Mrs. Gaskell.

4 ______ is the penname of Charles Lutwidge Dodgson, a university teacher of mathematics at ______. He is remembered more for his two books for children than for his excellent mathematics. Carroll's two Alice novels are ______ (1865) and ______ (1871).

II Find the relevant match from Column B for each item in Column A.

Column A	Column B
1 ( ) Charles Dickens	A. *Vanity Fair*
2 ( ) William M. Thackeray	B. *The Professor*
3 ( ) Charlotte Brontë	C. *Wuthering Heights*
4 ( ) Emily Brontë	D. *Treasure Island*
5 ( ) Anne Brontë	E. *How Do I Love Thee*
6 ( ) Mrs. Browning	F. *David Copperfield*
7 ( ) Thomas Hardy	G. *My Last Duchess*
8 ( ) Alfred Tennyson	H. *Agnes Grey*
9 ( ) Robert Browning	I. *Middlemarch*
10 ( ) Oscar Wilde	J. *Tess*
11 ( ) Robert Louis Stevenson	K. *The Eagle*
12 ( ) George Eliot	L. *The Picture of Dorian Gray*

III Choose the best answer for each statement.

1 In the 19th century English literature, a new literary trend, ______, appeared. And it flourished in the forties and in the early fifties.

A. Romanticism B. Naturalism

C. realism D. critical realism

2 Which of the following writers does not belong to English critical realists?

A. Charles Dickens B. Charlotte Brontë

C. Oscar Wilde D. Elizabeth Gaskell

3 In Dickens' novel *A Tale of Two Cities*, the "Two Cities" refer to London and ______.

A. Dublin B. Paris

C. New York D. Vienna

4 "I repeat, the woman I have been loving is not you.... Another woman in your shape." These words are taken from______.

A. Dickens' *Oliver Twist*

B. Charlotte Brontë's *Jane Eyre*

C. Emily Brontë's *Wuthering Heights*

D. Thomas Hardy's *Tess of the D'Urbervilles*

5 "Please, Sir, I want some more."

The master was a fat, healthy man, but he turned very pale...

This description is from ______.

A. *A Modest Proposal* B. *Oliver Twist*

C. *Tom Jones* D. *Hard Times*

6. Both two famous English writers, William Makepeace Thackeray and John Bunyan, once wrote ______.

A. *Paradise Lost* B. *Of Studies*

C. *Vanity Fair* D. *Oliver Twist*

IV Answer the following questions.

1 Heathcliff in *Wuthering Heights* is a complex character. Please make a brief comment on him with some examples.

2 Analyze Tess in the novel with some examples to support your idea.

3 Why is *Jane Eyre* a successful novel?

CHAPTER VII
English Literature in the Early Twentieth Century

General Introduction

For Britain, the 20th century was generally a time of declining national fortune and power. The century had to face two wars that cost many lives and the destruction of much property. The First World War tremendously weakened the British Empire. The Second World War marked the last stage of the disintegration of the British Empire. The once sun-never-set Empire finally collapsed. All these gave rise to all kinds of philosophical ideas in Western Europe, such as Karl Marx and Engels' theory of scientific socialism, Darwin's theory of evolution, Einstein's theory of relativity, and Freud's analytical psychology.

After the First World War, in the circle of literature, appeared various literary trends of **modernism**, which was a cultural movement in the first half of the twentieth century that rejected the literary conventions of the nineteenth century, opposed traditional values and techniques, and emphasized the importance of individual experience, including symbolism, expressionism, surrealism, cubism, futurism, Dadaism, imagism and stream of consciousness. Towards 1920s, these trends converged into a mighty torrent of modernist movement. The major figures that were associated with this movement were Kafka, Pound, Eliot, Joyce and Virginia Woolf.

During the period, the short lyric in poetry became popular. It flourished in the poetry of A. E. Housman, Thomas Hardy, and Yeats. Under the influence of impressionism, writers did not seek to interpret life, but focused on individual moments of experience. Major works of modernist fiction subvert the basic conventions of earlier prose fiction by the use of stream of consciousness and other innovative modes of narration. The subject matters of novels were also becoming more and more extensive.

E. M. Forster (1879-1970) is known best for his ironic and well-plotted novels examining class difference and hypocrisy in early 20th-century British society. His masterpiece *Howards End* (1910) is an ambitious "condition-of-England" novel concerned with different groups within the Edwardian middle classes. Forster achieved his greatest success with *A Passage to India* (1924). The novel takes as its subject the relationship between East and West, seen through the lens of India.

Joseph Conrad (1857-1924) was a Polish-British writer regarded as one of the greatest novelists to write in the English language. His novel reveals the transitional historical course of western expansion and gives a serious reflection on the course. His masterpiece *Heart of Darkness* raises questions about imperialism and racism, expressing his criticism on the expansion of imperialism, the exploitation and oppression of the nation. On the contrary, **Rudyard Kipling** (1865-1936) focused on advocating imperialism, calling upon England to "take up the White Man's burden" by dominating all "lesser breeds without law". His most popular works remain *The Jungle Book* (1894), which is written for children, and *Jim* (1901), which is his last novel with the feature of the imperialism. In 1907, he became the first Englishman to win the Nobel Prize in Literature.

H. G. Wells (1866-1946) is noted for his science fiction and is called a "father of science fiction". His masterpiece *The Time Machine* (1895) combines science fiction with social criticism. Other popular novels include *The Invisible Man* (1897), *The War of the Worlds* (1898), *The Island of Dr Moreau* (1896), *etc.*

Besides poetry and novels, drama also became popular. George Bernard Shaw, John Galsworthy and W. B. Yeats are famous dramatists.

George Bernard Shaw
(1856-1950)

INTRODUCTION

George Bernard Shaw, an Irish playwright, critic and polemicist, is considered the leading dramatist of his generation, and in 1925 was awarded the Nobel Prize in Literature.

Shaw was born in Dublin, Ireland. At 14, he dropped out of the school and worked in a land agent's office. In 1876, he moved to London and began his career as a novelist. Meanwhile, with a political awakening, he joined the gradualist Fabian Society and gradually became one of its most influential pamphleteers. In 1891, deeply influenced by Henrik Ibsen's *Doll's House*, he decided to engage in the drama creation. In 1892, he created his first play *Widowers' Houses*, then his first cycle of plays, "Plays Unpleasant" made their appearance. It contains *Widowers' Houses* (1892), *Mrs. Warren's Profession* (1894), and *The Philander* (1893). In 1894, *Arms and Man*, which belongs to "Plays Pleasant", made its appearance and achieved a great success. During the twentieth century, his famous plays included *Man and Superman* (1903), *Major Barbara* (1905), *Pygmalion* (1912), *Heartbreak House* (1919), *Saint Joan* (1923), and *The Apple Cart* (1929). He visited China in 1932 and was warmly received by the revolutionary writers represented by Lu Xun. In 1950 he died at the age of 95. He wrote over 50 plays in all. His last play, *Why She Would Not*, was unfinished and was published in1960.

SELECTED READING

Pygmalion[1]

Overview

Pygmalion is a play written by George Bernard Shaw in 1912, which was named after Pygmalion, a famous sculptor in Greek Mythology. In the play, Henry Higgins, a professor of phonetics, is Pygmalion, while Eliza

1 Pygmalion: King of Cyprus in Greek Mythology, a famous sculptor. He made an ivory image of a woman so lovely that he fell in love with it. He named her Galatea. He went to Aphrodite's shrine and begged the goddess to give him a wife as graceful as Galatea, and the goddess answered him. The work of his own hands became his wife.

Doolittle is the woman he creates and gives a new life to. Higgins makes a bet that he can train a bedraggled Cockney flower girl, Eliza Doolittle, to pass for a duchess at an ambassador's garden party, the most important element of which, he believes, is impeccable speech. The play is a sharp satire of the rigid British social hierarchy of the day and a commentary on women's independence. The play was adapted into the movie *My Fairy Lady*.

Act 1

Scene

[*Covent Garden at 11:15 p.m. Torrents of heavy summer rain. Cab whistles blowing frantically in all directions. Pedestrians running for shelter into the market and under the portico of St. Paul's Church, where there are already several people, among them a lady and her daughter in evening dress. They are all peering out gloomily at the rain, except one man with his back turned to the rest, who seems wholly preoccupied with a notebook in which he is writing busily.*

The church clock strikes the first quarter.]

THE DAUGHTER: [*in the space between the central pillars, close to the one on her left*] I'm getting chilled to the bone. What can Freddy be doing all this time? He's been gone twenty minutes.

THE MOTHER: [*On her daughter's right*] Not so long. But he ought to have got us a cab by this.

A BYSTANDER: [*on the lady's right*] He won't get no cab not until half-past eleven, missus, when they come back after dropping their theatre fares.

THE MOTHER: But we must have a cab. We can't stand here until half-past eleven. It's too bad.

THE BYSTANDER: Well, it ain't my fault, missus.

THE DAUGHTER: If Freddy had a bit of gumption, he would have got one at the theatre door.

THE MOTHER: What could he have done, poor boy?

THE DAUGHTER: Other people got cabs. Why couldn't he?

[*Freddy rushes in out of the rain from the Southampton Street side, and comes between them closing a dripping umbrella. He is a young man of twenty, in evening dress, very wet around the ankles.*]

THE DAUGHTER: Well, havn't you got a cab?

FREDDY: There's not one to be had for love or money.

THE MOTHER: Oh, Freddy, there must be one. You can't have tried.

THE DAUGHTER: It's too tiresome. Do you expect us to go and get one ourselves?

FREDDY: I tell you they're all engaged. The rain was so sudden: nobody was prepared; and everybody had to take a cab. I've been to Charing Cross one way and nearly to Ludgate Circus the other; and they were all engaged.

THE MOTHER: Did you try Trafalgar Square?

FREDDY: There wasn't one at Trafalgar Square.

THE DAUGHTER: Did you try?

FREDDY: I tried as far as Charing Cross Station. Did you expect me to walk to Hammersmith?

THE DAUGHTER: You havn't tried at all.

THE MOTHER: You really are very helpless, Freddy. Go again; and don't come back until you have found a cab.

FREDDY: I shall simply get soaked for nothing.

THE DAUGHTER: And what about us? Are we to stay here all night in this draught, with next to nothing on. You selfish pig—

FREDDY: Oh, very well: I'll go, I'll go. [*He opens his umbrella and dashes off Strandwards, but comes into collision with a flower girl, who is hurrying in for shelter, knocking her basket out of her hands. A blinding flash of lightning, followed instantly by a rattling peal of thunder, orchestrates*[1] *the incident.*]

THE FLOWER GIRL: Nah then, Freddy: look wh' y' gowin, deah.[2]

FREDDY: Sorry [*he rushes off*].

THE FLOWER GIRL: [*picking up her scattered flowers and replacing them in the basket*] Theres menners f' yer! Te-oo banches o voylets

1 orchestrates: to compose or arrange a piece of music for an orchestra to play. Here is the author's humor to compare the thunder and lightning to orchestral music.

2 wh' y' gowin, deah: Where are you going, dear?

trod into the mad.[1] [*She sits down on the plinth*[2] *of the column, sorting her flowers, on the lady's right. She is not at all an attractive person. She is perhaps eighteen, perhaps twenty, hardly older. She wears a little sailor hat of black straw that has long been exposed to the dust and soot of London and has seldom if ever been brushed. Her hair needs washing rather badly: its mousy color can hardly be natural. She wears a shoddy black coat that reaches nearly to her knees and is shaped to her waist. She has a brown skirt with a coarse apron. Her boots are much the worse for wear. She is no doubt as clean as she can afford to be; but compared to the ladies she is very dirty. Her features are no worse than theirs; but their condition leaves something to be desired; and she needs the services of a dentist.*]

THE MOTHER: How do you know that my son's name is Freddy, pray?

THE FLOWER GIRL: Ow, eez ye-ooa san, is e? Wal, fewd dan y' de-ooty bawmz a mather should, eed now bettern to spawl a pore gel's flahrzn than ran awy athaht pyin. Will ye-oo py me f'them?[3] [*Here, with apologies, this desperate attempt to represent her dialect without a phonetic alphabet must be abandoned as unintelligible outside London.*]

THE DAUGHTER: Do nothing of the sort, mother. The idea!

THE MOTHER: Please allow me, Clara. Have you any pennies?

THE DAUGHTER: No. I've nothing smaller than sixpence.

THE FLOWER GIRL: [*hopefully*] I can give you change for a tanner[4], kind lady.

THE MOTHER: [*to Clara*] Give it to me. [*Clara parts reluctantly*]. Now [*to the girl*] This is for your flowers.

THE FLOWER GIRL: Thank you kindly, lady.

THE DAUGHTER: Make her give you the change. These things are only a penny a bunch.

THE MOTHER: Do hold your tongue, Clara. [*To the girl*]. You can keep

1 Te-oo banches o voylets trod into the mad: Two bunches of violets were trodden into the mud.

2 plinth: square base or block on which a column or stature stands

3 Ow, eez ye-ooa san, is e?... Will ye-oo py me f'them?: Oh, he is your son, is he? Well, if you had done your duty as a mother should, he'd know better than to spoil a poor girl's flowers and then ran away without paying. Will you pay me for them?

4 tanner: sixpence

the change.

THE FLOWER GIRL: Oh, thank you, lady.

THE MOTHER: Now tell me how you know that young gentleman's name.

THE FLOWER GIRL: I didn't.

THE MOTHER: I heard you call him by it. Don't try to deceive me.

THE FLOWER GIRL: [*protesting*] Whos trying to deceive you? I called him Freddy or Charlie same as you might yourself if you was talking to a stranger and wished to be pleasant. [*She sits down beside her basket*].

THE DAUGHTER: Sixpence thrown away! Really, mamma, you might have spared Freddy that. [*She retreats in disgust behind the pillar*].

[*An elderly gentleman of the amiable military type rushes into shelter, and closes a dripping umbrella. He is in the same plight as Freddy, very wet about the ankles. He is in evening dress, with a light overcoat. He takes the place left vacant by the daughter's retirement.*]

THE GENTLEMAN: Phew!

THE MOTHER: [*to the gentleman*] Oh, sir, is there any sign of its stopping?

THE GENTLEMAN: I'm afraid not. It started worse than ever about two minutes ago. [*He goes to the plinth beside the flower girl; puts up his foot on it; and stoops to turn down his trouser ends*].

THE MOTHER: Oh, dear! [*She retires sadly and joins her daughter*].

THE FLOWER GIRL: [*taking advantage of the military gentleman's proximity to establish friendly relations with him*]. If it's worse it's a sign it's nearly over. So cheer up, Captain; and buy a flower off a poor girl.

THE GENTLEMAN: I'm sorry, I havn't any change.

THE FLOWER GIRL: I can give you change, Captain.

THE GENTLEMEN: For a sovereign? I've nothing less.

THE FLOWER GIRL: Garn! Oh do buy a flower off me, Captain. I can change half-a-crown[1]. Take this for tuppence[2].

THE GENTLEMAN: Now don't be troublesome: there's a good girl. [*Trying his pockets*] I really havn't any change—Stop: here's three hapence, if

1 crown: British coin worth 25 pence

2 tuppence: two pence

that's any use to you [*he retreats to the other pillar*].

THE FLOWER GIRL: [*disappointed, but thinking three halfpence better than nothing*] Thank you, sir.

THE BYSTANDER: [*to the girl*] You be careful: give him a flower for it. There's a bloke here behind taking down every blessed word you're saying. [*All turn to the man who is taking notes*].

THE FLOWER GIRL: [*springing up terrified*] I ain't done nothing wrong by speaking to the gentleman. I've a right to sell flowers if I keep off the kerb. [*Hysterically*] I'm a respectable girl: so help me, I never spoke to him except to ask him to buy a flower off me. [*General hubbub, mostly sympathetic to the flower girl, but deprecating her excessive sensibility. Cries of Don't start hollerin. Who's hurting you? Nobody's going to touch you. What's the good of fussing? Steady on. Easy, easy, etc., come from the elderly staid spectators, who pat her comfortingly. Less patient ones bid her shut her head, or ask her roughly what is wrong with her. A remoter group, not knowing what the matter is, crowd in and increase the noise with question and answer: What's the row? What she do? Where is he? A tec*[1] *taking her down. What! him? Yes: him over there: Took money off the gentleman, etc. The flower girl, distraught and mobbed, breaks through them to the gentleman, crying wildly*] Oh, sir, don't let him charge me. You dunno[2] what it means to me. They'll take away my character and drive me on the streets for speaking to gentlemen. They—

THE NOTE TAKER: [*coming forward on her right, the rest crowding after him*] There, there, there, there! who's hurting you, you silly girl? What do you take me for?

THE BYSTANDER: It's all right: he's a gentleman: look at his boots. [*Explaining to the note taker*] She thought you was a copper's nark[3], sir.

THE NOTE TAKER: [*with quick interest*] What's a copper's nark?

THE BYSTANDER: [*inapt at definition*] It's a—well, it's a copper's nark, as

1 tec: detective

2 dunno: don't know

3 nark: [GB slang] police decoy or spy

you might say. What else would you call it? A sort of informer.

THE FLOWER GIRL: [*still hysterical*] I take my Bible oath I never said a word—

THE NOTE TAKER: [*overbearing but good-humored*] Oh, shut up, shut up. Do I look like a policeman?

THE FLOWER GIRL: [*far from reassured*] Then what did you take down my words for? How do I know whether you took me down right? You just shew me what you've wrote about me. [*The note taker opens his book and holds it steadily under her nose, though the pressure of the mob trying to read it over his shoulders would upset a weaker man*]. What's that? That ain't proper writing. I can't read that.

THE NOTE TAKER: I can. [*Reads, reproducing her pronunciation exactly*] "Cheer ap, Keptin; n' baw ya flahr orf a pore gel.[1]"

THE FLOWER GIRL: [*much distressed*] It's because I called him Captain. I meant no harm. [*To the gentleman*] Oh, sir, don't let him lay a charge agen[2] me for a word like that. You—

THE GENTLEMAN: Charge! I make no charge. [*To the note taker*] Really, sir, if you are a detective, you need not begin protecting me against molestation by young women until I ask you. Anybody could see that the girl meant no harm.

THE BYSTANDERS GENERALLY: [*demonstrating against police espionage*[3]] Course they could. What business is it of yours? You mind your own affairs. He wants promotion, he does. Taking down people's words! Girl never said a word to him. What harm if she did? Nice thing a girl can't shelter from the rain without being insulted, etc., etc., etc. [*She is conducted by the more sympathetic demonstrators back to her plinth, where she resumes her seat and struggles with her emotion.*]

THE BYSTANDER: He ain't a tec. He's a blooming busybody: that's what he is. I tell you, look at his boots.

1 Cheer ap, Keptin; n' baw ya flahr orf a pore gel: Cheer up, Captain; and buy a flower off a poor girl.

2 agen: against

3 espionage: practice of spying or using spies

THE NOTE TAKER: [*turning on him genially*] And how are all your people down at Selsey?

THE BYSTANDER: [*suspiciously*] Who told you my people come from Selsey?

THE NOTE TAKER: Never you mind. They did. [*To the girl*] How do you come to be up so far east? You were born in Lisson Grove.

THE FLOWER GIRL: [*appalled*] Oh, what harm is there in my leaving Lisson Grove? It wasn't fit for a pig to live in; and I had to pay four-and-six a week. [*In tears*] Oh, boo—hoo—oo—

THE NOTE TAKER: Live where you like; but stop that noise.

THE GENTLEMAN: [*to the girl*] Come, come! he can't touch you: you have a right to live where you please.

A SARCASTIC BYSTANDER: [*thrusting himself between the note taker and the gentleman*] Park Lane, for instance. I'd like to go into the Housing Question with you, I would.

THE FLOWER GIRL: [*subsiding into a brooding melancholy over her basket, and talking very low-spiritedly to herself*] I'm a good girl, I am.

THE SARCASTIC BYSTANDER: [*not attending to her*] Do you know where I come from?

THE NOTE TAKER: [*promptly*] Hoxton.

[*Titterings. Popular interest in the note taker's performance increases.*]

THE SARCASTIC ONE: [*amazed*] Well, who said I didn't? Bly me! You know everything, you do.

THE FLOWER GIRL: [*still nursing her sense of injury*] Ain't no call to meddle with me, he ain't.

THE BYSTANDER: [*to her*] Of course he aint. Don't you stand it from him. [*To the note taker*] See here: what call have you to know about people what never offered to meddle with you? Where's your warrant?

SEVERAL BYSTANDERS: [*encouraged by this seeming point of law*] Yes: where's your warrant?

THE FLOWER GIRL: Let him say what he likes. I don't want to have no truck with him.

THE BYSTANDER: You take us for dirt under your feet, don't you? Catch you taking liberties with a gentleman!
THE SARCASTIC BYSTANDER: Yes: tell h i m where he come from if you want to go fortune-telling.
THE NOTE TAKER: Cheltenham, Harrow, Cambridge, and India.
THE GENTLEMAN: Quite right. [*Great laughter. Reaction in the note taker's favor. Exclamations of He knows all about it. Told him proper. Hear him tell the toff where he come from? etc.*]. May I ask, sir, do you do this for your living at a music hall?
THE NOTE TAKER: I've thought of that. Perhaps I shall some day.
[*The rain has stopped; and the persons on the outside of the crowd begin to drop off.*]
THE FLOWER GIRL: [*resenting the reaction*] He's no gentleman, he ain't, to interfere with a poor girl.
THE DAUGHTER: [*out of patience, pushing her way rudely to the front and displacing the gentleman, who politely retires to the other side of the pillar*] What on earth is Freddy doing? I shall get pneumonia if I stay in this draught any longer.
THE NOTE TAKER: [*to himself, hastily making a note of her pronunciation of "monia"*] Earlscourt.
THE DAUGHTER: [*violently*] Will you please keep your impertinent remarks to yourself?
THE NOTE TAKER: Did I say that out loud? I didn't mean to. I beg your pardon. Your mother's Epsom, unmistakeably.
THE MOTHER: [*advancing between her daughter and the note taker*] How very curious! I was brought up in Largelady Park, near Epsom.
THE NOTE TAKER: [*uproariously amused*] Ha! ha! What a devil of a name! Excuse me. [*To the daughter*] You want a cab, do you?
THE DAUGHTER: Don't dare speak to me.
THE MOTHER: Oh, please, please Clara. [*Her daughter repudiates her with an angry shrug and retires haughtily.*] We should be so grateful to you, sir, if you found us a cab. [*The note taker produces a whistle.*] Oh,

thank you. [*She joins her daughter.*] [*The note taker blows a piercing blast.*]

THE SARCASTIC BYSTANDER: There! I knowed[1] he was a plain-clothes copper.

THE BYSTANDER: That ain't a police whistle: that's a sporting whistle.

THE FLOWER GIRL:[*still preoccupied with her wounded feelings*] He's no right to take away my character. My character is the same to me as any lady's.

THE NOTE TAKER: I don't know whether you've noticed it; but the rain stopped about two minutes ago.

THE BYSTANDER: So it has. Why did'nt you say so before? and us losing our time listening to your silliness. [*He walks off towards the Strand.*]

THE SARCASTIC BYSTANDER: I can tell where you come from. You come from Anwell. Go back there.

THE NOTE TAKER: [*helpfully*] Hanwell.

THE SARCASTIC BYSTANDER: [*affecting great distinction of speech*] Thenk you[2], teacher. Haw haw! So long [*he touches his hat with mock respect and strolls off*].

THE FLOWER GIRL: Frightening people like that! How would he like it himself.

THE MOTHER: It's quite fine now, Clara. We can walk to a motor bus. Come. [*She gathers her skirts above her ankles and hurries off towards the Strand*].

THE DAUGHTER: But the cab—[*her mother is out of hearing*]. Oh, how tiresome! [*She follows angrily.*]

[*All the rest have gone except the note taker, the gentleman, and the flower girl, who sits arranging her basket, and still pitying herself in murmurs.*]

THE FLOWER GIRL: Poor girl! Hard enough for her to live without being worrited[3] and chivied.

THE GENTLEMAN: [*returning to his former place on the note taker's left*] How do you do it, if I may ask?

1 knowed: knew

2 Thenk you: Thank you.

3 worrited: worried

THE NOTE TAKER: Simply phonetics. The science of speech. That's my profession: also my hobby. Happy is the man who can make a living by his hobby! You can spot an Irishman or a Yorkshireman by his brogue[1]. I can place any man within six miles. I can place him within two miles in London. Sometimes within two streets.

THE FLOWER GIRL: Ought to be ashamed of himself, unmanly coward!

THE GENTLEMAN: But is there a living in that?

THE NOTE TAKER: Oh yes. Quite a fat one. This is an age of upstarts. Men begin in Kentish Town with 80 a year, and end in Park Lane with a hundred thousand. They want to drop Kentish Town; but they give themselves away every time they open their mouths. Now I can teach them—

THE FLOWER GIRL: Let him mind his own business and leave a poor girl—

THE NOTE TAKER: [*explosively*] Woman: cease this detestable boohooing[2] instantly; or else seek the shelter of some other place of worship.

THE FLOWER GIRL: [*with feeble defiance*] I've a right to be here if I like, same as you.

THE NOTE TAKER: A woman who utters such depressing and disgusting sounds has no right to be anywhere—no right to live. Remember that you are a human being with a soul and the divine gift of articulate speech: that your native language is the language of Shakespear and Milton and The Bible; and don't sit there crooning like a bilious pigeon.

THE FLOWER GIRL: [*quite overwhelmed, and looking up at him in mingled wonder and deprecation without daring to raise her head*] Ah-ah-ah-ow-ow-ow-oo!

THE NOTE TAKER: [*whipping out his book*] Heavens! what a sound! [*He writes; then holds out the book and reads, reproducing her vowels exactly*] Ah-ah-ah-ow-ow-ow-oo!

THE FLOWER GIRL: [*tickled by the performance, and laughing in spite of*

1 brogue: regional way of speaking

2 boohoo: howl, cry

herself] Garn[1]!

THE NOTE TAKER: You see this creature with her kerbstone English: the English that will keep her in the gutter to the end of her days. Well, sir, in three months I could pass that girl off as a duchess at an ambassador's garden party. I could even get her a place as lady's maid or shop assistant, which requires better English. That's the sort of thing I do for commercial millionaires. And on the profits of it I do genuine scientific work in phonetics, and a little as a poet on Miltonic lines.

THE GENTLEMAN: I am myself a student of Indian dialects; and—

THE NOTE TAKER: [*eagerly*] Are you? Do you know Colonel Pickering, the author of Spoken Sanscrit?

THE GENTLEMAN: I am Colonel Pickering. Who are you?

THE NOTE TAKER: Henry Higgins, author of Higgins's Universal Alphabet.

PICKERING: [*with enthusiasm*] I came from India to meet you.

HIGGINS: I was going to India to meet you.

PICKERING: Where do you live?

HIGGINS: 27A Wimpole Street. Come and see me tomorrow.

PICKERING: I'm at the Carlton. Come with me now and let's have a jaw over some supper.

HIGGINS: Right you are.

THE FLOWER GIRL: [*to Pickering, as he passes her*] Buy a flower, kind gentleman. I'm short for my lodging.

PICKERING: I really havn't any change. I'm sorry [*he goes away*].

HIGGINS: [*shocked at girl's mendacity*] Liar. You said you could change half-a-crown.

THE FLOWER GIRL:[*rising in desperation*] You ought to be stuffed with nails, you ought. [*Flinging the basket at his feet*] Take the whole blooming basket for sixpence.

[*The church clock strikes the second quarter.*]

---

1 garn: [slang] to go on speaking

HIGGINS: [*hearing in it the voice of God, rebuking him for his Pharisaic*[1] *want of charity to the poor girl*] A reminder. [*He raises his hat solemnly; then throws a handful of money into the basket and follows Pickering.*]
THE FLOWER GIRL: [*picking up a half-crown*] Ah-ow-ooh! [*Picking up a couple of florins*] Aaah-ow-ooh! [*Picking up several coins*] Aaaaaah-ow-ooh! [*Picking up a half-sovereign*] Aaaaaaaaaaaah-ow-ooh!!!
FREDDY: [*springing out of a taxicab*] Got one at last. Hallo! [*To the girl*] Where are the two ladies that were here?
THE FLOWER GIRL: They walked to the bus when the rain stopped.
FREDDY: And left me with a cab on my hands. Damnation!
THE FLOWER GIRL: [*with grandeur*] Never you mind, young man. I'm going home in a taxi. [*She sails off to the cab. The driver puts his hand behind him and holds the door firmly shut against her. Quite understanding his mistrust, she shews him her handful of money.*] Eightpence ain't no object to me, Charlie. [*He grins and opens the door*]. Angel Court, Drury Lane, round the corner of Micklejohn's oil shop. Let's see how fast you can make her hop it. [*She gets in and pulls the door to with a slam as the taxicab starts*].
FREDDY: Well, I'm dashed!

QUESTIONS

1 What is the daughter's family background?
2 What are the characters of the daughter?
3 What is the flower girl's family background?
4 What are the characters of the flower girl?
5 What does the writer mean by "in three months I could pass that girl off as a duchess at an ambassador's garden party"?
6 What social problem does the author mean to expose?

1 Pharisaic: of, relating to, or characteristic of the Pharisees

John Galsworthy (1867-1933)

INTRODUCTION

John Galsworthy was one of the most prominent novelists and playwrights in the early 20th century. He won the Nobel Prize in Literature in 1932.

John Galsworthy was born to a wealthy and well-established family on Kingston Hill in England. He studied law at Oxford University, but after graduation he began to devote himself to literary work. His first famous novel is *The Man of Property* (1906). His notable work is *The Forsyte Saga* (1906-1921), which is his first trilogy, including *The Man of Property* (1906), *In Chancery* (1920) and *To Let* (1921). His second trilogy *A Modern Comedy* made its appearance in 1929, including *The White Monkey* (1924), *The Silver Spoon* (1926) and *Swan Song* (1926). *End of the Chapter* (1934) is his third trilogy, including *Maid in Waiting* (1931), *The Flowering Wilderness* (1932), and *Over the River* (1933).

SELECTED READING

The Forsyte Saga

Overview

The Forsyte Saga, first published in 1922, is a series of three novels, which tell the ups and downs of the Forsyte family from 1886 to 1926. *The Man of Property* is the first novel of *the Forsyte Saga.* This novel focuses on the triangle relationship of Soames, Irene and Bosinney. Soames, who is a typical Forsyte, considers the sole aim of life is accumulating wealth and sees everything in terms of property. Irene, Soames's beautiful wife, loves art and cherishes noble ideals of life. After marriage, Soames finds Irene doesn't love him, which makes him concoct a plan to build a house in the country and imprison his wife in the house. During the designing and building of the house, Irene falls in love with and has an affair with the architect Philip Bosinney who has been hired by Soames to build the house. But Soames refuses to divorce and wants his revenge. He makes use of the financial dispute in the course of building the house to sue Bosinney at the court. At last, Bosinney dies from a car accident and Irene leaves Soames. Soames becomes the lonely winner.

The novel reveals the overwhelming desire of the Forsyte family and its influence on family members, and criticizes the relationship between the people and the property in the British society.

Man of Property

Chapter 3
Meeting at the Botanical

(Excerpt)

He discovered therefore one morning that an idea had come to him for making a series of water colour drawings of London. How the idea had arisen he could not tell; and it was not till the following year, when he had completed and sold them at a very fair price, that in one of his impersonal moods, he found himself able to recollect the Art critic, and to discover in his own achievement another proof that he was a Forsyte.

He decided to commence with the Botanical Gardens, where he had already made so many studies, and chose the little artificial pond, sprinkled now with an autumn shower of red and yellow leaves, for though the gardeners longed to sweep them off, they could not reach them with their brooms. The rest of the gardens they swept bare enough, removing every morning Nature's rain of leaves; piling them in heaps, whence from slow fires rose the sweet, acrid smoke that, like the cuckoo's note for spring, the scent of lime trees for the summer, is the true emblem of the fall. The gardeners' tidy souls could not abide the gold and green and russet pattern on the grass. The gravel paths must lie unstained, ordered, methodical, without knowledge of the realities of life, nor of that slow and beautiful decay which flings crowns underfoot to star the earth with fallen glories, whence, as the cycle rolls, will leap again wild spring.

Thus each leaf that fell was marked from the moment when it fluttered a good-bye and dropped, slow turning, from its twig.

But on that little pond the leaves floated in peace, and praised Heaven with their hues, the sunlight haunting over them.

And so young Jolyon found them.

Coming there one morning in the middle of October, he was disconcerted to find a bench about twenty paces from his stand occupied, for he had a proper horror of anyone seeing him at work.

A lady in a velvet jacket was sitting there, with her eyes fixed on the ground. A flowering laurel, however, stood between, and, taking shelter behind this, young Jolyon prepared his easel.

His preparations were leisurely; he caught, as every true artist should, at anything that might delay for a moment the effort of his work, and he found himself looking furtively at this unknown dame.

Like his father before him, he had an eye for a face. This face was charming!

He saw a rounded chin nestling in a cream ruffle, a delicate face with large dark eyes and soft lips. A black "picture" hat concealed the hair; her figure was lightly poised against the back of the bench, her knees were crossed; the tip of a patent-leather shoe emerged beneath her skirt. There was something, indeed, inexpressibly dainty about the person of this lady, but young Jolyon's attention was chiefly riveted by the look on her face, which reminded him of his wife. It was as though its owner had come into contact with forces too strong for her. It troubled him, arousing vague feelings of attraction and chivalry. Who was she? And what doing there, alone?

Two young gentlemen of that peculiar breed, at once forward and shy, found in the Regent's Park, came by on their way to lawn tennis, and he noted with disapproval their furtive stares of admiration. A loitering gardener halted to do something unnecessary to a clump of pampas grass; he, too, wanted an excuse for peeping. A gentleman, old, and, by his hat, a professor of horticulture, passed three times to scrutinize her long and stealthily, a queer expression about his lips.

With all these men young Jolyon felt the same vague irritation. She looked at none of them, yet was he certain that every man who passed would look at her like that.

Her face was not the face of a sorceress, who in every look holds out to men the offer of pleasure; it had none of the "devil's beauty" so highly prized among the first Forsytes of the land; neither was it of that type, no less adorable, associated with the box of chocolate; it was not of the spiritually passionate, or passionately spiritual order, peculiar to house-decoration and modern poetry; nor did it seem to promise to the playwright material for the production of the interesting and neurasthenic figure, who commits suicide in the last act.

In shape and colouring, in its soft persuasive passivity, its sensuous purity, this woman's face reminded him of Titian's "Heavenly Love," a reproduction of which hung over the sideboard in his dining-room. And her attraction seemed to be in this soft passivity, in the feeling she gave that to pressure she must yield.

For what or whom was she waiting, in the silence, with the trees dropping here and there a leaf, and the thrushes strutting close on grass, touched with the sparkle of the autumn rime? Then her charming face grew eager, and, glancing round, with almost a lover's jealousy, young Jolyon saw Bosinney striding across the grass.

Curiously he watched the meeting, the look in their eyes, the long clasp of their hands. They sat down close together, linked for all their outward discretion. He heard the rapid murmur of their talk; but what they said he could not catch.

He had rowed in the galley himself! He knew the long hours of waiting and the lean minutes of a half-public meeting; the tortures of suspense that haunt the unhallowed lover.

It required, however, but a glance at their two faces to see that this was none of those affairs of a season that distract men and women about town; none of those sudden appetites that wake up ravening, and are surfeited and asleep again in six weeks. This was the real thing! This was what had happened to himself! Out of this anything might come!

Bosinney was pleading, and she so quiet, so soft, yet immovable in her passivity, sat looking over the grass.

Was he the man to carry her off, that tender, passive being, who would never stir a step for herself? Who had given him all herself, and would die for him, but perhaps would never run away with him!

It seemed to young Jolyon that he could hear her saying: "But, darling, it would ruin you!" For he himself had experienced to the full the gnawing fear at the bottom of each woman's heart that she is a drag on the man she loves.

And he peeped at them no more; but their soft, rapid talk came to his ears, with the stuttering song of some bird who seemed trying to remember the notes of spring: Joy—tragedy? Which—which?

And gradually their talk ceased; long silence followed.

"And where does Soames come in?" young Jolyon thought. "People think she is concerned about the sin of deceiving her husband! Little they know of women! She's eating, after starvation—taking her revenge! And Heaven help her—for he'll take his."

He heard the swish of silk, and, spying round the laurel, saw them walking away, their hands stealthily joined....

QUESTIONS

1 What is the relationship between young Jolyon and the family when young Jolyon "discover in his own achievement another proof that he was a Forsyte"?
2 What is the relationship between nature and human that you can find in the second paragraph?
3 What are the major figures of speech the author uses?
4 What is it about the woman that aroused young Jolyon's feelings of attraction and chivalry?
5 Why does young Jolyon feel vague "irritation" and "jealousy"?
6 What does "Joy—tragedy? Which—which?" imply?

James Joyce
(1882-1941)

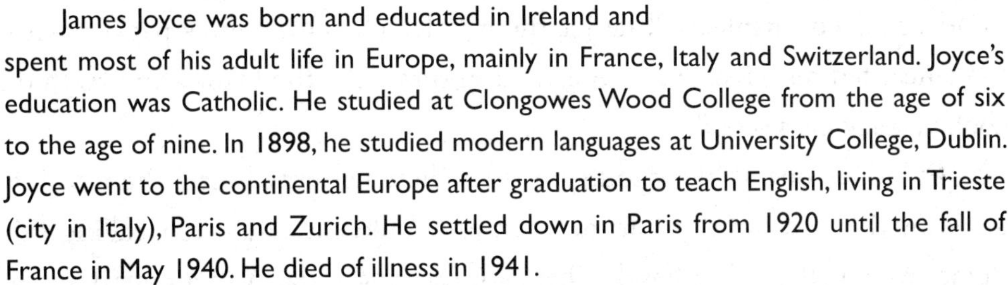

INTRODUCTION

James Joyce was an Irish novelist and poet, considered to be one of the most influential writers in modernism of the early 20th century.

James Joyce was born and educated in Ireland and spent most of his adult life in Europe, mainly in France, Italy and Switzerland. Joyce's education was Catholic. He studied at Clongowes Wood College from the age of six to the age of nine. In 1898, he studied modern languages at University College, Dublin. Joyce went to the continental Europe after graduation to teach English, living in Trieste (city in Italy), Paris and Zurich. He settled down in Paris from 1920 until the fall of France in May 1940. He died of illness in 1941.

On the Continent he was always the center of a literary circle. His works in his early times included *Dubliners* (1914) and an autobiographical novel *A Portrait of the Artist as a Young Man* (1916). Joyce is best known for *Ulysses* (1922), a landmark work in which the episodes of Homer's *Odyssey* are paralleled, perhaps most prominent among these works with the technique of "stream of consciousness", which is a literary style that is used to represent a character's feelings and thoughts in long continuous pieces of text that have little obvious organization or structure. It was first used in 1922 by James Joyce. James Joyce, Virginia Woolf, and Faulkner are three of the most distinguished exponents of the stream-of-consciousness.

His masterpiece is *Ulysses*, and the other main works include *Dubliners*, *A Portrait of the Artist as a Young Man* and *Finnegans Wake* (1939).

SELECTED READING

Ulysses

Overview

It was published in 1922. The novel tells of wanderings and "adventures" of Leopold Bloom, a modern Ulysses, during the 24 hours of a single day, July 16, 1904. The novel is divided into 18 chapters with each focusing on one hour of one single day. Each chapter parodies a specific episode in Homer's *Odyssey*.

Calypso is Episode 4. It is about the experience of the second protagonist of the book, Leopold Bloom, a part-Jewish advertising canvasser.

Calypso

(Excerpt)

…

He halted before Dlugacz's window, staring at the hanks of sausages, polonies, black and white. Fifty multiplied by. The figures whitened in his mind unsolved: displeased, he let them fade. The shiny links packed with forcemeat fed his gaze and he breathed in tranquilly the lukewarm breath of cooked spicy pig's blood.

A kidney oozed bloodgouts on the willow patterned dish: the last. He stood by the next door girl at the counter. Would she buy it too, calling the items from a slip in her hand. Chapped: washing soda. And a pound and a half of Denny's sausages. His eyes rested on her vigorous hips. Woods his name is. Wonder what he does. Wife is oldish. New blood. No followers allowed. Strong pair of arms. Whacking a carpet on the clothesline. She does whack it, by George. The way her crooked skirt swings at each whack.

The ferreteyed pork butcher folded the sausages he had snipped off with blotchy fingers, sausage pink. Sound meat there like a stallfed heifer.

QUESTIONS

1 What's the mood of the protagonist?
2 What do "oldish" and "New blood" mean?
3 What are the figures of speech the author uses?
4 Why does the author insert the narration with a lot of inner monologue of the protagonist?
5 How does the writer organize his writing?
6 What is the writing style of the work?

Virginia Woolf
(1882-1941)

INTRODUCTION

Virginia Woolf was one of the foremost modernists and one of the great innovative novelists of the writing style of "stream of consciousness" in the twentieth century. And she was also a central figure in the influential Bloomsbury Group of intellectuals.

Virginia Woolf was born in London. She grew up as a member of a large and talented family, with her father being a famous scholar and biographer in late Victorian time. After her father's death in 1904 she settled with her sister and two brothers in Bloomsbury. They entertained their literary and artistic friends at evening gatherings, and Woolf gradually became a central figure in the Bloomsbury Group, which was an influential group of associated English writers, intellectuals, philosophers and artists, the other best known members of which included John Maynard Keynes, E. M. Forster and Lytton Strachey. This loose collective of friends and relatives lived, worked or studied together near Bloomsbury, London, during the first half of the 20th century. Their works and outlook deeply influenced literature, aesthetics, criticism, and economics as well as modern attitudes towards feminism, pacifism, and sexuality.

Virginia married the writer Leonard Woolf in 1912 and founded Hogarth Press with her husband, publishing the writings of some notable authors including Sigmund Freud, T. S. Eliot and herself. In Virginia Woolf's writing, she attacked and rebelled against the traditional method of realism and tried her best to reduce the element of plot in the novel, to adopt the stream-of-consciousness and to explore problems of human personality and personal relationships. *The Mark on the Wall* (1921) is Woolf's first published short story with the feature of stream of consciousness. The novel *Mrs. Dalloway* published in 1925 displayed successfully the writing technique of stream-of-consciousness and made her reputation as an important psychological writer. After that, her other novels were published in succession. Her *Mrs. Dalloway* and *To the Lighthouse* (1927) are regarded as her masterpieces. Woolf is seen as the forerunner of feminism because of her focus on the women's rights and positions in her book *A Room of One's Own*. In her late years, she suffered painfully the periodic mental breakdown and in March 1941 she drowned herself.

The Mark on the Wall

Overview

The Mark on the Wall, published in 1917, is the first published story by Virginia Woolf. It is written in the first person, as a "stream of consciousness" monologue. The narrator notices a mark on the wall, and muses on the workings of the mind. The essence of the life and the eternal truth is revealed through the momentary impressions and meditation in the narrator's mind and the inner activities and mood swings of the narrator in the novel.

Perhaps it was the middle of January in the present year that I first looked up and saw the mark on the wall. In order to fix a date it is necessary to remember what one saw. So now I think of the fire; the steady film of yellow light upon the page of my book; the three chrysanthemums in the round glass bowl on the mantelpiece. Yes, it must have been the winter time, and we had just finished our tea, for I remember that I was smoking a cigarette when I looked up and saw the mark on the wall for the first time. I looked up through the smoke of my cigarette and my eye lodged for a moment upon the burning coals, and that old fancy of the crimson flag flapping from the castle tower came into my mind, and I thought of the cavalcade of red knights riding up the side of the black rock. Rather to my relief the sight of the mark interrupted the fancy, for it is an old fancy, an automatic fancy, made as a child perhaps. The mark was a small round mark, black upon the white wall, about six or seven inches above the mantelpiece.

How readily our thoughts swarm upon a new object, lifting it a little way, as ants carry a blade of straw so feverishly, and then leave it.... If that mark was made by a nail, it can't have been for a picture, it must have been for a miniature—the miniature of a lady with white powdered curls, powder-dusted cheeks, and lips like red carnations. A fraud of course, for the people who had this house before us would have chosen pictures in that way—an old picture for an old room. That is the sort of people they were—

very interesting people, and I think of them so often, in such queer places, because one will never see them again, never know what happened next. They wanted to leave this house because they wanted to change their style of furniture, so he said, and he was in process of saying that in his opinion art should have ideas behind it when we were torn as under, as one is torn from the old lady about to pour out tea and the young man about to hit the tennis ball in the back garden of the suburban villa as one rushes past in the train.

But as for that mark, I'm not sure about it; I don't believe it was made by a nail after all; it's too big, too round, for that. I might get up, but if I got up and looked at it, ten to one I shouldn't be able to say for certain; because once a thing's done, no one ever knows how it happened. Oh! dear me, the mystery of life; The inaccuracy of thought! The ignorance of humanity! To show how very little control of our possessions we have—what an accidental affair this living is after all our civilization—let me just count over a few of the things lost in one lifetime, beginning, for that seems always the most mysterious of losses—what cat would gnaw, what rat would nibble three pale-blue canisters of book-binding tools? Then there were the bird cages, the iron hoops, the steel skates, the Queen Anne coal-scuttle, the bagatelle board, the hand organ—all gone, and jewels, too. Opals and emeralds, they lie about the roots of turnips. What a scraping paring affair it is to be sure! The wonder is that I've any clothes on my back, that I sit surrounded by solid furniture at this moment. Why, if one wants to compare life to anything, one must liken it to being blown through the Tube at fifty miles an hour—landing at the other end without a single hairpin in one's hair! Shot out at the feet of God entirely naked! Tumbling head over heels in the asphodel meadows like brown paper parcels pitched down a shoot in the post office! With one's hair flying back like the tail of a race-horse. Yes, that seems to express the rapidity of life, the perpetual waste and repair; all so casual, all so haphazard....

But after life. The slow pulling down of thick green stalks so that the cup of the flower, as it turns over, deluges one with purple and red light. Why, after all, should one not be born there as one is born here, helpless, speechless, unable to focus one's eyesight, groping at the roots of the grass, at the toes of the Giants? As for saying which are trees, and which are men and women, or whether there are such things, that one won't be in a condition to do for fifty years or so. There will be nothing but spaces of light and dark, intersected by thick stalks, and rather higher up perhaps, rose-shaped blots of an indistinct colour—dim pinks and blues—which will, as time goes on, become more definite, become—I don't know what....

And yet that mark on the wall is not a hole at all. It may even be caused by some round black substance, such as a small rose leaf, left over from the summer, and I, not being a very vigilant housekeeper look at the dust on the mantelpiece, for example, the dust which, so they say, buried Troy three times over; only fragments of pots utterly refusing annihilation, as one can believe.

The tree outside the window taps very gently on the pane.... I want to think quietly, calmly, spaciously, never to be interrupted, never to have to rise from my chair, to slip easily from one thing to another, without any sense of hostility, or obstacle. I want to sink deeper and deeper, away from the surface, with its hard separate facts. To steady myself, let me catch hold of the first idea that passes.... Shakespeare.... Well, he will do as well as another. A man who sat himself solidly in an arm-chair, and looked into the fire, so—A shower of ideas fell perpetually from some very high Heaven down through his mind. He leant his forehead on his hand, and people, looking in through the open door—for this scene is supposed to take place on a summer's evening—But how dull this is, this historical fiction! It doesn't interest me at all. I wish I could hit upon a pleasant track of thought, a track indirectly reflecting credit upon myself, for those are the pleasantest thoughts, and very frequent even in the minds of modest mouse-coloured people, who believe genuinely that they dislike to hear their own praises. They are not thoughts directly praising oneself; that is the beauty of them; they are thoughts like this:

"And then I came into the room. They were discussing botany. I said how I'd seen a flower growing on a dust heap on the site of an old house in Kingsway. The seed, I said, must have been sown in the reign of Charles the First. What flowers grew in the reign of Charles the First?" I asked—(but I don't remember the answer). Tall flowers with purple tassels to them perhaps. And so it goes on. All the time I'm dressing up the figure of myself in my own mind, lovingly, stealthily, not openly adoring it, for if I did that, I should catch myself out, and stretch my hand at once for a book in self-protection. Indeed, it is curious how instinctively one protects the image of oneself from idolatry or any other handling that could make it ridiculous, or too unlike the original to be believed in any longer. Or is it not so very curious after all? It is a matter of great importance. Suppose the looking glass smashes, the image disappears, and the romantic figure with the green of forest depths all about it is there no longer, but only that shell of a person which is seen by other people—what an airless, shallow, bald, prominent world it becomes! A world not to be lived in. As we face each other in omnibuses and underground railways we are looking into the mirror; that accounts for the vagueness, the gleam of glassiness, in our eyes. And the novelists in future will realize more and more the importance of these reflections, for of course there is not one reflection but an almost infinite number; those are the depths they will explore, those the phantoms they will pursue, leaving the description of reality more and more out of their stories, taking a knowledge of it for granted, as the Greeks did and Shakespeare perhaps—but these generalizations are very worthless. The military sound of the word is enough. It recalls leading articles, cabinet ministers—a whole class of things indeed which as a child one thought the thing itself, the standard thing, the real thing, from which one could not depart save at the risk of nameless damnation. Generalizations bring back somehow Sunday in London, Sunday afternoon walks, Sunday luncheons, and also ways of speaking of the dead, clothes, and habits—like the habit of sitting all together in one room until a certain hour, although nobody liked it. There was a rule for everything. The rule for tablecloths at that particular period was that they should be made of tapestry with little yellow compartments marked upon them, such as you may see in photographs of the carpets in the corridors of the royal palaces. Tablecloths of a different kind were not real tablecloths. How shocking, and yet how wonderful it was to discover that these real things, Sunday luncheons, Sunday walks, country houses, and tablecloths were not entirely real, were indeed half phantoms, and the damnation which visited the disbeliever in them was only a sense of illegitimate freedom. What now takes the place of those things I wonder, those real standard things? Men perhaps, should you be a woman; the masculine point of view which governs our lives, which sets the standard, which establishes Whitaker's Table of Precedency[1], which has become, I suppose, since the war half a phantom to many men and women, which soon, one may hope, will be laughed into the dustbin where the phantoms go, the mahogany sideboards and the Landseer prints, Gods and Devils, Hell and so forth, leaving us all with an intoxicating sense of illegitimate freedom—if freedom exists....

In certain lights that mark on the wall seems actually to project from the wall. Nor is it entirely circular. I cannot be sure, but it seems to cast a perceptible shadow, suggesting that if I ran my finger down that strip of the wall it would, at a certain point, mount and descend a small tumulus, a smooth tumulus like those barrows on the South Downs which are, they say, either tombs or camps. Of the two I should prefer them to be tombs, desiring melancholy like most English people, and finding it natural at the end of a walk to think of the bones stretched beneath the turf.... There must be some book about it. Some antiquary must have dug up those bones and given them a name.... What sort of a man is an antiquary, I wonder? Retired Colonels for the most part, I daresay, leading parties of aged labourers to the top here, examining clods of earth and stone, and getting into correspondence with the neighbouring clergy, which, being opened at breakfast time, gives them a feeling of importance, and the comparison of arrowheads necessitates cross-country journeys to the county towns, an agreeable necessity both to them and to their elderly wives, who wish to make plum jam or to clean out the study, and have every reason for keeping that great question of the camp or the tomb in perpetual suspension, while the Colonel himself feels agreeably philosophic in accumulating evidence on

1 Whitaker's Table of Precedency: Whitaker's Table of Precedency shows the order in which the various ranks in public life and society proceed on formal occasions.

both sides of the question. It is true that he does finally incline to believe in the camp; and, being opposed, indites a pamphlet which he is about to read at the quarterly meeting of the local society when a stroke lays him low, and his last conscious thoughts are not of wife or child, but of the camp and that arrowhead there, which is now in the case at the local museum, together with the foot of a Chinese murderess, a handful of Elizabethan nails, a great many Tudor clay pipes, a piece of Roman pottery, and the wine-glass that Nelson[1] drank out of—proving I really don't know what.

No, no, nothing is proved, nothing is known. And if I were to get up at this very moment and ascertain that the mark on the wall is really—what shall we say? The head of a gigantic old nail, driven in two hundred years ago, which has now, owing to the patient attrition of many generations of housemaids, revealed its head above the coat of paint, and is taking its first view of modern life in the sight of a white-walled fire-lit room, what should I gain?—Knowledge? Matter for further speculation? I can think sitting still as well as standing up. And what is knowledge? What are our learned men save the descendants of witches and hermits who crouched in caves and in woods brewing herbs, interrogating shrew-mice and writing down the language of the stars? And the less we honour them as our superstitions dwindle and our respect for beauty and health of mind increases.... Yes, one could imagine a very pleasant world. A quiet, spacious world, with the flowers so red and blue in the open fields. A world without professors or specialists or house-keepers with the profiles of policemen, a world which one could slice with one's thought as a fish slices the water with his fin, grazing the stems of the water-lilies, hanging suspended over nests of white sea eggs.... How peaceful it is down here, rooted in the centre of the world and gazing up through the grey waters, with their sudden gleams of light, and their reflections—if it were not for Whitaker's Almanack[2]—if it were

1 Nelson (1758-1805): British admiral who defeated the French fleet in the Battle of the Nile (1798), thus ending Napoleon's attempt to conquer Egypt, and destroyed French and Spanish naval forces at Trafalgar (1805), where he was mortally wounded.

2 Whitaker's Almanack: It was initiated by the British publisher Joseph Whitaker in 1820-1875, and was honored as the best Almanack and a micro-encyclopedia.

not for the Table of Precedency!

I must jump up and see for myself what that mark on the wall really is—a nail, a rose-leaf, a crack in the wood?

Here is nature once more at her old game of self-preservation. This train of thought, she perceives, is threatening mere waste of energy, even some collision with reality, for who will ever be able to lift a finger against Whitaker's Table of Precedency? The Archbishop of Canterbury is followed by the Lord High Chancellor; the Lord High Chancellor is followed by the Archbishop of York. Everybody follows somebody, such is the philosophy of Whitaker; and the great thing is to know who follows whom. Whitaker knows, and let that, so Nature counsels, comfort you, instead of enraging you; and if you can't be comforted, if you must shatter this hour of peace, think of the mark on the wall.

I understand Nature's game—her prompting to take action as a way of ending any thought that threatens to excite or to pain. Hence, I suppose, comes our slight contempt for men of action—men, we assume, who don't think. Still, there's no harm in putting a full stop to one's disagreeable thoughts by looking at a mark on the wall.

Indeed, now that I have fixed my eyes upon it, I feel that I have grasped a plank in the sea; I feel a satisfying sense of reality which at once turns the two Archbishops and the Lord High Chancellor to the shadows of shades. Here is something definite, something real. Thus, waking from a midnight dream of horror, one hastily turns on the light and lies quiescent, worshipping the chest of drawers, worshipping solidity, worshipping reality, worshipping the impersonal world which is a proof of some existence other than ours. That is what one wants to be sure of.... Wood is a pleasant thing to think about. It comes from a tree; and trees grow, and we don't know how they grow. For years and years they grow, without paying any attention to us, in meadows, in forests, and by the side of rivers—all things one likes to think about. The cows swish their tails beneath them on hot afternoons; they paint rivers so green that when a moorhen dives one expects to see its feathers all green when it comes up again. I like to think of the fish balanced against the stream like flags blown out; and of water-beetles slowly raising domes of mud upon the bed of the river. I like to think of the tree itself: first the close dry sensation of being wood; then the grinding of the storm; then the slow, delicious ooze of sap. I like to think of it, too, on winter's nights standing in the empty field with all leaves close-furled, nothing tender exposed to the iron bullets of the moon, a naked mast upon an earth that goes tumbling, tumbling, all night long. The song of birds must sound very loud and strange in June; and how cold the feet of insects must feel upon it, as they make laborious progresses up the creases of the bark, or sun themselves upon the thin green awning of the leaves, and look straight in front of them with diamond-cut red eyes.... One by one the fibres snap beneath the immense cold pressure of the earth, then the last storm comes and, falling, the highest branches drive deep into the ground again. Even so, life isn't done with; there are a million patient, watchful lives still for a tree, all over the world, in bedrooms, in ships, on the pavement, lining rooms, where men and women sit after tea, smoking cigarettes. It is full of peaceful thoughts, happy thoughts, this tree. I should like to take each one separately—but something is getting in the way.... Where was I? What has it all been about? A tree? A river? The Downs? Whitaker's Almanack? The fields of asphodel? I can't remember a thing. Everything's moving, falling, slipping, vanishing.... There is a vast upheaval of matter. Someone is standing over me and saying,

"I'm going out to buy a newspaper."

"Yes?"

"Though it's no good buying newspapers.... Nothing ever happens. Curse this war; God damn this war!... All the same, I don't see why we should have a snail on our wall."

Ah, the mark on the wall! It was a snail.

QUESTIONS

1 What are the narrator's guess and imagination about the mark on the wall?

2 What is in fact the mark on the wall?

3 What is the symbolic meaning of "the mark on the wall"?
4 How is the technique of "stream of consciousness" displayed in the story?
5 What do you think of the narrator's identity?
6 What is the probable theme of the story?

D. H. Lawrence
(1885-1930)

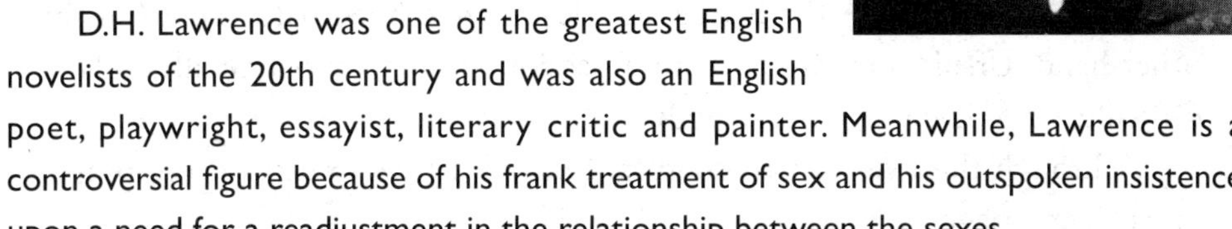

INTRODUCTION

D.H. Lawrence was one of the greatest English novelists of the 20th century and was also an English poet, playwright, essayist, literary critic and painter. Meanwhile, Lawrence is a controversial figure because of his frank treatment of sex and his outspoken insistence upon a need for a readjustment in the relationship between the sexes.

Lawrence was born in the Midland mining village of Eastwood, Nottinghamshire and he was one of five children of a miner and schoolteacher. He studied at Nottingham High School for three years and worked in a surgical goods factory at 15. In 1906 he entered Nottingham College to study the required courses for a teacher's certificate. Since 1908, he taught in a school in a southern suburb of London for two years. In 1911, his first famous novel *The White Peacock* made its appearance. Two years later, *Sons and Lovers* (1913) was published as an autobiographical novel about a mother's possessive love for her sons, which is regarded as Lawrence's earliest masterpiece.

He married Frieda in 1914. During World War I, due to Lawrence's anti-war sentiment, they had to seek refuge in Italy, Australia, Mexico, and France. During the time, Lawrence created his two probably most successful novels, *The Rainbow* (1915) and *Women in Love* (1921), which both expressed severe criticism of capitalist industrial civilization. *Lady Chatterley's Lover* is his most controversial novel which was first published in the United States in 1928. It is about an English noblewoman's love affair with a servant. The book was banned in England and America until 1960 for his frank treatment of sex in the novel. In 1930, he died of tuberculosis in France.

SELECTED READING

Women in Love

Overview

The novel, published in 1920, is a sequel to his earlier novel *The Rainbow* (1915). The novel continues to follow the love and life of the Brangwen sisters, Gudrun and Ursula. Ursula and Gudrun Brangwen live in the Midlands of

England in the 1910s. Ursula is a teacher, Gudrun an artist. They meet two men who live nearby, school inspector Rupert Birkin and coal-mine heir Gerald Crich. The four become friends. Ursula and Birkin become involved, and Gudrun eventually begins a love affair with Gerald. Because of the great differences in ideas and world outlook, the relationship between Gudrun and Gerald eventually broke up after numerous times of conflicts. At last, Gerald ended his life in the barren and dead ravine filled with snow. On the other hand, Ursula and Birkin, with a passion for life, overcame all kinds of difficulties and lived together happily.

Through the lives of two couples, Lawrence tries to explain the proper basis for marriage.

Chapter 3

(Excerpt)

…

She[1] reached for a bit of paper which had wrapped a small piece of chocolate she had found in her pocket, and began making a boat. He[2] watched her without heeding her. There was something strangely pathetic and tender in her moving, unconscious finger-tips, that were agitated and hurt, really.

"I *do* enjoy things—don't you?" she asked.

"Oh yes! But it infuriates me that I can't get right, at the really growing part of me. I feel all tangled and messed up, and I *can't* get straight anyhow. I don't know what really to *do*. One must do something somewhere."

"Why should you always be *doing*?" she retorted. "It is so plebeian. I think it is much better to be really patrician, and to do nothing but just be oneself, like a walking flower."

"I quite agree," he said, "if one has burst into blossom. But I can't get my flower to blossom anyhow. Either it is blighted in the bud, or has got the smother-fly, or it isn't nourished. Curse it, it isn't even a bud. It is a contravened knot."

Again she laughed. He was so very fretful and exasperated. But she was

1 She: Ursula

2 He: Birkin

anxious and puzzled. How was one to get out, anyhow. There must be a way out somewhere.

There was a silence, wherein she wanted to cry. She reached for another bit of chocolate paper, and began to fold another boat.

"And why is it," she asked at length, "that there is no flowering, no dignity of human life now?"

"The whole idea is dead. Humanity itself is dry-rotten, really. There are myriads of human beings hanging on the bush—and they look very nice and rosy, your healthy young men and women. But they are apples of Sodom[1], as a matter of fact, Dead Sea Fruit, gall-apples. It isn't true that they have any significance—their insides are full of bitter, corrupt ash."

"But there *are* good people," protested Ursula.

"Good enough for the life of today. But mankind is a dead tree, covered with fine brilliant galls of people."

Ursula could not help stiffening herself against this, it was too picturesque and final. But neither could she help making him go on.

"And if it is so, *why* is it?" she asked, hostile. They were rousing each other to a fine passion of opposition.

"Why, why are people all balls of bitter dust? Because they won't fall off the tree when they're ripe. They hang on to their old positions when the position is over-past, till they become infested with little worms and dry-rot."

There was a long pause. His voice had become hot and very sarcastic. Ursula was troubled and bewildered, they were both oblivious of everything but their own immersion.

"But even if everybody is wrong—where are you right?'" she cried, "where are you any better?"

"I?—I'm not right," he cried back. "At least my only rightness lies in the fact that I know it. I detest what I am, outwardly. I loathe myself as a human being. Humanity is a huge aggregate lie, and a huge lie is less than a small

1 Sodom: A city of ancient Palestine possibly located in the south of the Dead Sea. In the Old Testament, it was destroyed along with Gomorrah because of its wickedness and depravity.

truth. Humanity is less, far less than the individual, because the individual may sometimes be capable of truth, and humanity is a tree of lies. And they say that love is the greatest thing; they persist in *saying* this, the foul liars, and just look at what they do! Look at all the millions of people who repeat every minute that love is the greatest, and charity is the greatest — and see what they are doing all the time. By their works ye shall know them, for dirty liars and cowards, who daren't stand by their own actions, much less by their own words."

"But," said Ursula sadly, "that doesn't alter the fact that love is the greatest, does it? What they *do* doesn't alter the truth of what they say, does it?"

"Completely, because if what they say *were* true, then they couldn't help fulfilling it. But they maintain a lie, and so they run amok at last. It's a lie to say that love is the greatest. You might as well say that hate is the greatest, since the opposite of everything balances. What people want is hate—hate and nothing but hate. And in the name of righteousness and love, they get it. They distil themselves with nitroglycerine, all the lot of them, out of very love. It's the lie that kills. If we want hate, let us have it—death, murder, torture, violent destruction—let us have it: but not in the name of love. But I abhor humanity, I wish it was swept away. It could go, and there would be no *absolute* loss, if every human being perished tomorrow. The reality would be untouched. Nay, it would be better. The real tree of life would then be rid of the most ghastly, heavy crop of Dead Sea Fruit, the intolerable burden of myriad simulacra[1] of people, an infinite weight of mortal lies."

"So you'd like everybody in the world destroyed?" said Ursula.

"I should indeed."

"And the world empty of people?"

"Yes truly. You yourself, don't you find it a beautiful clean thought, a world empty of people, just uninterrupted grass, and a hare sitting up?"

The pleasant sincerity of his voice made Ursula pause to consider her own proposition. And really it *was* attractive: a clean, lovely, humanless world. It was the *really* desirable. Her heart hesitated, and exulted. But still,

1 simulacra: (sing. simulacrum) an unreal or vague semblance

she was dissatisfied with *him*.

"But," she objected, "you'd be dead yourself, so what good would it do you?"

"I would die like a shot, to know that the earth would really be cleaned of all the people. It is the most beautiful and freeing thought. Then there would *never* be another foul humanity created, for a universal defilement."

"No," said Ursula, "there would be nothing."

"What! Nothing? Just because humanity was wiped out? You flatter yourself. There'd be everything."

"But how, if there were no people?"

"Do you think that creation depends on *man*! It merely doesn't. There are the trees and the grass and birds. I much prefer to think of the lark rising up in the morning upon a human-less world. Man is a mistake, he must go. There is the grass, and hares and adders, and the unseen hosts, actual angels that go about freely when a dirty humanity doesn't interrupt them—and good pure-tissued demons: very nice."

It pleased Ursula, what he said, pleased her very much, as a phantasy. Of course it was only a pleasant fancy. She herself knew too well the actuality of humanity, its hideous actuality. She knew it could not disappear so cleanly and conveniently. It had a long way to go yet, a long and hideous way. Her subtle, feminine, demoniacal soul knew it well.

"If only man was swept off the face of the earth, creation would go on so marvellously, with a new start, non-human. Man is one of the mistakes of creation—like the ichthyosauri. If only he were gone again, think what lovely things would come out of the liberated days;—things straight out of the fire."

"But man will never be gone," she said, with insidious, diabolical knowledge of the horrors of persistence. "The world will go with him."

"Ah no," he answered, "not so. I believe in the proud angels and the demons that are our fore-runners. They will destroy us, because we are not proud enough. The ichthyosauri were not proud: they crawled and floundered as we do. And besides, look at elder-flowers and bluebells—they are a sign that pure creation takes place—even the butterfly. But humanity never gets beyond the caterpillar stage—it rots in the chrysalis, it never will have wings. It is anti-creation, like monkeys and baboons."

Ursula watched him as he talked. There seemed a certain impatient fury in him, all the while, and at the same time a great amusement in everything, and a final tolerance. And it was this tolerance she mistrusted, not the fury. She saw that, all the while, in spite of himself, he would have to be trying to save the world. And this knowledge, whilst it comforted her heart somewhere with a little self-satisfaction, stability, yet filled her with a certain sharp contempt and hate of him. She wanted him to herself, she hated the Salvator Mundi touch[1]. It was something diffuse and generalised about him, which she could not stand. He would behave in the same way, say the same things, give himself as completely to anybody who came along, anybody and everybody who liked to appeal to him. It was despicable, a very insidious form of prostitution.

"But," she said, "you believe in individual love, even if you don't believe in loving humanity—?"

"I don't believe in love at all—that is, any more than I believe in hate, or in grief. Love is one of the emotions like all the others—and so it is all right whilst you feel it. But I can't see how it becomes an absolute. It is just part of human relationships, no more. And it is only part of *any* human relationship. And why one should be required *always* to feel it, any more than one always feels sorrow or distant joy, I cannot conceive. Love isn't a desideratum—it is an emotion you feel or you don't feel, according to circumstance."

"Then why do you care about people at all?" she asked, "if you don't believe in love? Why do you bother about humanity?"

"Why do I? Because I can't get away from it."

"Because you love it," she persisted.

It irritated him.

"If I do love it," he said, "it is my disease."

"But it is a disease you don't want to be cured of," she said, with some cold sneering.

1 Salvator Mundi touch: the action of the savior. Salvator Mundi is the name of God.

He was silent now, feeling she wanted to insult him.

"And if you don't believe in love, what *do* you believe in?" she asked mocking. "Simply in the end of the world, and grass?"

He was beginning to feel a fool.

"I believe in the unseen hosts," he said.

"And nothing else? You believe in nothing visible, except grass and birds? Your world is a poor show."

"Perhaps it is," he said, cool and superior now he was offended, assuming a certain insufferable aloof superiority, and withdrawing into his distance.

Ursula disliked him. But also she felt she had lost something. She looked at him as he sat crouched on the bank. There was a certain priggish Sunday-school stiffness over him, priggish and detestable. And yet, at the same time, the moulding of him was so quick and attractive, it gave such a great sense of freedom: the moulding of his brows, his chin, his whole physique, something so alive, somewhere, in spite of the look of sickness.

And it was this duality in feeling which he created in her, that made a fine hate of him quicken in her bowels. There was his wonderful, desirable life—rapidity, the rare quality of an utterly desirable man: and there was at the same time this ridiculous, mean effacement into a Salvator Mundi and a Sunday-school teacher, a prig of the stiffest type.

He looked up at her. He saw her face strangely enkindled, as if suffused from within by a powerful sweet fire. His soul was arrested in wonder. She was enkindled in her own living fire. Arrested in wonder and in pure, perfect attraction, he moved towards her. She sat like a strange queen, almost supernatural in her glowing smiling richness.

"The point about love," he said, his consciousness quickly adjusting itself, "is that we hate the word because we have vulgarised it. It ought to be prescribed, tabooed from utterance, for many years, till we get a new, better idea."

There was a beam of understanding between them.

"But it always means the same thing," she said.

"Ah God, no, let it not mean that any more," he cried. "Let the old meanings go."

"But still it is love," she persisted. A strange, wicked yellow light shone at him in her eyes.

He hesitated, baffled, withdrawing.

"No," he said, "it isn't. Spoken like that, never in the world. You've no business to utter the word."

"I must leave it to you, to take it out of the Ark of the Covenant[1] at the right moment," she mocked.

Again they looked at each other. She suddenly sprang up, turned her back to him, and walked away. He too rose slowly and went to the water's edge, where, crouching, he began to amuse himself unconsciously. Picking a daisy he dropped it on the pond, so that the stem was a keel, the flower floated like a little water lily, staring with its open face up to the sky. It turned slowly round, in a slow, slow Dervish dance[2], as it veered away.

QUESTIONS

1 According to Ursula, how can a man be really patrician?
2 In Paragraph 5, Birkin said, "I can not get my flower to blossom anyhow". What is the symbolic meaning of the sentence?
3 What does Birkin think of "human life"? And why?
4 What kind of human life does Birkin expect?
5 What does Birkin think of "human's love"?
6 Try to analyze the character of Ursula.

1 the Ark of the Covenant: a gold-covered wooden chest, which is also known as the Ark of the Testimony

2 Dervish dance: a kind of whirling dance performed by dervish as acts of ecstatic devotion

William Butler Yeats
(1869-1939)

INTRODUCTION

William Butler Yeats was an Irish and British poet, one of the foremost figures of 20th century literature. He is considered a pillar of both the Irish and British literary establishments. In 1923 he got Nobel Prize in Literature, Ireland's first writer to win the Prize.

W. B. Yeats was born in Dublin. His father was an artist, so that Yeats naturally had frequent contacts with various artists in his childhood. He was educated in Dublin and London. Since 1881, he began to write some essays and poems. His early poetry was influenced by the romantic poets, but his Irish theme and his language with prose style showed him to be a poet of distinction. The beautiful Maud Gonne once drew him into the Irish National Movement. After 1896, Yeats devoted himself largely to drama and forming the Abby Theatre. Yeats focused on exploring the theory of symbolism and mask with the influence of Modern French poetry. In 1914, the poetry *Responsibilities* was published, marking the ending of Yeats' early creation.

During his poetic career, the mysticism of Blake, the Romantic idealism of Shelley, and the aesthetic ideas of the Pre-Raphaelites were mixed into Yeats' thought. He gave impetus to the modernist movement in poetry with Ezra Pound, T. S. Eliot and other poets to seek a fresh language, new rhythms, and wide poetic subjects.

Yeats is generally considered one of the few writers who completed their greatest works after being awarded the Nobel Prize; such works include *The Tower* (1928) and *The Winding Stair and Other Poems* (1929). He died in 1939 in Manton, France.

SELECTED READING

When You Are Old

The poem was written in 1893 and dedicated to Maud Gonne, a young lady he loved all his life. Maud Gonne was an English-born Irish revolutionary, feminist and actress. In 1891, he visited Gonne in Ireland and proposed marriage, but was rejected. Yeats proposed to Gonne three more times: in 1899, 1900 and 1901. She refused each proposal.

When you are old and gray and full of sleep
And nodding by the fire, take down this book,
And slowly read, and dream of the soft look
Your eyes had once, and of their shadows deep;

How many loved your moments of glad grace,
And loved your beauty with love false or true;
But one man loved the pilgrim soul in you,
And loved the sorrows of your changing face;

And bending down beside the glowing bars[1],
Murmur, a little sadly, how Love fled
And paced upon the mountains overhead,
And hid his face amid a crowd of stars.

QUESTIONS

1 What does the speaker love about the lady in the poem?
2 What is the rhyme scheme of each stanza?
3 In the beginning, what setting is created by the poet?
4 What are the figures of speech adopted in this poem? Give examples to illustrate your points.
5 In the poem, the poet uses three contrasts. What are they?
6 What is the symbolic meaning of "stars" in the last line?

1 bars: the barrier of fireplace

T. S. Eliot
(1888-1965)

INTRODUCTION

Thomas Stearns Eliot was one of the most influential modernist poets and literary critics of the 20th century. He was an essayist, publisher, playwright. He was awarded the Nobel Prize in Literature in 1948.

He was born in St. Louis, Missouri, educated at Harvard and Oxford. He settled in England and became a British citizen later in 1927. It was in London that Eliot met Ezra Pound, who had a great influence on Eliot, especially in his recognizing Eliot's poetic genius and helping with publication of his works.

He held that poetry should represent the complexities of modern civilization. An innovator of avant-garde as he was, he was influenced by the English metaphysical poets of the seventeenth century and the nineteenth century French symbolist poets. He used a lot of mythology, allusion, symbolism, and disconnected images as to make his works obscure to the readers. His poems gave voice to the disillusionment of the post World War I generation. Eliot's influence can be found in many writers, Virginia Woolf, Ezra Pound, and James Joyce.

Eliot's best-known poems include *The Love Song of J. Alfred Prufrock* (1915), *The Waste Land* (1922), *The Hollow Men* (1925), *Ash Wednesday* (1930) and *Four Quartets* (1945). He is also known for his seven plays, particularly *Murder in the Cathedral* (1935).

Eliot is also known for his contribution to the New Criticism, which was a movement in literary theory in American from the 1920s to the early 1960s. It emphasized close reading, particularly of poetry, without considering the biographical or historical circumstances. New criticism regarded a work of literature as independent of both author and reader. The New Critics also focused on paradox, ambiguity, irony, conflicts and tension to interpret the text.

SELECTED READING

The Waste Land

Overview

The Waste Land is a long poem of 434 lines. It is one of the most important poems of the 20th century and a masterpiece of modernist poetry.

With influence from the Western canon and mythology, and the Eastern Buddhism and the Hinduism, Eliot employs many literary and cultural allusions, metaphors and references for techniques. Structural complexity, abrupt changes of speaker, location and time, against a background of juxtapositions between past and present contribute to the obscurity of the poem. With a wide and disconnected range of cultures and literature works concerned, the poet tried to present the devastation and disorganization of the post-war world.

The poem is divided into five sections with some of Eliot's notes at the end. The first section, *The Burial of the Dead*, depicts a modern world of disillusionment and despair. The second, *A Game of Chess*, employs alternating narrations from different characters to reveal the morally deteriorating and spiritual barrenness of the modern society. *The Fire Sermon*, the third section, offers a philosophical meditation in relation to eastern religions. The fourth section includes a brief lyrical petition for death and purgatory. The concluding fifth section, *What the Thunder Said*, gives an image of judgment and a possible light of hope from religion.

I. The Burial of the Dead

(Excerpt)

April is the cruelest month, breeding
Lilacs out of the dead land, mixing
Memory and desire, stirring
Dull roots with spring rain.
Winter kept us warm, covering
Earth in forgetful snow, feeding
A little life with dried tubers.
Summer surprised us, coming over the Starnbergersee[1]
With a shower of rain; we stopped in the colonnade,
And went on in sunlight, into the Hofgarten[2],
And drank coffee, and talked for an hour.

1 Starnbergersee: It refers to Lake Starnberg, Germany's fifth largest freshwater lake, which was used by the poet to represent the modern wasteland in Central Europe.

2 Hofgarten: It is German for "court garden", a garden in the center of Munich, Germany.

Bin gar keine Russin[1], stamm' aus Litauen[2], echt deutsch[3].
And when we were children, staying at the arch-duke's
My cousin's, he took me out on a sled,
And I was frightened. He said, Marie,
Marie, hold on tight. And down we went,
In the mountains, there you feel free.
I read, much of the night, and go south in the winter.

QUESTIONS

1 Why is April the cruelest month?
2 Why is winter warm?
3 What is the possible theme of the poem?
4 What is the figure of speech used in the poem?

EXERCISES OF CHAPTER VII

I Fill in the following blanks.

1 George Bernard Shaw was awarded the Nobel Prize for ________.
2 James Joyce and Virginia Woolf are the two best-known novelists of the ________ school.
3 H. G. Wells is noted for his ________ and is called a ________.
4 ________ opposed traditional values and techniques, and emphasized the importance of individual experience.
5 ________, ________, and ________ are three of the most distinguished exponents of the stream-of-consciousness.

II Find the relevant match from Column B for each item in Column A.

Column A	Column B
1 ( ) John Galsworthy	A. *The Waste Land*
2 ( ) James Joyce	B. *The Man of Property*
3 ( ) Virginia Woolf	C. *Dubliners*

1 Bin gar keine Russin: (German) I am not Russion at all.
2 stamm' aus Litauen: (German) I come from Lithuania.
3 echt deutsch: (German) a true German.

4 ( ) Joseph Conrad | *D. A Passage to India*
5 ( ) D. H. Lawrence | *E. Heart of Darkness*
6 ( ) George Bernard Shaw | F. *The Rainbow*
7 ( ) E. M. Forster | G. *The Waves*
8 ( ) T. S. Eliot | *H. Saint Joan*

III Choose the best answer for each statement.

1 John Galsworthy was awarded the Nobel Prize in Literature because of his masterpiece _____.
A. *The End of the Chapter* B. *The Forsyte Saga*
C. *A Modern Comedy* D. *The Island Pharisees*

2 Which of the following is NOT written by D. H. Lawrence?
A. *The Waste Land* B. *The Rainbow*
C. *Lady Chatterley's Lover* D. *Women in Love*

3 ____ is the climax of Virginia Woolf's experiments through the novel form of "stream of consciousness".
A. *Jacob's Room* B. *To the Lighthouse*
C. *Orlando* D. *The Waves*

4 ____ is a collection of short stories which reflect three aspects of life in politics, culture and religion.
A. *A Portrait of the Artist as a Young Man* B. *Ulysses*
C. *Finnegans Wake* D. *Dubliners*

5 Which of the following is not written by Yeats? ____
A. *Four Quartets* B. *A Vision*
C. *The Winding Stair* D. *The Tower*

IV Answer the following questions.

1 What are the writing features of James Joyce?

2 What are the themes of *Pygmalion*?

CHAPTER VIII

English Literature Since 1945

General Introduction

After the transition from modernism to post-modernism, a number of modernists were still living and publishing in the 1950s and 1960s, including T. S. Eliot and Samuel Beckett. Beckett continued to produce significant works until the 1980s, though some view him as a post-modernist. Postmodern literature is both a continuation of the experimentation championed by writers of the modernist period and a reaction against Enlightenment ideas implicit in Modernist literature. This is a flourishing period of fiction, which should owe to the Nobel Prize in Literature and the Man Booker Prize for Fiction. The Man Booker Prize for Fiction (commonly known simply as the Booker Prize) is a literary prize awarded each year since 1969 for the best original full-length novel, written in the English language, and published in the UK.

The novelists who had been famous before World War Two still wrote novels after WWII, such as George Orwell, Graham Greene, Elias Canetti, Anthony Powell, etc.

George Orwell (1903-1950) published his *Animal Farm* in 1945 and *Nineteen Eighty-four* in 1949. Orwell's works bridge the big gulf in English literature between the two eras: before and after the Second World War. He wrote six novels all together. *Animal Farm* is Orwell's most popular book. This political fable tells the story of a political revolution that the animals on a farm drive out their master Jones and take control of the farm. Led by the pigs Snowball and Napoleon, the animals attempt to create a utopian society. However, the Farm becomes a world where all animals are equal but some are more equal than others. It turns out that the pigs are corrupted by power and a new tyranny has replaced the old. The novel criticizes and satirizes Stalin and the Russian government in the 1930s. Orwell's *Nineteen Eighty-four* describes a future world, which is divided into three countries that make up the entire globe: Oceania, Eurasia, and Eastasia. Oceania is a totalitarian society led by Big Brother, which censors everyone's behavior, even their thoughts. It is a political satire and also a forecast of what would happen when totalitarianism was able to take over not only the body but the soul. The novel tells us that all human beings need to be able to be private sometimes so that they can be themselves.

Graham Greene (1904-1991) was a very prolific and versatile writer. Through

67 years of writing, he wrote more than 27 novels, 9 volumes of short stories, and numerous plays, essays, children's books, travel books, and important film scripts. Greene's important novels include *The Power and the Glory* (1940), *The Heart of the Matter* (1948) and *The Human Factor* (1978). His last novel *The Captain and the Enemy* was published in 1988. In his novels, Greene explored the ambivalent moral and political issues of the modern world, often through a Catholic perspective.

Elias Canetti (1905-1994) was awarded Nobel Prize in Literature in 1981. He was born in Bulgaria, and later a British citizen. He was a modernist novelist, playwright, memoirist and non-fiction writer. His works were written in German.

Anthony Powell (1905-2000) was an English novelist best known for his twelve-volume work *A Dance to the Music of Time*, published between 1951 and 1975. His last novel *Fisher King* was published in 1986 and he was named by *The Times* newspaper among the list of "The 50 greatest British writers since 1945".

The novelists who became famous after WWII were active in writing during the second half of the twentieth century. They are William Golding (1911-1993), Anthony Burgess (1917-1993), Muriel Spark (1918-2006), Iris Murdoch (1919-1999), Doris Lessing (1919-2013), Kingsley Amis (1922-1995), John Fowles (1926-2005), William Trevor (1928-), etc.

Anthony Burgess's best-known book was probably *A Clockwork Orange* (1962) which is classified as science fiction with a satirical picture of future. Burgess eventually became one of the best known English literary figures of the latter half of the twentieth century. In 1980, his *Earthly Powers* should be awarded Booker Prize, but he refused to attend the ceremony unless it was confirmed to him in advance whether he had won.

Among the writers, **Muriel Spark** (1918-2006) was a Scottish female novelist. From her first novel *The Comforters* (1954) until her last novel *The Finishing School* (2004), she contributed 24 novels and pushed the boundaries of realism in her novels. In 2008, *The Times* newspaper named Spark as No. 8 in its list of "The 50 greatest British writers since 1945".

Iris Murdoch (1919-1999) was an English female novelist and philosopher, best known for her novels about good and evil, sexual relationships, morality, and the power of the unconscious. Her first published novel is *Under the Net* (1954) and her last or 26th novel is *Jackson's Dilemma* (1995). In 1978, she was awarded Booker Prize for her novel *The Sea, the Sea*. In 2008, *The Times* ranked Murdoch twelfth on a list of "The 50 greatest British writers since 1945".

Doris Lessing's first novel, *The Grass is Singing* (1959), explores the mind of the wife of a poor white farmer and follows the events that lead to her destruction. Her *The Golden Notebook* (1962) is a powerful attempt to write about women's lives, beliefs, and their pressures. After she was awarded the 2007 Nobel Prize in Literature, she continued her writing until her death in 2013.

Kingsley Amis (1922-1995) is remembered and frequently praised as a satirical novelist. He has written over 20 novels, 9 collections of short stories and poems. The novels of Kingsley Amis have greater comedy and less moral concern. The best known, *Lucky Jim* (1954), shows the attempts of a young university teacher to break the rules of his social class and connect with the working class and unusual characters outside any social group. As one of the representative writers of the "Angry Young Men" movement, Amis' *Lucky Jim* was perceived by many as part of the movement of the 1950s. Kingsley Amis' *The Old Devils* won the Booker Prize in 1986.

William Trevor (1928-) is widely regarded as one of the greatest contemporary writers of short stories in the English language.

The novelists who were born in 1930s and famous in the field of world literature are in the prime of their literary career, such as V. S. Naipaul (1932-) and David Lodge (1935-). In this group, many female novelists have made great contributions to English literature, such as A. S. Byatt (1936-), Margaret Drabble (1939-), and Angela Carter (1940-1992).

V. S. Naipaul (1932-) is an Indian-born British writer whose short stories, travel essays, and novels, such as *A Bend in the River* (1979), present an increasingly pessimistic view of the Third World. Over some 50 years, Naipaul has published more than 30 books, both of fiction and nonfiction. He published his latest novel *Magic Seeds* in 2004. Naipaul is generally regarded as the leading novelist produced by the English-speaking Caribbean. He has received many literary prizes, including the Booker Prize for *In a Free State* in 1971 and the Nobel Prize in Literature for his lifetime achievement in 2001. V. S. Naipaul was knighted in 1989 and has held honorary doctorates from Cambridge University and Columbia University.

A. S. Byatt (1936-) and **Margaret Drabble** (1939-) are sisters. **A. S. Byatt** is a novelist and poet. In 2008, *The Times* newspaper named her on its list of the 50 greatest British writers since 1945. A. S. Byatt was born Antonia Susan Drabble in 1936, in Sheffield, England, the eldest of four children of a judge and his wife, an English teacher. Byatt was appointed CBE in 1990 and DBE in 1999. Her masterpiece is *Possession: A Romance* which was published in 1990 and was awarded The Booker Prize for this novel. Her latest works include her novel *Ragnarok: The End of the Gods* (2011) and the novella *Dolls' Eyes* (2013). She once studied in Newnham College of Cambridge, University of Philadelphia in USA and Somerville College of Oxford. Byatt now lives in London. Her sister is the novelist Margaret Drabble.

Margaret Drabble (1939-) is a novelist, biographer, and critic who is named as realist novelist of the social manner. She has published 18 novels and the latest novel *The Pure Gold Baby* was published in 2013. Drabble edited two editions of *The Oxford Companion to English Literature* in 1985 and 2000. In 2006, the University of Cambridge awarded her an honorary Doctorate in Letters.

Angela Carter (1940-1992) was a novelist, short-story writer and critic, known for her feminist, magical realism, and picaresque works. In 2008, *The Times* ranked Carter tenth in their list of "The 50 greatest British writers since 1945". Her stories and novels take the form of fables, allegories, sophisticated fairy tales, Gothic melodramas and historical fantasies. She has been called fairy godmother of magic realism. Carter published 9 novels, 7 Short fiction collections, and other works. Her masterpieces include her novel *Nights at the Circus* (1984) and her short-story collection, *Burning Your Boats* (1996).

The novelists born after 1940 are called the new stars, such as Graham Swift (1949-), Martin Amis (1949-), Salman Rushdie (1947-), Howard Jacobson (1942-), Julian Barnes (1946-), Hilary Mantel (1952-) , J. K. Rowling (1965), etc.

Graham Swift (1949-) , born in London, is one of the most highly regarded British writers to appear in the 1980s. He was educated at the universities of London, Cambridge, and York, where he took his B.A., M.A., and PhD. Graham Swift is a Fellow of the Royal Society of Literature. *Waterland* is considered to be the author's premier novel and was shortlisted for the Booker Prize in 1983, but he finally achieved the Booker Prize in 1996 with his *Last Orders*. Now, he lives in London and has been the author of ten novels. Swift's latest novel is *Mothering Sunday: A Romance Knopf* which was published in 2016.

Martin Amis (1949-) is a novelist, once as the Professor of Creative Writing at the University of Manchester. He is Kingsley Amis' son, best-known for his novels *Money* (1984) and *London Fields* (1989). Martin Amis has been listed for the Booker Prize twice. In 2008, *The Times* named him one of "The 50 greatest British writers since 1945". He has published 14 novels and his latest novel is *The Zone of Interest* (2014).

Salman Rushdie (1947-) is a British Indian novelist and essayist. Rushdie was born in Bombay, then British India. He read history at King's College, Cambridge. After graduating, he once worked in television in Pakistan and as actor and freelance advertising copywriter in London. He is a Fellow of the Royal Society of Literature and Honorary Professor in the Humanities at the Massachusetts Institute of Technology. Rushdie has received eight honorary doctorates. In 2007, Queen Elizabeth II knighted him for his services to literature. In 2008 he was elected a Foreign Honorary Member of the American Academy of Arts and Letters. In 2015, he joined the New York University. He has been the author of ten novels. His second novel, *Midnight's Children* (1981), won the Booker Prize in 1981. In this novel, Rushdie combines magical realism with historical fiction. His fourth novel, *The Satanic Verses*, made Rushdie be sentenced to death in a religious decree and he was forced into hiding under police protection in England. The publishers and translators of this novel around the world once were the subject of attacks and even murder. Since 2000, Rushdie has lived in the United States and has worked at Emory University. He was elected to the American Academy of Arts and Letters. *Two Years Eight Months and Twenty-Eight Nights* (2015) is his latest novel.

Howard Jacobson (1942-) is a British novelist and journalist. He was born in Manchester in England and was educated at Cambridge University. Jacobson once worked at the University of Sydney for three years before returning to Britain to teach at Selwyn College, Cambridge. He has published 17 novels, known for writing comic novels that often revolve around the dilemmas of British Jewish characters. In 2010 Jacobson won the Man Booker Prize for his novel *The Finkler Question.* After that he published other three novels, *Zoo Time* (2012), *J* (2014), and *Shylock Is My Name: a Novel* (2016). Jacobson is known as a master of comic precision and the funniest British novelist since Kingsley Amis.

Julian Barnes (1946-) is an English writer, born in Leicester. He studied Modern Languages at Magdalen College, Oxford. Three of his earlier books had been shortlisted for the Booker Prize: *Flaubert's Parrot* (1984), *England, England* (1998), and *Arthur & George* (2005). However, Barnes won the Man Booker Prize for his book *The Sense of an Ending* in 2011. He has also written crime fiction under the pseudonym Dan Kavanagh. Barnes has published 16 novels and his latest novel is *The Noise of Time* (2016).

Ian McEwan (1948-) is an English novelist and screenwriter. He won the Man Booker Prize with *Amsterdam* (1998). In 2008, *The Times* featured him on their list of "The 50 greatest British writers since 1945". He has published 14 novels and 3 short story collections. The novels published since 2001 include *Atonement* (2001), *The Saturday* (2005), *On Chesil Beach* (2007), *Solar* (2010), *Sweet Tooth* (2012), and *The Children Act* (2014), and *Nutshell* (2016).

Hilary Mary Mantel (1952-) is an English novelist, short story writer and critic, whose work ranges in subject from personal memoir to historical fiction. She has twice been awarded the Booker Prize, the first woman to receive the prize twice. Her novel *Wolf Hall* was awarded the prize in 2009, which tells the story of Thomas Cromwell's rise to power in the court of Henry VIII. And the second novel of the Cromwell trilogy, *Bring Up the Bodies,* received the award in 2012. The trilogy of Thomas Cromwell is to be followed by *The Mirror and the Light.* Mantel has been awarded honorary degrees (DLitt) by the Universities of Cambridge, Oxford, Derby, Bath Spa, and Oxford Brookes.

J. K. Rowling (1965-) is the pen name of Joanne Rowling. She is a British novelist, screenwriter and film producer, best known as the author of the *Harry Potter* fantasy series.

As to drama, the absurdist play *Waiting for Godot* (1955), by the Irish writer **Samuel Beckett** (1906-1989), profoundly affected British drama. Beckett won the Nobel Prize in Literature in 1969. The Theatre of the Absurd influenced **Harold Pinter** (1930-2008), who was an English playwright, theater director, screenwriter and actor. He is regarded one of the most influential modern British dramatists, and his writing career spanned more than 50 years. Pinter was awarded the Nobel Prize in Literature in 2005. His plays are noted for the use of silence to increase tension, understatement and small talk. His best-known plays include *The Birthday Party* (1957), *The Homecoming* (1964), *Betrayal* (1978), and *Moonlight* (1993), each of which he adapted for the screen.

The major English poet, after T. S. Eliot, is **W. H. Auden** (1907-1973). Auden was best known for love poems, and he later became an American citizen. Probably the most common critical view from the 1930s onward ranked him as one of the three major 20th century British poets, and heir to Yeats and Eliot.

Samuel Beckett
(1906-1989)

Samuel Beckett was an Irish novelist, playwright, theatre director, and poet, most famous for his play *Waiting for Godot* (1953). Beckett is considered one of the last modernist writers, and he is regarded as one of the key figures in "Theatre of the Absurd". He was awarded the 1969 Nobel Prize in Literature "for his writing, which—in new forms for the novel and drama".

Samuel Beckett was born in the Dublin suburb of Foxrock in 1906. Beckett studied French, Italian, and English at Trinity College, Dublin from 1923 to 1927. In 1930, Beckett worked in Trinity College as a lecturer. Since 1937, he went abroad and lived in Paris for most of his adult life. He once was Joyce's secretary but he devoted his most energy and time to writing. Beckett wrote in both English and French. He is widely regarded as among the most influential writers of the 20th century. His notable works include *Murphy* (1938), *Molloy* (1951), *Malone Dies* (1951), *The Unnamable* (1953), *Waiting for Godot* (1953), *Watt* (1953), *Endgame* (1957), *Krapp's Last Tape* (1958), and *How It Is* (1961).

SELECTED READING

Waiting for Godot

Overview

Waiting for Godot was performed in 1953, the book form of which was published in 1952. The English language version was premiered in London in 1955. In the play, two characters, Vladimir and Estragon, wait endlessly and in vain for the arrival of someone named Godot. They are sitting there, talking about and doing some trivial and meaningless things. But the play ends with them still waiting. They only know that Godot promised to come. However, they are not clear who is Godot, why they wait for him, and whether he will come. Godot's absence has led to many interpretations since the première in 1953. It is a funny play that nothing happens on the stage without plot. The following selection is from Act I.

ACT I

A country road.

A tree.

Evening.

...

VLADIMIR[1]: Pah! [*He spits. Estragon moves to center, halts with his back to auditorium.*]

ESTRAGON[2]: Charming spot. [*He turns, advances to front, halts facing auditorium.*] Inspiring prospects. [*He turns to Vladimir.*] Let's go.

VLADIMIR: We can't.

ESTRAGON: Why not?

VLADIMIR: We're waiting for Godot[3].

ESTRAGON: [*despairingly*]. Ah! [*Pause.*] You're sure it was here?

VLADIMIR: What?

ESTRAGON: That we were to wait.

VLADIMIR: He said by the tree. [*They look at the tree.*] Do you see any others?

ESTRAGON: What is it?

VLADIMIR: I don't know. A willow.

ESTRAGON: Where are the leaves?

VLADIMIR: It must be dead.

ESTRAGON: No more weeping.

VLADIMIR: Or perhaps it's not the season.

ESTRAGON: Looks to me more like a bush.

VLADIMIR: A shrub.

ESTRAGON: A bush.

VLADIMIR: A—. What are you insinuating? That we've come to the wrong place?

ESTRAGON: He should be here.

---

1 Vladimir: Estragon calls him Didi, and the "boy" [appears later in the play] addresses him as Mr. Albert. He seems to be the more responsible and mature of the two main characters.

2 Estragon: Vladimir calls him Gogo. He seems weak and helpless, always looking for Vladimir's protection.

3 Godot: The man for whom Vladimir and Estragon wait unendingly. Godot never appears in the play. His name and character are often thought to refer to God.

VLADIMIR: He didn't say for sure he'd come.

ESTRAGON: And if he doesn't come?

VLADIMIR: We'll come back tomorrow.

ESTRAGON: And then the day after tomorrow.

VLADIMIR: Possibly.

ESTRAGON: And so on.

VLADIMIR: The point is—

ESTRAGON: Until he comes.

VLADIMIR: You're merciless.

ESTRAGON: We came here yesterday.

VLADIMIR: Ah no, there you're mistaken.

ESTRAGON: What did we do yesterday?

VLADIMIR: What did we do yesterday?

ESTRAGON: Yes.

VLADIMIR: Why... [*Angrily.*] Nothing is certain when you're about.

ESTRAGON: In my opinion we were here.

VLADIMIR: [*looking round*]. You recognize the place?

ESTRAGON: I didn't say that.

VLADIMIR: Well?

ESTRAGON: That makes no difference.

VLADIMIR: All the same... that tree... [*turning towards auditorium*] that bog...

ESTRAGON: You're sure it was this evening?

VLADIMIR: What?

ESTRAGON: That we were to wait.

VLADIMIR: He said Saturday. [*Pause.*] I think.

ESTRAGON: You think.

VLADIMIR: I must have made a note of it. [*He fumbles in his pockets, bursting with miscellaneous rubbish.*]

ESTRAGON: [*very insidious*]. But what Saturday? And is it Saturday? Is it not rather Sunday? [*Pause.*] Or Monday? [*Pause.*] Or Friday?

VLADIMIR: [*looking wildly about him, as though the date was inscribed *in the landscape*]. It's not possible!

ESTRAGON: Or Thursday?

VLADIMIR: What'll we do?

ESTRAGON: If he came yesterday and we weren't here you may be sure he won't come again today.

VLADIMIR: But you say we were here yesterday.

ESTRAGON: I may be mistaken. [*Pause.*] Let's stop talking for a minute, do you mind?

VLADIMIR: [*feebly*]. All right. [*Estragon sits down on the mound. Vladimir paces agitatedly to and fro, halting from time to time to gaze into distance off. Estragon falls asleep. Vladimir halts finally before Estragon.*] Gogo!... Gogo!... GOGO!

[*Estragon wakes with a start.*]

ESTRAGON: [*restored to the horror of his situation*]. I was asleep! [*Despairingly.*] Why will you never let me sleep?

VLADIMIR: I felt lonely.

ESTRAGON: I had a dream.

VLADIMIR: Don't tell me!

ESTRAGON: I dreamt that—

VLADIMIR: DON't TELL ME!

ESTRAGON: [*gesture toward the universe*]. This one is enough for you? [*Silence.*] It's not nice of you, Didi. Who am I to tell my private nightmares to if I can't tell them to you?

VLADIMIR: Let them remain private. You know I can't bear that.

ESTRAGON: [*coldly*]. There are times when I wonder if it wouldn't be better for us to part.

VLADIMIR: You wouldn't go far.

ESTRAGON: That would be too bad, really too bad. [*Pause.*] Wouldn't it, Didi, be really too bad? [*Pause.*] When you think of the beauty of the way. [*Pause.*] And the goodness of the wayfarers. [*Pause. Wheedling.*] Wouldn't it, Didi?

VLADIMIR: Calm yourself.

ESTRAGON: [*voluptuously*]. Calm... calm... The English say cawm[1]. [*Pause.*] You know the story of the Englishman in the brothel?

VLADIMIR: Yes.

ESTRAGON: Tell it to me.

VLADIMIR: Ah stop it!

ESTRAGON: An Englishman having drunk a little more than usual proceeds to a brothel. The bawd asks him if he wants a fair one, a dark one or a red-haired one. Go on.

VLADIMIR: STOP IT!

Exit Vladimir hurriedly. Estragon gets up and follows him as far as the limit of the stage. Gestures of Estragon like those of a spectator encouraging a pugilist. Enter Vladimir. He brushes past Estragon, crosses the stage with bowed head. Estragon takes a step towards him, halts.

ESTRAGON: [*gently*]. You wanted to speak to me? [*Silence. Estragon takes a step forward.*] You had something to say to me? [*Silence. Another step forward.*] Didi[2]...

VLADIMIR: [*without turning*]. I've nothing to say to you.

ESTRAGON: [*step forward*]. You're angry? [*Silence. Step forward.*] Forgive me. [*Silence. Step forward. Estragon lays his hand on Vladimir's shoulder.*] Come, Didi. [*Silence.*] Give me your hand. [*Vladimir half turns.*] Embrace me! [*Vladimir stiffens.*] Don't be stubborn! [*Vladimir softens. They embrace. Estragon recoils.*] You stink of garlic!

VLADIMIR: It's for the kidneys. [*Silence. Estragon looks attentively at the tree.*] What do we do now?

ESTRAGON: Wait.

VLADIMIR: Yes, but while waiting.

ESTRAGON: What about hanging ourselves?

VLADIMIR: Hmm. It'd give us an erection.

ESTRAGON: [*highly excited*]. An erection!

---

1 cawm: Estragon's spelling for the word "calm" according to the "English" accent. Estragon and Vladimir are not supposed to be English according to their names.

2 Didi: Vladimir

VLADIMIR: With all that follows. Where it falls mandrakes[1] grow. That's why they shriek when you pull them up. Did you not know that?

ESTRAGON: Let's hang ourselves immediately!

VLADIMIR: From a bough? [*They go towards the tree.*] I wouldn't trust it.

ESTRAGON: We can always try.

VLADIMIR: Go ahead.

ESTRAGON: After you.

VLADIMIR: No no, you first.

ESTRAGON: Why me?

VLADIMIR: You're lighter than I am.

ESTRAGON: Just so!

VLADIMIR: I don't understand.

ESTRAGON: Use your intelligence, can't you? [*Vladimir uses his intelligence.*]

VLADIMIR: [*finally*]. I remain in the dark.

ESTRAGON: This is how it is. [*He reflects.*] The bough... the bough... [*Angrily.*] Use your head, can't you?

VLADIMIR: You're my only hope.

ESTRAGON: [*with effort*]. Gogo[2] light—bough not break—Gogo dead. Didi heavy—bough break—Didi alone. Whereas—

VLADIMIR: I hadn't thought of that.

ESTRAGON: If it hangs you it'll hang anything.

VLADIMIR: But am I heavier than you?

ESTRAGON: So you tell me. I don't know. There's an even chance. Or nearly.

VLADIMIR: Well? What do we do?

ESTRAGON: Don't let's do anything. It's safer.

VLADIMIR: Let's wait and see what he says.

ESTRAGON: Who?

---

1 mandrake: It is the name of a southern European plant which has greenish-yellow flowers and a branched root. This plant is believed to have magical powers because its root resembles the human body.

2 Gogo: Estragon

VLADIMIR: Godot.

ESTRAGON: Good idea.

VLADIMIR: Let's wait till we know exactly how we stand.

ESTRAGON: On the other hand it might be better to strike the iron before it freezes.

VLADIMIR: I'm curious to hear what he has to offer. Then we'll take it or leave it.

ESTRAGON: What exactly did we ask him for?

VLADIMIR: Were you not there?

ESTRAGON: I can't have been listening.

VLADIMIR: Oh... Nothing very definite.

ESTRAGON: A kind of prayer.

VLADIMIR: Precisely.

ESTRAGON: A vague supplication.

VLADIMIR: Exactly.

ESTRAGON: And what did he reply?

VLADIMIR: That he'd see.

ESTRAGON: That he couldn't promise anything.

VLADIMIR: That he'd have to think it over.

ESTRAGON: In the quiet of his home.

VLADIMIR: Consult his family.

ESTRAGON: His friends.

VLADIMIR: His agents.

ESTRAGON: His correspondents.

VLADIMIR: His books.

ESTRAGON: His bank account.

VLADIMIR: Before taking a decision.

ESTRAGON: It's the normal thing.

VLADIMIR: Is it not?

ESTRAGON: I think it is.

VLADIMIR: I think so too.

[*Silence.*]

ESTRAGON: [*anxious*]. And we?

VLADIMIR: I beg your pardon?

ESTRAGON: I said, And we?

VLADIMIR: I don't understand.

ESTRAGON: Where do we come in?

VLADIMIR: Come in?

ESTRAGON: Take your time.

VLADIMIR: Come in? On our hands and knees.

ESTRAGON: As bad as that?

VLADIMIR: Your Worship wishes to assert his prerogatives?

ESTRAGON: We've no rights any more?

Laugh of Vladimir, stifled as before, less the smile.

QUESTIONS

1 Do you think Estragon and Vladimir are sure that Godot will come to meet them?
2 Why do they talk about the tree?
3 How long have they waited here from the conversation?
4 What do you think of the relationship between the two main characters?
5 What does Godot symbolize in the play?
6 Why do the two men keep waiting for Godot?

William Golding
(1911-1993)

INTRODUCTION

William Golding was a British novelist, playwright, and poet, best known for his novel *Lord of the Flies*. He was awarded the Booker Prize for literature in 1980 for his novel *Rites of Passage*, the first novel of a sea trilogy *To the Ends of the Earth*. In 1983 he was awarded the Nobel Prize in Literature. Golding was knighted by Elizabeth II in 1988. He was a fellow of the Royal Society of Literature.

William Golding was born and spent many childhood holidays in his grandmother's house. Golding went to Oxford University to study Natural Sciences for two years before transferring to English Literature. Then he was a schoolmaster teaching Philosophy and English in 1939. During World War II, Golding joined the Royal Navy in 1940. From 1945 to 1961 he worked at Bishop Wordsworth's School in Salisbury.

After his masterpiece *Lord of the Flies* was published in 1954, he continued his writing. His other famous novels include *The Inheritors* (1955), *Pincher Martin* (1956), *Free Fall* (1959), *The Spire* (1964), *The Pyramid* (1967), *Darkness Visible* (1979), and *Rites of Passage* (1980).

SELECTED READING

Lord of the Flies[1]

Overview

The novel tells us a story about a group of boys who are the only survivors after a British plane crashes on or near an isolated island in a remote region of the Pacific Ocean. The boys are in their middle childhood or preadolescence. Then the children split into two groups. The book portrays their descent into savagery. In the novel, the author seems to tell us that man is born evil and man is prone to evil. As a religious writer, he emphasizes original Sin in the Puritan tradition. At an allegorical level, the central theme is the conflicting

1 *Lord of the Flies:* The name "Lord of the Flies" is a translation of the name of the biblical Beelzebub, a powerful demon in hell.

human impulses toward civilization and social organization—living by rules, peacefully and in harmony—and toward the will to power. Themes include the tension between groupthink and individuality, between rational and emotional reactions, and between morality and immorality. The novel's characters, plot and environment description and so on have highly symbolic significance. The end of the book, a seemingly good denouement: a cruiser finally finds a fire on the island, Ralph has been saved. But he cries for the prospect of the collapse of human nature. He should be more painful because the cruiser to save them is only part of the war machine. Who will save them? The following selection is from Chapter 2, "Fire on the Mountain."

BY THE TIME Ralph[1] finished blowing the conch[2] the platform was crowded, there were differences between this meeting and the one held in the morning. The afternoon sun slanted in from the other side of the platform and most of the children, feeling too late the smart of sunburn, had put their clothes on. The choir, noticeably less of a group, had discarded their cloaks.

Ralph sat on a fallen trunk, his left side to the sun. On his right were most of the choir; on his left the larger boys who had not known each other before the evacuation; before him small children squatted in the grass.

Silence now. Ralph lifted the cream and pink shell to his knees and a sudden breeze scattered light over the platform. He was uncertain whether to stand up or remain sitting. He looked sideways to his left, towards the bathing-pool. Piggy[3] was sitting near but giving no help.

Ralph cleared his throat. "Well then."

All at once he found he could talk fluently and explain what he had to say. He passed a hand through his fair hair and spoke.

"We're on an island. We have been on the mountain-top and seen water all round. We saw no houses, no smoke, no foot-prints, no boats, no people. We're on an uninhabited island with no other people on it."

---

1 Ralph: He is the novel's protagonist, a twelve-year-old English boy, who represents the civilizing instinct within human beings.

2 conch: It becomes a symbol of civilization and order.

3 Piggy: Piggy is the most intelligent, rational boy in the group and his glasses represent the power of science. He was killed by Roger with the boulder.

Jack[1] broke in.

"All the same you need an army—for hunting. Hunting pigs—"

"Yes. There are pigs on the island."

All three of them tried to convey the sense of the pink live thing struggling in the creepers.

"We saw—"

"Squealing—"

"It broke away—"

"Before I could kill it—but—next time!"

Jack slammed his knife into a trunk challengingly.

The meeting settled down again.

"So you see," said Ralph, "we need hunters to get us meat. And another thing."

He lifted the shell on his knees and looked round the sun-slashed faces.

"There aren't any grown-ups. We shall have to look after ourselves."

The meeting hummed and was silent.

"And another thing. We can't have everybody talking once. We'll have to have 'Hands up' like at school."

He held the conch before his face and glanced mouth.

"Then I'll give him the conch."

"Conch?"

"That's what this shell's called. I'll give the conch to the next person to speak. He can hold it when he's speaking."

"But—"

"Look—"

"And he won't be interrupted. Except by me." Jack was on his feet.

"We'll have rules!" he cried excitedly. "Lots of rules! Then when anyone breaks'em

"Whee-oh!"

"Wacco!"

"Bong!"

1 Jack: Jack is the leader of the hunters. He represents the instinct of savagery, violence, and power.

"Doink[1]!"

Ralph felt the conch lifted from his lap. Then Piggy was standing cradling the great cream shell and the shouting died down. Jack, left on his feet, looked uncertainly at Ralph who smiled and patted the log. Jack sat down. Piggy took off his glasses and blinked at the assembly while he wiped them on his shirt.

"You're hindering Ralph. You're not letting him get to the most important thing."

He paused effectively.

"Who knows we're here? Eh?"

"They knew at the airport."

"The man with a trumpet-thing—"

"My dad."

Piggy put on his glasses.

"Nobody knows where we are," said Piggy. He was paler than before and breathless "Perhaps they knew where we was going to; and perhaps not. But they don't know where we are 'cos[2] we never got there." He gaped at them for a moment, then swayed and sat down. Ralph took the conch from his hands.

"That's what I was going to say," he went on, "when you all, all.... "He gazed at their intent faces. "The plane was shot down in flames. Nobody knows where we are. We may be here a long time."

The silence was so complete that they could hear the fetch and miss of Piggy's breathing. The sun slanted in and lay golden over half the platform. The breezes that on the lagoon had chased their tails like kittens were finding their way across the platform and into the forest. Ralph pushed back the tangle of fair hair that hung on his forehead.

"So we may be here a long time."

Nobody said anything. He grinned suddenly.

"But this is a good island. We—Jack, Simon and me—we climbed the

---

1 Doink: do

2 'cos: because

mountain. It's wizard. There's food and drink, and—"

"Rocks— "

"Blue flowers—"

Piggy, partly recovered, pointed to the conch in Ralph's hands, and Jack and Simon fell silent. Ralph went on.

"While we're waiting we can have a good time on this island."

He gesticulated widely.

"It's like in a book." At once there was a clamor.

"Treasure Island[1]— "

"Swallows and Amazons—"

"Coral Island[2]—"

Ralph waved the conch.

"This is our island. It's a good island. Until the grown-ups come to fetch us we'll have fun."

Jack held out his hand for the conch.

"There's pigs," he said. "There's food; and bathing-water in that little stream along there—and everything. Didn't anyone find anything else?"

He handed the conch back to Ralph and sat down. Apparently no one had found anything.

The older boys first noticed the child when he resisted. There was a group of little boys urging him forward and he did not want to go. He was a shrimp of a boy, about six years old, and one side of his face was blotted out by a mulberry-coloured birthmark[3]. He stood now, warped out of the perpendicular by the fierce light of publicity, and he bored into the coarse grass with one toe. He was muttering and about to cry.

The other little boys, whispering but serious, pushed him towards Ralph.

"All right," said Ralph, "come on then."

The small boy looked round in panic[4].

---

1 *Treasure Island:* an adventure novel written by R. L. Stevenson in 1883

2 *Coral Island:* an adventure story of plucky and resourceful boys written by R. M. Ballantyne in 1857

3 birthmark: mark on the skin at birth

4 panic: terror or anxiety

"Speak up!"

The small boy held out his hands for the conch and the assembly shouted with laughter; at once he snatched back his hands and started to cry.

"Let him have the conch!" shouted Piggy. "Let him have it!"

At last Ralph induced him to hold the shell but by then the blow of laughter had taken away the child's voice. Piggy knelt by him, one hand on the great shell, listening and interpreting to the assembly.

"He wants to know what you're going to do about the snake-thing."

Ralph laughed, and the other boys laughed with him. The small boy twisted further into himself.

"Tell us about the snake-thing."

"Now he says it was a beastie."

"Beastie?"

"A snake-thing. Ever so big. He saw it."

"Where?"

"In the woods."

Either the wandering breezes or perhaps the decline of the sun allowed a little coolness to lie under the trees. The boys felt it and stirred restlessly.

"You couldn't have a beastie, a snake-thing, on an island this size," Ralph explained kindly. "You only get them in big countries, like Africa, or India."

Murmur; and the grave nodding of heads.

"He says the beastie came in the dark."

"Then he couldn't see it!"

Laughter and cheers.

"Did you hear that? Says he saw the thing in the dark—"

"He still says he saw the beastie. It came and went away again an' came back and wanted to eat him."

"He was dreaming."

Laughing, Ralph looked for confirmation round the ring of faces. The older boys agreed; but here and there among the little ones was the dubiety that required more than rational assurance.

“He must have had a nightmare. Stumbling about among all those creepers.”

More grave nodding; they knew about nightmares.

“He says he saw the beastie, the snake-thing, and will it come back to-night?”

“But there isn’t a beastie!”

“He says in the morning it turned into them things like ropes in the trees and hung in the branches. He says will it come back to-night?”

“But there isn’t a beastie!”

There was no laughter at all now and graver watching. Ralph pushed both hands through his hair and looked at the little boy in mixed amusement and exasperation[1].

QUESTIONS

1 What does the conch shell symbolize?
2 What does the title mean?
3 What are the boys going to hunt?
4 How old is the youngest boy mentioned in the story?
5 Why does one boy say that he saw a beastie?
6 How is the relationship between Ralph and Jack?

1 exasperation: anger

John Fowles (1926-2005)

INTRODUCTION

John Fowles (1926-2005) was an English novelist, positioned between modernism and postmodernism.

He was born in Essex, England, and spent four years at Bedford School and New College, Oxford, to study both French and German. In 1950, Fowles took his BA degree in French. He was influenced by the writings of the French existentialists, such as Jean-Paul Sartre. After his graduation, he worked as a teacher in several universities in France, Greece and London.

In 1963, with the success of his novel *Collector* Fowles stopped his teaching and devoted himself full-time to a literary career. His representative is *The French Lieutenant's Woman* (1969), which has achieved not only critical acclaim but also popular success. It was eventually translated into more than ten languages, and established Fowles' international reputation. It was adapted as a feature film in 1981. Fowles' later novels include *Daniel Martin* (1977), *Mantissa* (1982) and *A Maggot* (1985).

He got many awards and honorary doctorates, including one from Oxford University. Fowles was named by *The Times* newspaper of UK as "one of the 50 greatest British writers since 1945".

SELECTED READING

The French Lieutenant's Woman

Overview

Fowles' masterpiece, *The French Lieutenant's Woman,* is regarded as postmodern historical fiction novel. It has been made into a well-received film.

The novel resembles a Victorian novel in structure and detail, while pushing the traditional boundaries of narrative in a very modern manner. The book explores the relationship of gentleman and amateur naturalist Charles Smithson and Sarah Woodruff, the former governess and independent woman with whom he falls in love. The novel builds on Fowles' authority in

Victorian literature. Part of the novel's reputation is based on its expression of postmodern literary concerns through thematic focus on metafiction, Marxist criticism and feminism. And he offered three alternative endings for the novel, one Victorian and two modern, with each one suggesting altogether different fates for the two main characters. The readers will face a trinity of possible conclusions according to the narrative.

Metafiction is a narrative technique and genre of fiction in which the central focus is on the nature of fiction itself or on the way in which fiction establishes and asserts its meaning. Metafiction deals, often playfully and self-referentially, with the writing of fiction or its conventions.

Chapter 55

(Excerpt)

...

For a while his traveling companion took no notice of the sleeping Charles. But as the chin sank deeper and deeper—Charles had taken the precaution of removing his hat—the prophet-bearded man[1] began to stare at him, safe in the knowledge that his curiosity would not be surprised.

His look was peculiar: sizing, ruminative, more than a shade disapproving, as if he knew very well what sort of man this was (as Charles had believed to see very well what sort of man he was) and did not much like the knowledge or the species. It was true that, unobserved, he looked a little less frigid and authoritarian a person; but there remained about his features an unpleasant aura of self-confidence—or if not quite confidence in self, at least a confidence in his judgment of others, of how much he could get out of them, expect from them, tax them.

A stare of a minute or so's duration, of this kind, might have been explicable. Train journeys are boring; it is amusing to spy on strangers; and so on. But this stare, which became positively cannibalistic in its intensity, lasted far longer than a minute. It lasted beyond Taunton[2], though it was briefly interrupted there when the noise on the platform made Charles wake for a few moments. But when he sank back into his slumbers, the eyes

1 The bearded man: Here the man refers to the writer himself. He put himself as a character in the story.

2 Taunton: the county town of Somerset, England

fastened on him again in the same leech-like manner.

You may one day come under a similar gaze. And you may—in the less reserved context of our own century—be aware of it. The intent watcher will not wait till you are asleep. It will no doubt suggest something unpleasant, some kind of devious sexual approach ... a desire to know you in a way you do not want to be known by a stranger. In my experience there is only one profession that gives that particular look, with its bizarre blend of the inquisitive and the magistral; of the ironic and the soliciting.

Now could I use you?

Now what could I do with you?

It is precisely, it has always seemed to me, the look an omnipotent god—if there were such an absurd thing—should be shown to have. Not at all what we think of as a divine look; but one of a distinctly mean and dubious (as the theoreticians of the nouveau roman have pointed out) moral quality. I see this with particular clarity on the face, only too familiar to me, of the bearded man who stares at Charles. And I will keep up the pretense no longer.

Now the question I am asking, as I stare at Charles, is not quite the same as the two above. But rather, what the devil am I going to do with you? I have already thought of ending Charles's career here and now; of leaving him for eternity on his way to London. But the conventions of Victorian fiction allow, allowed no place for the open, the inconclusive ending; and I preached earlier of the freedom characters must be given. My problem is simple—what Charles wants is clear? It is indeed. But what the protagonist wants is not so clear; and I am not at all sure where she is at the moment. Of course if these two were two fragments of real life, instead of two figments of my imagination, the issue of the dilemma is obvious: the one want combats the other want, and fails or succeeds, as the actuality may be. Fiction usually pretends to conform to the reality: the writer puts the conflicting wants in the ring and then describes the fight—but in fact fixes the fight, letting that want he himself favors win. And we judge writers of fiction both by the skill they show in fixing the fights (in other words, in persuading us that they were not fixed) and by the kind of fighter they fix in favor of: the good one, the tragic one, the evil one, the funny one, and so on.

But the chief argument for fight-fixing is to show one's readers what one thinks of the world around one—whether one is a pessimist, an optimist, what you will. I have pretended to slip back into 1867; but of course that year is in reality a century past. It is futile to show optimism or pessimism, or anything else about it, because we know what has happened since.

So I continue to stare at Charles and see no reason this time for fixing the fight upon which he is about to engage. That leaves me with two alternatives. I let the fight proceed and take no more than a recording part in it; or I take both sides in it. I stare at that vaguely effete but not completely futile face. And as we near London, I think I see a solution; that is, I see the dilemma is false. The only way I can take no part in the fight is to show two versions of it. That leaves me with only one problem: I cannot give both versions at once, yet whichever is the second will seem, so strong is the tyranny of the last chapter, the final, the "real" version.

I take my purse from the pocket of my frock coat, I extract a florin, I rest it on my right thumbnail, I flick it, spinning, two feet into the air and catch it in my left hand.

So be it. And I am suddenly aware that Charles has opened his eyes and is looking at me. There is something more than disapproval in his eyes now; he perceives I am either a gambler or mentally deranged. I return his disapproval, and my florin to my purse. He picks up his hat, brushes some invisible speck of dirt (a surrogate for myself) from its nap and places it on his head.

We draw under one of the great cast-iron beams that support the roof of Paddington station[1]. We arrive, he steps down to the platform, beckoning to a porter. In a few moments, having given his instructions, he turns. The bearded man has disappeared in the throng.

1 Paddington station: It is located on Praed Street in the Paddington area, which is also known as London Paddington, a central London railway terminus and London Underground station complex.

QUESTIONS

1 Who is the prophet-bearded man?
2 Where does the story take place?
3 Who asks the questions "Now could I use you? Now what could I do with you?"
4 What has happened between Charles and the bearded man on the train?
5 Where does the bearded man disappear?
6 How many characters have been described in this selection?

Doris Lessing
(1919-2013)

INTRODUCTION

Doris Lessing is now widely regarded as one of the most important post-war writers in the world. She was shortlisted for the Booker Prize three times and the nominees for the Nobel Prize in Literature three times. In 2007 she was awarded Nobel Prize in Literature. She earned her living by writing.

Doris Lessing was born just after the First World War in Iran. Her father was a captain in the British Army and ended his military service when she was five years old. Then the family moved to a farm in Rhodesia in Southern Africa. She was influenced by the important trends of thought in the 20th century, such as Freudianism, Marxism and existentialism. She became a Communist when she grew up. Lessing once worked as nursemaid, telephone operator, typist and journalist. She married twice and moved to London in 1949. In August 1991, she received an honorary title of Distinguished Fellow in Literature in the School of English and American Studies conferred by University of East Anglia. In June 1995, she received an Honorary Degree from Harvard University.

Doris Lessing was a prolific writer, who wrote 36 novels and 16 collections of short novels ranging in style from realistic novels to science fiction. Besides, she wrote 9 collections of non-fiction, and some short stories and plays. Her many novels and short stories are set either in Southern Africa or in England. Many of her characters are political activists of the left and women. Her politics of gender lead to her adoption by the feminist movement. Her literary career can be divided into three periods: Period I: 1950s-1970s; Period II: 1970s-1980s; Period III: since 1980s.

From the 1950s to about the 1970s, the most of her novels were realistic both inside and outside. *The Grass is Singing* (1959) is her first famous novel. Her five-novel sequence with the general title *Children of Violence* (1952-1969) tells a story about Martha Quest, the heroine, who tries to move away from the old ideas of the society in which she was brought up and wants to live her life according to her own beliefs. The quintet combines elements of psychological autobiography with powerful exploration of the relationship between black and white in southern Africa.

***The Golden Notebook* (1962)** is considered her masterpiece and also a milestone in feminist literature. The novel is a powerful attempt to write honestly about women's lives and beliefs and the pressures that political and social events in twentieth-century life and society put on them. The outside world and the people in it are often seen as unfriendly and wishing to hurt the female characters—the men in the novel often hurt and damage the women because they themselves are weak. The novel explores the sexual problems of an independent woman in a man's world with frankness and the political conscience of an ex-Communist. It consists of frame-stories about the lives of Molly and Anna Wulf, entitled *Free Woman*, with excerpts from Anna's four notebooks.

From the end of the 1970s to about the 1980s, Lessing turned to science fiction. In her series of novels with the general title *Canopus in Argos: Archives,* she draws on her reading of the Old and New Testaments, the Apocrypha, and the Koran and borrows conventions from science fiction to describe the efforts of a superhuman, extraterrestrial race to guide human history.

Since the 1980s, she came back to social analysis. Her last novels are *The Cleft* (2007), *Alfred and Emily* (2008) and *Adore* (2013).

SELECTED READING

The Cleft (2007)

Overview

In the novel, the history of human creation is retold by a Roman historian. The story he relates is the little-known saga of the Clefts, an ancient community of women with no knowledge nor need for men. Childbirth was controlled through the cycles of the moon, and only female offspring were born until a cleft gave birth to a male child, whom the clefts called "monster" and killed him. But more "monsters" were born one after another, so that the clefts left them on a rock to die. Eagles saw the dying babies and carried them into a nearby valley where they were suckled by deer. The male children gradually grew older and formed a tribe. At last the two tribes came into contact with each other.

In the novel Lessing explores how men and women, how similar and yet thoroughly distinct creatures, manage to live side by side in the world and how the specifics of gender affect every aspect of our existence. The following selection is from the beginning part of the novel.

(Excerpt)

You want to know about me? Very well, then. My name is Maire. There is always someone called Maire. I was born into the family of Cleft Watchers, like my mother and like her mother—these words are new. If everyone gives birth, as soon as they are old enough, everyone is a mother, and you don't have to say Mother. The Cleft Watchers are the most important family. We have to watch The Cleft. When the moon is at its biggest and brightest we climb up to above The Cleft where the red flowers grow, and we cut them, so there is a lot of red, and we let the water flow from the spring up there, and the water flushes the flowers down through The Cleft, from top to bottom, and we all have our blood flow. That is, all who are not going to give birth. Very well, have it your way, the moon's rays make the blood flow, not the red running down through The Cleft. But we *know* that if we don't cut the red flowers—they are small and soft like the blisters on seaweed, and they bleed red if you crush them—if we don't do that, we will not have our flow.

The Cleft is that rock there, which isn't the entrance to a cave, it is blind, and it is the most important thing in our lives. It has always been so. We are The Cleft[1], The Cleft is us, and we have always made sure it is kept free of saplings that might grow into trees, free of bushes. It is a clean cut down through the rock and under it is a deep hole. Every year when the sun touches the top of that mountain there, it is always the cold time, and we have killed one of us, and thrown the body down from the top of The Cleft into the hole. You say you have counted the bones, but I don't see how you can have, when some of the bones are dust by now. You say if a body and its bones has been thrown down every year, it is not so difficult to work out how long it has been going on. Well, if that is what you think is important...

No, I cannot say how it started. That isn't in our story.

The old Shes[2] must have known something.

We never called them that before the Monsters began being born. Why should we? We only had Shes, didn't we, only Clefts, and as for *old*, we didn't think like that. People were born, they lived for a time, unless they drowned swimming or had an accident or were chosen to be thrown into The Cleft. When they died they were put out on the Killing Rock.

---

1 The Cleft: The women in the tribe call themselves "Cleft," apparently naming after The Cleft, a huge stone which resembles female vagina.

2 Shes: Here "she" is used as a noun, referring to the woman of this female tribe.

...

Then a new thing began. When a Monster[1] was born, the young ones pretended to throw it away into the waves, but they went far away so they could not be seen, and knew that the babe's crying would fetch an eagle. Then they laid the babe down on the cliff and watched while the eagle swept down and took it. By then as many Monsters were being born as Clefts, the ones like us, the ones like you.

Have you ever thought how strange it is that you have nipples on those flat places in front there? You can't call them breasts, can you? Why have nipples at all when they aren't good for anything? You can't feed a babe with them, they are useless.

Yes, I am sure you have thought, because you are always noticing things and asking questions. Well, what is your reply, then?

Next, an Old She said we should keep one of the Monsters, one of you, and let it grow and see if it was fit for anything.

QUESTIONS

1 What kind of family was the narrator born in?
2 Where did the ancient women live?
3 What makes the women pregnant?
4 What is the Monster in the story?
5 How did the Clefts deal with the Monsters?
6 How did the eagles do when the babes were thrown on the cliff?
7 What are the nipples of the Monsters in the eyes of the Clefts?

1 Monster: The male baby is called "monster" by the Clefts because he is different from the clefts in physiology.

David Lodge
(1935-)

INTRODUCTION

David Lodge is an English author and literary critic, a Professor of English Literature at the University of Birmingham until 1987. He is best known for his novels satirising academic life, particularly the "Campus Trilogy": *Changing Places: A Tale of Two Campuses* (1975), *Small World: An Academic Romance* (1984), and *Nice Work* (1988). David Lodge is a Fellow of the Royal Society of Literature and was Chairman of the Judges for the Booker Prize for Fiction in 1989. Lodge has enjoyed an unusual dual status in English literary life over the past four decades, a leading comic novelist and one of the foremost literary critics of his generation. He is the fellow of the Royal Society of Literature. In 1998, Lodge was appointed CBE for his services to literature.

David Lodge was born in 1935 in South East London. His father was a professional musician and his mother, Mrs. Lodge, was an Irish-Belgian Catholic. Lodge was educated at a Catholic school and studied English at University College London (UCL) from 1952 to 1955 for his B.A. (Honours). And then he spent two years satisfying his National Service requirement in the Royal Armoured Corps. In 1957 he returned to UCL, and wrote a 700-page M.A. thesis on "Catholic Fiction since the Oxford Movement," receiving an M.A. in 1959. In 1960, he obtained a job as a lecturer at the University of Birmingham. It was in Birmingham that he met Malcolm Bradbury with whom he cooperated on two comic revues.

In 1964, he won a Harkness Travelling Scholarship which enabled him to travel in America whilst completing his first comic novel, *The British Museum Is Falling Down*. As a Harkness Fellow in the United States (1964-1965), he became a visiting professor at the University of California, Berkeley. In 1987 he retired from full-time teaching to concentrate on writing. He has produced fifteen novels and twelve volumes of critical analysis, reviews and essays. Two of Lodge's recent novels are *Author, Author* (2004) and *A Man of Parts* (2011). As a scholar, he is the author of numerous works of literary criticism, mainly about the English and American novel, and literary theory, such as *The Art of Fiction* (1992), *Modern Criticism and Theory: A Reader* (1992), *Consciousness and the Novel* (2002), *Lives in Writing* (2014). David Lodge is also a successful playwright and screenwriter, and has adapted both his own work and other writers' novels for television.

SELECTED READING

Small World

Overview

Small World: An Academic Romance (1984), the second novel of Lodge's "Campus Trilogy, develops Zapp and Swallow's story. Lodge used the theories of critics such as Roman Jakobson and Jacques Derrida in *Changing Places* and *Small World*. This may be Lodge's best book; it is certainly one of his best known, in part because it was the first to be made into a television program. Zapp and Swallow, together with other scholars, have involved in conference-attending and career-building. The explanation Lodge provides is that the "modern conference resembles the pilgrimage of medieval Christendom in that it allows the participants to indulge themselves in all the pleasures and diversions of travel while appearing to be austerely bent on self-improvement."

Prologue

When April with its sweet showers has pierced the drought of March to the root, and bathed every vein of earth with that liquid by whose power the flowers are engendered, when the zephyr, too, with its dulcet breath, has breathed life into the tender new shoots in every copse and on every heath, and the young sun has run half his course in the sign of the Ram, and the little birds that sleep all night with their eyes open give song (so Nature prompts them in their hearts), then, as the poet Geoffrey Chaucer observed many years ago, folk long to go on pilgrimages[1]. Only, these days, professional people call them conferences.

The modern conference resembles the pilgrimage of medieval Christendom in that it allows the participants to indulge themselves in all the pleasures and diversions of travel while appearing to be austerely bent on self-improvement. To be sure, there are certain penitential exercises to be performed—the presentation of a paper, perhaps, and certainly listening to the papers of others. But with this excuse you journey to new and interesting

1 This paragraph is the allusion of Chaucer's Prologue in the *Canterbury Tales*.

places, meet new and interesting people, and form new and interesting relationships with them; exchange gossip and confidences (for your well-worn stories are fresh to them, and vice versa); eat, drink and make merry in their company every evening; and yet, at the end of it all, return home with an enhanced reputation for seriousness of mind. Today's conferees have an additional advantage over the pilgrims of old in that their expenses are usually paid or at least subsidized, by the institution to which they belong, be it a government department, and commercial firm, or, most commonly perhaps, a university.

There are conferences on almost everything these days, including the works of Geoffrey Chaucer. If, like his hero Troilus at the end of *Troilus and Criseyde*[1], he looks down from the eighth sphere of heaven on

This little spot of erthe, that with the se
embraced is

and observes all the frantic traffic around the globe that he and other great writers have set in motion—the jet trails that criss-cross the oceans, making the passage of scholars from one continent to another, their paths converging and intersecting and passing, as they hasten to hotel, country house or ancient seat of learning, there to confer and carouse, so that English and other academic subjects may be kept up—what does Geoffrey Chaucer think?

Probably, like the spirit of Troilus, that chivalrous knight and disillusioned lover, he laughs heartily at the spectacle, and considers himself well out of it. For not all conferences are happy, hedonistic occasions; not all conference venues are luxurious and picturesque; not all Aprils, for that matter, are marked by sweet showers and dulcet breezes.

QUESTIONS

1 What does the first paragraph parody?
2 What does the modern conference resemble?

1 *Troilus and Criseyde*: It is a poem by Geoffrey Chaucer which re-tells the tragic story of the lovers Troilus and Criseyde. Shakespeare was also based in part on the material to write tragedy *Troilus and Cressida*.

3 What kind of advantages does the modern conference have?
4 Why do the scholars take part in today's conferences?
5 Are all conferences happy occasions? Discuss about today's conferences.
6 What is the tone of the Prologue?

EXERCISES OF CHAPTER VIII

I Fill the following blanks.

1 ________ is a literary prize awarded each year since 1969 for the best original ________ novel, written in the ________ language, and published in the ________.

2 George Orwell published two political novels which are ________ and ________.

3 The novelists who became famous after WWII and received Nobel Prize in Literature are ________, ________, ________ and ________;

4 The playwrights after WWII who got Nobel Prize in Literature include ________ and ________.

II Find the relevant match from Column B for each item in Column A.

Column A	Column B
1 ( ) Graham Greene	A. *The Sense of an Ending*
2 ( ) Anthony Burgess	B. *The Heart of the Matter*
3 ( ) Iris Murdoch	C. *The Sea, the Sea*
4 ( ) A.S. Byatt	D. *Last Orders*
5 ( ) Salman Rushdie	E. *Moonlight*
6 ( ) Howard Jacobson	F. *Possession: A Romance*
7 ( ) Julian Barnes	G. *A Clockwork Orange*
8 ( ) Ian McEwan	H. *Midnight's Children*
9 ( ) Harold Pinter	I. *Amsterdam*
10 ( ) Graham Swift	J. *The Finkler Question*

III Choose the best answer for each statement.

1 Who edited *The Oxford Companion to English Literature*?

A. David Lodge B. Margaret Drabble
C. Martin Amis D. Angela Carter

2 Who is the first woman to receive the Booker Prize twice?

A. J.K. Rowling B. A.S. Byatt

C. Iris Murdoch D. Hilary Mary Mantel

3 Sisters-novelists who are now still writing are ______.

A. Charlotte Brontë and Emily Brontë

B. Angela Carter and Iris Murdoch

C. A.S. Byatt and Margaret Drabble

D. Doris Lessing and Hilary Mantel

4 The famous novelists of father and son during 20th century are ______.

A. Howard Jacobson and Julian Barnes

B. Ian McEwan and Salman Rushdie

C. Graham Swift and Anthony Powell

D. Kingsley Amis and Martin Amis

5 What does the play *Waiting for Godot* symbolize?

A. Meaninglessness of existence

B. Happiness for waiting

C. Hope for getting money

D. Persistence of human being

IV Answer the following questions.

1 What does Lodge's *Small World* refer to?

2 What would Lessing in her novel *The Cleft* like to express about gender relationship?

PART II
AMERICAN LITERATURE

CHAPTER IX

American Literature of Romanticism (1820-1860)

General Introduction

Before the independence of the USA in 1783, Benjamin Franklin's (1706-1790) *Autobiography* was very popular and had become one of the classics of American literature. As a member of the Committee of Five, Franklin made fundamental contributions in writing the *Declaration of Independence,* but it was Thomas Jefferson (1743-1826) that was the principal author of the work which became the most representative and world-famous document. In the year of the USA independence, Noah Webster, called the "Father of American Scholarship and Education", declared, "America must be as independent in literature as she is in politics, as famous for the arts as for arms." Then American literature entered one of the most important periods, Romantic Period, which is also called "the American Renaissance" and stretches from the end of the 18th century to the mid-19th century.

Because of the risen level of education, more Americans began to read books, magazines, and newspapers during the 1850s. Therefore, a lot of professional writers appeared who strove to earn a living with a pen. During this period the first wave of feminist movement in the United States began with a host of notable women battling for their rights and asking for social reform. Fiction was a prime component of ladies' magazines. Novels were increasingly popular. The rapid development of American politics, economy, and culture, along with the rise of Romanticism and the prevalence of Transcendentalism, promoted the prosperity of American literature in the 19th century.

Romanticism was a reaction against Neoclassicism. This early 19th-century movement elevated the individual, the passions, and the inner life. It stressed strong emotion, imagination, freedom from classical correctness in art forms, and rebellion against social conventions. American Romanticism represented an attitude toward the realities of man, nature, and society.

American Romantic literature was influenced by Europe. The early appearance of American Romantic Gothic literature owed to Washington Irving (1783-1859), who is regarded as the "father of American literature". He is best known for his short stories Rip Van Winkle (1819) and The Legend of Sleepy Hollow (1820), both of which appeared in his book *The Sketch Book*. Washington Irving, along with James Fenimore Cooper, was among the first American writers to earn the fame in Europe, and Irving encouraged American authors such as Nathaniel Hawthorne, Herman Melville, Henry Wadsworth Longfellow, and Edgar Allan Poe. The famous poets such as Walt Whitman and Emily Dickinson also made contributions to the Romantic literature. American national literature began to form and flourish at their hands.

James Fenimore Cooper (1789-1851) was famous for his best-known five historical novels of the frontier period known as the *Leatherstocking Tales*, including *The Pioneers* (1823), *The Last of the Mohicans* (1826), *The Prairie* (1827), *The Pathfinder* (1840) and *The Deerslayer* (1841). In his series *The Last of the Mohicans* is often regarded as his masterpiece.

Herman Melville (1819-1891) was an American novelist, short story writer, and poet of the American Renaissance period, best known for *Typee* (1846). But his masterpiece was his whaling novel *Moby-Dick* (1851), which is an epic tale of the conflict between man and his fate. In the novel, Captain Ahab's obsessive quest to destroy the great white whale that tore off his leg leads the whaler "Pequod" and its crew to disaster.

The Romantic Movement gave rise to New England Transcendentalism. **Transcendentalism,** which was rooted in English and German Romanticism, was a religious and philosophical movement that was developed during the Romantic era (peaking between 1835-1845) in the Eastern region of the United States as a protest against the general state of spirituality. Among the transcendentalists' core beliefs was the inherent goodness of both people and nature. Transcendentalists were strong believers in the power of the individual. They stressed the role of divinity in nature and the individual's intuition, and exalted feeling over reason. Their beliefs were closely linked with those of the Romantics. Transcendentalists had faith that people were at their best when truly "self-reliant" and independent. The two monumental works of Transcendentalism to express their views are Emerson's *Nature* (1830) and Thoreau's *Walden* (1854).

Ralph Waldo Emerson (1803-1882) was an American essayist and poet who led the transcendentalist movement. His masterpiece was *Nature* (1836). In his essay *Nature*, Emerson put forth the foundation of Transcendentalism and suggested that reality could be understood by studying nature.

Henry David Thoreau (1817-1862) was a leading transcendentalist. He was an American author, poet, philosopher, and naturalist, best known for his book *Walden* (1854), a reflection upon simple living in natural surroundings.

Washington Irving
(1783-1859)

INTRODUCTION

Washington Irving was an American short story writer, essayist, biographer, historian, and diplomat of the early 19th century, who is largely credited as the first American Man of Letters. Irving was humorous and gentle. He was among the first of the moderns to write good history and biography as literary entertainment and is regarded as the Father of the American short stories. It was Irving that introduced the familiar essay from Europe to America.

Irving, the youngest of eleven children, was born and well educated in a very rich family of a New York merchant. He began his reading for the law at 16, but preferred literature then. He travelled to England, Holland, France, Germany, and Italy.

The Sketch Book appeared serially in 1819-1820 and then it was published in volume form in 1820.The book at once had an international success. It is the first great American juvenile literature.

From 1826 to 1829, he was in Spain on diplomatic business. Then from 1829 to 1831, he worked in London as secretary of the American legation for two years. These experiences helped his creation of works. In 1840, he began to write the *Life of George Washington* and finished the last volume in 1859.

As a writer, visitor, and diplomat, his influence abroad was that of a gifted cultural ambassador to let international readers know America. He, with Cooper and William Bryant, made great contributions to the establishment of American literature. Irving was one of the first American writers to earn an international reputation and he encouraged American authors such as Nathaniel Hawthorne, Herman Melville, H.W. Longfellow, and Edgar Allan Poe.

His masterpiece was *The Sketch Book*, which consisted of 34 stories, essays, and sketches. *The Sketch Book* marked the beginning of American Romanticism, in which Rip Van Winkle and The Legend of Sleepy Hollow are two best remembered stories full of humor and rich imagination.

SELECTED READING

Rip Van Winkle

(Excerpt)

Overview

The story of Rip Van Winkle is set in the years before and after the American Revolutionary War. Van Winkle was a good-natured, henpecked Dutch villager and he lived kindly in a pleasant village, at the foot of New York's Kaatskill Mountains. He enjoyed solitary activities in the wilderness and often roamed in the recesses of the mountains in order to escape his wife's nagging. One autumn day, Van Winkle wandered up the mountains with his dog, and he happened to see a group of odd-looking people who were playing ninepins. Rip did not ask who they were or how they knew his name. Instead, he joined them and dank some of their wine which soon led to his sound asleep. When he woke up, he discovered shocking changes. His faithful dog had gone and his gun had rotted and rusted. His beard was a foot long. Van Winkle returned to his village, where he recognized no one. He discovered that his wife had died and that his close friends had fallen in a war or moved away. He was not aware that the American Revolution had taken place. Rip Van Winkle was also disturbed to find another man called Rip Van Winkle, who in fact was his son. However, an old resident recognizes him and Rip's grown daughter took him in. His son and daughter helped him realize that his sleep on the top of the mountain had made him away from the village for at least twenty years. He resumed his usual idleness and lived happily with his children in easy circumstances without worrying about the harsh treatment of his wife. But his tale was taken to heart by other henpecked men in the village. They wished that they had had Rip's good luck and had a sound sleep to escape the hardships of the American Revolution.

...

Poor Rip was at last reduced almost to despair; and his only alternative, to escape from the labor of the farm and the clamor of his wife, was to take gun in hand, and stroll away into the woods. Here he would sometimes seat himself at the foot of a tree, and share the contents of his wallet with Wolf [1],

1 Wolf: name of Rip Van Winkle's dog

with whom he sympathized as a fellow-sufferer in persecution. "Poor Wolf," he would say, "thy mistress leads thee a dog's life of it[1]; but never mind, my lad, whilst I live thou shalt[2] never want a friend to stand by thee!" Wolf would wag his tail, look wistfully in his master's face, and if dogs can feel pity, I verily believe he reciprocated the sentiment with all his heart.

In a long ramble of the kind, on a fine autumnal day, Rip had unconsciously scrambled to one of the highest parts of the Kaatskill mountains. He was after his favorite sport of squirrel-shooting, and the still solitudes had echoed and re-echoed with the reports of his gun. Panting and fatigued, he threw himself, late in the afternoon, on a green knoll, covered with mountain herbage that crowned the brow of a precipice. From an opening between the trees, he could overlook all the lower country for many a mile of rich woodland. He saw at a distance the lordly Hudson, far, far below him, moving on its silent but majestic course, with the reflection of a purple cloud, or the sail of a lagging bark, here and there sleeping on its glassy bosom and at last losing itself in the blue highlands.

On the other side he looked down into a deep mountain glen, wild, lonely, and shagged, the bottom filled with fragments from the impending cliffs, and scarcely lighted by the reflected rays of the setting sun. For some time Rip lay musing on this scene; evening was gradually advancing; the mountains began to throw their long blue shadows over the valleys; he saw that it would be dark long before he could reach the village; and he heaved a heavy sigh when he thought of encountering the terrors of Dame Van Winkle[3].

As he was about to descend, he heard a voice from a distance hallooing: "Rip Van Winkle! Rip Van Winkle!" He looked around, but could see nothing but a crow winging its solitary flight across the mountain. He thought his fancy must have deceived him, and turned again to descend, when he heard the same cry ring through the still evening air, "Rip Van

1 thy mistress leads thee a dog's life of it: your mistress makes you live an unhappy life with many troubles. Here the author uses pun to produce humor.

2 thou shalt: [archaic] you shall

3 Dame Van Winkle: wife of Rip Van Winkle

Winkle! Rip Van Winkle!"—at the same time Wolf bristled up his back, and giving a low growl, skulked to his master's side, looking fearfully down into the glen. Rip now felt a vague apprehension stealing over him; he looked anxiously in the same direction, and perceived a strange figure slowly toiling up the rocks, and bending under the weight of something he carried on his back. He was surprised to see any human being in this lonely and unfrequented place, but supposing it to be some one of the neighborhood in need of his assistance, he hastened down to yield it.

On nearer approach, he was still more surprised at the singularity of the stranger's appearance. He was a short, square-built old fellow, with thick bushy hair, and a grizzled beard. His dress was of the antique Dutch fashion—a cloth jerkin strapped round the waist—several pairs of breeches, the outer one of ample volume, decorated with rows of buttons down the sides, and bunches at the knees. He bore on his shoulders a stout keg, that seemed full of liquor, and made signs for Rip to approach and assist him with the load. Though rather shy and distrustful of this new acquaintance, Rip complied with his usual alacrity; and mutually relieving each other, they clambered up a narrow gully, apparently the dry bed of a mountain torrent. As they ascended, Rip every now and then heard long rolling peals, like distant thunder, that seemed to issue out of a deep ravine, or rather cleft between lofty rocks, toward which their rugged path conducted. He paused for an instant, but supposing it to be the muttering of one of those transient thunder-showers which often take place in the mountain heights, he proceeded. Passing through the ravine, they came to a hollow, like a small amphitheatre, surrounded by perpendicular precipices, over the brinks of which impending trees shot their branches, so that you only caught glimpses of the azure sky, and the bright evening cloud. During the whole time Rip and his companion had labored on in silence; for though the former marvelled greatly what could be the object of carrying a keg of liquor up this wild mountain, yet there was something strange and incomprehensible about the unknown, that inspired awe, and checked familiarity.

On entering the amphitheatre, new objects of wonder presented themselves. On a level spot in the centre was a company of odd-looking personages playing at ninepins[1]. They were dressed in quaint outlandish fashion; some wore short doublets, others jerkins, with long knives in their belts, and most of them had enormous breeches, of similar style with that of the guide's. Their visages, too, were peculiar; one had a large head, broad face, and small piggish eyes; the face of another seemed to consist entirely of nose, and was surmounted by a white sugar-loaf hat, set off with a little red cock's tail. They all had beards, of various shapes and colors. There was one who seemed to be the commander. He was a stout old gentleman, with a weather-beaten countenance; he wore a laced doublet, broad belt and hanger[2], high-crowned hat and feather, red stockings, and high-heeled shoes, with roses[3] in them. The whole group reminded Rip of the figures in an old Flemish painting, in the parlor of Dominie Van Schaick, the village parson, and which had been brought over from Holland at the time of the settlement.

What seemed particularly odd to Rip was, that though these folks were evidently amusing themselves, yet they maintained the gravest faces, the most mysterious silence, and were, withal, the most melancholy party of pleasure he had ever witnessed. Nothing interrupted the stillness of the scene but the noise of the balls, which, whenever they were rolled, echoed along the mountains like rumbling peals of thunder.

As Rip and his companion approached them, they suddenly desisted from their play, and stared at him with such a fixed statue-like gaze, and such strange uncouth, lack-lustre countenances, that his heart turned within him, and his knees smote together. His companion now emptied the contents of the keg into large flagons, and made signs to him to wait upon the company. He obeyed with fear and trembling; they quaffed the liquor in profound silence, and then returned to their game.

By degrees, Rip's awe and apprehension subsided. He even ventured, when no eye was fixed upon him, to taste the beverage which he found had

1 ninepins: It is a game in which a ball is rolled along the floor at nine bottle-shaped blocks of wood in order to knock them down.

2 hanger: a short, curved sword worn at the side

3 roses: rosettes

much of the flavor of excellent Hollands[1]. He was naturally a thirsty soul, and was soon tempted to repeat the draught. One taste provoked another; and he reiterated his visits to the flagon so often, that at length his senses were overpowered, his eyes swam in his head, his head gradually declined, and he fell into a deep sleep.

On waking, he found himself on the green knoll whence he had first seen the old man of the glen. He rubbed his eyes—it was a bright sunny morning. The birds were hopping and twittering among the bushes, and the eagle was wheeling aloft, and breasting the pure mountain breeze. "Surely," thought Rip, "I have not slept here all night." He recalled the occurrences before he fell asleep. The strange man with the keg of liquor—the mountain ravine—the wild retreat among the rocks—the woe-begone party at ninepins—the flagon—"Oh! That flagon! That wicked flagon!" thought Rip—"What excuse shall I make to Dame Van Winkle?"

He looked round for his gun, but in place of the clean well-oiled fowling-piece, he found an old firelock lying by him, the barrel encrusted with rust, the lock falling off, and the stock worm-eaten. He now suspected that the grave roysterers of the mountains had put a trick upon him, and, having dosed him with liquor, had robbed him of his gun. Wolf, too, had disappeared, but he might have strayed away after a squirrel or partridge. He whistled after him and shouted his name, but all in vain; the echoes repeated his whistle and shout, but no dog was to be seen.

He determined to revisit the scene of the last evening's gambol, and if he met with any of the party, to demand his dog and gun. As he rose to walk, he found himself stiff in the joints, and wanting in his usual activity. "These mountain beds do not agree with me," thought Rip, "and if this frolic, should lay me up with a fit of the rheumatism, I shall have a blessed time with Dame Van Winkle." With some difficulty he got down into the glen: he found the gully up which he and his companion had ascended the preceding evening; but to his astonishment a mountain stream was now foaming down it, leaping from rock to rock, and filling the glen with babbling murmurs.

1 Hollands: a Dutch gin long famous for excellence

He, however, made shift to scramble up its sides, working his toilsome way through thickets of birch, sassafras, and witch-hazel; and sometimes tripped up or entangled by the wild grape vines that twisted their coils and tendrils from tree to tree, and spread a kind of network in his path.

At length he reached to where the ravine had opened through the cliffs to the amphitheatre; but no traces of such opening remained. The rocks presented a high impenetrable wall, over which the torrent came tumbling in a sheet of feathery foam, and fell into a broad deep basin, black from the shadows of the surrounding forest. Here, then, poor Rip was brought to a stand. He again called and whistled after his dog; he was only answered by the cawing of a flock of idle crows, sporting high in the air about a dry tree that overhung a sunny precipice; and who, secure in their elevation, seemed to look down and scoff at the poor man's perplexities. What was to be done? The morning was passing away, and Rip felt famished for want of his breakfast. He grieved to give up his dog and gun; he dreaded to meet his wife; but it would not do to starve among the mountains. He shook his head, shouldered the rusty firelock, and, with a heart full of trouble and anxiety, turned his steps homeward.

As he approached the village, he met a number of people, but none whom he knew, which somewhat surprised him, for he had thought himself acquainted with every one in the country round. Their dress, too, was of a different fashion from that to which he was accustomed. They all stared at him with equal marks of surprise, and whenever they cast eyes upon him, invariably stroked their chins. The constant recurrence of this gesture, induced Rip, involuntarily, to do, the same, when, to his astonishment, he found his beard had grown a foot long!

He had now entered the skirts of the village. A troop of strange children ran at his heels, hooting after him, and pointing at his gray beard. The dogs, too, not one of which he recognized for an old acquaintance, barked at him as he passed. The very village was altered: it was larger and more populous. There were rows of houses which he had never seen before, and those which had been his familiar haunts had disappeared. Strange names were over the doors—strange faces at the windows—everything was strange. His mind now misgave him; he began to doubt whether both he and the world around him were not bewitched. Surely this was his native village, which he had left but a day before. There stood the Kaatskill mountains—there ran the silver Hudson at a distance—there was every hill and dale precisely as it had always been—Rip was sorely perplexed—"That flagon last night," thought he, "has addled my poor head sadly!"

It was with some difficulty that he found the way to his own house, which he approached with silent awe, expecting every moment to hear the shrill voice of Dame Van Winkle. He found the house gone to decay—the roof had fallen in, the windows shattered, and the doors off the hinges. A half-starved dog that looked like Wolf, was skulking about it. Rip called him by name, but the cur snarled, showed his teeth, and passed on. This was an unkind cut indeed.—"My very dog," sighed poor Rip, "has forgotten me!"

He entered the house, which, to tell the truth, Dame Van Winkle had always kept in neat order. It was empty, forlorn, and apparently abandoned. This desolateness overcame all his connubial fears—he called loudly for his wife and children—the lonely chambers rang for a moment with his voice, and then all again was silence.

He now hurried forth, and hastened to his old resort, the village inn—but it too was gone. A large rickety wooden building stood in its place, with great gaping windows, some of them broken, and mended with old hats and petticoats, and over the door was painted, "The Union Hotel, by Jonathan Doolittle." Instead of the great tree that used to shelter the quiet little Dutch inn of yore[1], there now was reared a tall naked pole, with something on the top that looked like a red nightcap, and from it was fluttering a flag, on which was a singular assemblage of stars and stripes—all this was strange and incomprehensible. He recognized on the sign, however, the ruby face of King George[2], under which he had smoked so many a peaceful pipe, but even this was singularly metamorphosed. The red coat[3] was changed for

1 of yore: in the old days
2 King George: King George the Third
3 red coat: uniform of the British Army

one of blue and buff[1], a sword was held in the hand instead of a sceptre, the head was decorated with a cocked hat, and underneath was painted in large characters, "GENERAL WASHINGTON."

There was, as usual, a crowd of folk about the door, but none that Rip recollected. The very character of the people seemed changed. There was a busy, bustling, disputatious tone about it, instead of the accustomed phlegm and drowsy tranquillity. He looked in vain for the sage Nicholas Vedder, with his broad face, double chin, and fair long pipe, uttering clouds of tobacco-smoke, instead of idle speeches; or Van Bummel, the schoolmaster, doling forth the contents of an ancient newspaper. In place of these, a lean, bilious-looking fellow, with his pockets full of handbills, was haranguing, vehemently about rights of citizens-elections—members of Congress—liberty—Bunker's hill[2]—heroes of seventy-six—and other words, which were a perfect Babylonish jargon to the bewildered Van Winkle.

The appearance of Rip, with his long, grizzled beard, his rusty fowling-piece, his uncouth dress, and the army of women and children at his heels, soon attracted the attention of the tavern politicians. They crowded round him, eying him from head to foot, with great curiosity. The orator bustled up to him, and, drawing him partly aside, inquired, "on which side he voted?" Rip stared in vacant stupidity. Another short but busy little fellow pulled him by the arm, and rising on tiptoe, inquired in his ear, "whether he was Federal or Democrat[3]." Rip was equally at a loss to comprehend the question; when a knowing, self-important old gentleman, in a sharp cocked hat, made his way through the crowd, putting them to the right and left with his elbows as he passed, and planting himself before Van Winkle, with one arm akimbo, the other resting on his cane, his keen eyes and sharp hat penetrating, as it were, into his very soul, demanded in an austere tone, "What brought him to the election with a gun on his shoulder, and a mob at his heels; and whether he meant to breed a riot in the village?"

"Alas! Gentlemen," cried Rip, somewhat dismayed, "I am a poor, quiet

1 blue and buff: uniform of the American army
2 Bunker's hill: a hill near Boston, where the first battle of the American War of Independence took place
3 Federal or Democrat: the earliest American political parties

man, a native of the place, and a loyal subject of the King, God bless him!"

Here a general shout burst from the bystanders—"A Tory! A Tory! A spy! A refugee! Hustle him! Away with him!" It was with great difficulty that the self-important man in the cocked hat restored order; and having assumed a tenfold austerity of brow, demanded again of the unknown culprit, what he came there for, and whom he was seeking. The poor man humbly assured him that he meant no harm, but merely came there in search of some of his neighbors, who used to keep about the tavern.

"Well—who are they?—name them."

Rip bethought himself a moment, and inquired, "Where's Nicholas Vedder?"

There was a silence for a little while, when an old man replied, in a thin, piping voice, "Nicholas Vedder? Why, he is dead and gone these eighteen years! There was a wooden tombstone in the churchyard that used to tell all about him, but that's rotten and gone too."

"Where's Brom Dutcher?"

"Oh, he went off to the army in the beginning of the war; some say he was killed at the storming of Stony-Point[1]—others say he was drowned in a squall at the foot of Antony's Nose[2]. I don't know—he never came back again."

"Where's Van Bummel, the schoolmaster?"

"He went off to the wars, too; was a great militia general, and is now in Congress."

Rip's heart died away, at hearing of these sad changes in his home and friends, and finding himself thus alone in the world. Every answer puzzled him too, by treating of such enormous lapses of time, and of matters which he could not understand: war—Congress—Stony-Point; —he had no courage to ask after any more friends, but cried out in despair, "Does nobody here know Rip Van Winkle?"

"Oh, Rip Van Winkle!" exclaimed two or three. "Oh, to be sure! That's

1 Stony-Point: a famous strategic headland on the Hudson below West Point

2 Antony's Nose: a mountain near West Point

Rip Van Winkle yonder, leaning against the tree."

Rip looked, and beheld a precise counterpart of himself as he went up the mountain; apparently as lazy, and certainly as ragged. The poor fellow was now completely confounded. He doubted his own identity, and whether he was himself or another man. In the midst of his bewilderment, the man in the cocked hat demanded who he was, and what was his name?

"God knows!" exclaimed he at his wit's end; "I'm not myself—I'm somebody else—that's me yonder-no—that's somebody else, got into my shoes—I was myself last night, but I fell asleep on the mountain, and they've changed my gun, and everything's changed, and I'm changed, and I can't tell what's my name, or who I am!"

The bystanders began now to look at each other, nod, wink significantly, and tap their fingers against their foreheads. There was a whisper, also, about securing the gun, and keeping the old fellow from doing mischief; at the very suggestion of which, the self-important man with the cocked hat retired with some precipitation. At this critical moment a fresh, comely woman pressed through the throng to get a peep at the graybearded man. She had a chubby child in her arms, which, frightened at his looks, began to cry. "Hush, Rip," cried she, "hush, you little fool; the old man won't hurt you." The name of the child, the air of the mother, the tone of her voice, all awakened a train of recollections in his mind.

"What is your name, my good woman?" asked he.

"Judith Cardenier."

"And your father's name?"

"Ah, poor man, Rip Van Winkle was his name, but it's twenty years since he went away from home with his gun, and never has been heard of since, —his dog came home without him; but whether he shot himself, or was carried away by the Indians, nobody can tell. I was then but a little girl."

Rip had but one more question to ask; but he put it with a faltering voice:

"Where's your mother?"

"Oh, she too had died but a short time since; she broke a blood-vessel in a fit of passion at a New-England pedlar."

There was a drop of comfort, at least, in this intelligence. The honest man could contain himself no longer. He caught his daughter and her child in his arms. "I am your father!" cried he—"Young Rip Van Winkle once—old Rip Van Winkle now—Does nobody know poor Rip Van Winkle!"

All stood amazed, until an old woman, tottering out from among the crowd, put her hand to her brow, and peering under it in his face for a moment exclaimed, "Sure enough! It is Rip Van Winkle—it is himself. Welcome home again, old neighbor. Why, where have you been these twenty long years?"

Rip's story was soon told, for the whole twenty years had been to him but as one night. The neighbors stared when they heard it; some were seen to wink at each other, and put their tongues in their cheeks; and the self-important man in the cocked hat, who, when the alarm was over, had returned to the field, screwed down the corners of his mouth, and shook his head—upon which there was a general shaking of the head throughout the assemblage.

It was determined, however, to take the opinion of old Peter Vanderdonk, who was seen slowly advancing up the road. He was a descendant of the historian of that name, who wrote one of the earliest accounts of the province. Peter was the most ancient inhabitant of the village, and well versed in all the wonderful events and traditions of the neighborhood. He recollected Rip at once, and corroborated his story in the most satisfactory manner. He assured the company that it was a fact, handed down from his ancestor, the historian, that the Kaatskill mountains had always been haunted by strange beings. That it was affirmed that the great Hendrick Hudson[1], the first discoverer of the river and country, kept a kind of vigil there every twenty years, with his crew of the Halfmoon[2]; being permitted in this way to revisit the scenes of his enterprise, and keep a guardian eye upon the river and the great city called by his name. That his

1 Hendrick Hudson: Henry Hudson, an English navigator, who explored the new coast of North America
2 the Halfmoon: It refers to the ship Henry Hudson once used to explore.

father had once seen them in their old Dutch dresses playing at ninepins in the hollow of the mountain; and that he himself had heard, one summer afternoon, the sound of their balls, like distant peals of thunder.

To make a long story short, the company broke up, and returned to the more important concerns of the election. Rip's daughter took him home to live with her; she had a snug, well-furnished house, and a stout cheery farmer for a husband, whom Rip recollected for one of the urchins that used to climb upon his back. As to Rip's son and heir, who was the ditto of himself [1], seen leaning against the tree, he was employed to work on the farm; but evinced a hereditary disposition to attend to any thing else but his business.

Rip now resumed his old walks and habits; he soon found many of his former cronies, though all rather the worse for the wear and tear of time; and preferred making friends among the rising generation, with whom be soon grew into great favor.

Having nothing to do at home, and being arrived at that happy age when a man can be idle with impunity, he took his place once more on the bench, at the inn door, and was reverenced as one of the patriarchs of the village, and a chronicle of the old times "before the war." It was some time before he could get into the regular track of gossip, or could be made to comprehend the strange events that had taken place during his torpor. How that there had been a revolutionary war—that the country had thrown off the yoke of old England—and that, instead of being a subject to his Majesty George the Third, he was now a free citizen of the United States. Rip, in fact, was no politician; the changes of states and empires made but little impression on him; but there was one species of despotism under which he had long groaned, and that was—petticoat government[2]. Happily, that was at an end; he had got his neck out of the yoke of matrimony[3], and could go in and out whenever he pleased, without dreading the tyranny of Dame Van Winkle. Whenever her name was mentioned, however, he shook his head,

1 ditto of himself: the same with himself

2 petticoat government: The phrase refers to women running government or domestic affairs.

3 the yoke of matrimony: yoke, a frame encircled the necks of a pair of oxen or other draft animals working together to carry a load in two equal portions. Here it refers to the confine of freedom.

shrugged his shoulders, and cast up his eyes; which might pass either for an expression of resignation to his fate, or joy at his deliverance.

He used to tell his story to every stranger that arrived at Mr. Doolittle's hotel. He was observed, at first, to vary on some points every time he told it, which was, doubtless, owing to his having so recently awaked. It at last settled down precisely to the tale I have related, and not a man, woman, or child in the neighborhood, but knew it by heart. Some always pretended to doubt the reality of it, and insisted that Rip had been out of his head, and that this was one point on which he always remained flighty. The old Dutch inhabitants, however, almost universally gave it full credit. Even to this day, they never hear a thunder-storm of a summer afternoon about the Kaatskill, but they say Hendrick Hudson and his crew are at their game of ninepins; and it is a common wish of all henpecked husbands in the neighborhood, when life hangs heavy on their hands, that they might have a quieting draught out of Rip Van Winkle's flagon.

QUESTIONS

1 Why would Rip Van Winkle like to go out?
2 What do you think of the dog, Wolf?
3 What did Rip hear and who did he meet in the mountain?
4 What happened to Rip in the mountain then?
5 What did Rip see on waking?
6 What did Rip see when he came home?

Nathaniel Hawthorne
(1804-1864)

INTRODUCTION

Nathaniel Hawthorne was an American novelist and short-story writer. His novels concern moral or ethical problems. He is considered as the first great American writer of fiction, great democratic writer of the 19th century in America, and the master of psychological fiction.

Hawthorne was born in Salem, Massachusetts in 1804. His birthplace has been open to the public. His father was a sea captain who had died of yellow fever in Dutch when the boy was only four years old. Hawthorne had two sisters, but they lived in almost complete isolation from each other.

Hawthorne entered Bowdoin College in Maine, where he met two friends who had great impact upon his life. They were Henry Wadsworth Longfellow, who became a famous poet, and Franklin Pierce, who became the 14th President of the United States.

After college, Hawthorne published his first work, an anonymous novel titled *Fanshawe*, in 1828. He published several short stories in periodicals, which he collected in 1837 as *Twice-Told Tales*. During this period, he once worked as an editor for a magazine in Boston, then at the customs office. In 1841, he stayed for a few months at Brook Farm. After marrying Sophia Peabody, a transcendentalist, in 1842, Hawthorne left this farm and settled at the Old Manse. In 1846, his *Mosses from an Old Manse,* a short story collection, was first published. *The Scarlet Letter,* his masterpiece, was published in 1850, followed by other successful novels, *The House of the Seven Gables* (1851), *The Blithedale Romance* (1852), and *The Marble Faun* (1860). When his college friend Franklin Pierce became President, Hawthorne was appointed to a consular position in Liverpool in England in 1853. Then he spent the next six years in Europe.

Hawthorne gathered his material by observing and listening to others. He roamed around the town, moving among the old sailors, farmers, and the old wives of the town to get material for his writing. He also read the books of Puritan world.

Hawthorne shares with Allan Poe the master of short stories. Like Poe, Hawthorne often used grotesque or fantastic events in his fiction, but Hawthorne's works are broader in range and have more depth of thought. Hawthorne's unique gift to create strongly symbolic stories touches the deepest roots of man's moral nature. The finest example is the recreation of Puritan Boston, *The Scarlet Letter*. His ability to create vivid and symbolic images is also embodied in his short stories, such as *The Minister's Black Veil* and *Young Goodman Brown*.

SELECTED READING

The Scarlet Letter

Overview

Many of Hawthorne's stories are set in Puritan New England in the 17th century and *The Scarlet Letter* has become the classic portrayal of Puritan America. It tells of the story of passionate, forbidden love affair between beautiful Hester Prynne and the sensitive, religious young man, Author Dimmesdale. The main character, Hester Prynne, committed adultery. Two years ago, her husband, a scholar much older than she was, sent her on ahead to America. Alone in the small town in Boston, she had an affair and gave birth to a girl child. The Puritans of Boston were angry because she would not reveal her lover's identity. The usual penalty of adultery was death, but the Puritan judges decided to be merciful to her, declaring that her punishment would be to stand for several hours on the scaffold in public holding her infant, Pearl, in her arms. Hester would be wearing on the breast of her dress a piece of scarlet letter "A" for the rest of her life as her punishment for her sin and her secrecy. The scarlet letter "A" is meant to be a symbol of shame, originally a mark of Hester's adulterer; instead it becomes a powerful symbol of identity to Hester and shifts the letter's meaning as time passes. The novel highlights the Calvinistic obsession with morality, sexual repression, guilt and confession, and spiritual salvation.

The novel consists of 24 chapters. The following excerpt is from Chapter 2. As the story opens, a group of Puritan men and women gather in front of the prison waiting for Hester to appear. The conversation among the five Puritan women shows us that they severely criticized Hester for her adultery. The harsh, Puritanical point of view is noted in the unfriendly attitude of the townspeople toward Hester.

Chapter 2

The Market Place

(Excerpt)

...The bright morning sun, therefore, shone on broad shoulders and well-developed busts, and on round and ruddy cheeks, that had ripened in the far-off island[1], and had hardly yet grown paler or thinner in the atmosphere of New England. There was, moreover, a boldness and rotundity of speech among these matrons, as most of them seemed to be, that would startle us at the present day, whether in respect to its purport or its volume of tone.

"Goodwives," said a hard-featured dame of fifty, "I'll tell ye[2] a piece of my mind. It would be greatly for the public behoof, if we women, being of mature age and church-members in good repute, should have the handling of such malefactresses as this Hester Prynne. What think ye, gossips? If the hussy stood up for judgment before us five, that are now here in a knot together, would she come off with such a sentence as the worshipful magistrates have awarded? Marry, I trow not![3]"

"People say," said another, "that the Reverend Master Dimmesdale, her godly pastor, takes it very grievously to heart that such a scandal should have come upon his congregation."

"The magistrates are God-fearing gentlemen, but merciful overmuch—that is a truth," added a third autumnal matron. "At the very least, they should have put the brand of a hot iron on Hester Prynne's forehead. Madam Hester would have winced at that, I warrant me. But she—the naughty baggage—little will she care what they put upon the bodice of her gown! Why, look you, she may cover it with a brooch, or such like heathenish adornment, and so walk the streets as brave as ever!"

"Ah, but," interposed, more softly, a young wife, holding a child by the hand, "Let her cover the mark as she will, the pang of it will be always in her heart."

"What do we talk of marks and brands, whether on the bodice of her gown, or the flesh of her forehead?" cried another female, the ugliest as well as the most pitiless of these self-constituted judges. "This woman has brought shame upon us all, and ought to die. Is there not law for it? Truly

1 the far-off island: Here it refers to England.

2 ye: you

3 Marry, I trow not!: Indeed I believe not.

there is, both in the Scripture and the statute-book. Then let the magistrates, who have made it of no effect[1], thank themselves if their own wives and daughters go astray!"

"Mercy on us, goodwife," exclaimed a man in the crowd, "is there no virtue in woman, save what springs from a wholesome fear of the gallows? That is the hardest word yet! Hush, now, gossips! For the lock is turning in the prison-door, and here comes Mistress Prynne herself."

The door of the jail being flung open from within, there appeared, in the first place, like a black shadow emerging into sunshine, the grim and grisly presence of the town-beadle, with a sword by his side, and his staff of office[2] in his hand. This personage prefigured and represented in his aspect the whole dismal severity of the Puritanic code of law, which it was his business to administer in its final and closest application[3] to the offender. Stretching forth the official staff in his left hand, he laid his right upon the shoulder of a young woman, whom he thus drew forward; until, on the threshold of the prison-door, she repelled him, by an action marked with natural dignity and force of character, and stepped into the open air, as if by her own free will. She bore in her arms a child, a baby of some three months old, who winked and turned aside its little face from the too vivid light of day; because its existence, heretofore, had brought it acquainted only with the grey twilight of a dungeon, or other darksome apartment of the prison.

When the young woman—the mother of this child—stood fully revealed before the crowd, it seemed to be her first impulse to clasp the infant closely to her bosom; not so much by an impulse of motherly affection, as that she might thereby conceal a certain token, which was wrought or fastened into her dress. In a moment, however, wisely judging that one token of her shame would but poorly serve to hide another, she took the baby on her arm, and, with a burning blush, and yet a haughty smile, and a glance that would not be abashed, looked around at her townspeople and neighbours. On the breast of her gown, in fine red cloth, surrounded with an

1 who have made it of no effect: The word "it" refers to "the law".
2 staff of office: a pole as a symbol of authority or sign of office
3 closest application: physical application

elaborate embroidery and fantastic flourishes of gold thread, appeared the letter A. It was so artistically done, and with so much fertility and gorgeous luxuriance of fancy, that it had all the effect of a last and fitting decoration to the apparel which she wore; and which was of a splendour in accordance with the taste of the age, but greatly beyond what was allowed by the sumptuary regulations of the colony.

The young woman was tall, with a figure of perfect elegance on a large scale. She had dark and abundant hair, so glossy that it threw off the sunshine with a gleam, and a face which, besides being beautiful from regularity of feature and richness of complexion, had the impressiveness belonging to a marked brow and deep black eyes. She was ladylike, too, after the manner of the feminine gentility of those days; characterised by a certain state and dignity, rather than by the delicate, evanescent, and indescribable grace, which is now recognised as its indication. And never had Hester Prynne appeared more ladylike, in the antique interpretation of the term, than as she issued from the prison. Those who had before known her, and had expected to behold her dimmed and obscured by a disastrous cloud, were astonished, and even startled, to perceive how her beauty shone out, and made a halo of the misfortune and ignominy in which she was enveloped. It may be true, that, to a sensitive observer, there was something exquisitely painful in it. Her attire, which, indeed, she had wrought for the occasion, in prison, and had modelled much after her own fancy, seemed to express the attitude of her spirit, the desperate recklessness of her mood, by its wild and picturesque peculiarity. But the point which drew all eyes, and, as it were, transfigured the wearer—so that both men and women, who had been familiarly acquainted with Hester Prynne, were now impressed as if they beheld her for the first time—was that SCARLET LETTER, so fantastically embroidered and illuminated upon her bosom. It had the effect of a spell, taking her out of the ordinary relations with humanity, and enclosing her in a sphere by herself.

"She hath good skill at her needle, that's certain," remarked one of her female spectators; "but did ever a woman, before this brazen hussy, contrive such a way of showing it! Why, gossips, what is it but to laugh in the faces of our godly magistrates, and make a pride out of what they, worthy gentlemen, meant for a punishment?"

"It were well," muttered the most iron-visaged of the old dames, "if we stripped Madam Hester's rich gown off her dainty shoulders; and as for the red letter, which she hath stitched so curiously, I'll bestow a rag of mine own rheumatic flannel, to make a fitter one!"

"Oh, peace, neighbours, peace!" whispered their youngest companion; "do not let her hear you! Not a stitch in that embroidered letter, but she has felt it in her heart."

The grim beadle now made a gesture with his staff.

"Make way, good people, make way, in the King's name![1]" cried he. "Open a passage; and, I promise ye, Mistress Prynne shall be set where man, woman, and child, may have a fair sight of her brave apparel, from this time till an hour past meridian. A blessing on the righteous Colony of the Massachusetts[2], where iniquity is dragged out into the sunshine! Come along, Madam Hester, and show your scarlet letter in the market-place!"

...

QUESTIONS

1 What were the women's opinions to the punishment of Hester?
2 What were the punishing ways to Hester suggested by the five female spectators?
3 What is the image of the town-beadle?
4 What is the image of Hester Prynne?
5 What does one token refer to and what does another token mean?
6 What does scarlet "A" symbolize?

1 In the King's name: It refers to Charles I. At that time New England was colony of England, so Charles I was called their King.
2 Colony of the Massachusetts: one of the earliest thirteen colonies in New England whose capital was Boston

Edgar Allan Poe
(1809-1849)

INTRODUCTION

Edgar Allan Poe was an American poet, short story writer, editor, and literary critic, best known for his poetry and short stories, particularly his tales of mystery and horror. He is widely regarded as a central figure of Romanticism in the United States. Poe is generally considered a seminal figure in the development of science fiction and the detective story. He was the first well-known American professional writer to try to earn a living through writing alone, resulting in a financially difficult life and career.

He was born as Edgar Poe in Boston, Massachusetts, the child of struggling traveling actors. Poe was orphaned at the age of two when his mother died shortly after his father abandoned the family. Poe was taken in by John Allan, a merchant of Richmond, Virginia. Although Allan never formally adopted him, Poe later added Allan to his own name. Poe was happy with the Allan family only for a brief period; then tension began to develop between Poe and his foster father. He attended the University of Virginia for one semester but left due to lack of money. In 1827, Poe ran away to Boston to make his own way. In the same year, he published an anonymous collection of poems, *Tamerlane and Other Poems*. After a brief stay in the army, Allan helped him to work in West Point, but the discipline there proved to be too harsh for Poe's nature, so that Poe was discharged less than a year later in 1831.

Poe once lived in Baltimore with his father's sister, Mrs. Maria Clemm, and her daughter Virginia. He got a job as an editor, but lost the position because of excessive drinking and inability to meet deadlines. In 1835, Poe, then 26, married his 13-year-old cousin Virginia Clemm. They were married for 11 years until her early death, which might have inspired some of his writing.

From 1837, with his family he set out to try his luck in New York and Philadelphia. His drifted years from 1837 to 1845 were hard in poverty, but he wrote some famous short stories and poems. In 1845, Poe published his poem The Raven and obtained instant success. However, his wife died of tuberculosis two years after its publication. His works received more and more praise in Europe and his influence was especially strong on many French writers. However, Poe's European fame did not benefit him and poverty remained his typical condition. He died in Baltimore on October 7, 1849, only 40. His death remains a mystery and the cause of his death has been variously attributed to alcohol, brain congestion, cholera, drugs, heart disease, rabies, suicide, and tuberculosis, etc.

Now, Poe is widely recognized as the master of horror and mystery because some of his stories convey a sense of terror and mystery, such as The Masque of the Red Death and The Fall of the House of Usher. Poe is also called the father of the detective stories because of the influence of his The Purloined Letter, The Murders in the Rue Morgue, and The Cask of Amontillado.

Poe's poetry has the features of "Beauty is the sole purpose of the poem. Poetry is for pleasure, not for truth". Melancholy is the main tone of his poems. The Raven is his masterpiece. His poems Annabel Lee, The Bells, To Helen are very popular.

SELECTED READING

To Helen

Overview

This poem is believed to have been inspired by the beauty of Mrs. Jane Stith Stanard, the young mother of poet's classmate, Robert Stanard. As Robert's guest at his home in 1823 when the poet was only 14, Poe was greatly taken with the 27-year-old woman. He admitted that "the first purely ideal love of my soul". The lady died in 1824. But she appeared in this poetic work in the figure of Helen, the well-known ancient beauty, with all the adoration of Poe to her.

Helen, thy beauty is to me
    Like those Nicéan[1] barks[2] of yore[3],
That gently, o'er a perfumed sea,
    The weary, way-worn wanderer bore[4]
    To his own native shore.

On desperate seas long wont to[5] roam,
    Thy hyacinth hair, thy classic face,

1 Nicéan: of Nicaea, an ancient city in northwest Asia Minor
2 barks: boats
3 of yore: formerly; of long time ago
4 bore to: was brought to
5 wont to do sth.: in the habit of doing sth

Thy Naiad[1] airs[2] have brought me home
To the glory that was Greece,
And the grandeur that was Rome.

Lo![3] in yon brilliant window-niche
How statue-like I see thee stand,
The agate lamp within thy hand!
Ah, Psyche[4], from the regions which
Are Holy-Land![5]

QUESTIONS

1 What is the allusion in the first stanza?
2 What does "native shore" refer to?
3 Why does the poet mention Greece and Rome in the second stanza?
4 How many beauties have been mentioned? Who are they?
5 What does "Holy-Land" refer to in the third stanza?
6 What is the rhyme scheme in each stanza?

---

1 Naiad: one of the nymphs in Greek mythology, who lived in and presided over brooks, springs, and fountains
2 air: appearsance or manner
3 Lo: look
4 Psyche: goddess in Greek mythology and the name of Cupid's spouse
5 Holy Land: the biblical region of Palestine

Henry Wadsworth Longfellow (1807-1882)

INTRODUCTION

Henry Wadsworth Longfellow is called most beloved American poet of his time. He graduated from Bowdoin College and was Nathaniel Hawthorne's classmate. After spending time in Europe he became a professor at Bowdoin and, later, a professor of modern languages at Harvard. Longfellow received degrees from Cambridge and Oxford, and was given a private audience by Queen Victoria. After his death, Longfellow became the first non-British writer for whom a bust was placed in Poet's Corner of Westminster Abbey in London.

Longfellow wrote many lyric poems and became the most popular American poet of his day. His published poetry shows great versatility, using anapestic and trochaic forms, blank verse, heroic couplets, ballads and sonnets. His representative works include *Voices of the Night* (1839), which was his first major poetry collections, *Ballads and Other Poems* (1842), *Evangeline* (1847), and *The Song of Hiawatha* (1855). His popularity spread throughout Europe as well and his poetry was translated during his lifetime into Italian, French, German, and other languages. One of his poems, A Psalm of Life, was the first American poem to be introduced into China. Longfellow made poetry worth reading and worth writing.

I Shot an Arrow

Overview

This poem is written in a traditional iambic form with the feet *aabb*. In the poem, Longfellow sang the friendship implicitly and skillfully. The arrow and the song in this poem stand for the friendship. When he shot an arrow and breathed a song into the air, he did not expect to find them any more. But many years later, he came across with the arrow and found that his song was always in the heart of his friend. This suggests that the friendship is everlasting.

I shot an arrow in the air,

It fell to earth, I knew not where;
For, so swiftly it flew, the sight
Could not follow it in its flight.

I breathed a song into the air,
It fell to earth, I knew not where;
For who has sight so keen and strong,
That it can follow the flight of song.

Long, long afterward, in an oak
I found the arrow still unbroke;
And the song, from beginning to end,
I found again in the heart of a friend.

QUESTIONS

1 Why did the speaker fail to see the arrow he shot?
2 Why did the speaker lose sight of his song he breathed?
3 When did he find them again?
4 Where did he find the arrow and the song?
5 What do the arrow and the song stand for?
6 What is the theme of the poem?

Walt Whitman
(1819-1892)

INTRODUCTION

Walt Whitman was an American poet, essayist, and journalist. As a humanist, he was part of the transition between Transcendentalism and Realism. Whitman is among the most influential poets in America. His great contribution to American literature was his use of free verse, so he is often called the father of free verse.

Walt Whitman was born in West Hills, Town of Huntington in 1819, and the second of nine children in the family. At age four, Whitman moved with his family from West Hills to Brooklyn. He had very little schooling but read a great deal on his own. Whitman once was a volunteer nurse during the American Civil War.

Whitman's major work, *Leaves of Grass*, was first published in 1855 with his own money. He continued expanding and revising it until his death in 1892. *Leaves of Grass* was Whitman's lifelong work which consistd of 401 poems. This last version was published in 1892 and is referred to as the "deathbed edition". *Leaves of Grass* has been praised as "Democratic Bible" and as American Epic.

Whitman was one of the great innovators in American literature, both in the content and form of his poetry. He was the first American poet to write free verse. **Free verse** is poetry that is written without proper rules about form, rhyme, rhythm, meter, etc. The following poem is a typical example.

To the States

(Selection from *Leaves of Grass*)

To the States or any one of them or any city of the States, Resist much, obey little,
Once unquestioning obedience, once fully enslaved,
Once fully enslaved, no nation, state, city of this earth, ever afterward resumes its liberty.

SELECTED READING

O Captain! My Captain! [1]

Overview

O Captain! My Captain is a masterpiece to mourn the death of President Abraham Lincoln. It is the most outstanding elegy. In the poem, the poet uses the captain to symbolize Lincoln and the USA is represented by the ship. The leader is being conceived as the brave captain of a ship who falls dead on the deck just when the journey is over and victory is won.

O Captain! my Captain! our fearful trip[2] is done,
The ship has weather'd every rack, the prize[3] we sought is won,
The port is near, the bells I hear, the people all exulting,
While follow eyes the steady keel, the vessel grim and daring;
  But O heart! heart! heart!
    O the bleeding drops of red,
      Where on the deck my Captain lies,
        Fallen cold and dead.

O Captain! my Captain! rise up and hear the bells;
Rise up—for you the flag is flung—for you the bugle trills,
For you bouquets and ribbon'd wreaths—for you the shores a-crowding,
For you they call, the swaying mass, their eager faces turning;
  Here Captain! dear father!
    This arm beneath your head!
      It is some dream that on the deck,
        You've fallen cold and dead.

My Captain does not answer, his lips are pale and still,

1 captain: It here refers to President Abraham Lincoln, who was assassinated on April 14, 1865, in the Ford Theatre, Washington, D.C.
2 fearful trip: The trip symbolizes the hardship course of the Civil War.
3 the prize: It refers to the victory of the Civil War.

My father does not feel my arm, he has no pulse nor will,
The ship is anchor'd safe and sound, its voyage closed and done,
From fearful trip the victor ship comes in with object won;
  Exult O shores, and ring O bells!
    But I with mournful tread,
      Walk the deck my Captain lies,
        Fallen cold and dead.

QUESTIONS

1 Why is "Captain" capitalized in the poem?
2 What does "fearful trip" mean here?
3 What does "ship" symbolize in this poem?
4 What does "the prize" mean?
5 What are the possible themes of the poem?
6 What are the images the poet has given?

Emily Dickinson
(1830-1886)

INTRODUCTION

Emily Elizabeth Dickinson was an American female poet. She was a link between her era and the literary sensitivities of the turn of the century. As a writer of great power and beauty, she had no interest in having her poems published and fewer than a dozen of her nearly 1,800 poems were published during her lifetime. However, Dickinson has been ranked as one of America's great poets.

She was born to a successful family and spent her life in Amherst, Massachusetts. Her father was a prominent lawyer and politician who became a member of Congress. She had very close relationship with her family. Dickinson and her sister remained at home and never married. Most of her friendships therefore depended on correspondence. She loved nature and found deep inspiration in the birds, animals, plants, and changing seasons of the New England countryside.

Dickinson and her sister spent seven years at the Amherst Academy, taking classes in English and classical literature, Latin, botany, geology, history, etc. Then she briefly attended the Mount Holyoke Female Seminary for less than a year. Dickinson was certainly the most solitary literary figure of her time. This shy, withdrawn village young lady made time for her writing (she wrote about one poem a day). Miss Dickinson's greatest outpouring of poems occurred in the early 1860s, when she was so isolated and little influenced by the Civil War. She created some of the greatest American poetry of the 19th century and has fascinated the public since the 1950s. After Dickinson's death, her sister, Lavinia Dickinson, kept her promise and burned most of the poet's correspondence. Dickinson left no instructions about the 40 notebooks and loose sheets gathered in a locked chest. Her sister found nearly 1,800 poems that Dickinson had written. Lavinia recognized the poems' worth and became obsessed with seeing them published.

During her lifetime, her published poems were usually altered significantly by the publishers to fit the conventional poetic rules of the time, because her poems were unique for the era in which she wrote, such as short lines, without titles, slant rhyme, unconventional capitalization and punctuation. Emily refused to revise her poems to fit the standards of others. Dickinson complained that the edited punctuation (an added comma and a full stop substitution for the original dash) altered the meaning of the entire poem.

She never used two words when one would do, and combined concrete things with abstract ideas. Many of her poems deal with themes of death and immortality. Her poetry frequently uses humor, puns, irony and satire. Her poems are short, but come out in bursts, many of which are based on a single image or symbol. Dickinson is now considered to be one of the most significant of American poets.

Dickinson's poetry exhibits great intelligence. Her wit shines in the following poems. The titles were added by the editor Franklin for making them convenient to read in 1998.

SELECTED READING

Success

Success is counted sweetest
By those who ne'er succeed.
To comprehend a nectar[1]
Requires sorest need.

Not one of all the purple Host[2]
Who took the Flag to-day
Can tell the definition,
So clear, of Victory,

As he defeated—dying—
On whose forbidden ear
The distant strains of triumph
Burst agonized and clear!

QUESTIONS

1 What is required to "comprehend a nectar" in the first stanza?

1 nectar: the drink of the gods, a symbol of triumph
2 the purple host: people of very high rank. This comes from the fact that purple is the color of robes worn by Roman emperors and Catholic cardinals.

2 Who does "the purple host" refer to?
3 What does the poet convey to us?
4 Do you agree with her idea? Why?

I Died for Beauty

I died for Beauty—but was scarce[1]
Adjusted in the Tomb,
When One who died for Truth, was lain[2]
In an adjoining Room—

He questioned softly "Why I failed"?
"For Beauty," I replied—
"And I—for Truth,—Themself[3] are One;
We Bretheren[4], are," He said—

And so, as Kinsmen, met a Night[5]—
We talked between[6] the Rooms—
Until the Moss had reached our lips—
And covered up—our names—

QUESTIONS

1 What belief does the poet show us in the poem?
2 What are the characteristics in form of the poem?
3 The English famous poet Keats expressed that "Beauty is truth, truth beauty". Do you think this poem is closely related to that?
4 What is your idea about beauty and truth?

---

1 scarce: scarcely
2 lain: Here Emily Dickinson used "lain" for "laid".
3 Themself: They
4 Bretheren: brothers
5 a-night: at night
6 between: across

I'm Nobody

I'm Nobody! Who are you?
Are you—Nobody—Too?
Then there's a pair of us!
Don't tell! They'd advertise, you know!

How dreary—to be—Somebody!
How public—like a Frog—
To tell one's name—the livelong June—
To an admiring Bog!

QUESTIONS

1 What does "Nobody" mean? What does "Somebody" mean?
2 Who are the people of "pair of us" in the poem?
3 What does "they" here refer to?
4 What does "an admiring Bog" mean?
5 What is the image of frog in the poem?
6 Would you like to be "Nobody" or "Somebody"? Explain your idea.

Harriet Beecher Stowe (1811-1896)

INTRODUCTION

Harriet Beecher Stowe (1811-1896, or Mrs. Stowe) was an American abolitionist and author. She is famous for her anti-slavery novel *Uncle Tom's Cabin* (1852). She was born in a famous religious family and she was the seventh of 13 children. Mrs. Stowe attended Hartford Female Seminary founded by her eldest sister Catherine, and four years later became an assistant teacher there. In 1832, Harriet moved to Cincinnati, Ohio to join her father, where she met her husband Calvin Ellis Stowe, an anti-slavery professor.

Mrs. Stowe wrote 30 books, including novels, three travel memoirs, and collections of articles and letters. In June 1851, when she was 40, the first installment of her *Uncle Tom's Cabin* was published in the *National Era,* an anti-slavery paper. She originally used the subtitle "The Man That Was a Thing", but it was soon changed to "Life Among the Lowly". It depicts the harsh life of African Americans under slavery. In 1852, the story appeared in book form and soon set publishing records. The novel was very influential. When she met President Lincoln in 1862, he greeted her by saying, "so you are the little woman who wrote the book that started this Great War." She told her husband, "I had a real funny interview with the President."

SELECTED READING

Uncle Tom's Cabin

Overview

The anti-slavery novel *Uncle Tom's Cabin* was the best-selling novel of the 19th century with an initial print run of 5,000 copies. In less than a year, the book sold 300,000 copies. The story was inspired by the autobiography of Henson, an escaped-slave, and the moral outrage—The Fugitive Slave Law of 1850. Uncle Tom was a kind-hearted and honest black slave belonging to a Kentucky farmer named Arthur Shelby, who decided to sell Tom and Harry, son of a female black slave Eliza, to repay his debt. To stay with her son, Eliza ran away with Harry, reunited with her husband George Harris and the family managed to escape to Canada. On the other side, Tom was not as lucky as Eliza. He was sold first to Augustine St. Clare, a kind gentleman who decided to free Tom but died unexpectedly before he signed the paper, and then to a cruel slave owner Simon Legree. As Tom refused to tell Legree where the runaway slaves hid, Legree ordered his servant to beat Tom to death.

The following excerpt is the opening chapter of the novel. Mr. Shelby is discussing a deal of selling Tom with his guests. Readers can easily notice how black slaves were traded regardless of their willingness and how they were assessed by the white.

(Excerpt)

Late in the afternoon of a chilly day in February, two gentlemen were sitting alone over their wine, in a well-furnished dining parlor, in the town of P—, in Kentucky. There were no servants present, and the gentlemen, with chairs closely approaching, seemed to be discussing some subject with great earnestness.

For convenience sake, we have said, hitherto, two gentlemen. One of the parties, however, when critically examined, did not seem, strictly speaking, to come under the species. He was a short, thick-set man, with coarse, commonplace features, and that swaggering air of pretension which marks a low man who is trying to elbow his way upward in the world. He was much over-dressed, in a gaudy vest of many colors, a blue neckerchief, bedropped gayly with yellow spots, and arranged with a flaunting tie, quite in keeping with the general air of the man. His hands, large and coarse, were plentifully bedecked with rings; and he wore a heavy gold watch-chain, with a bundle of seals of portentous size, and a great variety of colors, attached to it, —which, in the ardor of conversation, he was in the habit of flourishing and jingling with evident satisfaction. His conversation was in free and easy defiance of Murray's Grammar[1], and was garnished at convenient intervals

1 Murray's Grammar: *English Grammar* (1795) by Lindley Murray (1745-1826), who was the most authoritative American grammarian of his day

with various profane expressions, which not even the desire to be graphic in our account shall induce us to transcribe.

His companion, Mr. Shelby, had the appearance of a gentleman; and the arrrangements of the house, and the general air of the housekeeping, indicated easy, and even opulent circumstances. As we before stated, the two were in the midst of an earnest conversation.

"That is the way I should arrange the matter," said Mr. Shelby.

"I can't make trade that way—I positively can't, Mr. Shelby," said the other, holding up a glass of wine between his eye and the light.

"Why, the fact is, Haley, Tom is an uncommon fellow; he is certainly worth that sum anywhere,—steady, honest, capable, manages my whole farm like a clock."

"You mean honest, as niggers go," said Haley, helping himself to a glass of brandy.

"No; I mean, really, Tom is a good, steady, sensible, pious fellow. He got religion at a camp-meeting, four years ago; and I believe he really did get it. I've trusted him, since then, with everything I have,—money, house, horses,—and let him come and go round the country; and I always found him true and square in everything."

"Some folks don't believe there is pious niggers Shelby," said Haley, with a candid flourish of his hand, "but I do. I had a fellow, now, in this yer[1] last lot I took to Orleans—'t was as good as a meetin, now, really, to hear that critter pray; and he was quite gentle and quiet like. He fetched me a good sum, too, for I bought him cheap of a man that was 'bliged to sell out; so I realized six hundred on him. Yes, I consider religion a valeyable[2] thing in a nigger, when it's the genuine article, and no mistake."

"Well, Tom's got the real article, if ever a fellow had," rejoined the other. "Why, last fall, I let him go to Cincinnati alone, to do business for me, and bring home five hundred dollars. 'Tom,' says I to him, 'I trust you, because I think you're a Christian—I know you wouldn't cheat.' Tom comes back,

1 yer: your
2 valeyable: valuable

sure enough; I knew he would. Some low fellows, they say, said to him—Tom, why don't you make tracks for Canada?' 'Ah, master trusted me, and I couldn't,'—they told me about it. I am sorry to part with Tom, I must say. You ought to let him cover the whole balance of the debt; and you would, Haley, if you had any conscience."

"Well, I've got just as much conscience as any man in business can afford to keep,—just a little, you know, to swear by, as't were," said the trader, jocularly; "and, then, I'm ready to do anything in reason to 'blige friends; but this yer, you see, is a leetle too hard on a fellow—a leetle too hard." The trader sighed contemplatively, and poured out some more brandy.

"Well, then, Haley, how will you trade?" said Mr. Shelby, after an uneasy interval of silence.

"Well, haven't you a boy or gal that you could throw in with Tom?"

"Hum!—none that I could well spare; to tell the truth, it's only hard necessity makes me willing to sell at all. I don't like parting with any of my hands, that's a fact."

Here the door opened, and a small quadroon boy, between four and five years of age, entered the room. There was something in his appearance remarkably beautiful and engaging. His black hair, fine as floss silk, hung in glossy curls about his round, dimpled face, while a pair of large dark eyes, full of fire and softness, looked out from beneath the rich, long lashes, as he peered curiously into the apartment. A gay robe of scarlet and yellow plaid, carefully made and neatly fitted, set off to advantage the dark and rich style of his beauty; and a certain comic air of assurance, blended with bashfulness, showed that he had been not unused to being petted and noticed by his master.

"Hulloa, Jim Crow!" said Mr. Shelby, whistling, and snapping a bunch of raisins towards him, "pick that up, now!"

The child scampered, with all his little strength, after the prize, while his master laughed.

"Come here, Jim Crow," said he. The child came up, and the master patted the curly head, and chucked him under the chin.

"Now, Jim, show this gentleman how you can dance and sing." The boy commenced one of those wild, grotesque songs common among the Negroes, in a rich, clear voice, accompanying his singing with many comic evolutions of the hands, feet, and whole body, all in perfect time to the music.

…

QUESTIONS

1 What are the gentlemen discussing?
2 How does Shelby assess Tom's character?
3 What is Mr. Haley's attitude towards the black slaves?
4 What does Jim look like?
5 How does Jim impress you?
6 What is Jim's talent?

EXERCISES OF CHAPTER IX

I Fill the following blanks.

1 Washington Irving, along with ______________ was among the first American writers to earn the international fame in Europe.

2 The American Romantic Movement gave rise to ______________, which was a religious and philosophical movement.

3 Transcendentalists were strong ______________ in the power of the individual. They stressed the role of ______________ and the individual's ______________, and exalted feeling over ______________.

4 The representative writers of American Romanticism are ____________, ______________, ______________ etc.

5 The two monumental works of Transcendentalism are ______________'s ______________ and ______________'s ______________.

II Find the relevant match from Column B for each item in Column A.

Column A	Column B
1 ( ) Washington Irving	A. *Uncle Tom's Cabin*
2 ( ) Edgar Allan Poe	B. *To Helen*
3 ( ) Nathaniel Hawthorne	C. *Walden*

4 ( ) Ralph Waldo Emerson — D. *Leaves of Grass*
5 ( ) Henry D. Thoreau — E. *The Sketch Book*
6 ( ) Herman Melville — F. *Nature*
7 ( ) Mrs. Stowe — G. *Moby-Dick*
8 ( ) Walt Whitman — H. *The Scarlet Letter*

III Choose the best answer for each statement.

1 Who was the principal author of the *Declaration of Independence*?
A. Benjamin Franklin B. Thomas Jefferson
C. George Washington D. Washington Irving

2 *To Helen* was written by Poe from the inspiration by the beauty of ______.
A. Greek beauty Helen B. mother of Poe's classmate
C. water nymph Naiads D. soulful beauty Psyche

3 The masters or fathers of American short stories are following writers except ______.
A. Washington Irving B. Edgar Allan Poe
C. Nathaniel Hawthorne D. H. W. Longfellow

4 ______ is regarded as the "father of American literature"?
A. Nathaniel Hawthorne B. James Fenimore Cooper
C. Thomas Jefferson D. Washington Irving

5 What does the ship symbolize in the poem *O Captain! My Captain*?
A. The Civil War B. The War of Independence
C. The United States D. The UK

6 The scarlet letter "A" on Hester's dress is a symbol, originally a mark of first letter of ______.
A. adulterer B. angel C. ability D. America

IV Answer the following questions.

1 What is the main image in the poem "O Captain! My Captain"?

2 Would you like to be Somebody or Nobody? Give your reasons to support your idea.

CHAPTER X

American Literature of Realism

(1860-1914)

General Introduction

From 1860 to 1914, the United States was transformed from an agricultural ex-colony to a huge, modern industrial nation, and one of the world's wealthiest states. The total population of the USA doubled. Urbanization and increased national income made the United States a major world power.

Originated in France, Realism called for a depiction of social reality and lives of ordinary people. In America, the term refers to the period from the mid-19th century to the early 20th century, during which American realists were devoted to interpretation of actualities of American lives in various contexts. **American Realism** was a style in art, music and literature that depicted contemporary social realities and the lives and everyday activities of ordinary people. The movement began in literature in the mid-19th century. American realist works attempted to define what was real.

There were several reasons for the coming of American Realism. The Civil War broke out in 1861 and overturned almost every aspect of American life. The moral value of American was changed and people began to question human nature and benevolence of God. Economically, America entered into a commercialized age. After the Civil War, the industrialization and mechanization flourished, giving rise to affluent mid-class. This was called the era of the millionaire. However, well-to-do Americans adored European dress styles and manners, sent their sons to Europe for education, and eagerly married off their daughters to European noblemen.

However, wealth and power lay in the hands of a few capitalists, producing the gap between the extremes of poverty and wealth. Politically, the frontier was closing, which deprived the value of American Dream. Besides, the age of Romanticism began to wane. The appearance of new writers such as Henry James and Mark Twain started a new literary age.

Generally speaking, the characteristics of American Realism are as follows. First, a straightforward and objective representation of everyday life reacted against Romanticism's emphasis on imagination and intuition. Second, the realists were interested in commonplace. Therefore, the protagonists of realistic works shifted from well-behaved mid-class young men to people from all social levels. Third, American

Realism did not seek abstract truth as Romanticism did and approached the harsh realities by experience.

There were several variations in American Realism. **Local colorism** was one of it, which focused on the description of local characters in a specific region. Mark Twain (1835-1910) was a representative writer of this school and he was noted by his vivid depiction of life along the Mississippi River. *The Adventures of Huckleberry Finn* in 1883 is a good example of local colorism.

Besides, **naturalism** held a pessimistic viewpoint that the fate of human being was controlled by the impersonal forces of nature. Some writers gave detailed descriptions of the lives of the human passion and sexuality, who are called naturalist novelists. Stephen Crane (1871-1900) was the pioneer of this school with *Maggie: A Girl of the Streets* (1893) as the first work and one of the best naturalistic American novels. *The Red Badge of Courage* (1895) was his haunting Civil War novel. Theodore Dreiser (1871-1945) was a master of naturalism, who concerned himself about the uncontrollable fate of lower-class people in the changing society. The naturalistic Jack London (1876-1916) became the highest paid writer in the United States of his time with his best-sellers *The Son of the Wolf* (1900), *The Call of the Wild* (1903), and *The Sea-Wolf* (1904). His masterpiece was *Martin Eden* which depicts the inner stress of the American dream as London experienced by himself. Henry James (1843-1916) was called **cosmopolitan novelist** because he was skilled in describing the contact and contrast between the New World (America) and the Old World (Europe). *The Portrait of a Lady* (1881) was one of his masterpieces. Other dominant figures of the realistic period include William Dean Howells (1837-1920), who was the champion of Realism, Kate Chopin (1850-1904), whose writing was characterized by its leading feminist awareness that could hardly be accepted by people of her age. The poet Robert Frost (1874-1963) is recognized as a link between Realism and Modernism.

Mark Twain
(1835-1910)

INTRODUCTION

Mark Twain (1835-1910), pen name of Samuel Langhorne Clemens, is a great literary giant praised for his wit and satire. He was a great humorist and one of the representative figures of Realism. William Faulkner regarded him as "the father of American literature".

Mark Twain was born and grew up in Missouri, a port town on the Mississippi River. When his father died in 1847, this young boy had to make his fortune by working as apprentice of a printer, and later an editorial assistant for a newspaper owned by his brother Orion where he earned his education and began writing. Later, he was a river pilot and his experience on the Mississippi River gave him the pen name Mark Twain, a term for a measured river depth of two fathoms or 12-feet, which was safe for a steamboat to navigate. Mark Twain worked as a journalist after the river trade was halted because of the Civil War.

In 1865, he published his tall tale The Celebrated Jumping Frog of Calaveras County and began to gain reputation as humorist. The short story brought international attention, and his wit and satire, in prose and in speech, earned praise from critics and readers. In 1869, Twain's first book *The Innocents Abroad* was published, which observes and criticizes the irreverent American manners in front of sacred ancient landmarks when he toured to Europe and the Middle East. In 1874, collaborated with Charles Dudley Warner, Twain published *The Gilded Age*, which satirizes the greed, materialism, hypocrisy, and corruption in almost every aspect of post-Civil War American society. Two years later, Twain made another important publication, *The Adventure of Tom Sawyer.* It is about Tom's adventures—some real, some imagined—with two friends down the Mississippi River. In 1883, *Life on the Mississippi* came out. As the name indicated, it is a travel book recounting Twain's journey along the Mississippi River. In the same year, *The Adventures of Huckleberry Finn* was published. It is listed among the Great American Novel and nourishes American literature from his time till the modern age. *The Man That Corrupted Hadleyburg* (1900) is a short fiction about how the responsible people in Hadleyburg are tempted to corrupt their honest town by a passing stranger. *The Prince and the Pauper* (1882) is Twain's first attempt at historical fiction.

Mark Twain tried many different literary styles including fiction, essays, and political satires and so on. His writing is featured by its strong local colors, colloquial speech and witty remarks. His works show a strong concern with social problems by portraying the life of lower-class people and satirizing the social injustice. The following short story embodies Twain's humorous and ironic writing features.

SELECTED READING

A Matter of Honor

Overview

This interesting short story tells us how the narrator tries to raise three dollars in an "honorable" way. Its lanauge is plain; the story is simple; but its humourous and ironic tone is quite impressive and profound.

I remember a time when a shortage occurred; my friend Swinton and I had to have it before the close of the day. I don't know now how we happened to want all that money at one time; I only know we had to have it. Swinton told me to go out and find it, and he said he would also go out and see what he could do. Being a man of strong religious faith, he didn't seem to have any doubt that we would succeed but I hadn't the same confidence. I had no idea where to turn to raise all that money, and I said so.

I think Swinton was ashamed of me, privately, because of my weak faith. He told me to give myself no uneasiness, no concern; and he said in a simple, confident, unquestioning way, "The Lord[1] will provide." I saw that he fully believed the Lord would provide, but it seemed to me that if he had had my experience—but never mind that. Before he was done with me, his strong faith had had its influence, and I went forth from the place almost convinced that the Lord really would provide.

I wandered around the streets for an hour trying to think up some way to get that money, but nothing suggested itself. At last, I walked into the Ebbitt Hotel and sat down. Presently a dog came over to me. He paused, glanced up at me, and said with his eyes, "Are you friendly?" I answered with my eyes that I was. He waved his tail happily and came forward and rested

1 the Lord: God

his head on my knee and lifted his brown eyes to my face in a loving way. He was charming creature, as beautiful as a girl, and he was all made of silk and velvet. I stroked his smooth brown head, and we were a pair of lovers right away.

Pretty soon, General Miles, the hero of the nation, came walking by in his blue and gold uniform with everyone's admiring gaze upon him. He saw the dog and stopped, and there was a light in his eyes which showed that he had a warm place in his heart for this handsome creature. The General then came forward and stroked the dog and said: "He is very fine. He is a wonder. Would you sell him?"

I was greatly moved; it seemed a marvellous thing to me, the way Swinton's faith had worked out.

I said, "Yes."

The General said, "How much do you ask for him?"

"Three dollars," I replied.

The General was obviously surprised. He said, "Three dollars? Only three dollars? Why, that dog is a most uncommon dog. He can't possible be worth less than fifty. If he were mine, I wouldn't take less than a hundred for him. I am afraid you are not aware of his value. Reconsider your price if you wish. I would not like to cheat you."

But I replied, "No. Three dollars. That is his price."

"Very well, since you insist upon it," said the General, and he gave me the three dollars and led the dog away, disappearing upstairs.

In about ten minutes a gentle-faced, middle-aged gentleman came along and began to look around, here and there, under tables and everywhere. I said to him, "Is it a dog you are looking for?"

His face had been worried before, and troubled; but it lighted up gladly now, and he answered, "Yes. Have you seen him?"

"Yes," I said. "He was here a minute ago, and I saw him follow a gentleman away. I think I could find him for you if you would like me to try."

I have seldom seen a person look so grateful. He said that he would like me to try. I assured him I would do it with great pleasure, but that as it might take a little time, I hope he would not mind paying me for my trouble. He replied that he would do it most gladly—repeating that phrase, "most gladly"—and asked me how much.

I said, "Three dollars."

He looked surprised and exclaimed, "Dear me, it is nothing! I will pay you ten quite willingly."

But I said, "No, three is the price," and it seemed to me that it would be wrong to take a penny more than was promised.

I got the number of the General's room from the clerk at the front desk of the hotel, and when I reached the room, I found the General there, stroking his dog and quite happy. I said, "I am sorry, but I have to take the dog back."

He seemed astonished and said, "Take him back? Why, he is my dog; you sold him to me, and at your own price."

"Yes," I said, "that's true. But I have to have him because the man wants him back."

"What man?"

"The man that owns him. He wasn't my dog."

The General looked even more astonished than before, and for a moment, he couldn't seem to find his voice. Then he said, "Do you mean to tell me that you were selling another man's dog—and knew it?"

"Yes, I knew it wasn't my dog."

"Then why did you sell him?"

I said, "Well, that is a strange question to ask. I sold him because you wanted him. You offered to buy the dog; you can't deny that. I was not anxious to sell him. I had not advertised him. I had not even thought of selling him, but it seemed to me that—"

He broke me off in the middle of my sentence and said, "It is the strangest thing I have ever heard of. The idea of your selling a dog that didn't belong to you—"

I interrupted him there and said, "you said yourself that the dog was probably worth a hundred dollars. I only asked you for three. Was there anything unfair about that? You offered to pay more; you know you did. I only asked you for three; you can't deny it."

"Oh, what in the world does that have to do with it? The truth of the matter is that you didn't own the dog—can't you see that? You seem to think if you sell it cheap. Now then—"

I said, "Please don't argue any more about it. You can't get around the fact that the price was perfectly fair, perfectly reasonable—considering that I didn't own the dog—and so arguing about it is only a waste of words. I have to have him back because the man wants him. Don't you see that I have no choice in the matter? Put yourself in my place. Suppose you had sold a dog that didn't belong to you. Suppose you—"

"Oh," he said, sighing, "don't mix me up any more with your crazy reasoning! Take him along and give me a rest."

So I paid him back the three dollars and led the dog downstairs and passed him over to his owner and collected three for my trouble.

I went away feeling quite satisfied with the whole matter because I had acted honourable. I could never have used the three dollars that I had sold the dog for because it was not rightly my own. But the three I got for returning him to his owner was rightly and properly mine because I had earned it. That man might never have gotten his dog back at all if it hadn't been for me. My principles have remained to this day what they were then. I was always honest; I know that I can never be otherwise. It is as I have always said: I was never able to use money which I had acquired in questionable ways.

Now then, that is the tale. Some of it is true.

QUESTIONS

1 What was the attitude of the narrator to the Lord?
2 Why did the narrator ask for three dollars only?
3 Do you think the narrator made a reasonable argument with General Miles? Why or why not?
4 Do you think the narrator got the money in an honorable way? Why or why not?
5 Can you find some examples of irony?
6 Can you explain the real intention of the writer?

Henry James
(1843-1916)

INTRODUCTION

Henry James (1843-1916) was a distinguished representative of American Realism. He explored European culture and American culture intensively in his works. James is noted for his "international theme", that is, the complex relationships between naïve Americans and cosmopolitan Europeans. Henry James has long been recognized as the major author to bridge the transition from the 19th century realism to the impressionistic and modernistic fiction of the 20th century, just as he leads us from America to Europe. Besides, he was an expert in describing the inner world of his characters.

Henry James was born to a wealthy cultured family in New York City. His father was an eminent philosopher and a friend of Emerson's; Henry James' elder brother, William James, was a famous philosopher, psychologist, and professor at Harvard University. In 1862, Henry James attended Harvard Law School, where he preferred reading and writing to studying law. At the age of six months James was taken to live near Windsor Castle and in the following year to Paris, where he met Turgenev, Flaubert, and Zola. By the time he was 21, James had spent almost one-third of his life in foreign countries and almost all of his time had been spent learning languages, including Latin and French. In 1876, he moved to England and spent the rest of his life in London. In 1911, he got honours degree from University of Harvard, and in 1912, he received honorary doctorate in literature from Oxford University. In 1915, Henry became a British citizen to show his support of England in World War I. He never married. In 1916, just before his death, he received the Order of Merit. As a master of psychological novel, he was a major influence on the 20th-century writing.

Henry James was a highly prolific writers who authored novels, short stories, travel papers, critical essays, autobiographies and many other literary styles. His famous works include *The American* (1877), a book recounting adventures of an American businessman, Christopher Newman, on his first trip in Europe; *Daisy Miller* (1878), which narrates the love story of a young American woman, Daisy Miller, who behaves unconventionally during her stay in Europe; *The Portrait of a Lady* (1881), a long novel about the tragic marriage of a young innocent American girl, Isabel Archer, after she inherits a large sum of money and rejects several European suitors; *The Turn of the Screw* (1898), a Gothic ghost story telling a sequence of mysterious events after a young governess is hired to take care of two kids; *The Ambassadors* (1903), one of the masterpieces of James' late period relating the journey of a middle-aged American man, Lambert Strether, to England and Paris with the mission of bringing Chad Newsome, son of Strether's patron, back home. *The Wings of the Dove* (1902), a love among Milly Theale, a rich American girl stricken with serious disease, and a pair of lovers Kate Croy and Merton Densher; *The Golden Bowl* (1904), a novel about the intricate relationship between a father and a daughter and their respective spouses.

Henry James published 100 volumes of stories (novellas), novels, plays, literary criticism, biography and autobiography and sketches of travels. He developed his own theory of novel-writing, such as *The Art of Fiction* (1884), and in his notebooks or the prefaces.

SELECTED READING

The Portrait of a Lady

Overview

The Portrait of a Lady is the most popular long novel of Henry James. The protagonist is a young American girl named Isabel Archer, who goes to London to visit her aunt after the death of her father. There, she meets several wealthy gentleman but rejects their proposals for the sake of freedom. Later, when she travels to Florence, Isabel is introduced to an American artist Gilbert Osmond and accepts his offer of marriage. However, the marriage is not a happy one because Osmond is a selfish person and lack of genuine affection. Although Isabel realizes her mistake, she, in the end of the novel, is still undecided whether to stay with Osmond or break away from him to pursue her own happiness. The following excerpt is from the ending of the novel, which is a good example of Henry James' skilled psychological description.

Chapter 55

(Excerpt)

…

Isabel[1] gave a long murmur, like a creature in pain; it was as if he[2]

1 Isabel: Isabel Archer, the protagonist in the novel and the wife of Gilbert Osmond

2 he: Caspar Goodwood, a young man, who wanted very much to marry Isabel and was refused by her on the very day that they met. He ashed her to reconsider their marriage.

were pressing something that hurt her. "The world's very small," she said at random; she had an immense desire to appear to resist. She said it at random, to hear herself say something; but it was not what she meant. The world, in truth, had never seemed so large; it seemed to open out, all round her, to take the form of a mighty sea, where she floated in fathomless waters. She had wanted help, and here was help; it had come in a rushing torrent. I know not whether she believed everything he said; but she believed just then that to let him take her in his arms would be the next best thing to her dying. This belief, for a moment, was a kind of rapture, in which she felt herself sink and sink. In the movement she seemed to beat with her feet, in order to catch herself, to feel something to rest on.

"Ah, be mine as I'm yours!" she heard her companion cry. He had suddenly given up argument, and his voice seemed to come, harsh and terrible, through a confusion of vaguer sounds.

This, however, of course, was but a subjective fact, as the metaphysicians say; the confusion, the noise of waters, all the rest of it, were in her own swimming head. In an instant she became aware of this. "Do me the greatest kindness of all," she panted. "I beseech you to go away!"

"Ah, don't say that. Don't kill me!" he cried. She clasped her hands; her eyes were streaming with tears. "As you love me, as you pity me, leave me alone!"

He glared at her a moment through the dusk, and the next instant she felt his arms about her and his lips on her own lips. His kiss was like white lightning, a flash that spread, and spread again, and stayed; and it was extraordinarily as if, while she took it, she felt each thing in his hard manhood that had least pleased her, each aggressive fact of his face, his figure, his presence, justified of its intense identity and made one with this act of possession. So had she heard of those wrecked and under water following a train of images before they sink. But when darkness returned she was free. She never looked about her; she only darted from the spot. There were lights in the windows of the house; they shone far across the lawn. In an extraordinarily short time—for the distance was considerable—he had moved through the darkness (for she saw nothing) and reached the door.

Here only she paused. She looked all about her; she listened a little; then she put her hand on the latch. She had not known where to turn; but she knew now. There was a very straight path.

Two days afterwards Caspar Goodwood knocked at the door of the house in Wimpole Street in which Henrietta Stackpole[1] occupied furnished lodgings. He had hardly removed his hand from the knocker when the door was opened and Miss Stackpole herself stood before him. She had on her hat and jacket; she was on the point of going out. "Oh, good-morning," he said, "I was in hopes I should find Mrs. Osmond.[2]"

Henrietta kept him waiting a moment for her reply; but there was a good deal of expression about Miss Stackpole even when she was silent. "Pray what led you to suppose she was here?"

"I went down to Gardencourt this morning, and the servant told me she had come to London. He believed she was to come to you." Again Miss Stackpole held him—with an intention of perfect kindness—in suspense. "She came here yesterday, and spent the night. But this morning she started for Rome."

Caspar Goodwood was not looking at her; his eyes were fastened on the doorstep. "Oh, she started—?" he stammered. And without finishing his phrase or looking up he stiffly averted himself. But he couldn't otherwise move.

Henrietta had come out, closing the door behind her, and now she put out her hand and grasped his arm. "Look here, Mr. Goodwood," she said; "just you wait!"

On which he looked up at her—but only to guess, from her face, with a revulsion, that she simply meant he was young. She stood shining at him with that cheap comfort, and it added, on the spot, thirty years to his life. She walked him away with her, however, as if she had given him now the key to patience.

1 Henrietta Stackpole: Isabel's friend. As a working and successful American woman, she was the consciousness of the American in Europe and wanted Isabel to marry Caspar.

2 Mrs. Osmond: Isabel Archer

QUESTIONS

1 What does the "world" in the first paragraph mean?
2 What has happened when Isabel and Caspar meet?
3 What psychological change does Isabel experience?
4 How does Henry James reveal her psychological activity?
5 Where would Isabel like to go in the end?
6 Do you think that Isabel and Caspar will get married?

Kate Chopin
(1850-1904)

INTRODUCTION

Kate Chopin (1850-1904) was an American short story writer and novelist. She is now considered by some to have been a forerunner of the feminist authors of the 20th century. She once was a conventional housewife but the course of her life was changed first by her husband's death which forced her to take over his plantation and make effort to repay a large sum of debt, and then by her beloved mother's death which left her in a state of depression. Therefore, to distract her attention and make some money, she began writing by the early 1890s for both children and adults.

Her representative work was *The Awakening* (1899). The novel is about a woman's doomed attempt to find her own identity through passion. In the novel, a young married woman with attractive children and successful husband gives up family, money, respectability, and eventually her life to search for self-realization. Chopin is most celebrated by *The Awakening* now, but at her time the book was severely criticized because the value opposed the social norms. She portrayed some independent women images who have their own wants and needs in her works. Her major works include two short story collections, in which *The Story of an Hour* is one of her important short stories.

SELECTED READING

The Story of an Hour

Overview

The story is about Louise Mallard's one-hour mental experience when she, at the beginning, hears the news that her husband died in a railway disaster and, in the end, finds out her husband is alive after all. At the news, Mrs. Mallard's first reaction is to lock herself into the room but gradually she finds out the benefit of his death. Therefore, when she discovers her husband is still alive, she dies of a heart attack out of shock.

Knowing that Mrs. Mallard was afflicted with a heart trouble, great care was taken to break to her as gently as possible the news of her husband's death.

It was her sister Josephine who told her, in broken sentences; veiled hints that revealed in half concealing.

Her husband's friend Richards was there, too, near her. It was he who had been in the newspaper office when intelligence of the railroad disaster was received, with Brently Maitard's name leading the list of "killed". He had only taken the time to assure himself of its truth by a second telegram, and had hastened to forestall any less careful, less tender friend in bearing the sad message.

She did not hear the story as many women have heard the same, with a paralyzed inability to accept its significance. She wept at once, with sudden, wild abandonment, in her sister's arms. When the storm of grief had spent itself she went away to her room alone. She would have no one follow her.

There stood, facing the open window, a comfortable, roomy armchair. Into this she sank, pressed down by a physical exhaustion that haunted her body and seemed to reach into her soul.

She could see in the open square before her house the tops of trees that were all aquiver with the new spring life. The delicious breath of rain was in the air. In the street below a peddler was crying his wares. The notes of a distant song which someone was singing reached her faintly, and countless sparrows were twittering in the leaves.

There were patches of blue sky showing here and there through the clouds that had met and piled one above the other in the west facing her window.

She sat with her head thrown back upon the cushion of the chair, quite motionless, except when a sob came up into her throat and shook her, as a child who has cried itself to sleep continues to sob in its dreams.

She was young, with a fair, calm face, whose lines bespoke repression and even a certain strength. But now there was a dull stare in her eyes, whose gaze was fixed away off yonder on one of those patches of blue sky. It was not a glance of reflection, but rather indicated a suspension of intelligent thought.

There was something coming to her and she was waiting for it, fearfully. What was it? She did not know, it was too subtle and elusive to name. But she felt it, creeping out of the sky, reaching toward her through the sounds, the scents, the color that filled the air.

Now her bosom rose and fell tumultuously. She was beginning to recognize this thing that was approaching to possess her, and she was striving to beat it back with her will—as powerless as her two white slender hands would have been.

When she abandoned herself, a little whispered word escaped her slightly parted lips. She said it over and over under her breath. "Free, free, free!" The vacant stare and the look of terror that had followed it went from her eyes. They stayed keen and bright. Her pulses beat fast, and the coursing blood warmed and relaxed every inch of her body.

She did not stop to ask if it were or were not a monstrous joy that held her. A clear and exalted perception enabled her to dismiss the suggestion as trivial.

She knew that she would weep again when she saw the kind, tender hands folded in death; the face that had never looked save with love upon her, fixed and gray and dead. But she saw beyond that bitter moment along procession of years to come that would belong to her absolutely. And she opened and spread her arms out to them in welcome.

There would be no one to live for her during those coming years, she would live for herself. There would be no powerful will bending hers in that blind persistence with which men and women believe they have a right to impose a private will upon a fellow creature. A kind intention or a cruel intention made the act seem no less a crime as she looked upon it in that brief moment of illumination.

And yet she had loved him—sometimes. Often she had not. What did it matter! What could love, the unsolved mystery, count for in face of this possession of self-assertion which she suddenly recognized as the strongest impulse of her being! "Free! Body and soul free!" she kept whispering.

Josephine was kneeling before the closed door with her lips to the keyhole, imploring for admission. "Louise, open the door! I beg, open the door—you will make yourself. What are you doing, Louise? For heaven's sake open the door."

"Go away. I am not making myself" No, she was drinking in a very elixir of life through that open window.

Her fancy was running riot along those days ahead of her. Spring days, and summer days, and all sorts of days that would be her own. She breathed a quick prayer that life might be long. It was only yesterday she had thought with a shudder that life might be long.

She arose at length and opened the door to her sister's importunities. There was a feverish triumph in her eyes, and she carried herself unwittingly like a goddess of Victory. She clasped her sister's waist, and together they descended the stairs. Richards stood waiting for them at the bottom.

Some one was opening the front door with a latchkey. It was Brently Mallard who entered, a little travel-stained, composedly carrying his gripsack and umbrella. He had been far from the scene of accident, and did not know there had been one. He stood amazed at Josephine's piercing cry, at Richards's quick motion to screen him from the view of his wife.

But Richards was too late.

When the doctors came they said she had died of heart disease—of joy that kills.

QUESTIONS

1 How is Mrs. Mallard's health condition?
2 What is the news about her husband?
3 What does the door symbolize?
4 What does the open window mean?
5 Why does the writer describe the natural scenery, such as the tops of trees, rain, distant song, sparrows , blue sky, etc.?
6 What are the possible themes of this short story?

Theodore Dreiser (1871-1945)

INTRODUCTION

Theodore Dreiser (1871-1945) is considered one of the great American realists, or naturalists. His novels deal with everyday life. As Dreiser described the characters and their actions in massive detail, he is called a master of Naturalism or an outstanding representative of Naturalism.

He was born to a poor and strict German-American family in Indiana. At the age of 16, he left home and made a living on his own. Dreiser attended Indiana University in the years 1889-1890 with the help of a former teacher but he dropped out one year later. Thereafter he worked as a reporter for several newspapers which prepared himself a lot for his future writing.

In 1900, Dreiser published his first novel *Sister Carrie*, a story of a country girl who flees the rural life for the city and degenerates in the pursuit of vanity and material interest. The book was a critical success but commercial failure because of the public objections to immoral character of the heroine. Discouraged by the poor acceptation and the ensuing family trouble, Dreiser did not complete and publish his second novel *Jennie Gerhardt* until 1911. Since then, Dreiser began a decade and a half of literary productivity. In 1912, he published *The Financier,* which is the first of his *Trilogy of Desire* to explore a male protagonist, Frank Cowperwood. The second book *The Titan* appeared in 1914, but the last volume, *The Stoic*, did not come out until 1945. Dreiser's first commercial success was *An American Tragedy* (1925), which was adapted for screen twice. This novel explores the dangers of the American dream. It is the dream of success, money, and social acceptance that has distorted human nature. Dreiser also wrote a number of short stories, poems, plays, and his autobiography.

As a writer of naturalist school, Dreiser portrayed the rural and urban American life in a very realistic way, paying particular attention to the fate of lower class in a changing society, which has an enormous influence on the generations to follow.

SELECTED READING

Sister Carrie

Overview

Sister Carrie is the first novel by Theodore Dreiser and is based partly on experience of his own sister Emma. A beautiful country girl, Carrie Meeber, in order to escape poverty, goes to Chicago to realize her American dream only to find life in the big city is not as easy as she imagined. To relieve hardship, she first cohabited with a salesman, Charles Drouet, that she met on the train to Chicago, and later became the mistress of a hotel manager, George Hurstwood. However, when Hurstwood goes bankrupt several years later, Carrie leaves him and turns to New York's theaters for employment. Finally, she becomes a famous actress and moves in the upper class, but finds that money and fame do not satisfy her desires. It has been called the "greatest of all American urban novels".

The following excerpt describes the harsh reality and possible fate that Carrie is going to meet after she travels to Chicago.

Chapter 1

The Magnet Attracting—A Walf Amid Forces

When Caroline Meeber boarded the afternoon train for Chicago, her total outfit consisted of a small trunk, a cheap imitation alligator-skin satchel, a small lunch in a paper box, and a yellow leather snap purse, containing her ticket, a scrap of paper with her sister's address in Van Buren Street, and four dollars in money. It was in August, 1889. She was eighteen years of age, bright, timid, and full of the illusions of ignorance and youth. Whatever touch of regret at parting characterised her thoughts, it was certainly not for advantages now being given up. A gush of tears at her mother's farewell kiss, a touch in her throat when the cars clacked by the flour mill where her father worked by the day, a pathetic sigh as the familiar green environs of the village passed in review, and the threads which bound her so lightly to girlhood and home were irretrievably broken.

To be sure there was always the next station, where one might descend and return. There was the great city, bound more closely by these very trains which came up daily. Columbia City was not so very far away, even once she was in Chicago. What, pray, is a few hours—a few hundred miles? She looked at the little slip bearing her sister's address and wondered. She gazed at the green landscape, now passing in swift review, until her swifter thoughts replaced its impression with vague conjectures of what Chicago might be.

When a girl leaves her home at eighteen, she does one of two things. Either she falls into saving hands and becomes better, or she rapidly assumes the cosmopolitan standard of virtue and becomes worse. Of an intermediate balance, under the circumstances, there is no possibility. The city has its cunning wiles, no less than the infinitely smaller and more human tempter. There are large forces which allure with all the soulfulness of expression possible in the most cultured human. The gleam of a thousand lights is often as effective as the persuasive light in a wooing and fascinating eye. Half the undoing of the unsophisticated and natural mind is accomplished by forces wholly superhuman. A blare of sound, a roar of life, a vast array of human hives, appeal to the astonished senses in equivocal terms. Without a counsellor at hand to whisper cautious interpretations, what falsehoods may not these things breathe into the unguarded ear! Unrecognised for what they are, their beauty, like music, too often relaxes, then weakens, then perverts the simpler human perceptions.

…

QUESTIONS

1 How old was Sister Carrie when she first went to Chicago?
2 Why did Carrie make her trip to Chicago?
3 What is your impression on Sister Carrie?
4 What is the writing style that the author uses in this part?
5 What ways would young girls find when they left hometown for big city?
6 What was the society like according to this part?

Robert Frost
(1874-1963)

INTRODUCTION

Robert Frost (1874-1963) is the most popular American poet of the 20th century. Frost's work looks simple, but many poems suggest a deeper meaning. Frost's work is distinguished by its simple style, colloquial speech and metaphorical images. Most of his poetry uses plain languages and depicts rural farm life to explore complexity such as existential crisis of mankind. The form of his poetry is traditional but the themes are mostly modern and, in this sense, Frost is regarded as a link between 19th-century American poetry and Modernism.

He was born in San Francisco and later moved to Lawrence Massachusetts with his mother and younger sister after the death of his father. In 1912, Frost moved to Great Britain with his family. There he made friends with Ezra Pound and Edward Thomas and published two poetry volumes, *A Boy's Will* (1913) and *North of Boston* (1914), which were favorably reviewed. In 1915, at the beginning of the World War I, Frost went back to farming in New Hampshire of America, where he began a career of writing, teaching and lecturing.

Frost was frequently honored during his lifetime. He won the Pulitzer Prize for Poetry four times and was awarded the Congressional Gold Medal in 1960 for his poetic works. He received honorary degrees from 44 institutions and was nation's unofficial Poet Laureate. At his age 86, he was invited to read his poems at John Kennedy's presidential inauguration in 1961, the first poet ever so honored.

SELECTED READING

The Road Not Taken

Two roads diverged in a yellow wood[1],
And sorry I could not travel both
And be one traveler, long I stood

1 yellow wood: It implies the season, autumn.

And looked down one[1] as far as I could
To where it bent[2] in the undergrown.

Then took the other, as just as fair[3],
And having perhaps the better claim[4],
Because it was grassy and wanted wear[5];
Though as for that the passing there
Had worn them really about the same[6].

And both that morning equally lay
In leaves no step had trodden black[7]
Oh, I kept the first for another day[8]!
Yet knowing how way leads on to way[9],
I doubted if I should even come back.

I shall be telling this with a sigh[10]
Somewhere ages and ages hence:
Two roads diverged in a wood, and I—
I took the one less traveled by,
And that has made all the difference[11].

QUESTIONS

1 What does the yellow wood mean in the first line?
2 What is the speaker sorry for?
3 What might the roads stand for in the poem?

---

1 looked down one: looked along one of the two roads
2 bent: disappeared
3 as just as fair: It is as reasonable as the choice of the first road to choose the second one.
4 claim: reason
5 wanted wear: It (the other road) was untrodden.
6 Had worn them really about the same: Two roads have been trodden in almost the same degree.
7 In leaves no step had trodden black: The fallen leaves of trees had not been trodden black.
8 I kept the first for another day: I would choose the first road next day.
9 how way leads on to way: how one road may diverge into many branches. It means that in human life one choice may lead to more choices.
10 I shall be telling this with a sigh: I will regret my decision because I was unable to take both.
11 all the difference: It refers to the different choice of life.

4 Why does the second road have the better claim?
5 Why should the speaker tell this with a "sigh"?
6 Does the speaker think he makes a wrong choice?
7 What would the poet like to convey to us?

Fire and Ice[1]

Some say the world will end in fire,
Some say in ice[2].
From what I've tasted of desire
I hold with[3] those who favor fire.
But if it had to perish twice,
I think I know enough of hate
To say[4] that for destruction ice
Is also great[5]
And would suffice.

QUESTIONS

1 Why does the poet put "ice" and "fire" together?
2 What kind of emotion does *ice* stand for in the poem?
3 What does *fire* represent here?
4 What are the most dangerous forces that could destroy the world?
5 What is the poetic style in this poem?
6 What is the theme of "Fire and Ice"?

1 The poet was inspired by Dante's *Inferno.*
2 in ice: the world will be destroyed by ice.
3 hold with: agree with
4 To say: If we talk about.
5 Is also great: Ice is destructive as fire.

EXERCISES OF CHAPTER X

I Fill in the following blanks.

1 Theodore Dreiser was a master of ____________ and ____________ of modern American novels.

2 ______________________ was Henry James' favorite theme in his works.

3 After the Civil War, the ____________ and ____________ flourished, giving rise to affluent mid-class.

4 Mark Twain was a great literary giant lauded for his ____________ and ____________.

5 Kate Chopin is now considered by some to have been a forerunner of the ____________ authors of the 20th century.

II Find the relevant match from Column B for each item in Column A.

Column A	Column B
1 ( ) cosmopolitan novelist	A. *The Adventures of Huckleberry Finn*
2 ( ) novel with local colorism	B. *Uncle Tom's Cabin*
3 ( ) a typical anti-slavery novel	C. Henry James
4 ( ) Robert Frost	D. *Sister Carrie*
5 ( ) Kate Chopin	E. *The Red Badge of Courage*
6 ( ) Theodore Dreiser	F. *The Awakening*
7 ( ) Stephen Crane	G. *Martin Eden*
8 ( ) Jack London	H. link between Realism and Modernism

III Choose the best answer for each statement.

1 Who does not belong to the novelists of Naturalism in the following list?
A. Mark Twain B. Theodore Dreiser
C. Stephen Crane D. Jack London

2 Theodore Dreiser believed that ______.
A. men can control their fate
B. man's fate is controlled by impersonal forces
C. men can change their fate by their personal effort
D. man's fate is not predetermined

3 Which of the following is not the work written by Mark Twain?
A. *The Adventure of Tom Sawyer* B. *An American Tragedy*
C. *The Man That Corrupted Hadleyburg* D. *The Gilded Age*

4. Kate Chopin's *The Awakening* received negative press at her time because ______.
A. the story is obscure B. the plot is too complicated

C. her writing is terrible D. its theme is far ahead of its time

5 Whom did William Faulkner regard as "the father of American literature"?

A. Henry James B. Samuel Langhorne Clemens

C. Theodore Dreiser D. Jack London

IV Answer the following questions.

1 Why is Kate Chopin regarded as a leading feminist of her time?

2 What is the contribution of Robert Frost to American poetry?

CHAPTER XI

American Literature of Modernism

(1914-1945)

General Introduction

The century had to face two wars that cost many lives and the destruction of much property. All these gave rise to all kinds of philosophical ideas in Western Europe, such as Einstein's theory of relativity and Freud's analytical psychology. These philosophical ideas made Modernism come into being. Then the establishment of Nobel Prize in Literature has promoted the development and prosperity of literature. During this period, the winners of the prize in the USA include Sinclair Lewis (1930), Eugene O'Neill (1936), and Pearl S. Buck (1938).

The 20th-century marked a new era for American literature. The First World War shocked and shattered the Victorian optimism and prosperity, rendering people were short of faith in science, progress, and rationality. In the wake of World War I, a group of writers and artists in America and Europe started a series of movements, which is called **Modernism**, seeking to find new ways of expression and a break from the literary tradition of the 19th century. This was an international cultural movement after World War I, expressing disillusionment with tradition and interest in new technologies and visions.

The Lost Generation grew up after the war and many novelists or poets expressed their loss, despair and disillusionment in their works. F. Scott Fitzgerald and Ernest Hemingway were the spokesmen for the Lost Generation. It refers to the young American writers caught up in the war and cut off from the old values, yet unable to come to terms with the new era when civilization went mad. The post war recovery and boom of economy boosted people's worship of capitalism and materialism, and deepened people's sense of loss and bewilderment, opening the era of the Jazz Age, or the Roaring 20s. The ensuing economic recession of the Great Depression in the 1930s overshadowed the prosperous Europe and America, destroyed people's optimism towards capitalism, democracy and individualism. Meanwhile, Marxism began to gain momentum, so people began to question the progress of human civilization, and to reflect upon the conflicts arising from the rapid growth of cities and industry.

Trying to create something new, modernist writers insisted on experimenting with new techniques of reprise, incorporation, rewriting, recapitulation, revision, parody to show a chaotic world. There appeared various literary trends, Imagism, Expressionism, Dadaism, Symbolism, New Criticism, etc. The avant-garde writers include some poets, dramatists, and novelists. In poetry, Ezra Pound was the prominent figure of Imagism whose works focused on presentation of the images of concrete objects with simple language. Wallace Stevens, William Carlos Williams, and E. E. Cummings were influenced by Imagism. T. S. Eliot enjoyed a great reputation for his most daring innovation in his writing techniques and the contents of the poems. Langston Hughes was one of the earliest innovators to use the new literary art form called jazz poetry. In drama, American playwrights imitated English and European theater until well into the 20th century. It was Eugene O'Neill who did great contribution to American literature. With the influence of modern psychology, especially Freudian psychoanalysis, modernist writers began to explore into people's mind, using the technique of Stream of Consciousness. In novel, William Faulkner was one of the most influential Southern writers. He adopted various techniques of symbolism, multiple points of view and Stream of Consciousness.

Gertrude Stein (1874-1946) was an American novelist, poet, playwright and art collector. Raised in Oakland, California, Stein moved to Paris in 1903, and spent the remainder of her life in France. She hosted a Paris salon, where the leading figures in Modernism in literature and art would meet, such as Pablo Picasso, Ernest Hemingway, F. Scott Fitzgerald, Sinclair Lewis, and Ezra Pound.

Sinclair Lewis (1885-1951) was the first American to win the Nobel Prize in Literature in 1930. He was famous for his insightful criticism of American capitalism and materialism. Lewis graduated from Yale University. His *Main Street* (1920) satirizes the hypocritical small-town life; his other famous novel is *Babbitt* (1922), which added a new word to the American language: babbittry, meaning narrow-minded, complacent, bourgeois ways.

Pearl S. Buck (1892-1973), an American writer, also known by her Chinese name Sai Zhenzhu, was the first woman to win the Nobel Prize in Literature in 1938. She spent most of her life before 1934 in Zhenjiang, China. Her masterpiece, *The Good Earth* (1931) gives a rich description of the peasant life of China from the eyes of a Westerner. She is honored and commemorated for her great effort in crossing the cultural boundaries between China and America, though she also suffered greatly from a mixed identity, denied by both cultures.

Margaret Mitchell (1900-1949) was an American writer, whose masterpiece *Gone with the Wind* won her the National Book Award for Most Distinguished Novel of 1936 and the Pulitzer Prize for Fiction in 1937. The novel is set in the time before and after the Civil War, filled with nostalgia for the old hard working, simple, harmonious, and elegant South, which is destroyed by the cruelty of the war, and capitalist development of the vulgar North.

Richard Wright (1908-1960) was a black writer in America. His works focus on racism, especially the plight of African Americans during the late 19th to mid-20th centuries. His best known novel, *The Native Son,* is a protest novel against the oppression and division between the white and the black in a white-dominant society.

Ezra Pound
(1885-1972)

INTRODUCTION

Ezra Pound was an American poet and critic, and the leading figure of the development of Imagism, which was a literary movement launched by British and American poets, chiefly by Ezra Pound between 1912 and 1917. **Imagism** used free verse, common speech pattern, and clear concrete images. For the imagist poets, a visual image and concrete instances can be poetic and abstract. Other imagists included William Carlos Williams and Amy Lowell.

Pound found his technique from classical Chinese and Japanese poetry, which emphasized clarity, precision, and economy of language, instead of traditional rhyme. Pound held that flowery words, particularly adjectives, should be avoided, as well as expressions which mix the abstract with the concrete to the detriment of the visual image.

Ezra Pound was born in Hailey, Idaho, on October 30, 1885. He completed two years of college at the University of Pennsylvania and earned a degree from Hamilton College in 1905. He had mastered 9 languages as well as English before he graduated from university. Pound became a professor at the age of 22. After teaching at Wabash College for two years, he travelled abroad to Spain, Italy, and London, where he became interested in Japanese and Chinese poetry. In 1914, he married Dorothy Shakespear, daughter of the novelist Olivia Shakespear, a former lover of Yeats, who had a great influence on Pound. In 1924, Pound moved to Italy and became involved in Fascist politics. In 1945, he was arrested and convicted in America on charges of treason. He spent many months in a prison camp to wait his trial. He then translated *Confucius* and finished his best poetry *Cantos* (1968). Due to a mental breakdown, he was released and imprisioned in a mental house for 12 years before he returned to Italy and died there.

Working in London in the early 20th century as a foreign editor of several American literary magazines, Pound helped discover and shape the works of contemporaries such as T. S. Eliot, James Joyce, Robert Frost and Ernest Hemingway.

Pound wrote 70 books, over 1,500 articles of his own, and contributed to 70 books of other writers as an editor. Pound's poetry is best known for its clear, visual images, fresh rhythms, and muscular, intelligent, unusual lines, such as *In a Station of the Metro* (1913).

SELECTED READING

In a Station of the Metro[1]

Overview

The poem is considered one of the leading poems of the Imagist Literature. Pound's process of deleting the poem from 30 lines to only 14 words typifies Imagism's focus on economy of language, precision of imagery and experimenting with non-traditional verse forms.

The apparition[2] of these faces in the crowd;
Petals on a wet, black bough.

QUESTIONS

1 Where does this image of the poem take place?
2 What do the "petals" symbolize?
3 Why is the "bough" wet and black?
4 What are the colors, smell, feelings from the poem?
5 What does the contrast between the "petals" and the "bough" imply?
6 The word "apparition" has double meanings in this poem. What are they?
7 What are the two images juxtaposed, or placed next to each other, in the poem?

1 Here the station refers to the Paris subway.

2 apparition: It has double meanings. One is "appearance", in the sense of something which appears, or shows up; the other is the spirit of a dead person appearing in a form which can be seen.

E. E. Cummings
(1894-1962)

INTRODUCTION

E. E. Cummings was an American poet, painter, essayist, author, and playwright. He was an eminent writer of the 20th century American literature. Cummings is celebrated as an avant-garde poet conducting daring experiments with language.

A number of his poems feature a typographical style, with words, parts of words, or punctuation scattered across the page to form a visual pattern. The lines may be broken as not to make sense until to read aloud, and then the meaning and emotion become clear. While Cummings uses typography to "paint a picture" with some of his poems, some of his poems are purely syntactic ones. His poetry often deals with themes of love and nature, as well as the relationship of the individual to the masses and to the world.

Cummings was born in 1894 in the town of Cambridge, Massachusetts. His father was a professor of Sociology and Political Science at Harvard University. Attending Harvard, Cummings was introduced to the writing and artistry of Ezra Pound, who was a great influence on Cummings and many other writers in his time. His works included approximately 2,900 poems, two autobiographical novels, four plays and several essays.

SELECTED READING

in Just-

Overview

The poem contains Cummings' inventive formations of compound words, such as "mud-luscious", "puddle-wonderful", and "eddieandbill." It compares the "balloonman" to Pan, the mythical creature that is half-goat and half-man. This poem is written with added spaces and line breaks to add tempo and rhythm changes while being innovative and impressive.

in Just—
spring   when the world is mud-
luscious the little
lame balloonman

whistles   far   and   wee

and eddieandbill[1] come
running from marbles[2] and
piracies and it's
spring

when the world is puddle-wonderful

the queer
old balloonman whistles
far   and   wee
and bettyandisbel[3] come dancing

from hop-scotch[4] and jump-rope[5] and

it's
spring
and
    the
        goat-footed

balloonMan   whistles

1 eddieandbill: "eddie" and "bill" are two boys' names which are put together by Cummings. The normal form should be "Eddie and Bill".

2 marbles: children's games played with small hard balls, usually of glass

3 bettyandisbel: "betty" and "isbel" are names for two kids: Betty and Isbel.

4 hop-scotch: a children's game in which players toss a small object into the numbered spaces of a pattern of rectangles outlined on the ground and then hop or jump through the spaces to retrieve the object

5 jump-rope: rope skipping

far

and

wee

QUESTIONS

1 What does the "balloonman" symbolize?
2 Why did Cummings invent words like "mud-luscious", "puddle-wonderful", "eddieandbill", and "bettyandisbel"?
3 Why are the lines broken in this way?
4 How is the poem arranged in typography? And why is it?
5 What is the tone of the poem?
6 What is the theme of the poem?

Langston Hughes
(1902-1967)

INTRODUCTION

Langston Hughes was a foremost black poet in America. As a prominent social activist, novelist, playwright, poet, and columnist, Hughes is best known as a leader of the Harlem Renaissance in New York City. He is also known for his engagement with the music world of jazz, which had a great influence on his writing, embracing African-American jazz rhythms. Hughes incorporated blues, spirituals, colloquial speech, and folkways in his poetry. His works make insightful and colorful portraits of the struggle, joy, laughter, and music of the working-class blacks in America. His works are filled with pride in the African-American identity and culture, the best reflection of which can be found in his signature poem, *The Negro Speaks of Rivers*.

Langston Hughes was born in Missouri in 1902 and was one of the first black writers to attempt to make a profitable career out of writing. After his parents separated during his early years, he and his mother often lived a life of poverty. He once attended Columbia University for a year. However, he graduated from Lincoln University in Pennsylvania in 1929. By then Hughes was already one of the central figures of the Harlem Renaissance. He also became a tireless promoter of African American culture. In his last years he became a spokesman for the Civil Rights Movement.

Harlem Renaissance was a literary, artistic, and intellectual movement that took place in Harlem, New York, from the 1920s to the mid-1930s. It's considered to be a rebirth of African American arts and literature, which endowed the African Americans a new black cultural identity, and gave voice to the formerly silent group. Langston Hughes was one of the prominent writers and the nucleus of the movement.

SELECTED READING

Dreams

Overview

The author describes the importance of dreams in the first poem. In the second poem, the author describes the position of black men in America.

Hold fast[1] to dreams,
For if dreams die,
Life is a broken winged bird
That cannot fly.

Hold fast to dreams,
For when dreams go,
Life is a barren field,
Frozen only with snow.

QUESTIONS

1 What images does the poet employ to describe the life once we lose our dreams?
2 Why must we stick to our dreams?
3 What would the poet like to convey to readers?
4 What do dreams stand for here?

I, Too

I, too, sing America.

I am the darker brother.
They send me to eat in the kitchen
When company comes,
But I laugh,
And eat well,
And grow strong.

Tomorrow,
I'll be at the table
When company comes.
Nobody'll dare

1 hold fast: hold tightly

Say to me,
"Eat in the kitchen,"
Then.

Besides,
They'll see how beautiful I am
And be ashamed—

I, too, am America.

QUESTIONS

1 What is the meaning of "the darker brother"?
2 What does "eat in the kitchen" refer to ?
3 What does "I, too, am America" refer to?
4 What is the speaker's feeling in the poem?
5 What is the speaker's dream?
6 What is the theme of the poem?

Wallace Stevens (1879-1955)

INTRODUCTION

Wallace Stevens was an American modernist and gifted nonprofessional poet, born in Reading, Pennsylvania, educated at Harvard and then New York Law School. He won the Pulitzer Prize for Poetry for his *Collected Poems* in 1955. Stevens became an insurance executive in 1916. Because he never concerned himseif more about promoting his literary reputation than about perfecting what he wrote, his associates in the insurance company did not know that he was a major poet.

Stevens focused on the transformative power of imagination and description of concrete objects. His works feature aesthetic philosophy with an influence from impressionist painting. Some of his best-known poems include "Anecdote of the Jar", "Disillusionment of Ten O'Clock", "The Emperor of Ice-Cream".

Wallace Stevens ranks with Pound, Eliot, and Frost as one of America's major poets. His later poems imply more philosophical ideas which are more difficult and obscure to understand.

SELECTED READING

Anecdote of the Jar

Overview

Stevens presents the jar with nature to show the power of human imagination and creation to change the chaotic and bewildering world. Imagination can bring order and hope to the confusion and wilderness of human spirit and life.

I placed a jar in Tennessee,
And round it was, upon a hill.
It made the slovenly wilderness
Surround that hill.

The wilderness rose up to it,
And sprawled around, no longer wild.
The jar was round upon the ground
And tall and of a port in air[1].

It took dominion[2] everywhere.
The jar was gray and bare.
It did not give of bird or bush,
Like nothing else in Tennessee.

QUESTIONS

1 Where does the speaker place the "jar"?
2 What does the "jar" symbolize?
3 What does "slovenly wilderness" imply?
4 What does "dominion" imply?
5 Why is the jar "gray and bare"?
6 What is the theme of the poem?

1 tall and of a port in air: towering and lofty
2 dominion: rulling power

Williams Carlos Williams (1883-1963)

INTRODUCTION

William Carlos Williams was a poet closely associated with Modernism and Imagism. William Carlos Williams was born in Rutherford, New Jersey. He received his MD from the University of Pennsylvania, where he met Ezra Pound, who became a great influence on his writing. Following Pound, he was one of the eminent poets of the Imagist movement. Disagreement with Imagism later on led him to another way. Experimenting with new techniques of meter and lineation, Williams tried to invent entirely new American poetry, whose theme concerned everyday life of common people. He came up with the concept of the "variable foot", a method of determining line breaks. Williams' poetry is noted for its precision and he has great ability to compose poems from the most ordinary objects and experiences.

His best known and loved poem is "The Red Wheelbarrow". Just as a photographer to capture an instant of time like an unposed snapshot, he gave us a vivid picture.

SELECTED READING

The Red Wheelbarrow

Overview

Williams presents a picture of the commonplace rural life on a farm. The simple language lends the poem color, moisture, sound, peace, motion, and life.

so much depends
upon

a red wheel
barrow

glazed with rain

water

beside the white
chickens.

QUESTIONS

1 Is there a picture or painting in your mind when reading the poem?
2 What is the purpose of the poet to set it in a rainy day?
3 Three items are mentioned in the poem. What are they?
4 Do you think the poem shows us the elements of Imagism?
5 What makes sharp contrast in the poem?
6 What do "the wheelbarrow", "rain" and "chickens" symbolize respectively?
7 Make a comparison of the Chinese poem Ode to Goose by Luo Binwang and The Red Wheelbarrow to find out the similarities.

F. Scott Fitzgerald
(1896-1940)

INTRODUCTION

F. Scott Fitzgerald was one of the most celebrated American writers in the 1920s, one of the Lost Generation. He is also deemed as a chronicler of the Jazz Age of America. His works are tainted with biographical traces, focused on satire and criticism of the worship of money, and the unbridgeable gulf between the different classes in the rigid hierarchy of the society.

Born to an upper-middle-class family, Fitzgerald received good education, but he dropped off from Princeton University to join the U.S. Army in World War I. During World War I, he fell in love with a rich and beautiful girl, Zelda Sayre, who lived in Alabama. Zelda broke off their engagement because he was relatively poor. Coming back from the war, he went to seek his literary fortune in New York City in order to marry her. His first novel, *This Side of Paradise* (1920), became a best-seller, which was the voice of modern American youth. Then, he married Zelda, who is the prototype of Daisy in *The Great Gatsby*. For four years, this good-looking, dashing young couple plunged into the gaudy, wealthy society of their generation and they were treated like a prince and princess. Therefore, they spent all their money and had to move to France in1924, where he met and befriended many American expatriate writers, notably Ernest Hemingway. In 1940, he died before completing his final novel, *The Last Tycoon*.

Fitzgerald's masterpiece is *The Great Gatsby* (1925), and other major works include *This Side of Paradise* (1920), *Tender Is the Night* (1934), about a young psychiatrist whose life is doomed by his marriage to an unstable woman, and *The Last Tycoon* (1941).

SELECTED READING

The Great Gatsby

Overview

The Great Gatsby was written in 1925, deemed as Fitzgerald's masterpiece and one of the best novels of America in his time. The novel explores the theme of aspiration and desire, reality and fantasy, innocence and hypocrisy, idealism and decadence, illusion and disillusion, using technique of symbolism.

It is a story about Jay Gatsby's pursuit of American Dream. It took place in New York in the 1920s. Nick Carraway, the narrator, is a veteran from the war, who rents a house in the West Egg district of Long Island, a district of the new rich people who have made their fortunes but without social connections. However, Nick has connection with the well-established upper-class in the East Egg, his cousin Daisy Buchanan, and her husband Tom. Nick's neighbor in West Egg is a mysterious millionaire, Jay Gatsby, who lives in a mansion and throws extravagant parties every Saturday night, but never participates in them. When Nick finally gets invited to Gatsby's party, he knows that Daisy is Gatsby's first love, and Gatsby throws parties for her attention. With the help of Nick, Gatsby and Daisy get reunited and have an affair. When Tom gets violent with jealousy, tragedy is brewing. Gatsby takes the blame of killing Tom's mistress in a car accident for Daisy, and ends up being shot by the husband of the victim.

The following excerpt of Chapter 3 is about the first meeting of Nick and Gatsby, the latter is depicted as a mysterious millionaire.

Chapter 3

(Excerpt)

There was music from my neighbor's house through the summer nights. In his blue gardens men and girls came and went like moths among the whisperings and the champagne and the stars. At high tide in the afternoon I watched his guests diving from the tower of his raft or taking the sun on the hot sand of his beach while his two motor-boats slit the waters of the Sound[1], drawing aquaplanes over cataracts of foam. On week-ends his Rolls-Royce[2] became an omnibus[3], bearing parties to and from the city, between nine in the morning and long past midnight, while his station wagon scampered like a brisk yellow bug to meet all trains. And on Mondays eight servants including an extra gardener toiled all day with mops and scrubbing-brushes and hammers and garden-shears, repairing the ravages[4] of the night before.

Every Friday five crates of oranges and lemons arrived from a fruiterer

1 the Sound: Long Isand Sound, east of New York City
2 Rolls-Royce: a very expensive and luxurious British automobile
3 omnibus: a vehicle carrying many passengers
4 ravages: destructive effect, damage

in New York—every Monday these same oranges and lemons left his back door in a pyramid of pulpless halves. There was a machine in the kitchen which could extract the juice of two hundred oranges in half an hour, if a little button was pressed two hundred times by a butler's thumb.

At least once a fortnight a corps of caterers came down with several hundred feet of canvas and enough colored lights to make a Christmas tree of Gatsby's enormous garden. On buffet tables, garnished with glistening hors-d'oeuvre, spiced baked hams crowded against salads of harlequin designs and pastry pigs and turkeys bewitched to a dark gold.

In the main hall a bar with a real brass rail was set up, and stocked with gins and liquors and with cordials so long forgotten that most of his female guests were too young to know one from another.

...

I believe that on the first night I went to Gatsby's house I was one of the few guests who had actually been invited. People were not invited—they went there. They got into automobiles which bore them out to Long Island and somehow they ended up at Gatsby's door. Once there they were introduced by somebody who knew Gatsby and after that they conducted themselves according to the rules of behavior associated with amusement parks. Sometimes they came and went without having met Gatsby at all, came for the party with a simplicity of heart that was its own ticket of admission.

I had been actually invited. A chauffeur in a uniform of robin's egg blue crossed my lawn early that Saturday morning with a surprisingly formal note from his employer—the honor would be entirely Gatsby's, it said, if I would attend his "little party" that night. He had seen me several times and had intended to call on me long before but a peculiar combination of circumstances had prevented it—signed Jay Gatsby in a majestic hand.

Dressed up in white flannels[1] I went over to his lawn a little after seven and wandered around rather ill-at-ease among swirls and eddies of people I didn't know—though here and there was a face I had noticed on

1 white flannels: casual men's trousers made of flannel

the commuting train. I was immediately struck by the number of young Englishmen dotted about; all well dressed, all looking a little hungry and all talking in low earnest voices to solid and prosperous Americans. I was sure that they were selling something: bonds or insurance or automobiles. They were, at least, agonizingly aware of the easy money in the vicinity and convinced that it was theirs for a few words in the right key.

As soon as I arrived I made an attempt to find my host but the two or three people of whom I asked his whereabouts stared at me in such an amazed way and denied so vehemently any knowledge of his movements that I slunk off in the direction of the cocktail table—the only place in the garden where a single man could linger without looking purposeless and alone.

I was on my way to get roaring drunk from sheer embarrassment when Jordan Baker came out of the house and stood at the head of the marble steps, leaning a little backward and looking with contemptuous interest down into the garden.

Welcome or not, I found it necessary to attach myself to someone before I should begin to address cordial remarks to the passers-by.

…

There was dancing now on the canvas in the garden, old men pushing young girls backward in eternal graceless circles, superior couples holding each other tortuously, fashionably and keeping in the corners—and a great number of single girls dancing individualistically or relieving the orchestra for a moment of the burden of the banjo or the traps. By midnight the hilarity had increased. A celebrated tenor had sung in Italian and a notorious contralto had sung in jazz and between the numbers people were doing "stunts" all over the garden, while happy vacuous bursts of laughter rose toward the summer sky. A pair of stage "twins"—who turned out to be the girls in yellow—did a baby act in costume and champagne was served in glasses bigger than finger bowls.

The moon had risen higher, and floating in the Sound was a triangle of silver scales, trembling a little to the stiff, tinny drip of the banjoes on the lawn.

I was still with Jordan Baker. We were sitting at a table with a man of about my age and a rowdy little girl who gave way upon the slightest provocation to uncontrollable laughter. I was enjoying myself now. I had taken two finger bowls of champagne and the scene had changed before my eyes into something significant, elemental and profound.

At a lull in the entertainment the man looked at me and smiled.

"Your face is familiar," he said, politely. "Weren't you in the Third Division during the war?"

"Why, yes. I was in the Ninth Machine-Gun Battalion."

"I was in the Seventh Infantry until June nineteen-eighteen. I knew I'd seen you somewhere before."

We talked for a moment about some wet, grey little villages in France.

Evidently he lived in this vicinity for he told me that he had just bought a hydroplane and was going to try it out in the morning.

"Want to go with me, old sport[1]? Just near the shore along the Sound."

"What time?"

"Any time that suits you best."

It was on the tip of my tongue to ask his name when Jordan looked around and smiled.

"Having a gay time now?" she inquired.

"Much better." I turned again to my new acquaintance. "This is an unusual party for me. I haven't even seen the host. I live over there—" I waved my hand at the invisible hedge in the distance, "and this man Gatsby sent over his chauffeur with an invitation."

For a moment he looked at me as if he failed to understand.

"I'm Gatsby," he said suddenly.

"What!" I exclaimed. "Oh, I beg your pardon."

"I thought you knew, old sport. I'm afraid I'm not a very good host."

1 old sport: Gatsby's pet phrase, like Old Brother

QUESTIONS

1 What is the color of Nick's clothes when he goes to the party?
2 Why do some of the guests go to the party uninvitedly?
3 What is the implication of the description of the party?
4 What is the implication of the extravagant parties?
5 What is the aim of Gatsby holding the parties?
6 What is the relationship between Nick and Gatsby? Do you think they had Known each other before?

John Steinbeck
(1902-1968)

INTRODUCTION

John Steinbeck was the winner of the 1962 Nobel Prize in Literature, deemed as "a giant of American letters". Steinbeck was born and brought up in California's Salinas Valley, a place with a rich migratory and immigrant history. Many of his works were set here, featuring a distinct sense of place and love of the land. His works explore social injustice with his characterization of the struggling characters and depiction of the plight of the working class and migrant workers in the rural areas during the Great Depression. Steinbeck studied English Literature at Stanford University, leaving without a degree in 1925. He traveled to New York City where he took odd jobs while trying to write.

Steinbeck wrote 27 books, including 16 novels, 6 non-fiction books, and 5 collections of short stories. *The Grapes of Wrath* (1939) is considered Steinbeck's masterpiece and his other major works include *Tortilla Flat* (1935), *Cannery Row* (1945), *East of Eden* (1952), *Of Mice and Men* (1937), and *The Red Pony* (1937).

SELECTED READING

The Grapes of Wrath

Overview

The Grapes of Wrath is a realist novel about the economic and social plight of farmers in the rural areas in the Great Depression, celebrated as one of the canon of American literature. It won John Steinbeck National Book Award, Pulitzer Prize, and the Nobel Prize in literature.

The novel depicts the Joads, a poor family of Oklahoma farmers, are forced to leave their home by natural disaster, economic depression, and agricultural industry development and go West to seek a living in California. Along the trip to the West, the family begins to crumble, grandparents despairing and dying, young men giving up and running away. The conditions in California turn out no better with oversupplied labors. The migrant workers fight against the unfair low wages by organizing strikes which end with violence and death. At the end of the novel, the Joads go to an old barn to take shelter from the flood where they saved a boy and his dying father, humanity giving the last shelter for the people in the throes of suffering.

Chapter 21

The moving, questing people were migrants now. Those families which had lived on a little piece of land, who had lived and died on forty acres, had eaten or starved on the produce of forty acres, had now the whole West to rove in. And they scampered about, looking for work; and the highways were streams of people, and the ditch banks were lines of people. Behind them more were coming. The great highways streamed with moving people. There in the Middle- and Southwest had lived a simple agrarian folk who had not changed with industry, who had not farmed with machines or known the power and danger of machines in private hands. They had not grown up in the paradoxes of industry. Their senses were still sharp to the ridiculousness of the industrial life.

And then suddenly the machines pushed them out and they swarmed on the highways. The movement changed them; the highways, the camps along the road, the fear of hunger and the hunger itself, changed them. The children without dinner changed them, the endless moving changed them. They were migrants. And the hostility changed them, welded them, united them—hostility that made the little towns group and arm as though to repel an invader, squads with pick handles, clerks and storekeepers with shotguns, guarding the world against their own people.

In the West there was panic when the migrants multiplied on the highways. Men of property were terrified for their property. Men who had never been hungry saw the eyes of the hungry. Men who had never wanted anything very much saw the flare of want in the eyes of the migrants. And the men of the towns and of the soft suburban country gathered to defend themselves; and they reassured themselves that they were good and the invaders bad, as a man must do before he fights. They said, these goddamned Okies are dirty and ignorant. They're degenerate, sexual maniacs. These goddamned Okies are thieves. They'll steal anything. They've got no sense of property rights.

And the latter was true, for how can a man without property know the ache of ownership? And the defending people said, They bring disease, they're filthy. We can't have them in the schools. They're strangers. How'd you like to have your sister go out with one of 'em?

The local people whipped themselves into a mold of cruelty. Then they formed units, squads, and armed them—armed them with clubs, with gas, with guns. We own the country. We can't let these Okies get out of hand. And the men who were armed did not own the land, but they thought they did. And the clerks who drilled at night owned nothing, and the little storekeepers possessed only a drawerful of debts. But even a debt is something, even a job is something. The clerk thought, I get fifteen dollars a week. S'pose a goddamn Okie would work for twelve? And the little storekeeper thought, How could I compete with a debtless man?

And the migrants streamed in on the highways and their hunger was in their eyes, and their need was in their eyes. They had no argument, no system, nothing but their numbers and their needs. When there was work for a man, ten men fought for it—fought with a low wage. If that fella'll work for thirty cents, I'll work for twenty-five.

If he'll take twenty-five, I'll do it for twenty.

No, me, I'm hungry. I'll work for fifteen. I'll work for food. The kids. You ought to see them. Little boils, like, comin' out, an' they can't run aroun'. Give 'em some windfall fruit, an' they bloated up. Me. I'll work for a little piece of meat.

And this was good, for wages went down and prices stayed up. The great owners were glad and they sent out more handbills to bring more people in. And wages went down and prices stayed up. And pretty soon now we'll have serfs again.

And now the great owners and the companies invented a new method. A great owner bought a cannery. And when the peaches and the pears were ripe he cut the price of fruit below the cost of raising it. And as cannery owner he paid himself a low price for the fruit and kept the price of canned goods up and took his profit. And the little farmers who owned no canneries lost their farms, and they were taken by the great owners, the banks, and the companies who also owned the canneries. As time went on, there were fewer farms. The little farmers moved into town for a while and exhausted their credit, exhausted their friends, their relatives. And then they too, went on the highways. And the roads were crowded with men ravenous[1] for work, murderous for work.

And the companies, the banks worked at their own doom and they did not know it. The fields were fruitful, and starving men moved on the roads. The granaries[2] were full and the children of the poor grew up rachitic, and the pustules of pellagra swelled on their sides. The great companies did not know that the line between hunger and anger is a thin line. And money that might have gone to wages went for gas, for guns, for agents and spies, for blacklists, for drilling. On the highways the people moved like ants and searched for work, for food. And the anger began to ferment[3].

QUESTIONS

1 What is the economic background of the novel?
2 What does the first paragraph describe?
3 Why do people hold hostility towards the migrants?
4 What does it mean when a storekeeper said that "How could I compete with a debtless man" in the fifth paragraph?
5 What do "ravenous" and "murderous" imply in "men ravenous for work, murderous for work" in the tenth paragraph?
6 What does the author blame for the plight of the migrants?

---

1 ravenous: extremely hungry
2 granary: a storehouse for grain
3 ferment: excite, stir up

William Faulkner
(1897-1962)

INTRODUCTION

William Faulkner was one of the most celebrated writers in American literature and Southern literature. He wrote novels, short stories, poetry, and screenplays. Faulkner was awarded the Nobel Prize in Literature in 1949.

Faulkner is famous for his experimental style which features techniques of stream of consciousness, symbolism, multiple points of view, and complex sentence structures. He shared the master of stream of consciousness with James Joyce. He adjusted his complex style to mirror the complexity of the characters. The more complex the sentence, the more psychologically complex a character. The themes of his works focus on the historical development and decadence of the South and the politics of sexuality and race. Faulkner ranks with Hemingway as one of the leading American authors of the 20th century.

Born to an old Southern family, Faulkner was greatly influenced by the history of his family and his hometown of Lafayette County, where he lived for most of his life, and based on which Faulkner created the fictional Yoknapatawpha County, the setting for most of his novels and short stories. Except for staying in Hollywood as a scriptwriter, he worked mainly on his novels and short stories on a farm in Oxford. Although Faulkner received many awards, he lived in obscurity until he was nearly 50 years old. For most of his life he struggled with alcoholism, debt, and infidelity. He was a man of perseverance, failure, talent, and great success.

Faulkner's representative is *The Sound and the Fury* (1929). The main story of the novel is about the family history of the Compsons, who were once the owner of a plantation. The story was divided into four parts and narrated by four characters. Most parts of the novel were written in stream-of-consciousness. The traditional time order was totally broken in this novel. The sentences of the most parts have no capitalization and no proper punctuation, which are the fragments with mistaken information. The other major works include *As I Lay Dying* (1930), *Light in August* (1932), *Absalom, Absalom!* (1936). His first short story collection, *These 13* (1931), includes many of his most readable stories, including "A Rose for Emily".

SELECTED READING

A Rose for Emily

Overview

"A Rose for Emily" is Faulkner's best known short story, written in a Gothic genre with symbolism.

The story begins with the funeral of Emily Grierson, an old aristocratic lady in a Southern town, and also the last one of her class in the town. Before her father's death, they had lived a life as if in the past South. His father wouldn't bear marrying his daughter to someone below their status. When he died, he left Emily nothing but a house. Emily fell in love with a Northern laborer, which met opposition from the town people. And the laborer turned out a not marrying man. When word got spread that they would get married, the laborer disappeared, never being seen again. It was said that he was last seen entering Emily's house. From then on, Emily behaved strangely, never left her house, and sent off all the servants except for one who helped her with the chores. After her funeral, the people broke into the mysterious room which had not been opened for 30 years and found out Miss Emily's secret.

I

When Miss Emily Grierson died, our whole town went to her funeral: the men through a sort of respectful affection for a fallen monument[1], the women mostly out of curiosity to see the inside of her house, which no one save an old man-servant—a combined gardener and cook—had seen in at least ten years.

It was a big, squarish frame house that had once been white, decorated with cupolas and spires and scrolled balconies[2] in the heavily lightsome style of the seventies, set on what had once been our most select street. But garages and cotton gins had encroached and obliterated even the august names of that neighborhood; Only Miss Emily's house was left, lifting its stubborn and *coquettish* decay above the cotton wagons and the gasoline

1 a fallen monument: Here the author implies that Miss Emily is the symbol of an old tradition and certain values. Her death is like a monument fallen to the ground.

2 cupolas and spires and scrolled balconies: This is a typical Western-style building.

pumps—an eyesore among eyesores. And now Miss Emily had gone to join the representatives of those august names where they lay in the cedar-bemused cemetery among the ranked and anonymous graves of Union and Confederate soldiers[1] who fell at the battle of Jefferson.

Alive, Miss Emily had been a tradition, a duty, and a care; a sort of hereditary obligation upon the town, dating from that day in 1894 when Colonel Sartoris, the mayor—he who fathered the edict that no Negro woman should appear on the streets without an apron—remitted her taxes, the dispensation dating from the death of her father on into perpetuity. Not that Miss Emily would have accepted charity. Colonel Sartoris invented an involved tale to the effect that Miss Emily's father had loaned money to the town, which the town, as a matter of business, preferred this way of repaying. Only a man of Colonel Sartoris' generation and thought could have invented it, and only a woman could have believed it.

When the next generation, with its more modern ideas, became mayors and aldermen[2], this arrangement created some little dissatisfaction. On the first of the year they mailed her a tax notice. February came, and there was no reply. They wrote her a formal letter, asking her to call at the sheriff[3]'s office at her convenience. A week later the mayor wrote her himself, offering to call or to send his car for her, and received in reply a note on paper of an archaic shape, in a thin, flowing calligraphy in faded ink, to the effect that she no longer went out at all. The tax notice was also enclosed, without comment.

They called a special meeting of the Board of Aldermen. A deputation waited upon her, knocked at the door through which no visitor had passed since she ceased giving china-painting lessons eight or ten years earlier. They were admitted by the old Negro into a dim hall from which a stairway mounted into still more shadow. It smelled of dust and disuse—a close, dank smell. The Negro led them into the parlor. It was furnished in heavy, leather-covered furniture. When the Negro opened the blinds of one window, they

1 Union and Confederate soldiers: Here Union is the United States of America and the Confederate is the Confederate States of America. It refers to the American Civil War (1861-1865).

2 aldermen: members of the governing council of a city

3 sheriff: chief officer

could see that the leather was cracked; and when they sat down, a faint dust rose sluggishly about their thighs, spinning with slow motes in the single sun-ray. On a tarnished gilt easel before the fireplace stood a crayon portrait of Miss Emily's father.

They rose when she entered—a small, fat woman in black, with a thin gold chain descending to her waist and vanishing into her belt, leaning on an ebony cane with a tarnished gold head. Her skeleton was small and spare; perhaps that was why what would have been merely plumpness in another was obesity in her. She looked bloated, like a body long submerged in motionless water, and of that pallid hue. Her eyes, lost in the fatty ridges of her face, looked like two small pieces of coal pressed into a lump of dough as they moved from one face to another while the visitors stated their errand.

She did not ask them to sit. She just stood in the door and listened quietly until the spokesman came to a stumbling halt. Then they could hear the invisible watch ticking at the end of the gold chain.

Her voice was dry and cold. "I have no taxes in Jefferson. Colonel Sartoris explained it to me. Perhaps one of you can gain access to the city records and satisfy yourselves."

"But we have. We are the city authorities, Miss Emily. Didn't you get a notice from the sheriff, signed by him?"

"I received a paper, yes," Miss Emily said. "Perhaps he considers himself the sheriff ... I have no taxes in Jefferson."

"But there is nothing on the books to show that, you see We must go by the—"

"See Colonel Sartoris. I have no taxes in Jefferson."

"But, Miss Emily—"

"See Colonel Sartoris." (Colonel Sartoris had been dead almost ten years.) "I have no taxes in Jefferson. Tobe!" The Negro appeared. "Show these gentlemen out."

II

So she vanquished them, horse and foot[1], just as she had vanquished

1 horse and foot: [idiom] one and all; completely

their fathers thirty years before about the smell.

That was two years after her father's death and a short time after her sweetheart—the one we believed would marry her—had deserted her. After her father's death she went out very little; after her sweetheart went away, people hardly saw her at all. A few of the ladies had the temerity to call, but were not received, and the only sign of life about the place was the Negro man—a young man then—going in and out with a market basket.

"Just as if a man—any man—could keep a kitchen properly, "the ladies said; so they were not surprised when the smell developed. It was another link between the gross, teeming world and the high and mighty Griersons.

A neighbor, a woman, complained to the mayor, Judge Stevens, eighty years old.

"But what will you have me do about it, madam?" he said.

"Why, send her word to stop it," the woman said. "Isn't there a law?"

"I'm sure that won't be necessary," Judge Stevens said. "It's probably just a snake or a rat that nigger of hers killed in the yard. I'll speak to him about it."

The next day he received two more complaints, one from a man who came in diffident deprecation. "We really must do something about it, Judge. I'd be the last one in the world to bother Miss Emily, but we've got to do something." That night the Board of Aldermen met—three graybeards[1] and one younger man, a member of the rising generation.

"It's simple enough," he said. "Send her word to have her place cleaned up. Give her a certain time to do it in, and if she don't..."

"Dammit, sir," Judge Stevens said, "will you accuse a lady to her face of smelling bad?"

So the next night, after midnight, four men crossed Miss Emily's lawn and slunk about the house like burglars, sniffing along the base of the brickwork and at the cellar openings while one of them performed a regular sowing motion with his hand out of a sack slung from his shoulder. They broke open the cellar door and sprinkled lime there, and in all the

1 grey-beards: the aged men with grey beard; old men

outbuildings. As they recrossed the lawn, a window that had been dark was lighted and Miss Emily sat in it, the light behind her, and her upright torso[1] motionless as that of an idol. They crept quietly across the lawn and into the shadow of the locusts that lined the street. After a week or two the smell went away.

That was when people had begun to feel really sorry for her. People in our town, remembering how old lady Wyatt, her great-aunt, had gone completely crazy at last, believed that the Griersons held themselves a little too high for what they really were. None of the young men were quite good enough for Miss Emily and such. We had long thought of them as a tableau[2], Miss Emily a slender figure in white in the background, her father a straddled silhouette in the foreground, his back to her and clutching a horsewhip[3], the two of them framed by the back-flung front door. So when she got to be thirty and was still single, we were not pleased exactly, but vindicated; even with insanity in the family she wouldn't have turned down all of her chances if they had really materialized.

When her father died, it got about that the house was all that was left to her; and in a way, people were glad. At last they could pity Miss Emily. Being left alone, and a pauper, she had become humanized. Now she too would know the old thrill and the old despair of a penny more or less.

The day after his death all the ladies prepared to call at the house and offer condolence and aid, as is our custom Miss Emily met them at the door, dressed as usual and with no trace of grief on her face. She told them that her father was not dead. She did that for three days, with the ministers calling on her, and the doctors, trying to persuade her to let them dispose of the body. Just as they were about to resort to law and force, she broke down, and they buried her father quickly.

We did not say she was crazy then. We believed she had to do that. We remembered all the young men her father had driven away, and we knew that with nothing left, she would have to cling to that which had robbed her,

1 torso: the trunk of the human body

2 tableau: dramatic situation

3 horsewhip: the legendary weapon used by American fathers to protect their daughters from unwelcome suitors

as people will.

III

She was sick for a long time. When we saw her again, her hair was cut short, making her look like a girl, with a vague resemblance to those angels in colored church windows—sort of tragic and serene.

The town had just let the contracts for paving the sidewalks, and in the summer after her father's death they began the work. The construction company came with riggers and mules and machinery, and a foreman named Homer Barron, a Yankee[1]—a big, dark, ready man, with a big voice and eyes lighter than his face. The little boys would follow in groups to hear him cuss the riggers, and the riggers singing in time to the rise and fall of picks. Pretty soon he knew everybody in town. Whenever you heard a lot of laughing anywhere about the square, Homer Barron would be in the center of the group. Presently we began to see him and Miss Emily on Sunday afternoons driving in the yellow-wheeled buggy and the matched team of bays[2] from the livery stable.

At first we were glad that Miss Emily would have an interest, because the ladies all said, "Of course a Grierson would not think seriously of a Northerner, a day laborer." But there were still others, older people, who said that even grief could not cause a real lady to forget noblesse oblige—without calling it noblesse oblige[3]. They just said, "Poor Emily. Her kinsfolk[4] should come to her." She had some kin in Alabama[5]; but years ago her father had fallen out with them over the estate of old lady Wyatt, the crazy woman, and there was no communication between the two families. They had not even been represented at the funeral.

And as soon as the old people said, "Poor Emily," the whispering began. "Do you suppose it's really so?" they said to one another. "Of course it is.

1 Yankee: a native of a northern U.S. state, especially a Union soldier during the Civil War
2 matched team of bays: two reddish-brown horses similar in size and appearance
3 noblesse oblige: [French] usual nobility; obligations of the upper class
4 kinsfolk: relatives
5 Alabama: a state of the southeast United States

What else could..." This behind their hands; rustling of craned silk and satin behind jalousies closed upon the sun of Sunday afternoon as the thin, swift clop-clop-clop of the matched team passed: "Poor Emily."

She carried her head high enough—even when we believed that she was fallen. It was as if she demanded more than ever the recognition of her dignity as the last Grierson; as if it had wanted that touch of earthiness to reaffirm her imperviousness. Like when she bought the rat poison, the arsenic. That was over a year after they had begun to say "Poor Emily", and while the two female cousins were visiting her.

"I want some poison," she said to the druggist. She was over thirty then, still a slight woman, though thinner than usual, with cold, haughty black eyes in a face the flesh of which was strained across the temples and about the eye sockets as you imagine a lighthouse-keeper's face ought to look. "I want some poison," she said.

"Yes, Miss Emily. What kind? For rats and such? I'd recom—"

"I want the best you have. I don't care what kind."

The druggist named several. "They'll kill anything up to an elephant. But what you want is—"

"Arsenic," Miss Emily said. "Is that a good one?"

"Is... arsenic? Yes, ma'am. But what you want—"

"I want arsenic."

The druggist looked down at her. She looked back at him, erect, her face like a strained flag. "Why, of course," the druggist said. "If that's what you want. But the law requires you to tell what you are going to use it for."

Miss Emily just stared at him, her head tilted back in order to look him eye for eye, until he looked away and went and got the arsenic and wrapped it up. The Negro delivery boy brought her the package; the druggist didn't come back. When she opened the package at home there was written on the box, under the skull and bones: "For rats".

IV

So the next day we all said, "She will kill herself"; and we said it would be the best thing. When she had first begun to be seen with Homer Barron, we had said, "She will marry him." Then we said, "She will persuade him yet," because Homer himself had remarked—he liked men, and it was known that he drank with the younger men in the Elks' Club—that he was not a marrying man. Later we said, "Poor Emily" behind the jalousies as they passed on Sunday afternoon in the glittering buggy, Miss Emily with her head high and Homer Barron with his hat cocked and a cigar in his teeth reins and whip in a yellow glove.

Then some of the ladies began to say that it was a disgrace to the town and a bad example to the young people. The men did not want to interfere, but at last the ladies forced the Baptist minister—Miss Emily's people[1] were Episcopal[2]—to call upon her. He would never divulge what happened during that interview, but he refused to go back again. The next Sunday they again drove about the streets, and the following day the minister's wife wrote to Miss Emily's relations in Alabama.

So she had blood-kin[3] under her roof again and we sat back to watch developments. At first nothing happened. Then we were sure that they were to be married. We learned that Miss Emily had been to the jeweler's and ordered a man's toilet set in silver, with the letters H. B.[4] on each piece. Two days later we learned that she had bought a complete outfit of men's clothing, including a nightshirt, and we said, "They are married." We were really glad. We were glad because the two female cousins were even more Grierson than Miss Emily had ever been.

So we were not surprised when Homer Barron—the streets had been finished some time since—was gone. We were a little disappointed that there was not a public blowing-off, but we believed that he had gone on to prepare for Miss Emily's coming, or to give her a chance to get rid of the cousins. (By that time it was a cabal, and we were all Miss Emily's allies to help circumvent the cousins.) Sure enough, after another week they departed.

1 Emily's people: the members of Emily's family
2 Episcopal: the Episcopal Church (an American religious group)
3 blood-kin: close relative
4 H.B.: an abbreviation for the name of Homer Barron, Emily's lover

And, as we had expected all along, within three days Homer Barron was back in town. A neighbor saw the Negro man admit him at the kitchen door at dusk one evening.

And that was the last we saw of Homer Barron. And of Miss Emily for some time. The Negro man went in and out with the market basket, but the front door remained closed. Now and then we would see her at a window for a moment, as the men did that night when they sprinkled the lime, but for almost six months she did not appear on the streets. Then we knew that this was to be expected too; as if that quality of her father which had thwarted her woman's life so many times had been too virulent and too furious to die.

When we next saw Miss Emily, she had grown fat and her hair was turning gray. During the next few years it grew grayer and grayer until it attained an even pepper-and-salt[1] iron-gray, when it ceased turning. Up to the day of her death at seventy-four it was still that vigorous iron-gray, like the hair of an active man.

From that time on her front door remained closed, save for a period of six or seven years, when she was about forty, during which she gave lessons in china-painting. She fitted up a studio in one of the downstairs rooms, where the daughters and granddaughters of Colonel Sartoris' contemporaries were sent to her with the same regularity and in the same spirit that they were sent to church on Sundays with a twenty-five-cent piece for the collection plate[2]. Meanwhile her taxes had been remitted[3].

Then the newer generation became the backbone and the spirit of the town, and the painting pupils grew up and fell away and did not send their children to her with boxes of color and tedious brushes and pictures cut from the ladies' magazines. The front door closed upon the last one and remained closed for good. When the town got free postal delivery, Miss Emily alone refused to let them fasten the metal numbers above her door and attach a mailbox to it. She would not listen to them.

Daily, monthly, yearly we watched the Negro grow grayer and more

1 pepper-and-salt: (colour) with small dark and light dots
2 the collection plate: the plate used to collect money during church services
3 remit: to excuse payment of a debt

stooped, going in and out with the market basket. Each December we sent her a tax notice, which would be returned by the post office a week later, unclaimed. Now and then we would see her in one of the downstairs windows—she had evidently shut up the top floor of the house—like the carven torso of an idol in a niche, looking or not looking at us, we could never tell which. Thus she passed from generation to generation—dear, inescapable, impervious, tranquil, and perverse.

And so she died. Fell ill in the house filled with dust and shadows, with only a doddering[1] Negro man to wait on her. We did not even know she was sick; we had long since given up trying to get any information from the Negro.

He talked to no one, probably not even to her, for his voice had grown harsh and rusty, as if from disuse.

She died in one of the downstairs rooms, in a heavy walnut bed with a curtain, her gray head propped on a pillow yellow and moldy with age and lack of sunlight.

V

The Negro met the first of the ladies at the front door and let them in, with their hushed, sibilant voices and their quick, curious glances, and then he disappeared. He walked right through the house and out the back and was not seen again.

The two female cousins came at once. They held the funeral on the second day, with the town coming to look at Miss Emily beneath a mass of bought flowers, with the crayon face of her father musing profoundly above the bier and the ladies sibilant and macabre[2]; and the very old men—some in their brushed Confederate uniforms—on the porch and the lawn, talking of Miss Emily as if she had been a contemporary of theirs, believing that they had danced with her and courted her perhaps, confusing time with its mathematical progression, as the old do, to whom all the past is not a

1 doddering: too old to walk in balance
2 the ladies sibilant and macabre: the ladies whispering and gossiping about the death.

diminishing road but, instead, a huge meadow which no winter ever quite touches, divided from them now by the narrow bottleneck of the most recent decade of years.

Already we knew that there was one room in that region above stairs which no one had seen in forty years, and which would have to be forced. They waited until Miss Emily was decently in the ground before they opened it.

The violence of breaking down the door seemed to fill this room with pervading dust. A thin, acrid pall as of the tomb seemed to lie everywhere upon this room decked and furnished as for a bridal: upon the valance curtains of faded rose color, upon the rose-shaded lights, upon the dressing table, upon the delicate array of crystal and the man's toilet things backed with tarnished silver, silver so tarnished that the monogram was obscured. Among them lay a collar and tie, as if they had just been removed, which, lifted, left upon the surface a pale crescent in the dust. Upon a chair hung the suit, carefully folded; beneath it the two mute shoes and the discarded socks.

The man himself lay in the bed.

For a long while we just stood there, looking down at the profound and fleshless grin. The body had apparently once lain in the attitude of an embrace, but now the long sleep[1] that outlasts love, that conquers even the grimace of love[2], had cuckolded him[3]. What was left of him, rotted beneath what was left of the nightshirt, had become inextricable from the bed in which he lay; and upon him and upon the pillow beside him lay that even coating of the patient and biding dust.

Then we noticed that in the second pillow was the indentation of a head. One of us lifted something from it, and leaning forward, that faint and invisible dust dry and acrid in the nostrils, we saw a long strand of iron-gray hair.

1 the long sleep: euphemism for death

2 the grimace of love: the imitation of love

3 cuckold: if a wife cuckolds her husband, she has sex with another man

QUESTIONS

1 What does the rose in the story symbolize?
2 Are there any other symbols? What are they?
3 Why does the author use "we" instead of "I"? Who are "we"?
4 What does the old house look like? And why is it?
5 Whose body is in bed?
6 What are the attitudes of the people towards Miss Emily? Why?

Ernest Hemingway (1899-1961)

INTRODUCTION

Ernest Hemingway was an American novelist, short story writer, and journalist. Hemingway won the Nobel Prize in Literature in 1954. He is most celebrated for his economical and understated writing style which has greatly influenced the American literature. He also enjoyed a reputation as a legendary hero for his life of adventures. Many of his works are considered classics of American literature.

Hemingway was raised in a well-educated family in Oak Park, Illinois, a Protestant upper middle-class suburb of Chicago. His father taught him how to hunt, fish, and box, which became his lifelong interests. After high school, he left for the Italian Front to serve as an ambulance driver in World War I. In 1918, he was seriously wounded and returned home. His novel *The Sun Also Rises* published in 1926 brought him fame. Hemingway's experiences became the story of his novel, *A Farewell to Arms* (1929), about the tragic love affair of an American soldier and an English nurse during the war. In 1921, with his first wife, Hemingway moved to Paris, where he met and came under the great influence of the modernist writers and artists of the "Lost Generation", especially Gertrude Stein, James Joyce, and Ezra Pound. In 1933, Hemingway went on safari to East Africa, which provided material for *Green Hills of Africa* (1935), and the short story "*The Snows of Kilimanjaro*" (1936). In 1937, Hemingway was sent to report on the Spanish Civil War for the North American Newspaper Alliance, which served as the background for his novel *For Whom the Bell Tolls* (1940). *The Old Man and the Sea* (1952) helped to establish his international reputation as a great writer. Car accidents, plane crashes and war wounds brought him intense pains physically and mentally for the rest of his life after his returning from World War I. On the early morning of July 2, 1961, Hemingway shot himself with his favorite shotgun.

The greatest contribution of Hemingway to the world literature is his terse writing style, featuring simple syntax with no subordination, omission of internal punctuation and adjectives, short declarative sentences, objective and detached point of view, which is referred to as the "iceberg theory". His works were written in a deceptively simple way for the readers to fill in the gaps he left in his novels. The themes of his works are love, war, despair, disillusionment, wilderness, death, and loss. His code-heroes are men with inner moral discipline, who remain their "grace under pressure" in a decaying post-war world. Hemingway often put his characters in dangerous situations in order to reveal their inner natures. In some of his works, the danger sometimes becomes an occasion for masculine assertion.

And he was the leading figure of the Lost Generation, which includes the writers living in the period from the end of World War I to the beginning of the Great Depression. Their works depicted a sense of emotional confusion and disillusionment stemming from World War I, which destroyed the innocence and optimism of the 19th century. Some well-known members of the group include Ernest Hemingway, Ezra Pound, John Dos Passos and F. Scott Fitzgerald.

SELECTED READING

A Clean, Well-Lighted Place

Overview

A Clean, Well-Lighted Place is a short story. Deep into a night in a small café in Spain, there are three men, a deaf old man drinking alone, an older waiter, and a young waiter. The younger waiter wants to go off work to go back home to his wife but the old man keeps ordering more wine. The two waiters talk about the old man trying to kill himself a week ago. The younger waiter gets more and more impatient and impolite, and finally refuses the old man's ordering of another drink. The old man pays the bill and leaves the tip, stepping out, "unsteadily but with dignity".

Hemingway uses symbolism and existentialism in the story to show the theme of nihilism of the human existence. **Existentialism** was a movement in the mid-19th century, and reached its peak in mid-20th century France. It is based on the view that humans make their own choice and define their own meaning in life in an absurd universe. It concerns the essence of human existence, and the feeling that there is no purpose or explanation at the core of existence. Existentialism holds that, as there is no God or any other transcendent force, the only way to counter this nothingness is by embracing existence.

It was late and every one had left the cafe except an old man who sat in the shadow the leaves of the tree made against the electric light. In the day time the street was dusty, but at night the dew settled the dust and the old man liked to sit late because he was deaf and now at night it was quiet and he felt the difference. The two waiters inside the café knew that the old man was a little drunk, and while he was a good client they knew that if he became too drunk he would leave without paying, so they kept watch on him.

"Last week he tried to commit suicide," one waiter said.

"Why?"

"He was in despair."

"What about?"

"Nothing."

"How do you know it was nothing?"

"He has plenty of money."

They sat together at a table that was close against the wall near the door of the café and looked at the terrace where the tables were all empty except where the old man sat in the shadow of the leaves of the tree that moved slightly in the wind. A girl and a soldier went by in the street. The street light shone on the brass number on his collar. The girl wore no head covering and hurried beside him.

"The guard will pick him up," one waiter said.

"What does it matter if he gets what he's after?"

"He had better get off the street now. The guard will get him. They went by five minutes ago."

The old man sitting in the shadow rapped on his saucer[1] with his glass. The younger waiter went over to him.

"What do you want?"

The old man looked at him. "Another brandy," he said.

"You'll be drunk," the waiter said. The old man looked at him. The waiter went away.

"He'll stay all night," he said to his colleague. "I'm sleepy now. I never get into bed before three o'clock. He should have killed himself last week."

The waiter took the brandy bottle and another saucer from the counter inside the café and marched out to the old man's table. He put down the saucer and poured the glass full of brandy.

"You should have killed yourself last week," he said to the deaf man.

1 saucer: It is used to calculate the number of the cups.

The old man motioned with his finger. "A little more," he said. The waiter poured on into the glass so that the brandy slopped over and ran down the stem into the top saucer of the pile. "Thank you," the old man said. The waiter took the bottle back inside the café. He sat down at the table with his colleague again.

"He's drunk now," he said.

"He's drunk every night."

"What did he want to kill himself for?"

"How should I know?"

"How did he do it?"

"He hung himself with a rope."

"Who cut him down?"

"His niece."

"Why did they do it?"

"Fear for his soul."[1]

"How much money has he got?"

"He's got plenty."

"He must be eighty years old."

"Anyway I should say he was eighty."

"I wish he would go home. I never get to bed before three o'clock. What kind of hour is that to go to bed?"

"He stays up because he likes it."

"He's lonely. I'm not lonely. I have a wife waiting in bed for me."

"He had a wife once too."

"A wife would be no good to him now."

"You can't tell. He might be better with a wife."

"His niece looks after him. You said she cut him down."

"I know."

"I wouldn't want to be that old. An old man is a nasty thing."

"Not always. This old man is clean. He drinks without spilling. Even

1 Fear for his soul: For religious reasons, the old man's niece did not let him die, even though she would have inherited his money. Roman Catholics believe that the soul of a person who commits suicide will not be admitted into Heaven.

now, drunk. Look at him."

"I don't want to look at him. I wish he would go home. He has no regard for those who must work."

The old man looked from his glass across the square, then over at the waiters.

"Another brandy," he said, pointing to his glass. The waiter who was in a hurry came over. "Finished," he said, speaking with that omission of syntax stupid people employ when talking to drunken people or foreigners. "No more tonight. Close now."

"Another," said the old man.

"No. Finished." The waiter wiped the edge of the table with a towel and shook his head.

The old man stood up, slowly counted the saucers, took a leather coin purse from his pocket and paid for the drinks, leaving half a peseta tip. The waiter watched him go down the street, a very old man walking unsteadily but with dignity.

"Why didn't you let him stay and drink?" the unhurried waiter asked. They were putting up the shutters. "It is not half past two."

"I want to go home to bed."

"What is an hour?"

"More to me than to him."

"An hour is the same."

"You talk like an old man yourself. He can buy a bottle and drink at home."

"It's not the same."

"No, it is not," agreed the waiter with a wife. He did not wish to be unjust. He was only in a hurry.

"And you? You have no fear of going home before your usual hour?"

"Are you trying to insult me?"

"No, hombre[1], only to make a joke."

"No," the waiter who was in a hurry said, rising from pulling down the

1 hombre: Spanish for "man" in the sense of "my good man".

metal shutters. "I have confidence. I am all confidence."

"You have youth, confidence, and a job," the older waiter said. "You have everything."

"And what do you lack?"

"Everything but work."

"You have everything I have."

"No. I have never had confidence and I am not young."

"Come on. Stop talking nonsense and lock up."

"I am of those who like to stay late at the café." the older waiter said.

"With all those who do not want to go to bed. With all those who need a light for the night."

"I want to go home and into bed."

"We are of two different kinds," the older waiter said. He was now dressed to go home. "It is not only a question of youth and confidence although those things are very beautiful. Each night I am reluctant to close up because there may be someone who needs the café."

"Hombre, there are bodegas[1] open all night long."

"You do not understand. This is a clean and pleasant café. It is well lighted. The light is very good and also, now, there are shadows of the leaves."

"Good night," said the younger waiter.

"Good night," the other said. Turning off the electric light he continued the conversation with himself, It was the light of course but it is necessary that the place be clean and pleasant. You do not want music. Certainly you do not want music. Nor can you stand before a bar with dignity although that is all that is provided for these hours. What did he fear? It was not a fear or dread, It was a nothing that he knew too well. It was all a nothing and a man was a nothing too. It was only that and light was all it needed and a certain cleanness and order. Some lived in it and never felt it but he knew it all was nada[2] y[3] pues[4] nada y nada y pues nada. Our nada who art in nada,

1 bodega: It refers to a shop to sell wine and food, especially in a Spanish-speaking country.

2 Nada: [Spanish] nothing. He parodies a well-known Christian prayer, substituting the Spanish word nada (nothing) for the usual words. Religion can offer him no comfort.

3 y: [Spanish] and

4 pues: [Spanish] then

nada be thy name thy kingdom nada thy will be nada in nada as it is in nada. Give us this nada our daily nada and nada us our nada as we nada our nadas and nada us not into nada but deliver us from nada; pues nada. Hail nothing full of nothing, nothing is with thee. He smiled and stood before a bar with a shining steam pressure coffee machine.

"What's yours?" asked the barman.

"Nada."

"Otro loco mas[1]," said the barman and turned away.

"A little cup," said the waiter.

The barman poured it for him.

"The light is very bright and pleasant but the bar is unpolished," the waiter said.

The barman looked at him but did not answer. It was too late at night for conversation.

"You want another copita[2]?" the barman asked.

"No, thank you." said the waiter and went out. He disliked bars and bodegas. A clean, well-lighted café was a very different thing. Now, without thinking further, he would go home to his room. He would lie in the bed and finally, with daylight, he would go to sleep. After all, he said to himself, it's probably only insomnia. Many must have it.

QUESTIONS

1 List the images of light and darkness in the story.
2 What are the old waiter and young waiter's attitudes towards life?
3 Why would the old man like to commit suicide?
4 What does a clean, well-lighted place mean to the old man?
5 The older waiter said to the younger waiter: "we are of two different kinds". In what ways do you think they are different?
6 Why does the old man choose to drink in the café instead of at home?
7 What does the old waiter's long conversation with himself suggest?
8 What is the style of language in this story?

---

1 Otro loco mas: [Spanish] Another lunatic
2 Copita: a small cup

Eugene O'Neill
(1888-1953)

INTRODUCTION

Eugene O'Neill was one of the greatest playwrights in American literature, the first one to promote drama to be as important and influential as poetry and novels in American literature, and he was also the first American dramatist to win the Nobel Prize in Literature.

O'Neill was born in a hotel at Broadway, New York, in 1888. His father was an Irish immigrant actor always on tour with a theatrical company, who suffered from alcoholism; his mother was also of Irish descent, who suffered from an addiction to morphine. He had worked at many odd jobs, as a secretary, sailor, actor, reporter, before he settled on writing as his calling.

O'Neill's masterpiece works include *Anna Christie* (1920), *The Emperor Jones* (1920), *The Hairy Ape* (1922), *Desire Under the Elms* (1924), *The Iceman Cometh* (1939), *Long Day's Journey into Night* (1941).

SELECTED READING

The Hairy Ape

Overview

Written in 1922, *The Hairy Ape* was an expressionist work to expose the dehumanization and oppression of capitalism, and the disillusionment and loss of the working class.

Yank Smith, a brutish and strong fireman on board a cruise ship, worked happily and confidently with his fellow workers until Mildred Douglas, a young lady from the upper class, got appalled and faint at the sight of the filthy cursing Yank, who called Yank a "filthy beast". It threw Yank into an abyss of fury, depression, and bewilderment concerning his identity. He left the ship to go to New York, only to find that he didn't belong to anywhere. The only solace he could find was an ape in a zoo, but he got killed by the ape when he tried to set the ape free.

Scene VIII

(Excerpt)

SCENE—Twilight of the next day. The monkey house at the Zoo. One spot of clear gray light falls on the front of one cage so that the interior can be seen. The other cages are vague, shrouded in shadow from which chatterings pitched in a conversational tone can be heard. On the one cage a sign from which the word "gorilla" stands out. The gigantic animal himself is seen squatting on his haunches on a bench in much the same attitude as Rodin's "Thinker".[1] *YANK enters from the left. Immediately a chorus of angry chattering and screeching breaks out. The gorilla turns his eyes but makes no sound or move.*

YANK—[*With a hard, bitter laugh.*] Welcome to your city, huh? Hail, hail, de gang's all here! [*At the sound of his voice the chattering dies away into an attentive silence.* YANK *walks up to the gorilla's cage and, leaning over the railing, stares in at its occupant, who stares back at him, silent and motionless. There is a pause of dead stillness. Then* YANK *begins to talk in a friendly confidential tone, half-mockingly, but with a deep undercurrent of sympathy.*] Say, yuh're some hard-lookin' guy, ain't yuh? I seen lots of tough nuts dat de gang called gorillas, but yuh're de foist real one I ever seen. Some chest yuh got, and shoulders, and dem arms and mits! I bet yuh got a punch in eider fist dat'd knock 'em all silly! [*This with genuine admiration. The gorilla, as if he understood, stands upright, swelling out his chest and pounding on it with his fist.* YANK *grins sympathetically.*] Sure, I get yuh. Yuh challenge de whole woild, huh? Yuh got what I was sayin' even if yuh muffed de woids. [*Then bitterness creeping in.*] And why wouldn't yuh get me? Ain't we both members of de same club—de Hairy Apes? [*They stare at each other—a pause—then* YANK *goes on slowly and bitterly.*] So yuh're what she seen when she looked at me, de white-faced tart! I was you to her, get me? On'y outa de cage—broke out—free to moider her, see? Sure! Dat's what she tought. She wasn't wise dat I was in a cage, too—worser'n yours—sure—a damn sight—'cause you got some chanct to bust loose—but me— [*He grows confused.*] Aw, hell! It's

1 Rodin's "The Thinker": Rodin was a great French sculptor, especially known for "The Thinker", one of his masterpiece.

all wrong, ain't it? [*A pause.*] I s'pose yuh wanter know what I'm doin' here, huh? I been warmin' a bench down to de Battery[1] —ever since last night. Sure. I seen de sun come up. Dat was pretty, too—all red and pink and green. I was lookin' at de skyscrapers—steel—and all de ships comin' in, sailin' out, all over de oith—and dey was steel, too. De sun was warm, dey wasn't no clouds, and dere was a breeze blowin'. Sure, it was great stuff. I got it aw right—what Paddy said about dat bein' de right dope—on'y I couldn't get *in* it, see? I couldn't belong in dat. It was over my head. And I kept tinkin'—and den I beat it up here to see what youse was like. And I waited till dey was all gone to git yuh alone. Say, how d'yuh feel sittin' in dat pen all de time, havin' to stand for 'em comin' and starin' at yuh—de white-faced, skinny tarts and de boobs what marry 'em—makin' fun of yuh, laughin' at yuh, gittin' scared of yuh—damn 'em! [*He pounds on the rail with his fist. The gorilla rattles the bars of his cage and snarls. All the other monkeys set up an angry chattering in the darkness.* YANK *goes on excitedly.*] Sure! Dat's de way it hits me, too. On'y yuh're lucky, see? Yuh don't belong wit 'em and yuh know it. But me, I belong wit 'em—but I don't, see? Dey don't belong wit me, dat's what. Get me? Tinkin' is hard—[*He passes one hand across his forehead with a painful gesture. The gorilla growls impatiently.* YANK *goes on gropingly.*] It's dis way, what I'm drivin' at. Youse can sit and dope dream in de past, green woods, de jungle and de rest of it. Den yuh belong and dey don't. Den yuh kin laugh at 'em, see? Yuh're de champ of de woild. But me—I ain't got no past to tink in, nor nothin' dat's coming', on'y what's now—and dat don't belong. Sure, you're de best off! Yuh can't tink, can yuh? Yuh can't talk neider. But I kin make a bluff at talkin' and tinkin'—a'most git away wit it—a'most!—and dat's where de joker comes in. [*He laughs.*] I ain't on oith and I ain't in heaven, get me? I'm in de middle tryin' to separate 'em, takin' all de woist punches from bot' of 'em. Maybe dat's what dey call hell, huh? But you, yuh're at de bottom. You belong! Sure! Yuh're de on'y one in de woild dat does, yuh lucky stiff! [*The gorilla growls proudly.*] And dat's why dey gotter put yuh in a cage, see? [*The gorilla roars angrily.*] Sure! Yuh get me. It beats it when you try

1 de Battery: the Battery, a park at the southern end of Manhattan Island in New York

to tink it or talk it—it's way down—deep—behind—you 'n' me we feel it. Sure! Bot' members of dis club! [*He laughs—then in a savage tone.*] What de hell! T' hell wit it! A little action, dat's our meat! Dat belongs! Knock 'em down and keep bustin' 'em till dey croaks yuh wit a gat—wit steel! Sure! Are yuh game? Dey've looked at youse, ain't dey—in a cage? Wanter git even? Wanter wind up like a sport 'stead of croakin' slow in dere? [*The gorilla roars an emphatic affirmative.* YANK *goes on with a sort of furious exaltation.*] Sure! Yuh're reg'lar! Yuh'll stick to de finish! Me 'n' you, huh?—bot' members of this club! We'll put up one last star bout dat'll knock 'em offen deir seats! Dey'll have to make de cages stronger after we're trou! [*The gorilla is straining at his bars, growling, hopping from one foot to the other.* YANK *takes a jimmy from under his coat and forces the lock on the cage door. He throws this open.*] Pardon from de governor! Step out and shake hands! I'll take yuh for a walk down Fif' Avenoo. We'll knock 'em offen de oith and croak wit de band playin'. Come on, Brother. [*The gorilla scrambles gingerly out of his cage. Goes to* YANK *and stands looking at him.* YANK *keeps his mocking tone—holds out his hand.*] Shake—de secret grip of our order. [*Something, the tone of mockery, perhaps, suddenly enrages the animal. With a spring he wraps his huge arms around* YANK *in a murderous hug. There is a crackling snap of crushed ribs—a gasping cry, still mocking, from* YANK.] Hey, I didn't say, kiss me. [*The gorilla lets the crushed body slip to the floor; stands over it uncertainly, considering; then picks it up, throws it in the cage, shuts the door, and shuffles off menacingly into the darkness at left. A great uproar of frightened chattering and whimpering comes from the other cages. Then* YANK *moves, groaning, opening his eyes, and there is silence. He mutters painfully.*] Say—dey oughter match him—with Zybszko[1]. He got me, aw right. I'm trou. Even him didn't tink I belonged. [*Then, with sudden passionate despair.*] Christ, where do I get off at? Where do I fit in? [*Checking himself as suddenly.*] Aw, what de hell! No squakin', see! No quittin', get me! Croak wit your boots on![2] [*He grabs hold of the bars of the cage and hauls himself painfully to his feet—looks around him bewilderedly—*

1 Zybszko: a well-known American wrestler of the 1920s
2 Croak wit your boots on! : Die with your boots on! Die while sill fighting!

forces a mocking laugh.] In de cage, huh? [*In the strident tones of a circus barker.*] Ladies and gents, step forward and take a slant at de one and only—[*His voice weakening*]—one and original—Hairy Ape from de wilds of—[*He slips in a heap on the floor and dies. The monkeys set up a chattering, whimpering wail. And, perhaps, the Hairy Ape at last belongs.*]

QUESTIONS

1 What are the features of the language?
2 What does Yank mean by saying that "Ain't we both members of de same club—de Hairy Apes?"
3 When Yank says that "But me, I belong wit 'em—but I don't, see? Dey don't belong wit me, dat's what", what does he imply?
4 What does the ape symbolize?
5 Are there any similarities and differences between Yank and the ape?
6 What does the title mean?

EXERCISES OF CHAPTER XI

I Fill in the following blanks.

1 American writers after World War I self-consciously acknowledged that they were the " ____________", devoid of faith and alienated from the Western civilization.

2 ____________'s drama marks the coming of the age of American drama.

II Find the relevant match from Column B for each item in Column A.

Column A	Column B
Part I	
1 ( ) John Steinbeck	A. *The Old Man and the Sea*
2 ( ) William Faulkner	B. *The Grapes of Wrath*
3 ( ) Eugene O'Neill	C. *Tender Is the Night*
4 ( ) Ernest Hemingway	D. *The Emperor Jones*
5 ( ) Scott Fitzgerald	E. *The Sound and the Fury*
Part II	
7 ( ) Imagism	G. E. E. Cummings
8 ( ) black poet	H. Ezra Pound

9 ( ) Lost generation — I. William Faulkner
10 ( ) gifted nonprofessional poet — J. Langston Hughes
11 ( ) stream of consciousness — K. Ernest Hemingway
12 ( ) typographical style — L. Wallace Stevens

III Choose the best answer for each statement.

1 Which of the following figures does not belong to the Lost Generation?
A. Ezra Pound B. William Carlos Williams
C. Ernest Hemingway D. Theodore Dreiser

2 The following writers were awarded Nobel Prize in Literature except for ______.
A. William Faulkner B. F. Scott Fitzgerald
C. John Steinbeck D. Ernest Hemingway

3 In Faulkner's novel *The Sound and the Fury*, he used a typical technique called ______.
A. stream of consciousness B. imagism
C. symbolism D. naturalism

4 What does the jar in *Anecdote of the Jar* symbolize?
A. Ground and hill B. Artistic imagination
C. Disordered wilderness D. Bird or bush

5 The two striking contrast words in *The Red Wheelbarrow* are ______.
A. red and white B. water and rain
C. rain and barrow D. glazed and red

IV Answer the following questions.

1 What is the social background of Modernism?
2 What are the features of Hemingway's writing style?

CHAPTER XII

American Literature Since 1945

General Introduction

American literature since 1945 reflects the complexity, the unrest, and the multiculturalism of contemporary American society. After the dropping of the atomic bombs on Japan, the USA got even more involved in the international affairs, such as the lost Korean War, Vietnam War, and Cold War with Soviet Union, which left permanent dark shadow in the memory of Americans. The Second World War caused a long pause in literary creation, but a group of war novels appeared. Herman Wouk's (1915-) historical novels about World War II are highly acclaimed, including *The Caine Mutiny* (1951), *The Winds of War* (1971) and *War and Remembrance* (1978). A new generation of authors appeared to write in the skeptical and ironic tradition. More experimental and unconventional American works in the post-war period, including *Catch-22* (1961) and *Gravity's Rainbow* (1973), are also war novels. The life of the 1960s was enriched by the Civil Rights Movement, the appearance of a counter culture, and a climax of feminism. Kennedy's assassination in 1963 coincided with the beginning of riots and uprisings by poor people and blacks in the cities.

In order to relieve the mental trauma caused by World War II and express the disaffection with American life, the writers of so-called "Beat Generation" appeared in the 1950s with their poetry and fiction. Beat poetry is oral, repetitive, and immensely effective in readings, largely because it developed out of poetry readings in underground clubs. It might be correct to see it as a great-grandparent of the rap music that became prevalent in 1990s.

The Beat Generation was a group of authors whose literature explored and influenced American culture in the post-World War II era. The bulk of their work was published and popularized throughout the 1950s. Central elements of Beat culture were rejection of standard narrative values, the spiritual quest, and exploration of American and Eastern religions, rejection of materialism, explicit portrayals of the human condition, experimentation with psychedelic drugs, and sexual liberation and exploration. Some ideas such as drugs, sex were not good for teenager and caused society's chaos indirectly. Beat Generation was to relieve the spiritual burden and sorrow. It was also an exploration of new value. Because of its totally criticizing the tradition and emphasizing the individual freedom too much, it seemed to mislead the young people to pursue a negative life. The representatives of Beat Generation were the novelist Jack Kerouac (*On the Road,* 1957) and the poet Allen Ginsberg (*Howl,* 1955). The expression of Beat Generation can be found in other famous books, such as J. D. Salinger's *The Catcher in the Rye* (1951), Ralph Ellison's *Invisible Man* (1952), Norman Mailer's *The Man Who Studied Yoga* (1952), and Saul Bellow's *Seize the Day* (1956).

Since World War II, extremely various and multifaceted narration has been influenced by international currents such as European Surrealism, Existentialism and Latin American Magical Realism. But they did not take root in the United States. As World War II offered prime material, a group of post-war writers influenced by philosophical ideas like Existentialism sought to differentiate their works from the tradition of realism to present the theme of absurdity in war fiction. Joseph Heller's *Catch-22* (1961) and Thomas Pynchon's *Gravity's Rainbow* (1973) are the representative works. This way to feature absurdity and bitter satire is known as black humor. **Black humor** is an amusing way of looking at or treating something that is serious or sad. It often describes terrible events, which are normally associated with pleasant occasions, thus producing the suitable effect for humor. Black humor attacks on social mores through shocking language and offensive imagery, which provides readers with a kind of desperate humor to bring laughter at tragic things. Besides Joseph Heller and Thomas Pynchon, Kurt Vonnegut's *Slaughterhouse-Five* (1969) and John Barth's *The Sot-weed Factor* (1961) contain the elements of black humor.

After WWII, the American literature has been diversifying flourish, including Jewish fiction, African-American fiction, feminist fiction, short stories, psychological fiction, Chinese-American fiction, etc. William Faulkner (1949), Ernest Hemingway (1954), John Steinbeck (1962), Saul Bellow (1976), Isaac Bashevis Singer (1978), Joseph Brodsky (1987, born in Soviet Union), Toni Morrison (1993), and Bob Dylan (2016) are the winners of the Nobel Prize in Literature.

Famous Jewish novelists include Norman Mailer, J. D. Salinger, Saul Bellow, and Isaac Singer. Saul Bellow was awarded the Nobel Prize in Literature in 1976, and Isaac Singer won the prize in 1978. Herman Wouk was born in a Jewish family, but he wrote war novels. Philip Roth (1933-) is an American novelist. His 1959 novella *Goodbye, Columbus*, an irreverent and humorous portrait of American Jewish life, won the 1960 US National Book Award for Fiction.

Norman Mailer (1923-2007) was an American novelist, journalist, essayist, playwright, film-maker, actor and political activist, born to a well-known Jewish family in Long Branch, New Jersey. In World War II, he served in the Philippines. He was not involved in much combat and completed his service as a cook, but the experience provided enough material for his masterpiece *The Naked and the Dead* (1948). His other major works are: *T Barbary Shore* (1951), *The Deer Park* (1955), *An American*

Dream (1965), *Why are We in Vietnam?* (1967), etc.

J. D. Salinger (1919-2010) was a Jewish American novelist and short story writer. He was born wan New York City and grew up in a fashionable neighborhood in Manhattan. His best known work was *The Catcher in the Rye* (1951), a story about a rebellious teenage schoolboy and his quixotic experiences in New York. His other famous works were: *The Laughing Man* (1949), *Nine Stories* (1953), *Teddy* (1953), *Zooey* (1957), etc.

Isaac Singer (1904-1991) was a Polish-born Jewish-American waiter. Singer was the author of 24 novels, many short stories, children's books and memoirs. He grew up in a poor section of Warsaw and emigrated to the United States from Poland in 1935. He was a most untypical American who wrote in Yiddish. Singer did not become an American citizen until 1943. His novels are moving depictions of Jewish life in Poland and America. *The Magician of Lublin* (1960), *The Slave* (1962), *The Estate* (1972), etc. are very popular.

Herman Wouk (1915-) was born in New York City into a Jewish family that had emigrated from Russia. He was a bestselling Pulitzer Prize-winning Jewish American author with a number of notable novels to his credit, including *The Caine Mutiny* (1951), *The Winds of War* (1971), and *War and Remembrance* (1978). At the age of 98, he published his latest novel, *The Lawgiver* in 2012.

Black writers began to promote racial and social integration through production of African-American fiction, such as Richard Wright's *Native Son* (1940), Ralph Ellison's *Invisible Man* (1952), James Baldwin *Go Tell it on the Mountain* (1953). Alice Walker and Toni Morrison have been active to express their longing for rights and power in their works. Black literature reached the climax when Toni Morrison who won the Nobel Prize in Literature as the first black writer in 1993.

Alice Walker (1944-) is an African-American woman novelist, short story writer, poet, and activist. She is recognized as a representative of a new generation of the Southern writers and is a realistic, feminist writer of racial minorities. She was born in the rural community of Eatonton, Georgia. Walker called herself "womanist" and has long been associated with feminism, presenting black existence from the female perspective. Her books deal with the Civil Rights Movement. Walker's dialect novel *The Color Purple* (1982) has been highly claimed, for which she won the National Book Award for Fiction and the Pulitzer Prize for Fiction. *The Color Purple* is the story of the love between two poor black sisters that survives a separation over years. The novel portrays men as basically unaware of the needs and reality of women.

American major short story writers are Katherine Anne Porter and John Cheever. Isaac Singer is called novelist and short story master. And Saul Bellow contributes more than a dozen short story collections to American literature.

Katherine Anne Porter (1890-1980) was a famous short story writer in this period, and was also American journalist, essayist, novelist and political activist. She was born in Indian Creek, Texas. Her family tree can be traced back to O. Henry, who was her father's second cousin. Her novel *Ship of Fools* was published in 1962 and was the best-selling novel in America that year. *The Collected Stories of Katherine Anne Porter* appeared in 1965, winning the Pulitzer Prize and the National Book Award.

John Cheever (1912-1982) is known for his elegant, suggestive short stories and has been called a "novelist of manners". His representative *The Stories of John Cheever* (1978) won the 1979 Pulitzer Prize for Fiction and a National Book Critics Circle Award. Cheever also wrote four novels and was awarded the National Medal for Literature by the American Academy of Arts and Letters in 1982.

John Updike (1932-2009) was an American novelist, poet, short story writer, art critic, and literary critic. Updike is regarded as a writer of manners. He was born in Reading, Pennsylvania, United States. He is best known for his Rabbit series: *Rabbit, Run* (1960), *Rabbit Redux* (1971), *Rabbit is Rich* (1981), *Rabbit at Rest* (1990), and the novella *Rabbit Remembered* (2000). Both of his *Rabbit is Rich* and *Rabbit at Rest* received the Pulitzer Prize. Updike is one of only three authors to win the Pulitzer Prize for Fiction more than once. He published more than 20 novels and more than a dozen short story collections, as well as poetry, art criticism, literary criticism and children's books. He is widely considered to be one of the great American writers of his time.

Thomas Pynchon (1937-) is an American novelist, one of the representatives of black humor. He is more commonly classified as a postmodernist author. Pynchon was born in Long Island, New York in 1937 and graduated from Cornell University as an English major in 1959. His novel *V* was published in 1963. Pynchon's most celebrated novel is *Gravity's Rainbow* (1973). Some scholars called it as the greatest American post-WWII novel and it was described as "literally an anthology of postmodernist themes and devices". The major portion of the novel takes place in London and Europe in the final months of World War II. The novel has multiple plots involving some 400 characters. For this novel Pynchon won the U.S. National Book Award for Fiction in 1974.

Vladimir Nabokov (1899-1977) was a Russian-American novelist. His first nine novels were in Russian, and he achieved international prominence after he began writing English prose. He was a finalist for the National Book Award for Fiction seven times. His representative work *Lolita* (1955) is ranked fourth in the list of the Modern Library 100 Best Novels. In *Lolita*, Nabokov began to explore forbidden desire and sexuality.

Plays after WWII faced the challenge of the fast boom of movies and television, which gave pressure to the playwrights. They must broaden the ways and forms. The influence of Europe's Theatre of the Absurd and other experimental forms pushed modern drama to emerge in new faces. Arthur Miller, Tennessee Williams, and Edward

Albee are famous American playwrights after Eugene O'Neill.

The Theatre of the Absurd was a new school of drama in the 1950s, appeared in France and then came into vogue in Europe as well as in America. Their work focused largely on the idea of Existentialism and expressed what happens when human existence has no meaning or purpose and therefore all communication breaks down, in fact alerting their audience to pursue the opposite. French writer Samuel Beckett's *Waiting for Godot* is considered the monument of the plays. Edward Albee is the representative writer in America.

Tennessee Williams (1911-1983) was an American playwright, born in Columbus, Mississippi. Some works were inspired by his family members. Williams adapted much of his best known works for the cinema. His major works were *The Glass Menagerie* (1945), which won the New York Drama Critics' Circle Award, *A Streetcar Named Desire* (1947), which won Pulitzer Prize, and *Cat on a Hot Tin Roof* (1955) claiming another Drama Critics' Circle Award and another Pulitzer Prize.

Arthur Miller (1915-2005) was a prolific American playwright, essayist, and prominent figure in the 20th-century American theatre. He is considered to be one of the greatest dramatists of the 20th century. He was born in New York City. Most of his works were influenced by his particular life experiences. An early influential event was the Great Depression of the 1930s. Miller won many awards for his plays. Among them were a Pulitzer Prize, New York Drama Critics' Circle prizes and Tony awards. His representative work was *Death of a Salesman* (1949). Other major works were *All My Sons* (1947), which won several awards in 1947, *A View from the Bridge* (1955), *After the Fall* (1964), and *The Archbishop's Ceiling* (1977).

Edward Albee (1928-2016) was an American playwright known for works such as *The Zoo Story* (1958), *American Dream* (1960), and *Who's Afraid of Virginia Woolf?* (1963). His early works reflected a mastery and Americanization of the Theatre of the Absurd that found its peak in works by European playwrights. His works were often considered as well-crafted, realistic examinations of the modern condition. During his life time, Albee won three Pulitzer Prize for *A Delicate Balance* (1966), *Seascape* (1974), and *Three Tall Women* (1990-1991). His latest work *The Goat or Who is Sylvia?* (2000) won Tony Award.

American poetry after WWII flourished in various forms. The poets are grouped under poetical schools, such as Black Mountain, the Beat Generation, Black poets, etc.

Allen Ginsberg (1926-1997), as the representative of the Beat Generation, was famous for his masterpiece *Howl* (1956). **Robert Lowell** (1917-1977) was known as one of the most brilliant poets after the war. **Joseph Brodsky** (1940-1996) was a Russian and American poet and essayist. He was born in Soviet Union and settled down in United States in 1972. He got Nobel Prize in Literature in 1987. The Nobel Prize in Literature 2016 was awarded to **Bob Dylan** (1941-) "for having created new poetic expressions within the great American song tradition", who is an American songwriter, singer, artist, and writer.

Chinese American writers have begun to flower since the 20th century. **Amy Tan** (1952-) explores mother-daughter relationships with her most well-known work *The Joy Luck Club* (1989), which focuses on four Chinese American immigrant families in San Francisco. **Maxine Hong Kingston** (1940-) is a Chinese American author and Professor Emerita at the University of California, Berkeley. She has contributed to the feminist movement with her memoir *The Woman Warrior* (1976). She won the National Book Award for Nonfiction in 1981 for *China Men*. In 2014, Kingston was awarded the 2013 National Medal of Arts by President Obama.

Saul Bellow
(1915-2005)

INTRODUCTION

Saul Bellow (1915-2005) was a Canadian-American writer. He was born in Lachine, Quebec, two years after his parents emigrated from Saint Petersburg, Russia. When he was nine, his family moved to Chicago, the city that was to form the backdrop of many of his novels. He entered the University of Chicago, and later transferred to nearby Northwestern University, in which he received his Bachelor's degree in 1937. In 1941, Bellow became an American citizen.

Bellow was awarded American National Book Award three times; Pulitzer Prize for Fiction in 1975; Nobel Prize in Literature in 1976; the Foundation's lifetime Medal for Distinguished Contribution to American Letters in 1990. His representative work was *The Adventures of Augie March* (1953), which won National Book Award for Fiction. His other major works were *Dangling Man* (1944), *The Victim* (1947), *Seize the Day* (1956), *Henderson the Rain King* (1959), *Herzog* (1964) for National Book Award, *Mr. Sammler's Planet* (1970) for National Book Award, *Humboldt's Gift* (1975) for the 1976 Pulitzer Prize for Fiction.

The Adventures of Augie March is a picaresque novel, published in 1953. Everyone around Augie finds a greater measure of success, because they commit themselves to some pursuit or goal, even if it is not the most noble.

SELECTED READING

The Adventures of Augie March

Overview

The story describes Augie March's growth from childhood to a fairly stable maturity. Augie, his brother Simon, and the mentally abnormal Georgie are brought up by their mother, who is losing her eyesight, and a tyrannical grandmother in the rough parts of Chicago. Augie drifts from one situation to another in a free-wheeling manner.

Chapter 1

(Excerpt)

I'm an American, Chicago born—Chicago, that somber city—and go at things as I have taught myself, freestyle, and will make the record in my own way: first to knock, first admitted; sometimes an innocent knock, sometimes a not so innocent. But a man's character is his fate, says Heraclitus, and in the end there isn't any way to disguise the nature of the knocks by acoustical work on the door or gloving the knuckles[1].

Everybody knows there is no fineness or accuracy of suppression; if you hold down one thing you hold down the adjoining[2].

My own parents were not much to me, though I cared for my mother. She was simple-minded, and what I learned from her was not what she taught, but on the order of object lessons. She didn't have much to teach, poor woman. My brothers and I loved her. I speak for them both; for the elder it is safe enough; for the younger one, Georgie, I have to answer—he was born an idiot—but I'm in no need to guess, for he had a song he sang as he ran dragfooted with his stiff idiot's trot, up and down along the curl-wired fence in the backyard:

Georgie Mahchy, Augie, Simey
Winnie Mahchy, evwy, evwy love Mama.

He was right about everyone save Winnie, Grandma Lausch's poodle, a pursy old overfed dog. Mama was Winnie's servant, as she was Grandma Lausch's. Loud-breathing and wind-breaking, she lay near the old lady's stool on a cushion embroidered with a Berber aiming a rifle at a lion. She was personally Grandma's, belonged to her suite; the rest of us were the governed, and especially Mama. Mama passed the dog's dish to Grandma, and Winnie received her food at the old lady's feet from the old lady's hands. These hands and feet were small; she wore a shriveled sort of lisle on her

---

1 knuckle: one of the joints of the fingers
2 adjoining: with nothing in between, or touching

legs and her slippers were gray—ah, the gray of that felt, the gray despotic to souls—with pink ribbons. Mama, however, had large feet, and around the house she wore men's shoes, usually without strings, and a dusting or mobcap like somebody's fanciful cotton effigy of the form of the brain. She was meek and long, round-eyed like Georgie—gentle green round eyes and a gentle freshness of color in her long face. Her hands were work-reddened, she had very few of her teeth left—to heed the knocks as they come—and she and Simon wore the same ravelly coat-sweaters. Besides having round eyes, Mama had circular glasses that I went with her to the free dispensary on Harrison Street to get. Coached by Grandma Lausch, I went to do the lying. Now I know it wasn't so necessary to lie, but then everyone thought so, and Grandma Lausch especially, who was one of those Machiavellis of small street and neighborhood that my young years were full of. So Grandma, who had it all ready before we left the house and must have put in hours plotting it out in thought and phrase, lying small in her chilly small room under the featherbed, gave it to me at breakfast. The idea was that Mama wasn't keen enough to do it right. That maybe one didn't need to be keen didn't occur to us; it was a contest. The dispensary would want to know why the Charities didn't pay for the glasses. So you must say nothing about the Charities, but that sometimes money from my father came and sometimes it didn't, and that Mama took boarders. This was, in a delicate and choosy way, by ignoring and omitting certain large facts, true. It was true enough for *them*, and at the age of nine I could appreciate this perfectly. Better than my brother Simon, who was too blunt for this kind of maneuver and, anyway, from books, had gotten hold of some English schoolboy notions of honor. *Tom Brown's Schooldays*[1] for many years had an influence we were not in a position to afford.

QUESTIONS

1 What does "knock" mean?

2 What does this sentence "if you hold down one thing you hold down

1 *Tom Brown's School Days*: a novel by Thomas Hughes in 1857.

the adjoining" mean?

3 Why did Augie say "My own parents were not much to me"?
4 What is the mother's image in Augie's mind?
5 Who was Georgie in the novel?
6 What do you know about Augie March according to this text?

Joseph Heller
(1923-1999)

INTRODUCTION

Joseph Heller (1923-1999) was an American satirical novelist, short story writer and playwright, born in New York In 1942. At age 19, he joined the U S Army Air Corps. After the World War II, he studied at the University of Southern California and New York University. In 1949, he received his MA in English from Columbia University. As a Fulbright scholar, he spent one year at the University of Oxford in England. After his graduation from these universities, he taught composition at Pennsylvania State University for two years and also taught fiction and dramatic writing at Yale University. Since 1961, he has been a full-time writer. He died of a heart attack in his home in 1999. On hearing of Heller's death, his friend Kurt Vonnegut said, "Oh, God, how terrible. This is a calamity for American letters."

His representative work is *Catch-22* (1961), which is the best anti-war novel based on World War II and a most typical work of black humor. The title of the novel, "Catch-22", entered the English lexicon to refer to an impossible situation.

SELECTED READING

Catch-22

Overview

Catch-22 is a key-stone work in American literature, and even added a new term to the dictionary. Joseph Heller shows his view of the American society in the sight of the reader. This society is in a kind of organized chaos, a kind of institutionalized craze, and all in the society obey "Catch-22", an absurd logic. Only Heller's imagination can tolerate such a morbid, absurd society, and only "black humor" can perform it well. Through the symbol "Catch-22", readers can also see the absurdity of war, and crazy and unreasonable American society and its bureaucracy. The main plot of the novel is set on a US air force base eight miles south from the Italian island at the end of World War II. Captain Yossarian struck to save his own life in confusion, absurdity and terror, and ignored all authorities. On this island, his sole purpose was to escape the operational flight. But he could not disobey Catch-22. Suddenly, he found the sick man could escape flying. So, he pretended to be sick and were sent to a hospital again and again, because he found it the best hiding place. Finally, he fled to Sweden. In this novel, Mr. Heller supposed the Peano Island as a stage to display the American society, and let people see clearly in this crazy world how people become "completely mad".

The novel satirizes the utter absurdity and the absolute power of the military bureaucracy.

Chapter 42

(Excerpt)

…

"What about the disgrace?" demanded Major Danby.

"What disgrace? I'm more in disgrace now." Yossarian tied a hard knot in the second shoelace and sprang to his feet. "Well, Danby, I'm ready. What do you say? Will you keep your mouth shut and let me catch a ride?"

Major Danby regarded Yossarian in silence, with a strange, sad smile. He had stopped sweating and seemed absolutely calm. "What would you do if I did try to stop you?" he asked with rueful mockery. "Beat me up?"

Yossarian reacted to the question with hurt surprise. "No, of course not. Why do you say that?"

"I will beat you up," boasted the chaplain, dancing up very close to Major Danby and shadowboxing. "You and Captain Black, and maybe even Corporal[1] Whitcomb. Wouldn't it be wonderful if I found I didn't have to be afraid of Corporal Whitcomb any more?"

"Are you going to stop me?" Yossarian asked Major Danby, and gazed at him steadily.

Major Danby skipped away from the chaplain and hesitated a moment longer. "No, of course not!" he blurted out, and suddenly was waving both arms toward the door in a gesture of exuberant[2] urgency. "Of course I won't stop you. Go, for God sakes, and hurry! Do you need any money?"

---

1 corporal: a person in the military of low rank, below a sergeant

2 exuberant: (esp. of people and their behavior) very energetic, and showing the happiness of being alive

"I have some money."

"Well, here's some more." With fervent, excited enthusiasm, Major Danby pressed a thick wad of Italian currency upon Yossarian and clasped his hand in both his own, as much[1] to still his own trembling fingers as to give encouragement to Yossarian. "It must be nice to be in Sweden now," he observed yearningly. "The girls are so sweet. And the people are so advanced."

"Goodbye, Yossarian," the chaplain called. "And good luck. I'll stay here and persevere, and we'll meet again when the fighting stops."

"So long, Chaplain. Thanks, Danby."

"How do you feel, Yossarian?"

"Fine. No, I'm very frightened."

"That's good," said Major Danby. "It proves you're still alive. It won't be fun."

Yossarian started out. "Yes it will."

"I mean it, Yossarian. You'll have to keep on your toes every minute of every day. They'll bend heaven and earth to catch you."

"I'll keep on my toes every minute."

"You'll have to jump."

"I'll jump."

"Jump!" Major Danby cried.

Yossarian jumped. Nately's whore was hiding just outside the door. The knife came down, missing him by inches, and he took off.

QUESTIONS

1 What does "disgrace" mentioned by Major Dandy and Yossarian refer to?
2 Why did Yossarian react to the question in surprise?
3 What does the conversation mean in the text?
4 Why did Dandy say "You will have to keep on your toes every minute of every day"?
5 What do you think of the relationship between Major Danby and Yossarian?
6 Why is *Catch-22* known as a typical novel of black humor?

1 as much: the same

Jack Kerouac
(1922-1969)

INTRODUCTION

Jack Kerouac (1922-1969) was an American novelist and poet, who did most to spread the philosophy of the Beat Generation. It was he who gave the movement its name in the 1950s. He was born to a French Canadian worker's family in Lowell, Massachusetts. Kerouac studied in Columbia University along with Ginsberg, but he did not graduate. He joined the Merchant Marine, starting the travels of his youth, which would become the basis of *On the Road* (1951).

SELECTED READING

On the Road

Overview

On the Road gave voice to a rising, dissatisfied fringe of the young generation of the late 1940s and early 1950s. It was after the Great Depression and World War II, and more than a decade before the Civil Rights Movement and the turmoil of the 1960s.

In the winter of 1947, Sal Paradise, a young writer, met Dean Moriarty, who came to New York City. Dean and Sal's friendship began with three-year restless journeys back and forth across America. Sal, in pursuit of personality, with Dean, Marylou, several young men and women, drove across the continent of United States several times, finally to Mexico. Along the way, they were crazy with binge drink, drug and entertainment.

Chapter 1

(Excerpt)

I first met Dean not long after my wife and I split up[1]. I had just

1 split up: divorced

gotten over a serious illness that I won't bother to talk about, except that it had something to do with the miserably weary split-up and my feeling that everything was dead. With the coming of Dean Moriarty began the part of my life you could call my life on the road. Before that I'd often dreamed of going West to see the country, always vaguely planning and never taking off. Dean is the perfect guy for the road because he actually was born on the road, when his parents were passing through Salt Lake City in 1926, in a jalopy[1], on their way to Los Angeles. First reports of him came to me through Chad King, who'd shown me a few letters from him written in a New Mexico reform school. I was tremendously interested in the letters because they so naively and sweetly asked Chad to teach him all about Nietzsche and all the wonderful intellectual things that Chad knew. At one point Carlo and I talked about the letters and wondered if we would ever meet the strange Dean Moriarty. This is all far back, when Dean was not the way he is today, when he was a young jail kid shrouded in mystery. Then news came that Dean was out of reform school and was coming to New York for the first time; also there was talk that he had just married a girl called Marylou.

One day I was hanging around the campus and Chad and Tim Gray told me Dean was staying in a cold-water pad in East Harlem, the Spanish Harlem. Dean had arrived the night before, the first time in New York, with his beautiful little sharp chick Marylou; they got off the Greyhound bus at 50th Street and cut around the corner looking for a place to eat and went right in Hector's, and since then Hector's cafeteria has always been a big symbol of New York for Dean. They spent money on beautiful big glazed cakes and creampuffs.

All this time Dean was telling Marylou things like this: "Now, darling, here we are in New York and although I haven't quite told you everything that I was thinking about when we crossed Missouri and especially at the point when we passed the Booneville reformatory which reminded me of my jail problem, it is absolutely necessary now to postpone all those leftover

1 jalopy: an old car in bad condition

things concerning our personal love things and at once begin thinking of specific work life plans ...” and so on in the way that he had in those early days.

QUESTIONS

1 Why did Sal feel that everything was dead?
2 Why did Sal say Dean was the perfect guy for the road?
3 How did Sal know about Dean?
4 What does “leftover things” refer to in Paragraph 3?
5 What is a big symbol of New York for Dean?
6 What have you got from the text?

Toni Morrison
(1931-)

INTRODUCTION

Toni Morrison (1931-) is a Black American woman novelist, editor, and Professor Emeritus at Princeton University. She was born in Lorain, Ohio. As a child, Morrison read constantly and her favorite authors were Jane Austen and Leo Tolstoy. Morrison's father also told her numerous folktales of the black community. She is perhaps the most successful writer to emerge from this ear in which African American writers explored new means of expressing both their engagement with contemporary political issues and their interest in rediscovering their ethnic and cultural roots. Her major works are: *The Bluest Eye* (1970), *Sula* (1973), *Song of Solomon* (1975), *Tar Baby* (1981), *Beloved* (1987), *Paradise* (1998), Love (2003), *A Mercy* (2008), *Home* (2012), and *God Help the Child* (2015). Morrison explores the connection between language, identity, and memory. Morrison won the Pulitzer Prize and the American Book Award in 1988 for *Beloved* and the Nobel Prize in Literature in 1993. On May 29, 2012, Morrison received the Presidential Medal of Freedom.

Toni Morrison wrote *Beloved* on a foundation of historical events. The most significant event within the novel—Sethe's murder of Beloved—is based on the 1856 murder by Margaret Garner of her children to prevent them from being recaptured and taken back into slavery with the passage of the Fugitive Slave Act of 1850.

SELECTED READING

Beloved

Overview

The novel concerns the story of the protagonist Sethe and her daughter Denver after their escape from slavery. Their home in Cincinnati of Ohio is haunted by a revenant, whom they believe to be the ghost of Sethe's the other daughter, who was killed by Sethe herself for avoiding slavery. A woman presumed to be her daughter, called Beloved, returns years later to haunt Sethe's home on 124 Bluestone Road, Cincinnati, Ohio. In the climax of the novel, the youngest daughter Denver reaches out and seek help from the black community, and some of the village women arrive at the house to exorcise Beloved. Unaware of the situation, Sethe attacks the white man who once helped the blacks, and she is brought down by the village women. While Sethe is confused and has a "re-memory" of her master coming again, Beloved disappears. The novel resolves with Denver becoming a working member of the community and Paul D returning to Sethe and pledging his love. The story opens with an introduction to the ghost.

124[1] was spiteful. Full of a baby's venom. The women in the house knew it and so did the children. For years each put up with the spite in his own way, but by 1873 Sethe and her daughter Denver were its only victims. The grandmother, Baby Suggs, was dead, and the sons, Howard and Buglar, had run away by the time they were thirteen years old—as soon as merely looking in a mirror shattered it (that was the signal for Buglar); as soon as two tiny hand prints appeared in the cake (that was it for Howard). Neither boy waited to see more; another kettleful of chickpeas smoking in a heap on the floor; soda crackers crumbled and strewn in a line next to the door sill. Nor did they wait for one of the relief periods: the weeks, months even, when nothing was disturbed. No. Each one fled at once—the moment the house committed what was for him the one insult not to be borne or witnessed a second time. Within two months, in the dead of winter, leaving their grandmother, Baby Suggs; Sethe, their mother; and their little sister, Denver, all by themselves in the gray and white house on Bluestone Road. It didn't have a number then, because Cincinnati didn't stretch that far. In fact, Ohio had been calling itself a state only seventy years when first one brother and then the next stuffed quilt packing into his hat, snatched up his shoes, and crept away from the lively spite the house felt for them.

Baby Suggs didn't even raise her head. From her sickbed she heard them go but that wasn't the reason she lay still. It was a wonder to her that her grandsons had taken so long to realize that every house wasn't like the one on Bluestone Road. Suspended between the nastiness of life and the meanness of the dead, she couldn't get interested in leaving life or living

1 124: a place which is outside of Cincinnati, Ohio

it, let alone the fright of two creeping-off boys. Her past had been like her present—intolerable—and since she knew death was anything but forgetfulness, she used the little energy left her for pondering color.

"Bring a little lavender in, if you got any. Pink, if you don't."

And Sethe would oblige her with anything from fabric to her own tongue. Winter in Ohio was especially rough if you had an appetite for color. Sky provided the only drama, and counting on a Cincinnati horizon for life's principal joy was reckless indeed. So Sethe and the girl Denver did what they could, and what the house permitted, for her. Together they waged a perfunctory battle against the outrageous behavior of that place; against turned-over slop jars, smacks on the behind, and gusts of sour air. For they understood the source of the outrage as well as they knew the source of light.

Baby Suggs died shortly after the brothers left, with no interest whatsoever in their leave-taking or hers, and right afterward Sethe and Denver decided to end the persecution by calling forth the ghost that tried them so. Perhaps a conversation, they thought, an exchange of views or something would help. So they held hands and said, "Come on. Come on. You may as well just come on."

The sideboard took a step forward but nothing else did.

"Grandma Baby must be stopping it," said Denver. She was ten and still mad at Baby Suggs for dying.

Sethe opened her eyes. "I doubt that," she said.

"Then why don't it come?"

"You forgetting how little it is," said her mother. "She wasn't even two years old when she died. Too little to understand. Too little to talk much even."

"Maybe she don't want to understand," said Denver.

"Maybe. But if she'd only come, I could make it clear to her." Sethe released her daughter's hand and together they pushed the sideboard back against the wall. Outside a driver whipped his horse into the gallop local people felt necessary when they passed 124.

"For a baby she throws a powerful spell," said Denver.

"No more powerful than the way I loved her," Sethe answered and there it was again.

…

Counting on the stillness of her own soul, she had forgotten the other one: the soul of her baby girl.

Who would have thought that a little old baby could harbor so much rage? Rutting among the stones under the eyes of the engraver's son was not enough. Not only did she have to live out her years in a house palsied by the baby's fury at having its throat cut, but those ten minutes she spent pressed up against dawn-colored stone studded with star chips, her knees wide open as the grave, were longer than life, more alive, more pulsating than the baby blood that soaked her fingers like oil.

"We could move," she suggested once to her mother-in-law.

"What'd be the point?" asked Baby Suggs. "Not a house in the country ain't packed to its rafters with some dead Negro's grief. We lucky this ghost is a baby."

QUESTIONS

1 Where was No. 124 located?
2 Why were Sethe and Denver the spite's only victims?
3 Who were Howard and Buglar? What had they done?
4 What happened in the house?
5 What did Sethe and Denver decide after Baby Suggs died?
6 What does the conversation between Sethe and Denver reflect?

Bob Dylan
(1941-)

INTRODUCTION

Bob Dylan (born Robert Allen Zimmerman, in 1941) is an American songwriter, singer, artist, and writer. For more than five decades, he has been influential in popular music and culture. Bob Dylan was born in Duluth, Minnesota of USA. 1959, he was enrolled at the University of Minnesota.Then, his focus on rock and roll gave way to American folk music. During his spanning of 50 years, Bob has explored the traditions in American song—from folk, blues, country, rock and roll, rockabilly, jazz to folk music.

Much of his most celebrated work dates from the 1960s, his early songs such as "Blowing in the Wind" and "The Times They Are a-Changin" became anthems for the American civil rights and anti-war movements. In 2015, Dylan released *Shadows in the Night*, which has been described as part of the Great American Songbook. He has received numerous awards including eleven Grammy Awards, a Golden Globe Award, and an Academy Award. In 2008, he was awarded the Pulitzer Prize for "his profound impact on popular music and American culture, marked by lyrical compositions of extraordinary poetic power". In May 2012, Dylan got the Presidential Medal of Freedom from President Obama in the White House. In 2016, he was awarded the Nobel Prize in Literature.

SELECTED READING

Blowing in the Wind

Overview

This song raises a series of rhetorical questions about peace, war and freedom. Dylan originally wrote and performed only a two-verse version of the song. Shortly after this performance, he added the middle verse to the song. It has been described as a protest song.

How many roads must a man walk down

Before they call him a man
How many seas must a white dove sail
Before she sleeps in the sand
How many times must the cannon balls fly
Before they're forever banned
The answer, my friend, is blowing in the wind
The answer is blowing in the wind

How many years must a mountain exist
Before it is washed to the sea
How many years can some people exist
Before they're allowed to be free
How many times can a man turn his head
And pretend that he just doesn't see
The answer, my friend, is blowing in the wind
The answer is blowing in the wind

How many times must a man look up
Before he can see the sky
How many ears must one man have
Before he can hear people cry
How many deaths will it take
'Till he knows that too many people have died
The answer, my friend, is blowing in the wind
The answer is blowing in the wind.

QUESTIONS

1 Why does the songwriter question a man?
2 What do "cannon balls" refer to?
3 What figures of speech have been used in the song?
4 What are the possible themes in this song?
5 Write out each stanza's rhyme scheme.
6 What is the repeated answer in the song?

EXERCISES OF CHAPTER XII

I Fill in the following blanks.

1 The representative writer of Theatre of the Absurd in American literature is ____________.

2 Since 1945, eight American authors won the Nobel Prize in Literature. They are ____________, ____________, ____________, ____________, ____________, ____________, ____________, ____________,

3 The representative writers of Black Humor are ____________and ____________.

II Find the relevant match from Column B for each item in Column A.

Column A	Column B
1 ( ) Saul Bellow	A. *The Naked and the Dead*
2 ( ) Edward Albee	B. *Death of a Salesman*
3 ( ) Arthur Miller	C. *A Streetcar Named Desire*
4 ( ) Toni Morrison	D. *The Adventures of Augie March*
5 ( ) Joseph Heller	E. *The Color Purple*
6 ( ) Jack Kerouac	F. *The Catcher in the Rye*
7 ( ) Tennessee Williams	G. *Beloved*
8 ( ) Norman Mailer	H. *On the Road*
9 ( ) J. D. Salinger	I. *Catch-22*
10 ( ) Alice Walker	J. *The Zoo Story*

III Choose the best answer for each statement.

1 To which country did Yossarian decide to desert?

A. Sweden B. Swiss C. The USA D. Spain

2 Sethe said to her younger daughter Denver "No more powerful than the way I loved her". What did she imply?

A. Sethe had more power than Beloved.

B. Sethe killed Beloved for her real love to avoid being a slave again.

C. Sethe killed Beloved for her poverty and madness.

D. Sethe regreted killing her own daughter.

3 A group of authors whose literature explored and influenced American culture in the 1950s to criticize the tradition and emphasize the individual freedom too much were the so-called ______.

A. Lost Generation B. war novelists

C. Beat Generation D. Jewish novelists

4 One of the representative works written by writers of Beat Generation is ______.

A. *The Catcher in the Rye* by J. D. Salinger

B. *Howl* by Allen Ginsberg

C. *Invisible Man* by Ralph Ellison

D. *Seize the Day* by Saul Bellow

5 Besides Joseph Heller's *Catch-22*, another representative work of the black humor is ______.

A.Tomas Pynchon's *Gravity's Rainbow*

B. John Barth's *The Sot-weed Factor*

C. Kurt Vonnegut's *Slaughterhous-Five*

D. Toni Morrison's *Beloved*

IV Answer the following question.

1 Discuss the theme of race in the novel of *On the Road*?

2 Why did Sethe kill her two-year-old daughter in Toni Morrison's novel *Beloved*?

BIBLIOGRAPHY

Abrams, M. H. *The Norton Anthology of English Literature* (6th edition). New York: W. W. Norton & Company, 1993.

Bold, Carl. *Highlights of American Literature*. Washington D.C.: University of Maryland, 1971.

Booz, Elisabeth. *A Brief Introduction to Modern American Literature*. Shanghai: Shanghai Foreign Language Education Press, 1982.

Booz，Elisabeth, *A Brief Introduction to Modern English Literature*. Shanghai: Shanghai Foreign Language Education Press,1986.

Bradbury, Malcolm. *The Modern British Novel: 1878-2001*. Beijing: Foreign Language Teaching and Research Press, 2005.

Brooks, Cleanth & Robert Penn Warren. *Understanding Poetry* (4th edition). Beijing: Foreign Language Teaching and Research Press, 2004.

Cassill, R.V. *The Norton Anthology of Short Fiction* (5th edition). New York: W. W. Norton & Company, 1995.

Cooperman, Stanley, Charlotte Alexander, et al. 世界经典文学赏析（英汉对照系列）. 北京：外语教学与研究出版社，1996.

Crystal, David. *The New Penguin Encyclopedia*. London: Penguin Books Ltd., 2002.

Drabble, Margaret. *The Oxford Companion to English Literature*. Oxford: Oxford University Press, 2000.

Eagleton, Terry. *The English Novel: An Introduction*. Malden, Blackwell Publishing, 2005.

Elliott, Emory. *The Columbia History of the American Novel.* New York: Columbia University Press,1991.

Gioia, Kennedy. *Literature: An Introduction to Fiction, Poetry, Drama, and Writing* (10th edition). New York: Pearson Longman, 2007.

Hogins, James Burl. *Literature* (3rd Edition*).* Chicago: Science Research Associates, Inc., 1984.

Laurence, Perrine. *Sound and Sense: An Introduction to Poetry*. New York: Harcourt, Brace &World, Inc., 1963.

Lawall, Sarah. *The Norton Anthology of World Masterpieces:The Western Tradition* 1 & 2 (7th edition). New York: W.W. Norton & Company, 1999.

Leavitt, Charles. Nathaniel Hawthorne's *The Scarlet Letter* and *The House of Seven Gables, The Blithedale Romance & The Marble Faun*. Beijing: Foreign Language Teaching and Research Press, 1997.

Lodge, David. ed. *Modern Criticism and Theory: A Reader*. Harlow: Longman Group, 1999.

Mack, Maynard. *The Norton Anthology: World Masterpieces*: Volume 1 & 2 (6th edition). New York: W. W. Norton & Company, 1992.

Marin, Melissa, Brian Phillips, et al. *Today's Most Popular Study Guides*. Tianjin: Tianjin Publishing Company of Science and Technology Translation, 2003.

Rosenthal, M. L. *The Modern Poets: A Critical Introduction*. Beijing: Foreign Language Teaching and Research Press, 2004.

Sanders, Andrew. *The Short Oxford History of English Literature*. Oxford: Oxford University Press, 2000.

Schwarts, Grace. George Bernard Shaw's *Pygmalion*. Beijing: Foreign Language Teaching and Research Press, 1997.

Thornley, G. C. & Gwyneth Roberts. *An Outline of English Literature*. Essex: Longman Group Ltd., 1984.

VanSpanckeren, Kathryn. *Outline of American Literature*. Florida: University Press of Florida, 2009.

Wiki: https://en.wikipedia.org/wiki/Main_Page.

蔡龙权，叶华年．美国文学名作研读．上海：上海交通大学出版社，2011.

曹曼．美国文学教程．武汉：武汉大学出版社，2007.

常耀信．美国文学简史．天津：南开大学出版社，2011.

陈嘉．英国文学史（1-4 卷）．北京：商务印书馆，1999.

陈嘉．英国文学作品选读（1-4）．北京：商务印书馆，1981.

陈立华．经典诗歌欣赏．武汉：武汉测绘科技大学出版社，1997.

戴桂玉．新编英美文学欣赏教程．北京：中国社会科学出版社，2001.

戴桂玉．英美文学选读应试指南．广州：华南理工大学出版社，2005.

桂扬清，吴翔林．英美文学选读．北京：中国对外翻译出版公司，1985.

郭群英．英国文学新编．北京：外语教学与研究出版社，2011.

胡家峦．英国名诗详注．北京：外语教学与研究出版社，2003.

胡荫桐，刘树森．美国文学教程．天津：南开大学出版社，2002.

胡荫桐．美国文学新编．北京：外语教学与研究出版社，2010.

李公昭．新编美国文学选读．西安：西安交通大学出版社，2009.

李宜燮，常耀信．美国文学选读（上、下册）．天津：南开大学出版社，2008.

李正栓．美国诗歌研究．北京：北京大学出版社，2007.

李正栓．英语诗歌教程．北京：高等教育出版社，2008.

刘炳善．英国文学简史．郑州：河南人民出版社，1993.

刘俐俐．外国经典短篇小说文本分析．北京：北京大学出版社，2004.

刘守兰．英美名诗解读．上海：上海外语教育出版社，2003.
刘意青，刘炅．简明英国文学史．北京：外语教学与研究出版社，2008.
罗经国．新编英国文学选读（上、下册）．北京：北京大学出版社，1997.
陶洁．美国文学选读（第三版）．北京：高等教育出版社，2011.
田祥斌．欧美文学名篇选读．北京：外语教学与研究出版社，2006.
童明．美国文学史．北京：外语教学与研究出版社，2008.
万培德．美国二十世纪小说选读．上海：华东师范大学出版社，1981.
王丽丽．二十世纪英国文学史．济南：山东大学出版社，2001.
王守仁．英国文学选读（第二版）．北京：高等教育出版社，2005.
王佐良，李赋宁．英国文学名篇选注．北京：商务印书馆，1989.
王佐良．英国诗选（注释本）．上海：上海译文出版社，1993.
吴伟仁．英国文学史及选读（重排版，第 1-2 册）．北京：外语教学与研究出版社，2013.
吴伟仁．美国文学史及选读（重排版，第 1-2 册）．北京：外语教学与研究出版社，2013.
杨岂深，孙铢．英国文学选读．上海：上海译文出版社，1982.
张伯香．英国文学教程（上下册）．武汉：武汉大学出版社，2004.
张丽娟，张艳波．英美文学史及精要选读．北京：中国经济出版社，2013.
左金梅等．英国文学．青岛：中国海洋大学出版社，2004.